MW00579356

The Trees Inspire

Joyce L. Kieffer

The Trees Remember

Book 1

Book two: The Trees Endure

Book three: The Trees Remember

THE TREES INSPIRE

Joyce L. Kieffer

The Trees Inspire

This book is a work of fiction. Although many names and places are historically accurate and gleaned from the author's ancestors and own life experiences, any references to historical events, real people or real places are used fictitiously. Other names, characters, places and events are products of the author's imagination, and any resemblance to actual events, places or persons, living or dead, is entirely coincidental.

Print ISBN: 978-1-66780-9-076
eBook ISBN: 978-1-66780-9-083

THIS NOVEL IS DEDICATED TO MY FAMILY, WHOSE PATIENCE, TECHNICAL ASSISTANCE AND ENCOURAGEMENT ENABLED ME TO ENDURE THE SIX-YEAR JOURNEY TO WRITE THIS BOOK AND THE TWO BOOKS TO FOLLOW...

AND ALL THE STRONG WOMEN AND MEN WHOSE LIVES ARE INSPIRED TO SAVE OUR FORESTS.

JUNIATA COUNTY, PENNSYLVANIA, 1897

CHAPTER 1

THE YOUNG WOMAN WAS FREE—AT LEAST THIS MORNING IN early May. Free to ride into the purple-blue Shade Mountains. Free to smell the oxygen-infused air created by endless acres of trees on the family's mountain land. Free to dream about finishing school and becoming something other than a farm girl.

Jenny nickered when Rebecca tossed the saddle over the animal's back. Pausing a moment to stroke the filly's neck, Rebecca appreciated how hard her father worked to buy his white horses. But this was a farm, and these animals were primarily muscled workhorses—sturdy with large feet—horses that didn't mind a saddle and a rider on their backs.

Joining her father when her brother refused to go with him to examine the trees after a severe storm that had raged through the mountains a few weeks ago, the two rode along a path that meandered upwards toward their vast expanse of virgin timber. She bounced under the rhythm of the horse's gait, inhaling the fresh pine. In less than an hour, they reached a switchback trail that had been cut through a deciduous and evergreen forest with an understory of hawthorn, serviceberry, and ironwood trees. Deep green leafy branches of mountain laurel peppered the lush mountainsides. Soon they reached a thick stand of hemlocks and white pines so tall their tops were enclosed in billowy morning mist. As they rode further along the trail, cool mountain breezes greeted them under the dense canopy. The cacophony of sounds—songbirds, wind-blown trees squeaking, moaning, clicking, and a raptor's sharp cry—made Rebecca smile. "Pop, do you hear that?" she asked. But her father, Elwood, looked intensely at his prized trees as though seeing them for the first time… the vast eight-hundred-acre forest land his father had given him nearly nineteen years ago.

Pausing near the top of Little Round Top, they led their horses to a spring nestled under a pile of rocks. The air smelled clean, like air-dried sheets. Just as Rebecca's eyes adjusted to the dimness under the trees, she saw a flash of movement. A hawk closed its tendons on a mink crawling beside the small spring-fed stream. She watched in fascination as the long-tailed, red-eyed raptor clutched its prey and dodged through the trees until it finally alighted over the tops.

"Did you see that, Pop?"

"See what?"

"The Cooper's hawk."

"Nope. All I see is timber. Trees. Our trees. Probably worth more than our entire farm."

Rebecca's eyes swept upward toward the overstory of the tall trees. So many greens up there. Malachite. Emerald. Jade. Hunter. Apple. But it was pointless to talk to her father about the colors of the trees. He was only interested in the timber. "I can't even see where that tornado went through a couple of years ago."

"Yeah, Yoder lost a big swath of trees on the north side. Good thing he had them cut into timber before they rotted—though hemlock wood isn't much good for anything. So tough the nails just bend when you try to hammer them in. Had to take about another acre of good trees down and put in a road to set up a small lumber camp. Never going to cut our trees unless I'm desperate."

Rebecca felt a chill and rubbed her arms. Desperate. What does that mean? Which greens would disappear? No sense in questioning him. He'd only tell her more if he wanted to.

The bed of pine needles beckoned her to sit on them under a copse of white pine trees. She inhaled their sweet, sharp scent. Her father followed without speaking. Finally, after a deep breath, he said, "Know what bothers me about our hemlocks? Just want the bark—use it to tan leather." Elwood took off his straw hat and scratched his head. "Heard they use smaller ones to make posts."

Rebecca frowned. "What kind of posts? They look too big for fence posts."

"Use them for posts in the mines. Prop up boards of the mine shafts."

"Is that why they cut all the hemlocks, even the half-grown ones?"

Elwood wiped his face with his red bandanna. "Yep."

The picture in her mind of the adolescent hemlock posts, one end stuck in the hard ground and the other against the cold, damp ceiling of a dark mine shaft, made Rebecca shiver. She imagined sap oozing from their cuts like teardrops crawling down into the black dust.

Pointing to the trees below them, her father interrupted her thoughts. "Look down the mountain. Heard tell our mountains are small compared to the ones way north of here. At least that's what some lumberman told us at the Grange meeting last week. Said those big giants up there have been mostly timbered—hemlock and pine nearly gone, and the hardwoods."

Rebecca's eyes swept up the gigantic white pine she leaned against. "Gary told me the same thing could happen here in Juniata County—and Perry and Snyder." She scooped up a handful of pine needles and sniffed their pungent aroma. "He calls it 'cut and run.'"

"That's just his opinion." Elwood stood and reached for a dead branch. He struggled to snap it, violently shaking it back and forth until it gave way with a loud crack. "Damn it… your brother thinks he knows everything. Doesn't realize some of our neighbors need jobs—no place else to work. Can't make a living by farming anymore."

Rebecca studied this man beside her. She saw a proud, handsome near-stranger, with light brown wavy hair, hazel eyes, and a hard body that told the story of his work as a farmer. His hands were callused, and his right thumb had a split nail that grew together in the center ever since he hit it with a hammer. But that accident was just a minor one compared to those that often happened on a farm. Just last week he had fallen off the back of the plow when the blade hit a rock, and nearly ran over his leg. Rebecca put a poultice of black snakeroot on the bruise that spread from his ankle to his knee, one of many medicinal plants Back So Straight, her Iroquois friend and mentor, taught her to find in the woods.

Father and daughter slowly rode down the mountain, gently guiding their mounts between trees and boulders. Rebecca was puzzled that Elwood made no mention of the tree stumps protruding from a large, barren mountainside just north of their woodland. Several other portions of the nearby Shade Mountains were bare too. Though she knew he would do everything he could to hold on to their land and timber, she suspected her father was afraid he would someday have to sell it.

After reaching the farm, they unsaddled their horses and wiped the frothy loam from their sides. "Pop, please let me see your leg again. That bruise is a bad one. I need to put a new poultice on it… and keep it on for an hour or so."

"Can't do that. Need to fix the plow."

"But Back So Straight told me the poultice needs to stay on to prevent more blood from accumulating under the skin."

"Don't care what she says. Have work to do."

"But Pop"—Rebecca turned around to the sound of gravel crunching under foot. Her brother stood by the open barn door, a knife in one hand and wooden stakes in the other.

"I'm glad you're here," she said. "I wish you had ridden with us today. I saw a Cooper's hawk swoop down on a mink—carried it away like it was a mouse."

Gary kicked up a cloud of dust with his boot. "I didn't want to see the ugly tree stumps next to our mountain. Before you know it, all the timber will be gone and there won't be any game to hunt or trap. Nothin' but bald hills and scrub brush."

Whenever his son and daughter bantered, which was often, Elwood bristled. More times than not, he came down hard on Gary. "If you worried about the farm as much as you do about the trees, you'd be helping me instead of traipsing all over Juniata County."

The boy-man glared at his father whose angry stance—hands on his hips and feet wide apart—made it clear he was not to be challenged. Neither moved. Rebecca held her breath and closed her eyes. The sound of the stakes falling on the gravel made her open them in time to see a knife strike the rafter above her father's head.

"Gary!" Rebecca screamed.

"I'm tired of his bullshit. All he does is complain about me not wanting to check our forests, as if I had something to do with the trees being cut next to us. But he doesn't do anything about it—"

Just then the farmhand jumped down from the loft and landed in front of Gary. His awkward gait slowed him down, but he managed to scurry toward the barn door.

Gary tried to grab his arm, but missed. "Howard—where're you going? Why were you up in the loft 'stead of mucking the stalls?"

Elwood pulled the knife out of the rafter and shook it at his son. "Let him go. He's not the problem. You are. Ever throw a knife at me again, you can get the hell out of here—and don't come back."

She may have been free from doing farm chores this morning, but there was no escaping the arguments between her father and brother. But this was the first time either of them had threatened violence.

CHAPTER 2

THE NEXT MORNING JUST BEFORE DAWN, HOWARD BURST through the cabin door and ran to the stairway. "Mr. Vagner! Da barn iss on fi-yurrh," his heavy accent cutting through his words. By then smoke had seeped through the cracks in the rough logs and hung below the ceiling like thick gunpowder gray clouds. He shouted again. "Fi-yurrh! Da barn burning."

Gary opened his bedroom door and coughed. "Pop, Ma, get up. Barn's on fire. Hurry. Wake Rebecca. I'm going downstairs to wake Grandpa and Grandma." He jumped by twos down the steps and warned the elder Wagners asleep in the back bedroom. Once he was sure they were up, he sprinted out the front door, followed by the farmhand who turned and ran away from the burning barn. Flames had already crawled up its sides—giant orange tentacles reaching the roof. Only the back corner where the horses were kept wasn't burning. Gary raced inside the barn and minutes later stumbled out leading Jenny, her eyes covered with his bandanna. He slapped the horse on the rump and ran back in for another. A minute later he led a mare through the encroaching fire and saw the flames reflected in her eyes. She reared up on her hind legs, straining against the rope around her neck.

By then Elwood reached the burning structure. "Jane—fill the buckets at the pump. Rebecca—let the pigs out of their pen. And the chickens. Where the hell's Howard?"

After Gary managed to get the horse under control, he handed its rope to his father. "He ran away… not sure where. I'm going back in for the last one. Give me that bucket to throw water on the hay."

"No, son. Too dangerous. Roof looks like it's gonna cave in."

But Gary couldn't hear his father's warning above the fire's roar. He grabbed the bucket, charged blindly back into the barn and threw the water on the hay in front of him. But the fire was already creeping forward. He groped his way along the stalls, eyes burning, and gasping with each breath from the dense smoke. By the time the young man reached the first stall, his lungs felt as though they were on fire too. A wooden beam fell in front of him, catching more hay on fire. He heard a wild scream and the saw the blurred shape of the horse as it crashed through the boards in the side of the barn and ran outside. Staggering and gasping, Gary tried to find his way out through the opening, but he couldn't see anything.

He leaned up against the wall and closed his eyes. He pictured the fire consuming his father's prize horse. A deep sense of regret overcame him. Regret at not being able to save it. But there were more. Regret for arguing. Throwing a knife at his father. Regret he may never see him and his family again. Maybe he should just breathe in the smoke until he suffocated rather than burn to death. Then he heard a faint voice but couldn't tell where it was coming from.

"Gary, this way! Come here—it's the only way out. Gary. Where are you? Can you hear me?"

Gary tried to follow the sound of his father's voice, but everywhere he turned, he met with more flames and smoke. Suddenly, he heard boards shatter and saw a flash of white. Confused and terrified, the stallion did what horses often do unless they're blindfolded—gallop back into the burning building. The smell of singed hair made him gag. Gary groped toward the sound and felt the splintered edges of the hole. He closed his eyes against the smoke and heat. In desperation, he blindly jumped head first through the ragged opening and tumbled to the ground. The fall knocked the wind out of him. He tried to take a breath, but his chest muscles tightened in fear. Searing pain shot up his arms. The last thing he heard was a horse, its screams echoing off the mountains like the sound of a saw blade slicing through a newly harvested tree.

CHAPTER 3

As the Iroquois healer stood over Gary and looked carefully at his arms and face, everyone listened to her instructions. "I am going to the forest to find some medicine to put on his burns. Mr. Wagner, carry him into the cabin. I will return shortly. Jane, do not put anything on the blisters, but give him cold water to drink. Rebecca—have a pan and wooden spoon ready for us as soon as I come back."

Living in a small cabin on the Wagner farm for the past seventeen years, Back So Straight was a mystery to most people living in this rural, tight-knit community. She managed to avoid contact with them, staying mostly on the farm and in the mountain land surrounding it. On moonless nights, she walked the fields and meadows, communing with the wildlife that came alive after sundown. There, she was never alone.

Before she moved to the farm, she lived in Strausstown, a small town in Eastern Pennsylvania, with her son and two daughters. Back So Straight never talked about her children; she was alone except for her dog, Wind. The Indian woman had piercing black eyes and brown skin, her face unlined except for slight crow's feet at the corner of her eyes. Slightly older than Rebecca's mother, she carried her tall frame with the grace of a white-tailed deer.

Her moccasins didn't make a sound as she ran into the forest to find a nearly one hundred feet tall slippery elm, a tree she had watched grow through the years. Towering over the dense overstory of the forest, its brown samaras yielded a single seed. Just above the lowest branches, a pair of black and white streaked woodpeckers plucked the seeds and buds from the branches. When she approached the tree, they flew away, their crimson-capped heads contrasted against their white bellies. It was the inner bark she needed.

In a clear soft voice she said, "Thank you for yielding your medicine, Mother tree." Then she took a sharp knife and cut away a small patch of dense outer bark and let it fall to the ground to replenish the earth. Her next cut removed slices of slippery, sappy inner bark, letting them fall into a gourd.

With agile steps she descended the mountain until she reached the understory. There she found a small tree among the moist slopes near the foothills. Its woody pods held two black seeds, but it was the leaves she needed. "Give me your medicine once again, sacred tree." The witch hazel yielded its oval leaves as she striped them into a small basket. Then she sliced small patches of scaly bark with her knife and placed them on top of the leaves. She hurried back to the farm. The girl-healer and the boy-man awaited her.

CHAPTER 4

After helping to carry Gary into the cabin and covering him with a blanket, Rebecca stayed with him while the rest of the family gathered in the kitchen. Elwood's father, Joseph, pounded his fat fist on the kitchen table. "It must have been Howard. No storms… no lightning. Maybe he kicked over a lantern."

"Don't know. Farmhand worked for us for nearly three years. Sure, he was slow and clumsy, but worked hard and never made any trouble," Elwood responded.

Howard was a drifter who had landed up at the Wagner farm dirty and hungry. Since Rebecca's mother Jane wouldn't let him live outside like an animal, he was hired in exchange for room and board. They gave him a small room in the hayloft and fed him from their table. He had no family and couldn't read or write. Although Rebecca pitied Howard, she hated being relentlessly teased by her brother and his friend, Jake, who told her she would marry Howard and live in the hayloft.

Everyone sat quietly at their usual places around the farm table. They were still in their nightclothes except for Elwood, who had managed to pull on trousers in the wee hours that morning when they heard Howard yelling. But after today, his mud-stained pants, riddled with holes from burning sparks, would be thrown away. Gary looked the worst; one sleeve of his nightshirt was torn off and the other hung in burned tatters. His arms and fingers were red and blistered and his eyebrows were singed off. His soft moans added to the melancholy mood in the room.

Without speaking, Jane got up and cooked oatmeal, setting bowls and spoons on the table. Rebecca followed. She sliced a loaf of homemade bread and took jelly from the cupboard. But everyone else sat as though in a stupor.

The kitchen door opened and Back So Straight came into the kitchen carrying a small gourd and a basket. She nodded to Rebecca, who emptied their contents into a pan and mashed them with a wooden spoon. Because Rebecca recognized the moist slippery elm and witch hazel, she knew exactly what to do—create a dressing to seal the burns and ease the pain. Once the concoction was ready, Rebecca and Back So Straight gently smeared the mixture onto Gary's arms and hands. His screams echoed off the log walls, making Rebecca nearly drop the pan.

However, Back So Straight grabbed the pan and continued to spread the medicine over the wounds. "Gary, you must be brave. This medicine may sting at first. In a breath or two, you will feel it cool." Gary nodded and closed his eyes. A moment later, he opened his eyes and nodded, but Rebecca recognized the pain and fear in his clenched jaws.

Jane smoothed the singed hair from her son's forehead while Back So Straight coached Rebecca to smear another layer of the mixture of slippery elm and witch hazel onto each burn. Although Gary winced, he sat still while his sister and the Indian woman worked. When each blister and red skin was covered with the gooey mixture, Back So Straight held the cloths flat while Rebecca laid Gary's outstretched arms on white muslin, and wrapped them firmly.

Once the bandages were in place, Back So Straight said, "The medicine will keep the cloth from sticking to your flesh. You will keep your arms straight for a while, but then carefully bend them this afternoon and when the sun goes down. Rebecca will help you. Do this each morning, in the middle of the day when the sun is highest, and when the moon appears. It will keep your arms from stiffening and the skin from tightening like a drum. I will come at these times and help your sister put more medicine on your wounds." Back So

Straight turned to Rebecca and Jane. "Make him drink much water. I will give him Echinacea but go to your medicine man and ask him for strong medicine to ease Gary's pain so he can sleep."

Rebecca stared at her brother. "Gary, you were so brave to go into the barn after the gelding. Especially after you and Pop argued a few days ago. I know he was mad at you—that's why he said you had to leave if you ever did anything like that again. But he saved your life. Wouldn't give up finding you. If you left the farm, where would you go?"

"Don't know. I hope I don't have to. Especially now. Been burned and it hurts like hell. Besides, I have no place to go. Just don't like being ordered around all the time like I'm a farmhand like Howard."

"I don't blame you. I hate hearing you two at each other's throats all the time. It must be hard for our mother, too. I see her flinch every time it happens."

"Yeah, I know. Got to go upstairs. Had enough."

Rebecca watched Gary get up and make his way toward the stairway. His smell was almost as putrid as the outside air. The stench of burning flesh, along with the acrid smoke of tar from the roof shingles, had seeped its way into the cabin and nearly made her gag. But she was also worried about her father. Poor Pop. He must be thinking about what we're going to do now that we lost the barn and nearly everything inside. Plows and harvesting equipment—gone. Tools—gone. Shelter and hay to feed the animals come winter—gone. Horse—burned to death. Worse than anything, Gary could have died.

After Back So Straight left the cabin, Jane put her arm around her husband and said, "Come, eat something. We've done everything we can. At least the summer kitchen didn't catch fire."

Elwood ate a piece of bread, followed by the rest of the family. Except Gary, who had gone upstairs to bed. Rebecca ate a few bites, more to please her mother than because she was hungry.

"Where's Howard anyway?" Jane asked, but no one answered. "Elwood, he'll have no food and no place to sleep tonight—go find him and talk to him, please. He must be scared to death."

Elwood nodded. He shuffled out of the cabin and into the smoky residue in the air. The barn, now a burned-out shell—a ghost smoldering in the morning air—stood before him. Blackened farm implements rested inside, their twisted frames silent reminders of what he had lost. There among the ruins were white bones, a rib cage leaning against what was once a plow blade. Before he could turn turned his face away from the horror, he felt saliva gather in his mouth. He spit and tried not to gag.

The corncrib, a small rectangular building made of pine planks, stood between the smoke house and the tool shed. Luckily, it was far enough from the barn to spare it from the fire. He stormed toward the structure. "Howard, you better be in here and you better tell me what happened to my barn." When he reached the corncrib, he saw the door latch was open.

Stepping into the corncrib, he walked around the space left where corn had been removed earlier that year to feed their livestock. There, in a dark back corner, Howard was curled up like a baby. When he heard his boss coming, he flung his arms over his face.

"What the hell are you doing? Howard, sit up. Just want to talk to you."

Howard didn't move.

"Damn it, I said sit up."

Howard let out a desperate cry but remained on the floor. Despite the young man's bulky frame, Elwood grabbed his arms and forced him to sit up. "Tell me what happened."

"I don know how started. Von minute I sleepin' and den I smelt da smoke. I not hurt horses." Howard's wailing and sobbing echoed through the narrow room, cutting through Elwood's anger. He released Howard's arms and backed away. The farmhand crumpled to the floor. Elwood stomped out of the corncrib and closed the door, but left the latch open. He walked back to the cabin turning his head away when he passed the remains of the smoldering barn.

"What did he say? How did the fire start?" Jane asked, as soon as her husband walked in the door.

Elwood looked down at the floor and spoke so softly she could hardly hear him. "Don't know, but I'm going to find out even if it kills me." He slumped into his favorite chair, an overstuffed wine-colored relic with arms and headrest worn shiny with age and body oil. He closed his eyes and sat still for several minutes. When he opened them, he blurted out to no one in particular, "Let the poor boy alone."

The next day dawned gray and drizzling. The smell of barn smoke still lingered. Rebecca wanted to go back to the day before the fire, as if it hadn't happened. Everyone was long-faced and quiet. They had lost everything they needed to continue farming.

A short time after daylight, Back So Straight quietly entered the cabin. The usual sounds of people talking their way through breakfast were missing. Walking directly into the front room, she saw the family in their nightclothes. Without asking, she went to the henhouse and collected eggs from chickens that had returned to their nests. Then she took her knife to cut slices of ham in the smokehouse from last fall's butchering and added sliced potatoes and onions to the mixture. Soon everything was sizzling in the big iron skillet over the wood stove.

"Rebecca, has your brother awakened yet?" Back So Straight whispered.

"No, Ma's upstairs with him this morning. He's still sleeping after a hard night."

"This is good. After we eat we will put more poultices on his burns." Then, pointing toward the door to the cellar, she said in a soft voice, "Now get peaches in the cold cellar."

Still in a stupor, Rebecca got up and walked down the crude steps to the basement and across the damp floor. She bent low because the space under the cabin was just dirt that was dug out to about four feet deep. Cut out of the ground floor, the whitewashed cave-like room was the only part that was deep enough to stand. When she opened the door, spiders darted from their webs into cracks in the ceiling. She sniffed the moist, musty air and looked for the striped garter snake that lived under the wooden apple and potato crates. But the olive green reptile was nowhere in sight.

Row after row of vegetables, fruits, soups and meats lined the sagging shelves—food they had grown, harvested, butchered, and canned in these jars to last them through the long winter months. Rebecca thought back to those monotonous days and evenings spent in the summer kitchen in the backyard where the heat from the hot fire in the wood stove was kept from the cabin. Baskets of vegetables, aluminum pots of boiling water, lines of Ball jars, and the bright metal discs that sealed them flashed in her mind. At least they still have food to eat for a while... and thank God the fields didn't burn.

She grabbed a jar of peaches and brought it up the rickety ladder toward the kitchen. The smell of ham, onions, and potatoes reminded her of how hungry she was.

Back So Straight turned over the last spatula of the browned mixture. "You will all come and eat now. I will serve you."

It was unusual for the Indian woman to come into the cabin without being asked. Rebecca was curious. Since the fire, the healer had taken care of all of them—even Jane, who seemed to be absorbed in making sure her son and husband were all right.

The Wagner family sat at the long farm table and let the Indian woman spoon food onto their plates until everyone was served. Wooden-handled forks and knives scraped the blue speckled enamelware plates in the otherwise silent cabin.

Finally, Jane spoke. "Howard didn't show for supper last night or breakfast today. He never misses a meal."

Rebecca kept her eyes on her food, suspecting what would come next.

"Rebecca, fetch him from the corncrib. Ask him to come for breakfast. He can eat out there if he wants to."

"All right," Rebecca said reluctantly, "but I don't see why someone else can't do it. Everyone makes fun of me when I talk to Howard."

"You can either clean up breakfast or go get Howard."

"I'm going, but afterwards I want to go for a walk where I don't smell smoke anymore."

Rebecca walked upstairs, one slow step after another. She was in no hurry to get dressed. Howard. Dumb Howard. Why couldn't he just go hungry? Returning downstairs, she found her boots on the porch and slipped her feet into them, sitting on the bench her father had made last year for her sixteenth birthday. The gray paint was starting to show chips from shoes and boots propped against it to scrape off mud—and probably some manure too. At least they smelled that way. She thought she'd get used to the smell of manure. But that hadn't happened yet.

She walked behind what was left of the barn, small tendrils of smoke still rising from the ashes. Holding her breath and running toward the corncrib, she saw the small wooden latch on the door was open. She stood for a moment before calling out, "Hey… Howard, where are you? Ma wants you to come in and have something to eat." She waited, expecting a reply. "Come on, you know you're hungry."

"Howard? Pop said you're in here." No answer, no sound of movement. Finally, she tired of waiting and swung the door open wide. When she stepped on the wooden floor, she heard mice scrambling across the floorboards, their tiny feet making soft scratching noises. Several crows watched overhead, waiting to steal corn kernels between the slits in the sideboards. Except for their cawing, it was unusually quiet.

It was dusky in the corncrib. Slits of daylight peeped in between the weathered boards only to be trapped by piles of field corn. Her eyes struggled to adjust, but when they did, she saw nothing but ears of corn peeping out from their parchment husks and stacked like tossed pick-up-sticks. Except for one corner that caught her attention. It was strangely empty but for an old wooden ladder oddly propped against the wall. She couldn't recall that being there—ever.

Next to the ladder was a shadow. As her eyes followed the shadowy image up the wall, there he was. Hanging.

CHAPTER 5

SLEEP DIDN'T COME EASILY THAT NIGHT. WHEN REBECCA closed her eyes, the image of Howard, his grotesquely contorted face staring straight ahead, appeared and lingered, despite her efforts to picture trees or flowers—or anything else. She thought about this poor man, alone and frightened. Even if he did set the fire, he didn't deserve to die.

But why would he do such a thing? He lived in the barn. He had no place else to go.

Morning came, and with it her sense of guilt and shame.

Her grandmother, Mary, rescued her from her torment. "Rebecca, would you take me to get coffee? Folks may want to come inside after Howard's burial." Mary stood waiting at the front door dressed in her usual ankle-length black cotton skirt and long-sleeved blouse with an apron made from cotton feedbag cloth. Above her low-heeled shoes, her heavy black stockings clung to her legs. Her long braided hair was pulled back in a silver bun.

Eager to get away from the smell of the fire, Rebecca hitched up the wagon and helped her grandmother climb onto the seat. When they arrived at Zarker's store, it was empty except for a group of men sitting in the back corner talking loudly. She was curious to hear if they were talking about the fire. Pretending to be interested in buying something, she said, "Grandma,

I'll be in the back to see if there's any new bolts of cotton while you buy the coffee. Please wait for me."

As she got nearer, the words 'fire' and 'squaw' slammed against Rebecca's ears. Not already. Can't believe how quickly news travels in this town.

Rebecca hid behind the bolts of cloths and heard a raspy voice say, "So, what happened at the Wagner farm? First the barn burned down and then the hired man hung himself. What's going on over there? It's bad enough they have that squaw hanging around all the time."

Another deep voice responded. "Yep, maybe she set the fire. Can't trust those Indians. They sneak around not making a sound—just show up when you least expect it."

Rebecca knew the old geezer. He minded everyone's business but his own. His body odor wafted toward her, making her holds her nose. Probably hadn't taken a bath in a month. A small, skinny man with a wad of tobacco in his cheek chimed in, his Pennsylvania Dutch accent thickening his words. "Isn't dat old Mary Vagner over there? Mary and Choseph Vagner? Have you ever hert of a stoopider thing?"

The other two men mumbled something Rebecca couldn't hear, then laughed until one of them coughed up phlegm and hawked it into a spittoon. Rebecca swallowed and stifled a gag. The skinny man continued. "Dit she marry dat fat red-haired bastard years ago chust to say 'Mary and Choseph' like dey was holy?"

Rebecca felt the blood rush to her head but stayed hidden. They were nothing but mean-mouthed old men. So what if she married a man named Joseph? The only time that old geezer could have seen her grandfather in town was years ago when he sold their tobacco crop. And they didn't know Back So Straight or what a brilliant healer she was.

A few moments later, Mr. Zarker came out from behind the wooden counter. "All right fellas, that's enough. The Wagners are decent, hardworking people. Time for you to gossip somewhere else."

The old men mumbled as they walked between the narrow aisles of cloth and kitchenware until they reached the front of the store. Glaring at Mary without saying a word, one of them bumped her elbow before he slammed the door behind him.

When Rebecca came out from behind the bolts, she took her grandmother's arm. "Thank you, Mr. Zarker. Here's the money for the coffee."

Shoving the money in a drawer under the counter, Zarker said to the women, "Don't pay those old-timers no mind. They love to gossip."

Just as Rebecca and Mary reached the front of the store, a man dressed in a tweed suit with a matching vest and white shirt opened the door. "Good morning, ladies." He took off his hat and placed it against his chest. "May I ask if this is a good place to get some information?"

"It may be." Rebecca pointed to Mr. Zarker. "This is the owner. I'm sure he knows just about everything in this town."

But before the storekeeper responded, the man said, "My name's Hugh Eastman. I'm trying to find out where the fire was two nights ago. My family and I are spending summers here in McAlisterville—our new house is just west of town and we smelled the smoke."

"I can answer that question. I'm Rebecca Wagner. Our barn burned down and everything in it, including one of our horses—and my brother was burned trying to rescue them," blurted Rebecca, trying to control her emotions. "Thank God it didn't spread to our cabin or out in the fields where our other animals are kept for the summer."

The man took a monogrammed handkerchief out of his pocket and wiped his forehead. "That's too bad. Would it be all right if I stopped by to see for myself and ask if there's anything your family needs?" He held Rebecca and her grandmother in a steady gaze.

"Of course... but it would be best if you wait until tomorrow."

Rebecca turned the wagon toward the farm in the distance—the flat shell of a barn barely visible. The two women rode past a mound of earth beside the newly dug grave nestled in the family graveyard. Old tombstones, some black with age, some tiny and barely visible, contrasted the surrounding white picket fence with purple-blue morning glories climbing up each wooden post. In the distance Elwood and Gary appeared beside the woodshed where they nailed the last few boards together for Howard's coffin, while Grandpa and Grandma Wagner watched from the porch.

The women pulled up beside the woodshed. Mary took the coffee into the cabin while Rebecca walked toward the meadow. No use standing around to hear father and Gary argue like they always did.

As she expected, the arguing began. Her father pointed to the small wooden barrel of nails while Gary stood with his hands on his hips. Elwood said, "Quit dragging your feet. Get hammering. Let's get this the hell over with as soon as possible."

Gary spit on the ground, took his hammer and pounded the first nail, only to drop the tool from his bandaged hands. "Damn, hurts too much. Can't do it."

"Never mind." Elwood shaded his eyes and scanned the meadow before yelling, "Rebecca. Come here and help me."

Though she wanted to run in the opposite direction, Rebecca rushed to the woodshed, heart throbbing in her chest. She needed to help her father, but pitied her brother who stood watching, his face flushed and eyes narrowed in pain. She pounded the nails as though her life depended on it. Howard dead. Poor Gary—doing his best but his arms still hurting. Barn gone. Just let anyone dare to tell her she couldn't pound nails as good as a man.

Howard's body lay on the floor in the parlor where he and Gary moved it yesterday after Dr. Headings, the local doctor, pronounced the man dead. Jane and Mary had bathed him and changed his soiled clothes. Even though they worked as quickly as possible, their noses couldn't escape the odors of urine and feces.

Still tormented by the way he confronted the farmhand, Elwood snapped at his wife. "Quit fussing with that cloth and get the coffin ready. Ain't got much time till things start to stink worse than the manure pile."

The two women hurriedly lined the simple pine box with feedbag cloth. They stood aside while Gary and Elwood struggled to lift Howard's stiff body into the coffin. His neck had ligature marks and his tongue protruded from the side of his mouth. Jane held her hand over her eyes. "I can't stand to see his purple face again. Poor Howard." Once she composed herself, she said to Rebecca, "the flowers."

Rebecca placed a handful of wildflowers on top of Howard's chest and quickly drew her hand away. Memories haunted her. Memories of the corncrib… hearing the eerie cawing of the crows… the ladder leaning against the boards… Howard's dark shadow on the wall… his body hanging. Why did he kill himself? Why did she have to find him? Why her?

After Elwood placed the lid on the coffin, he nailed it shut. The crisp bang of his hammer echoed against the mountains. Squeezing her eyes closed and holding her hands over her ears, Rebecca tried to block everything out. When she felt someone gently press against her shoulder, she opened her eyes. Gary stood next to her, his face stoic. Rebecca smelled the witch hazel bandages on his arms. More memories flooded her mind. The burning barn… her brother trapped inside… the horse jumping back into the inferno… the sound of it screaming.

Gary's muffled voice brought her back to the present moment. "Hey, people are staring at you."

Finally, she realized she had been daydreaming. Neighbors from the nearby farms stood close by. Only a dozen or so bothered to pay their respects—somber-faced farmers and their wives who barely knew the deceased man, but came anyway. They listened as the young preacher from the Evangelical church where the Wagners worshiped every Sunday read from Genesis Chapter three, verse 19. "In the sweat of thy face shalt thou eat bread, till thou return unto the ground, for out of it wast thou taken; for dust thou art, and unto dust shall thou return." After a brief pause, the preacher led them in the Lord's Prayer.

All the men except Gary shoveled rocky ground over the coffin, Howard's final resting place. Only a reddish brown mound of earth remained of his life. Rebecca focused on the dirt, thinking about Howard's body inside: dust thou art and unto dust shall thou return. She glanced at her father. His chin quivered as he stared at the dirt mound and kicked a small stone that had toppled off. Tears slipped down his cheeks and dripped from his nose, and a moment later, he wiped them away with his sleeve. Even though neighbors still lingered about, Jane took his hand and led him into the cabin.

Despite the customary meal after the funeral, Rebecca's father and mother never returned to invite folks to stay. Rebecca waited while their neighbors started to talk among themselves. She turned to her grandmother and whispered, "Do you think we should invite the folks inside for just for coffee?"

"I don't think so. Your Pop's too upset to talk to anyone."

Rebecca nodded and turned to the small group of people lingering at the graveside. "I apologize for not inviting you in for coffee and eats, but I hope you forgive us under the circumstances."

After the neighbors left the farm, Gary followed grandpa and grandma into the cabin. Now everyone was gone except Rebecca. She lingered until everyone was out of sight, hoping she had done the right thing. But she suspected the old men at Zarker's store would eventually find out they hadn't offered hospitality after the burial, and gossip about the Wagners again. Well, she thought—they can just go jump in a lake. Most of the neighbors were good people and would help no matter what. But she was weary of folks who minded their business and passed judgment on them just because they were different.

That night when the rest of the family had gone to bed, sounds of Rebecca's mother and father talking kept her awake. Then Elwood's sobbing filtered through the log walls. She thought about all the horror she had seen and heard these past few days. Guilt flooded her conscience. Maybe she was mean to Howard, just like Gary and his friend Jake. Maybe if she had hurried to find him the morning after the fire, he'd still be alive. Soon her sobbing echoed her father's.

CHAPTER 6

RIDING A MAGNIFICENT SORREL HORSE WITH FOUR WHITE stockings and a white blaze, a handsomely dressed man rode up the dirt road toward the Wagner cabin. Elwood stopped chopping firewood and wiped his forehead with a red bandanna. The stranger sat with his shoulders squared and his hand-tooled boots sticking out of shiny stirrups. Squinting from underneath his straw hat and looking around the yard, he rode closer to where Elwood stood, ax in hand.

"Hello. Am I correct in saying this is the Wagner farm?" He spoke rapidly, not waiting for an answer as though he already knew it. "I understand you had a fire here... lost your barn and some implements. I'm really sorry to hear it." His suit was made of fine wool and tailored to fit his lean, muscular frame. The man was taller than most. As he spoke, his hands slipped into his pockets and jiggled come coins. When he withdrew his hand, the wide gold band on his left hand glinted in the sun.

"I'm Hugh Eastman. I live just outside town and thought I'd stop by and find out if there's anything you might need."

"Elwood Wagner. Mighty nice of you to come by. Yep. Lost my barn and a whole lot of equipment, not to mention one of my horses. Where'd you say you live?"

"Just down Main Street West a few miles from here. My wife and family and I recently moved into our new home—although there's still some work to do."

"Want to sit on the porch for a spell? My wife just baked an apple pie."

"That's very kind of you, Mr. Wagner. I can't stay for pie but I have a little time before I have to get back to my workers."

The two men walked up to the porch and sat in rocking chairs Elwood had made years ago from curly maple wood.

"Call me Elwood. What kind of business are you in, Mr. Eastman?"

"I'm in the lumber business. Buy and sell."

Elwood frowned. "Are you part of the outfit that's cutting the hemlocks and pines here in the Shade Mountains?"

"That's me. And my partner, Peter North. We both recently built summer homes across the road from each other. We actually live in Philadelphia."

"Been wondering who's been timbering the woods around here. Do you intend to stay for a while?"

The visitor hesitated a bit before answering. "It depends. I'm always looking for good timber. As long as there are trees to cut and men to cut them, I'll be interested in providing jobs for those who want to work for me."

Jane opened the kitchen door, a surprised look on her face to see a strange man sitting on the porch with her husband. "Hello, I'm Jane. I didn't hear anyone out here. I was just about to ask my husband to come in for lunch and some apple pie. "Elwood, would you and Mr. ..." she fished for an introduction.

"This is Mr. Hugh Eastman. Stopped by to ask if we needed anything because of the fire," Elwood said.

Before Jane could respond, Eastman said, "Very nice to meet you, Mrs. Wagner. Sorry, but I really must be going. Maybe next time I'll take you up on the pie. And bring along my family. We're building a home on Main Street West just part way to Mifflintown."

"That would be nice, Mr. Eastman. Our daughter Rebecca is just inside. Let me quickly introduce her to you before you leave." Jane opened the door and called to her daughter. “Rebecca, come outside. This is Mr. Eastman. He and his family live in one of the new houses just west of town.”

The man smiled and bowed slightly. “Hello. Nice to meet you again.”

Rebecca nodded. “Yes, we met in town yesterday.” She studied the stranger—fascinated by his manners and different way of pronouncing his words.

As if on cue, Eastman turned to Elwood and shook his hand. “Let me know if there is anything we can do. Anything. Please.”

Elwood walked Hugh Eastman to his horse and ran his hand over the handsome animal’s rump. “Thanks for stopping by. Short of building a new barn and replacing my tools—can’t think of anything we need right now.”

After their visitor rode away, Jane called out, “Come on, let’s eat lunch.” She had made fried smoked sausage, dandelion salad with hard-boiled eggs and hot bacon dressing, along with fresh tomatoes topped with sliced onions, sugar and vinegar. Meadow tea and apple pie followed.

“Grandpa and Grandma Wagner, time for lunch.” Jane held the door opened until Mary and Joseph got up from their bench under the apple tree and walked into the cabin.

After Elwood said a blessing, Jane’s curiosity got the best of her. “Elwood, what do you think of the stranger who stopped by asking about the barn?”

Her father-in-law Joseph stabbed a hunk of sausage and bit off a large piece. “What stranger?”

“I’m talking about the man who came to offer us help a little bit ago,” said Jane.

After Elwood cleared his throat and took a long drag of tea, he said, “Don’t know. Seems he’s in the lumber business. Need lumber to build houses and barns, but the mountains look pretty empty where they’ve been cut.”

Joseph stopped eating and looked at his son. “I wonder if he owns the sawmills?”

The sound of the sawmill was familiar to Rebecca. Her bedroom faced the side of the valley where the screeching saws woke her up in the morning if she overslept.

"If he does, I'll bet he knows about the accident that just happened there last week," said Joseph. "The worker lost his arm to the saw blade when he was distracted by a bee."

Closing her eyes, Rebecca pictured the severed arm lying in the sawdust, hand splayed like a glove and blood dripping from the stump. Always curious about things like that, she wondered who took care of the injured man and what happened to the severed arm.

Elwood added, "Most likely he does know." Then he pointed to Gary's empty place at the table. "Where's Gary today? Haven't seen him since breakfast."

When no one answered, he raised his voice. "Goddamnit. His arms are getting better. Why is it that whenever there's firewood to be cut, he's nowhere to be found? Don't have Howard to help me anymore—have to do everything myself."

Wanting to avoid their son's anger, Mary and Joseph silently left the kitchen, leaving dirty plates on the table. Even Jane retreated to the sink and pumped water into a metal dishpan.

Rebecca tried to diffuse the tension. "I'm not sure where Gary went."

"One of these days, I'm going to take the belt to him."

"Come on, Pop. I'll help you bring firewood into the woodshed as soon as I finish cleaning up lunch."

It was true. Gary hated farm work and fought his father's expectation that he follow in his footsteps. Trouble was, he resembled his father more every year and, in many ways, they were exactly alike. Quick tempered. Stubborn. Opinionated. Had to be right. Loved the forests, but for different reasons: Elwood for the value of the trees, Gary for hunting, fishing, and trapping.

But Gary was more of a mountain man—same light-brown hair but worn longer. Same stocky build, but instead of hazel eyes, his were brown and set below thick eyebrows. He liked to wear a broad-brimmed hat with a hawk feather tucked into the braided leather band around the crown, and canvas trousers.

Neither of them seemed to want to mend their relationship. Maybe it was because they relied on Jane and Rebecca to be the mediators instead of trying to understand each other. After all, they had their awe of the mountains as common ground. And both were intent on saving them from being clear cut.

Rebecca loved them both but didn't know what to do when they argued. She watched her mother try to diffuse the tension between father and son, and saw the price Jane paid to be the peacemaker. Worry lines on her pretty face. Tears when no one was looking. Quickly made excuses for both when they lost their tempers. Good thing she didn't see Gary throw his knife.

CHAPTER 7

HER FORTY-SECOND SUMMER WAS NEAR. SHE LOOKED UP AT a giant oak tree—an alerce—the mother of all trees. The tree's mature habit was so large when she looked up, the Indian woman's eyes could only see the arm branch that sheltered her from the rain dripping down from finger-shaped leaves. Their glossy backs rippled with each falling drop that escaped through the dense canopy.

Brown button acorns lay at her feet. Some had lost their hats. Others were cracked open by hungry foragers.

Back So Straight was not the only one giving thanks for the rain. A red spotted newt scampered from underneath a rock toward a bog, now filled with water once again. Having been vindicated from certain drying death, the creature wormed its way under the black-brown leaf sludge lining the underbelly of the pool.

She smelled the rain-washed air. Pure. Clean. Earthen. She placed her hands on the damp furrowed trunk and asked the tree spirit to give her wisdom when the girl-woman arrived to seek her council.

CHAPTER 8

WHEN REBECCA WAS JUST YARDS AWAY FROM BACK SO Straight's cabin, Wind trotted to her, tail wagging and blue eyes looking straight into her face. She kneeled down and wrapped her arms around the dog's neck, burying her face in the soft, thick fur.

"Do you wish to come in?" Back So Straight stood at the opened door.

"No, but I need your advice."

Back So Straight walked to a nearby fallen tree, silver and smooth with age, its bark long gone, and sat down. "Come. Sit with me."

A scarlet tanager called its chip-purr from the canopy above. The Indian woman said, "This is a bird not often seen unless it comes down to feed on sumac berries and bugs. It is a wise bird to avoid being seen by predators who are attracted by its red color."

Rebecca looked up. She saw nothing, but wondered if she could learn something from what Back So Straight said about the bird being wise enough to protect itself. Maybe her mentor would teach her how to do the same. Finding it difficult to know where to begin, Rebecca finally said, "Every day there's another disagreement between my Pop and brother. They argue and shout at each other. Gary leaves the farm without saying where he's going or when he'll be back. He doesn't help Pop with the farm work unless he has to."

The Indian woman sat quietly, stroking Wind, waiting for Rebecca to continue.

"I don't know what to do. Ma tries to smooth things out between them but she looks so sad and tired. I dread to see what would happen if I weren't here anymore to help her."

"Does she ask them to stop saying the angry words?"

"No, not exactly. She tries to make peace by helping Pa herself or asking me to help him."

Back So Straight look directly into Rebecca's eyes. "Is this what you want her to do?"

"I don't know." Rebecca wasn't sure she was being honest. Maybe she did resent having to do Gary's work.

"Do you think it is your place to bring peace between them?"

Rebecca bit her cheek, stalling for time to think. "That's why I came to talk to you."

Back So Straight stopped stroking her dog. "I am not able to walk their walk. Nor are you."

"What does that mean?"

"When people are not on the same path, there is little you can do."

"But a few weeks ago, my brother threw a knife near my father's head."

Back So Straight took a deep breath and looked up at the sky. "One can only love them."

"I do. But I want them to stop fighting with each other."

"They will only do this when they are ready. Nothing you or your mother do or say will make their path smooth."

Rebecca didn't like what she heard. "But just this morning, Pa threatened to beat Gary with his belt if he didn't help him. Ma always says things will get better when my brother gets older. But that isn't happening. When they argue, everyone disappears. I'm left with the shouting and name-calling."

As usual, Back So Straight said nothing. She simply sat, listening to the sounds of the forest. A pileated woodpecker's staccato pounding echoed against the surrounding trees. Wind's ears stood straight up. Finally the Indian woman said, "What is it you wish, my child?"

"I wish they would get along—but they both act like they're stupid."

The older woman smiled, the corner of her mouth lifting slightly. "Getting along would be wiser, would it not?"

"I can't understand why people act like that. It makes me want to run away."

Back So Straight looked directly into Rebecca's eyes and held her gaze for a few moments before she spoke. "My dear Rebecca, let me tell you the story my grandmother told me of things my own people did. Many said they were, as you say, stupid."

Rebecca laughed. She had never heard Back So Straight use that word.

"Long before I was born, most of my family moved north to the reservations where they would not be persecuted by white people. Before they left, a young brave led an angry raiding party to a farm where they heard whisky was hidden in a large wooden chest. The brave's father did not want him to do this and stayed behind. But his son did not listen. They broke open the chest. When they did not find the whiskey, they killed the whole family."

"That's not stupid, it's horrible! What happened?"

"They carved the chest with ancient symbols of their clan, foolishly revealing who did that terrible thing."

Rebecca's eyes grew wide. "Were they punished?"

They were all hanged. Even the father. So you see my child, there are times when all people do and say stupid things. Sometimes we can learn from them but other times it is too late. I do not know what will happen to your father and brother. Only time knows."

"But I must do something to stop them from hurting each other."

The Indian woman's shoulders drew back. "Remember what I said: this is not your journey. It is theirs. All you can do is love them."

Rebecca sat quietly, thinking about this wise woman—this mysterious healer who always seemed to look right through her. In the past all Rebecca's mother would tell her was that she had known Back So Straight for many years and they were friends. Then she'd change the subject. Maybe now was a good time to find out more. But before Rebecca could gather her courage to ask more questions, Back So Straight stood up and looked into the forest. Then she sat down on the ground with her legs crossed and leaned her back against the log. Rebecca did the same. They were still and quiet for a few minutes.

Turning toward the Indian woman, Rebecca said, "How did you come to live here on the farm? I asked my mother but she only told me that you met when she was nearly nineteen and had gone to Strausstown to visit relatives."

Back So Straight didn't answer for what seemed like a long time. Finally she spoke in a soft voice, "I came to live on your farm before you were born. I have lived here ever since. Your mother has been good to me."

Because Rebecca hoped Back So Straight might finally reveal more about herself, she asked, "How did you get your name?" It was a question she had asked many times before, but had never received a complete answer.

Back So Straight searched Rebecca's face, then smiled widely. "This much I will tell you. When I was born, I was a very long baby and my back was like an arrow. Not like a baby who curls up like a sleeping dog by the fire. My mother told me I always slept on my back so I could stretch out my legs in front of me. I was happiest when strapped in a baby carrier—your people call it a papoose—so my back and legs were straight."

The Indian woman paused, a faraway look on her face. She fingered the beads on her blouse, rolling them between her thumb and middle finger. Before continuing, she reached down and petted her dog.

"Since babies often died before their first year, I was not named at my birth. When it became more certain that I would live, my mother named me Back So Straight. As a girl I hated my name but I came to accept it out of respect for my mother and my grandmother's status as the daughter of a great shaman."

Rebecca's eyes filled with tears. "You learned a lot from them, didn't you? I'm so lucky because I have a mother and grandmother Mary, but I also have you."

The peaceful look on Back So Straight's face radiated like the sun as it breaks through the clouds. She got up from her perch on the ground, and placed her hand on Rebecca's head. "I am teaching you to be a healer. But there is still much you do not know. You will have to learn how to be strong, my child."

CHAPTER 9

WHEN REBECCA TOSSED A BLANKET OVER JENNY'S BACK, THE filly that had escaped the fire, she was careful to smooth it down so there would be no edges to rub her favorite horse under the saddle. She hoisted the plain leather saddle over the blanket—an easy task for someone who was used to working on a farm. She had just finished helping her mother wash and hang up line after line of overalls and barn clothing, bedding, and empty feed bags. Doing laundry was a constant task. Hauling buckets of clean water from the pump to the house. Heating it on the wood stove. Emptying dirty water from the washtubs. She was looking forward to escaping this endless chore.

As she rode the few miles toward town, fields of wheat, hay and barley spread before her, their golden tips of grain contrasting the rich brown earth beneath them. Rows of half-grown field corn with silky tassels drooping over their green husks reached toward the foothills. Rebecca loved to inhale the nutty scent of ripening fields. But as her eyes swept up the mountains, she saw the patchwork of bald forests where the trees had been cut. Next to them were vast stands of hemlocks, pine and hardwoods, broken into segments by tiny dark brown ribbons of smoke from the lumber camps.

A few miles west of town, two magnificent houses stood across the road from one other. They were larger than any homes she had ever seen. Rebecca tried to think of a word to describe them. Colossal. Maybe palatial. She tried to imagine the number of rooms—and how it might feel to live there. How many bedrooms? Did they have a library? How could anyone possibly clean a house that big?

One mansion on the right side of the road was mostly constructed of stone but part of the front was built of wood siding painted brilliant white. A long horseshoe driveway meandered through the large portico on the side of the house and back to the road. Surrounding the entire estate stood a stone wall. Small white pines sat like miniature watchmen throughout the yard. Encircled by white wooden railing, a gazebo held enormous pots of ferns and flowers that drooped their colors onto the grass below.

Workmen stood on ladders painting lavishly carved trim around the soffit. Others carried furniture into the massive dwelling, while a well-dressed woman yelled directions. Rebecca stared at the workmen with rapt attention and failed to see a young woman rocking on a swing in the gazebo.

"Hello, Miss. Have you come to visit?"

"Oh, hello there. Yes, I have. A man came to our farm the other day and told us you just moved here."

"I'm Maggie Eastman. Glad to meet you. The man you met is my father. He told me about you. Please, come sit with me in the gazebo."

"My name's Rebecca Wagner. Glad to meet you too." Rebecca wiped her sweaty forehead on her sleeve and swung down from Jenny's back.

The red-haired young woman patted the flowered cushion next to her, and waited for Rebecca to sit down. Her hair was as coppery as the roof on the McAlisterville General Store. Freckles dotted her face and arms like drops of apple cider. Maggie vigorously brushed off bits of dried weeds that clung to her dress, and tried to tie the sash that had come undone. "My mother tells me I'm messy."

"I live on a farm," Rebecca said. "Nothing is messier."

Green eyes sparkled beneath Maggie's thick orangey-gold eyelashes. "It must be fun living with animals and hiding in a hayloft."

Rebecca grinned at the girl's suggestion. They didn't actually live with animals, and the hayloft was just one of many spaces needed for a farm to function. But it was probably a lost cause to try to correct her. She decided on, "Well, sometimes it's fun, but our barn burned down so we don't have a hayloft anymore." She glanced ahead at the enormous building. "Is this your new house?"

"We're going to live here in the summertime from now on, but our regular home is in Philadelphia. My mother's inside talking to the painters. Would you like to meet her?"

Rebecca and Maggie walked through the ornately carved double doors that led to a foyer as big as the cabin's living room. A slightly plump woman with red hair piled on top of her head stood at the base of a stairway with carvings etched into rich chestnut spokes and posts, writing in a ledger. She put down her pen when she heard footsteps. "Maggie, who is this lovely girl?"

"Mother, this is Rebecca Wagner. She lives on a farm, but she doesn't have a hayloft."

"Very delighted to meet you, Rebecca. Now if you will excuse me, I must supervise the painters. They'll ruin everything. Maggie, why don't you take Rebecca to meet Lilly? I think you're all about the same age."

Taking Rebecca's arm, Maggie led her down the long driveway, chattering away. "Lilly and I go to the Shipley School in Bryn Mawr, and her father works with mine."

Kicking a stone out of her way, she pulled Rebecca along. "Lilly's my best friend. Our families will both be living here until we must return to Philadelphia in September. You're going to just love her."

Across the street from Maggie's house, sat an L-shaped, two-story red brick home with an enormous porch on three sides. Curtains were visible through dozens of tall windows. The mansion was surrounded by a white picket fence—an extravagance that extended around the entire property and beyond to the fields and meadows. White wooden shutters and intricately carved trim gave the house the look of gentility and warmth. Five cupolas and weathervanes in the shape of tall sailing ships sat on the rooftop of a long, rectangular barn. Rebecca's imagination cranked into full swing. Must have many horses and cows. But who took care of them? Hope they had better luck with hired hands than we did.

A colored woman opened the front door. "Howdy do, Miss Maggie. You lookin' for Miss Lilly? She's out on the back porch wit Missus North. You go back there and see fo' yoself." Rebecca tried not to stare but she had never seen a colored person before or heard one speak.

Holding their skirts up to their knees, the two sprinted to the back of the house.

Maggie's lacy petticoats and white silk stockings caught Rebecca's eye. She wondered if Maggie noticed her cotton slip and bare legs.

"Lilly… Lilly, come see who came to visit us. Rebecca Wagner. She lives on a farm near here."

A young woman with the grace of a gazelle walked toward them as though she were skating on ice. She looked directly into Rebecca's eyes. "My name's Lilly North. Glad to meet you, Rebecca." She spoke in a soft, hushed voice, but her smile was warm and reached her eyes.

"Hello. I'm… " But Rebecca was too captivated by Lilly's face to continue. Her skin was milky white and she had eyes bluer than the wild hickory flowers that grew along the dirt roads around McAlisterville. Taller than Maggie, her silky, light brown hair was pinned back at the sides of her high cheekbones and tied on top of her head with a pink ribbon.

Finally, she said, "I'm pleased to meet you, Lilly. You sure have a beautiful place."

"Thank you. That's nice of you to say. Would you like to have some lemonade? Let's go into the porch where the insects won't bother us." The three young women filed in through the door. Soft, mauve-colored rugs sat beneath white wicker furniture.

Lilly lowered herself with the grace of a cat, her slender frame perched on the edge of a cushioned chair. "Rebecca, where do you go to school?"

The young woman's beauty and grace distracted Rebecca again. "I… um… at McAlisterville School. I start my last year come September. How about you?"

"Maggie and I attend a private school in Philadelphia. Then we'll be attending Bryn Mawr College after we graduate."

Rebecca listened carefully as they told her about Philadelphia and their families. She found herself drawn into their lives and fascinated by their way of speaking and their manners. Yes, Ma'am. No, Ma'am. Clear diction—no you'ens or yous' like many people in and around McAlisterville. Rebecca was also delighted when she discovered they all had something in common: brothers but no sisters.

Her new acquaintances peppered her with questions about what it was like to live on a farm. "Do you have animals? What kind? Do you have to milk cows? Do you have to work in the fields?"

It was easy for Rebecca to answer their questions. She enjoyed the attention of these lovely young women. But she studied them the whole time, wondering why they seemed so inquisitive. It never occurred to her that living on a farm was interesting.

Lilly stood and put her hand to her mouth. "I forgot my manners. Please excuse me while I ask the maid to bring us some lemonade." Moments later, she walked back into the porch followed by a colored, older woman carrying a silver tray with a glass pitcher, three dainty cups and linen napkins. "Thank you, Lucy."

Before taking a cup, Maggie and Lilly placed a linen napkin on their laps. Rebecca followed their lead. She waited until they began sipping before she tasted the sweet-tart lemonade, savoring its icy coolness in her mouth.

Lilly put her cup down and turned her attention to Rebecca. "What do you want to do when you graduate from school?"

"I… I'm not sure. Most girls in McAlisterville don't graduate because they're needed on the farm. And sometimes they either get married or go to work as a domestic. If they earn money, they have to give it to their parents to help support the family."

Maggie and Lilly stared at each other with wide open eyes.

Seeing their reaction, Rebecca added, "I… like to help a friend of mine use plants to heal people when they're injured or sick. I'm getting pretty good at it. My family thinks so too."

Lilly lifted her hand to her mouth and started to speak, then changed her mind. Rebecca looked down at her lap, smoothing an imaginary wrinkle in her skirt. She wasn't ready to reveal too much about herself, at least not yet.

Rebecca was in awe of her friends and their magnificent homes, but uncertain how she fit in. Should she visit them again? Would they accept her if they knew she lived in a log cabin? However, one thing was clear: her new friends had no desire to get married or work as a domestic.

And neither did she.

CHAPTER 10

JULY WAS PEAK HARVEST FOR GARDEN VEGETABLES, PARTICularly green and yellow beans. Rebecca and her mother spent long days canning beans and other vegetables for the winter. It was hot and monotonous work. First, Ball jars and lids had to be sterilized in boiling water. While they were being prepared, Rebecca and her mother carried baskets of vegetables to the sink, and using the hand pump, washed them with cold water to remove dirt and bugs still clinging to their skins.

Once they were washed the women nicked the ends of the beans off with a sharp paring knife. Next, they snapped the crisp vegetables into pieces and packed them into the jars. Bean after bean.

After covering the beans with a mixture of water, pickling salt and white vinegar, they placed flat lids on top. Then the jars were set in a large pot filled with a few inches of water and cooked in boiling water for thirty minutes. When they cooled and the flat lids sealed, they tightly screwed lids on each jar. Rebecca carried tray after tray of sealed jars to the cold cellar. The two women canned all day, sometimes joined by grandmother Mary, until the day fell away and it was time to clear the table and prepare for supper.

Rebecca hated canning and cooking. It was hot and monotonous work. She wanted to spend more time with Maggie and Lilly—resentful that her work on the farm made it difficult to get away. However, she was hesitant to ask her new friends to visit the farm, knowing the log cabin was humble compared to their summer homes. And afraid the smell of animals and manure that permeated the air when the fields were plowed would turn them away.

On a dreary, cloudy day when she finished her chores early, Rebecca eagerly rode Jenny the three miles to Lilly's house. The young women spent the afternoon lounging on Lilly's large four-poster bed looking at pictures of the latest fashions in *Philadelphia Public Ledger* newspaper. Philadelphia's Gimbles, New York's Macy's and Chicago's Marshall Fields boasted ads for clothing, hats, gloves, and shoes. Occasionally, Lilly circled an item and later ask her father to purchase it for her when he traveled to New York or Chicago. Rebecca pictured Lilly going shopping for new dresses and shoes in a fancy carriage and tried to imagine what it would be like to have whatever she wanted.

Lukewarm when it came to fashion, Maggie told Rebecca she would rather dress in plain skirts and blouses. But Rebecca found the ads interesting and daydreamed about owning one of the high-necked, puffy-sleeved dresses with a bustle in the back. Even Lilly and Maggie's mothers wore beautiful dresses and blouses with sleeves that narrowed above the elbow and gathered at the wrist every day despite the heat of summer. They often wiped their faces with embroidered handkerchiefs and fanned themselves with ornate paper fans. Servants did the housecleaning, cooking, gardening, and laundry so the women could rest and tend to their stitchery—plus manage the household workers. Rebecca dreamed of a life where others did the work for her. It would be wonderful to be matron of a mansion. No farm work. No laundry… cleaning… canning. Children cultured and well-mannered like Maggie and Lilly. But most of all, being free to choose what you wanted to be.

Rebecca grew more fascinated with her new friends every time they were together. She listened as they talked about life in Philadelphia—libraries, socials, teas, and dances. Some of Maggie and Lilly's girlfriends went to finishing school. Rebecca often lay awake at night thinking about all of them, wondering what it would be like to live in their world—more curious than jealous. But she was envious they went to private school and the expectation they would go to Bryn Mawr. As far back as Rebecca remembered, no one she knew went to college. Particularly if she were a woman.

CHAPTER 11

The Indian woman stood still at the edge of the forest. Her eyes searched the understory for white flowers. Back So Straight watched the sun's rays filter through the trees, landing on some thick, spongy moss. Next to the moss grew small black elderberry bushes. She memorized their location. Must remember to show Rebecca. Leaf and root bark will make poultices for many injuries.

Then she walked soundlessly ahead through the baby trees and drooping shrubs. Delicate ferns, dipping and swaying in the gentle breeze pleased her eyes. She stopped. A five-lined skink, its bright azure tail glowing in a patch of sunlight, skittered across the ground and hid under a rock. She smiled. Then, behind the waving green fern-arms she saw them. Yarrow. Their lacy white faces grew on top of feathery leaves. Hello. She greeted them and whispered a prayer of thanks. Only harvesting three plants, she saved the rest for the future.

CHAPTER 12

ON A RARE AUGUST DAY WHEN HER EARLY MORNING chores—hunting eggs, feeding the pigs, hoeing weeds in the garden—were finished, Rebecca took advantage of the lull in the never-ending work to be done on the farm. "Ma, what do you think about Lilly and Maggie going berry picking with me before they have to go back to Philadelphia?"

Her mother stopped kneading the bread she was baking and smiled. "That's a good idea, Rebecca. They may never have had the chance to pick wild berries before coming to McAlisterville. Just be careful. You know there are animals that like berries too."

"I'm going to ask Back So Straight if I can take Wind along. She'd warn us of any danger." Rebecca was careful when it came to her new friends, always aware of their lack of experience living in the country.

Back So Straight spoke to her dog. "Go with Rebecca and guard her." Then she emptied three pails of dried moss and roots and handed the metal buckets to Rebecca. Attaching them to her horse, Rebecca set out for the big houses at the end of town, her guardian bringing up the rear.

As she entered Maggie's backyard and approached the house, lace curtains billowed in the wind through opened windows. She paused, taking in the scene before her: white wicker furniture on the veranda accented by fuchsia, green, and lilac cushions. Flowers everywhere. A grassy lawn with shrubbery defining walking paths. What she wouldn't give to sit here any time she wanted… drink lemonade… no farm work. Maybe read books.

Her thoughts were interrupted by a familiar voice. "Rebecca! Hello," Maggie called from the portico. "Why are you carrying buck—she stopped short when she saw Wind. "Where'd you get that dog? It looks odd with those blue eyes. Is it a wolf?" Rebecca didn't have a chance to answer before Maggie grabbed one of the buckets. "Are we going to pick berries? Wait here. I'll have to ask my father." A short time later, Maggie returned and said, "Let's go."

The young women ran across the road to Lilly's house. A maid was hanging wash on the clothesline near the main house. The rope stretched clear across the yard to the smaller brick building where the servants lived. White sheets hung like sails in the wind the entire length of the line. The maid stopped fastening a sheet with wooden clothespins and stepped back. But when Wind didn't come any closer, she resumed placing another clothespin on the billowing sheet. "Good mornin' girls. Miss Lilly be in the kitchen eatin' some scones I baked this mornin'. Would you like me to fetch her?"

"No, thank you, we'll find her," Maggie said, and proceeded to take Rebecca's hand and led them running to the backyard. Lilly greeted them but the moment she saw Wind, she retreated into the house. Rebecca shouted through the door, "Lilly, the dog won't hurt you. She belongs to my friend." The door opened a crack and Lilly's face peeked out.

"I'm not coming outside. I'm afraid of that dog."

Feeling guilty about frightening her friend, Rebecca replied, "It's okay, Lilly. She's harmless. I promise she won't hurt you. She can wait outside."

Maggie ignored the dog and Lilly's fear. "May we come in and have some of those scones your maid told us about?"

Opening the door slightly and looking to make sure the dog was a safe distance away, Lilly answered, "Yes, of course. Come in." She set two delicate china plates on a table covered with a crocheted lace tablecloth. A massive crystal vase sat in the middle with yellow and orange daylilies fanning out on all sides. "Please sit down. Here's some honey to put on top if you wish."

After taking her first bite, Rebecca closed her eyes and smiled. It was the smoothest, most buttery thing she had ever tasted—even better than her mother's biscuits. "This is so good. Thank you very much."

"We always have scones for breakfast as soon as the rosemary plants have seeds. Other times, Lucy puts raisins on top. But… why do you have buckets?" Lilly's eyebrows lifted toward the widow's peak on her perfectly unblemished forehead, and her long slender arms perched on her tiny waist. Rebecca studied her, then looked at Maggie's freckled face and slouched shoulders. How different her new friends were. One a fancy lady and one a rough and tumble girl. Wonder what they thought about her, a farm girl?

Finally, Rebecca answered, "We're going berry picking, Lilly. The wild raspberries are almost over this time of year, but I think there're still plenty left. Do you have to ask your mother if you can go?"

When Lilly's mother, Sarah, heard voices, she walked into the kitchen and immediately greeted her daughter's friends—hugging them gently and giving them a light kiss on the cheek. Rebecca could see where Lilly got her beauty. Same shining hair with sunshine glowing through, same graceful posture, same delicate body, and the same sweet spirit.

"Yes, you may go…" but when she looked into the backyard she hesitated. "What's that strange dog doing in our yard?"

"Oh, she's a good guard dog," Rebecca answered.

Sarah looked again at the blue-eyed dog, then Rebecca. "I guess it's all right if you say so, Rebecca. Be careful, now. Hear me?"

"Yes, Ma'am, we will," Rebecca assured her.

Rebecca led her friends, pails dangling over their arms, across the road and through the foothills. She knew the way to the berry patches—she had picked berries there ever since she was a little girl—and was careful to avoid rocky ridges where footing was difficult. Maggie and Lilly chattered as they walked, pausing now and then to ask her questions. When they nearly stepped on a small mound of poop in their pathway, they giggled and quizzed Rebecca about what animal it came from.

Rebecca offered a bemused smile. "A deer passed through here recently, probably a female. The droppings are still wet. If it was a male, a buck, the pile would be much bigger."

Squinting and drawing her lips together, Lilly gave a sideward glance at her friends. But Maggie's eyes grew big and bright. Their questions delighted Rebecca. It never occurred to her that the ordinary things she saw in the mountains would take on such significance to her new friends. Every time she answered a question, her newfound sense of importance grew.

Before long, they reached the edge of the woods. The forests that hid the high meadow were thick with evergreens. They were so massive the patches of blue sky above them barely showed through. The ground smelled musty from layers of evergreen needles. Fallen pinecones dotted the forest floor. As they walked over the dried lacy spheres, it sounded like glass being ground into shards under their shoes.

At the edge of the forest stood a high meadow covered with masses of wildflowers: black-eyed Susan, dark pink smartweed, tall ironweed, and golden ragwort. Their subtle fragrance lifted on the breezes. Wild raspberry bushes, their shiny berries hanging from thin branches, grew among the flowers. Rebecca led her friends, their buckets swaying wildly in their hands, to the densest cluster.

"Look. There're still plenty of berries," Rebecca said, voicing a challenge. "Let's see who can fill her bucket first."

Maggie took her seriously, and ran to the bushes most heavy with berries. She stuffed them in her mouth by the handfuls.

"Your mouth is purple," Lilly scolded. "You must be eating more berries than you put in your bucket. Your hands are stained too. Don't wipe them on your dress or your mother will be angry." Rebecca suspected Lilly, always the lady, was deterred from eating berries to avoid tainting her flawless skin and clothing.

Maggie darted from bush to bush. She was on a mission. Her red hair flashed in the sunlight, more vibrant than any of the flowers. Beads of perspiration built under her nose and slipped down onto her lips. Berry juice dripped onto her dress. Maggie's hair was damp with sweat, and she had a wine-colored smudge over one eyebrow where she wiped her forehead with her hand. Lilly and Rebecca bent over with laughter.

"What are you laughing at? My bucket's fuller than yours. And look," pointing to the ground, "I found some cute baby snakes with yellow tips on their tails."

Rebecca's drew in her breath, leaving her nearly speechless. She finally managed to scream. "Don't move! Those are baby copperheads. They're poisonous. There may be a nest of them. Maggie, step back slowly. Lilly, stay where you are behind me. Whatever you do, don't step on them."

She turned to see Lilly with a look of terror on her face, foot in mid-air. Coiled up where she was about to step was a thick snake with hourglass markings on its back and a penny-colored head. Rebecca heard something move through the bushes. Only when she saw a blur of black fur did she realize it was Wind. Barking and teeth bared, the dog ran toward the snake.

"Wind, watch out!" Rebecca yelled. But it was too late. The snake struck the dog on her chest. Just as quickly, Wind grabbed the snake's tail with her teeth and flung it into the woods.

"Leave the buckets here. I must go home and get help. Do you know the way back to your house?"

Maggie said firmly, "No, I don't think I can find my way. Lilly, do you?" But her friend shook her head, tears spilling down her cheeks. She dropped her bucket and wiped them away.

"We must all go to the farm." Rebecca pleaded, "Can you run fast?"

"Yes, I can," answered Maggie. Lilly just looked at Rebecca and gave a slight nod.

By then the dog had difficulty holding up her head. Her chest was bleeding heavily, blood forming furrows on her fur and dripping onto the ground. Finally she laid down, her swollen tongue hanging out her mouth.

"Let's go," Rebecca shouted.

The three girls ran as fast as they could, Rebecca and Maggie slowing down now and then so they wouldn't lose sight of Lilly. Dead trees and brush made them stop to help each other, and the rough, rocky banks of the forest threatened their footing. A branch caught Rebecca's face, scratching her cheeks. Thoughts of Wind, wounded and bleeding, raced through her mind. What if Wind dies?

Lilly tripped over a fallen log and fell into a shallow wet bog, but she managed to pull herself up and began running again. Mud smeared across her dress, arms, and face. When they reached the edge of the farm, Lilly and Maggie collapsed against a fence post out of breath, but Rebecca ran the rest of the way to the cabin. "Pop! Pop! Where are you? Gary... someone... help me." Rebecca could hardly breathe, her screams slipping between gasps.

"Rebecca?" Jane shouted as she ran from the garden in back of the cabin, her apron bulging, tomatoes flying out from each side.

"Ma... Wind was bitten... by a copperhead. She's still in the... berry patch in the high meadow. We walked into... a nest of them." Rebecca tried to catch her breath before continuing. "Where's... where's Pop and Gary? We have to go back for her. She may... already be dead."

Back So Straight appeared near the burned-out barn and was already jumping on Jenny's back.

Frozen to the ground and confused by what she saw, Rebecca momentarily lost her sense of what to do next. "Back So Straight must have heard me screaming. She's riding my horse."

"Let her go. Saddle the mare," Jane said. "Ride with me and show me where the dog is lying..."

Dragging their feet, Lilly and Maggie finally reached the cabin. "Please stay here," Rebecca shouted. Get a drink at the pump. The men will be back shortly. Tell them what happened. We'll be back as soon as we can."

By the time Rebecca saddled the horse, Back So Straight was already approaching the woods. The way she rode the filly amazed Rebecca. It was the first time she had ever seen her Indian friend ride a horse. She galloped away—bareback—like she had been doing it all her life.

Nearly a half hour later, Back So Straight reached the high meadow and cautiously approached the bushes where snakes might still be hiding, nearly invisible in the twigs and leaves. Following the sound of whimpering, she saw Wind on her side, a trail of blood where she must have dragged herself away from the bushes. Her neck and face were swollen to twice their normal size. She was lifeless except for the opening and closing of her eyelids.

When Back So Straight whispered in the dog's ear, the animal's legs twitched slightly. The dog's chest was still bleeding. She opened a small pack and removed a wad of yarrow leaves, spat on them, and made a poultice to pack on the wound. After tearing a piece of her long skirt into a wide strip of cloth, the Indian woman gently wound it around the dog's upper body. Wind, now motionless, didn't make a sound.

Rebecca and her mother approached through the tall flowers. They watched carefully where they put their feet. When they reached Back So Straight, the Indian woman said, "I must take Wind back to my hut. She is near death. Rebecca, bring Jenny to me and help lift Wind onto the horse's back. We must be very careful. Do not disturb the cloth over her chest."

While Jane held the horse steady, Back So Straight and Rebecca hoisted the dog, laying her belly across the animal's back just below its mane. The cloth around Wind's chest seeped dark red blood that made the horse's back wet and slippery. Back So Straight climbed on the horse and sat behind the dog, steadying Wind with her knee.

The ride to the farm was agonizingly slow. Back So Straight rode carefully so as to not dislodge the dog. But several times Wind nearly slipped off the horse and the Indian woman carefully pulled the dog in the opposite direction. Dark blood stained the horse's white shoulders.

When they reached the farm, Elwood and Gary carried Wind to her hut where they gently laid her on the old wooden table inside the door. Back So Straight ordered everyone out of the cabin except Rebecca. "Snake bites may bleed for a long time, especially those on the head and chest. I will use more fresh yarrow and flowers leaves to stop it. Crush those in my basket and give me some to chew. Then get some water. Make yarrow tea like I taught you."

While Rebecca did as she was told, Back So Straight chanted as she made a thick green poultice of the chewed and crushed leaves and pressed it onto the lifeless dog's chest. Her mentor's soulful chanting somehow sounded familiar, but she didn't know how or why.

Rebecca listened to the rhythmic sounds of words and phrases she didn't understand. She closed her eyes and felt the gravity of what had happened in the mountains. Placing her friends in harm's way. Wind bitten by a poisonous snake. Having to face Back So Straight if her dog dies—facing her friends and their parents.

About ten minutes later when the tea had cooled, the Indian woman soaked a cloth in the tea and dribbled some into Wind's mouth. The dog made a few lapping movements with her grossly swollen tongue and swallowed. Placing her hands on the dog's head, Back So Straight whispered, "Only the common frog has bitten you."

Rebecca stood aside and watched in fascination as Back So Straight took a turtle shell rattle and walked around the table. She recalled her mentor telling her about the sacredness of the turtle and the meaning of the bear-fur mustache and the beads attached to the deer-bone handle. Back So Straight's grandmother, a beloved shaman, had given it to her when she became a woman. Dried corn, small shot, tobacco, and sage-sweet grass inside gave the rattle a sound like acorns dropping on a bed of leaves.

"You may go now," Back So Straight said. "I wish to be alone."

Her two young friends sat with Rebecca's mother on the edge of the cabin's porch. Their clothes were streaked with dirt, twigs stuck in their hair. Lilly tried to brush the stains off her dress and pull the little bits of wood out of her hair, but Maggie made no attempt to make herself look more presentable.

As Rebecca approached, Jane said, "Let's go into the cabin. You too, Rebecca," She opened the door and stood aside while the young ladies entered. "Here are some clean washcloths. Use the water pump at the sink." While they washed their hands and face, Jane poured some meadow tea.

Rebecca approached her friends, barely able to speak. "I… I'm sorry about the snakes. I should have been more careful." She felt drained, like she did the morning after the barn fire.

Both Lilly Maggie spoke at the same time. "It's not your fault."

"But Wind may die. She's very sick and it's my fault." Rebecca was close to tears but didn't want her friends see her cry. Despite her effort to blink them back, they seeped out of her eyes. She took her washcloth and pretended to wash her face a second time.

Jane patted her daughter on the back. "It's nobody's fault. Come, Rebecca, we must take your friends home before their folks come looking for them."

The wagon ride to the mansions seemed to take forever. Maggie and Lilly tried to talk to Rebecca about Wind and the snakes, but she only managed to nod now and then. When they reached the stone house, Maggie gave Rebecca a hug before jumping off the wagon. "I hope the dog gets better." Without waiting for an answer, she ran to the front door and dashed inside.

All was quiet as Jane drove the wagon to the brick house across the street. Before Lilly climbed down, Rebecca took her hand. "Lilly, please explain to your mother and father what happened to you and Maggie. My Ma and Pop and I will stop by in a day or two to speak with them. But now we must get back and make supper for everyone."

Lilly nodded and walked to the sun porch. When she got to the door, she turned around and waved.

Rebecca waved back. But all she could think of was how the copperhead snakes could have bitten all of them. The terrified look on her friends' faces. The dog's bleeding chest. Her swollen and lifeless body. All her fault.

CHAPTER 13

LATER THAT WEEK JANE AND ELWOOD RETURNED TO THE BIG houses outside town to ask if Lilly and Maggie had recovered from their harrowing experience. The Eastmans were sitting in the gazebo when they arrived.

Jane called out, "Hello. We came to see how Maggie's doing."

"Nice to see you," said Hugh Eastman. "Maggie's doing quite well but she's worried about Rebecca and the dog. We're thankful the girls weren't hurt."

"Yes, we are too," Jane agreed.

"Please come join us in the gazebo," said Maggie's mother.

Jane and Elwood climbed down from the wagon and stepped into the gazebo. Rebecca followed, her steps measured, reluctant to face Maggie's mother and father. "I'm sorry about the snakes. I should have been more careful."

"I am sure you did what you could to keep everyone safe," Mrs. Eastman said, taking Rebecca's hand.

Just then Lilly's mother and father, Hugh and Sarah North, walked into the yard and over to the gazebo. "Hello, everyone. Rebecca, how are you… and how is the dog?"

Rebecca's stomach turned flip-flops and the saliva in her mouth disappeared. "I… I'm fine but the dog is still very sick. We aren't sure she'll make it." The gravity of her statement gripped her. This dog her mentor raised from a puppy that became her companion… her protector. If she dies…

Hugh Eastman stood, took a step forward and rested his hands on his waist. "I'm sure I speak for all of us when I say thank you to Rebecca and that dog. It could have been a far more serious incident for all of them."

After a brief moment of awkwardness when Rebecca didn't respond, Elwood turned to Mr. Eastman. "Yep, could have. Proud of my daughter's quick thinking."

"You certainly can be. Now about another matter. Mr. Wagner, perhaps we could talk privately?"

Elwood nodded and followed Mr. Eastman as he walked away from the gazebo.

"I've been thinking about the barn you lost. Maybe you can come work for me."

"That's a kind of you, Mr. Eastman. But I have a farm to run. Only thing to show for my twenty years of being tied to that land. Rather leave the barn unfinished."

"Mr. Wagner, we're neighbors. I want to help you. How about I make you an offer to purchase some of your mountain land. Then you can buy lumber and replace the equipment and tools you lost. What do you say? Shall I have my attorney work up an agreement?"

"Don't know," Elwood said, scratching his head. "How many acres would you need?"

"Well, I'd say… about a hundred of your big pine and hemlock stand. There're probably some hardwoods mixed in there too."

Elwood took a deep breath and clenched his fists. He looked at the ground and spit. After grinding the wet spot into the ground, he stared at Mr. Eastman with slanted eyes.

Neither spoke until Hugh Eastman cleared his throat. "I know this is a hard decision, but you won't regret it once you have your farm back in operation again."

"I just don't know. Seems like a lot of land to sell." Elwood's released his fists, his arms hanging limp at his sides. "All right, but only a hundred acres. No more." He took a deep breath and held out his hand. "I'm used to a promise and a handshake to do my business. That's all you'll need from me."

"Wait a minute. I always have agreements in writing." Hugh studied Elwood for a minute or two and shrugged his shoulders. "I guess in this case I'll make an exception. I won't even tell my attorney. Peter North may not agree, but I trust you, Mr. Wagner."

Elwood studied Hugh Eastwood before responding. "All right. But we have to agree on which land I sell. Assume you'll cut the trees down. Give me time—have to figure out how much lumber I'll need to build my barn and how much money I'll need to buy new equipment. Can't do it until next week. Have hay that needs to be cut in a few days."

"Let me know when you're ready to mark off your land, but don't take too long. I'd like to get a crew up to the new timberland and start cutting. How does two weeks sound?"

"Hmmm, don't know. Harvesting hay's tricky work. Depends on the weather. Couple of years ago, a hailstorm came through and flattened my hay before I could cut it. Couldn't even save more'n half an acre."

"Two weeks, no later. Let me know when you're ready." Hugh jiggled coins in his pockets as he turned and walked back to the gazebo.

Elwood stood hunched over. His stomach felt like someone had landed a punch in his midsection. He had just agreed to sell one hundred acres of his beloved woodland.

He said nothing about the conversation with Hugh Eastman when he drove back to the farm, but Jane and Rebecca were quiet too. As they approached their property, Rebecca searched the trees near Back So Straight's hut. There, behind the tree the Indian woman used as a bench, movement caught her eye. Back So Straight was walking into the trees with a basket hung on her arm and a small spade in her hand. Her dog was not with her.

"Ma, Back So Straight went into the woods. That must mean that Wind is better, doesn't it?"

"Probably."

Her mother didn't sound convincing. The fear Wind had died made her breath catch in her throat. "Do you think… I should talk to her?"

"Why don't you wait until after supper? By that time she should be back in her cabin and you can take some food to her."

Rebecca wanted to argue but she sensed something was bothering her mother and father. Their faces looked pinched around the eyes.

"Would you like me to start cooking?" Rebecca asked her mother.

"Sure. Fetch some canned pork and a jug of sauerkraut from the cold cellar, and some potatoes. Start to peel. I'll help you mash as soon as Pop and I tend to the horses."

Grandma Mary came out of the back bedroom when she heard the cabin door open. "How's that dog doing?"

"I don't know exactly, but I hope to find out after supper."

The old woman put her arm around Rebecca and squeezed her shoulder. Grandma didn't say very much but she always seemed to know when someone needed a hug. Rebecca and her grandmother cooked supper together, each doing the familiar peeling, stirring, and mixing without having to ask what to do next. By the time the food was ready, the rest of the family trickled in.

After giving thanks, Elwood was unusually quiet. No one seemed to notice except Rebecca. She looked at her mother for clues, but Jane joined the others in table conversation. Hadn't rained in over two weeks. Cat had more kittens. Neighbor lost a cow. Grange meeting Thursday evening. Gary bragged about shooting a groundhog.

After supper, Rebecca took a basket of food to the hut. She gingerly knocked on the door and stood waiting. And waiting. But just as she lifted her hand to knock again, her mother tapped her on the shoulder.

"I saw what happened from the cabin window. Leave her be. She needs time to be alone. Try to understand. She's caring for her beloved dog. She's not blaming you for the accident. That's what it was: an accident. Wind probably saved Lilly's life and maybe yours too. Give her time. Let's take a walk around the back meadow to clear our heads of all this worry."

Sensing her mother was trying to placate her and avoid saying more about Back So Straight, Rebecca agreed reluctantly.

Jane took her daughter's hand. But Rebecca still wasn't convinced. "She won't let me inside her cabin. What if she never forgives me? I'm so lonely. Lilly and Maggie are soon going back to Philadelphia and I'll be left here with nothing to do but chores."

"I know, Rebecca. I have your grandma and grandpa Wagner, but since my parents are gone, Back So Straight has become..." She hesitated. "Like family to me."

Rebecca thought about Jane's relationship with Back So Straight. They spent a lot of time together. Her mother went to visit Back So Straight, but she hardly ever came into the cabin unless there was an important reason or she was invited.

Just as Rebecca and Jane rounded the back corner of the cabin, the Indian woman came out of her hut and left the door standing open. Wind slowly walked over the threshold. She was thin, the wound on her chest raw and black around the edges. Her legs trembled when she put weight on them, but she stayed upright. Dark circles covered the skin around her swollen eyes, making them look like patches of blue sky on a cloudy day. After following Back So Straight for a short distance, the dog measured each step as she turned around and went back inside. The Indian woman followed silently, but there was the hint of a smile on her face.

"Wind's alive. Thank God," said Rebecca.

"What do you say we butcher a chicken tomorrow and make pot pie for supper. Maybe Back So Straight will join us."

Rebecca nodded, forgetting her mother's reluctance to tell her more about Back So Straight. "I'll ask her first thing in the morning."

Jane grasped her daughter's elbow. "Let's go home."

For the first time since Wind was injured, Rebecca felt happy. She raised her head and let out a deep breath. But something caught her eye in the foothills behind the cabin. There at the base of the mountain, her father stood still as a tree on a windless day. His head was tilted sharply upward toward the sky. Then he abruptly jerked off his straw hat and slammed it on the ground.

CHAPTER 14

LATE SUMMER MORNINGS STILL HELD CHORES TO BE TENDED to. After gathering the eggs, feeding the pigs, and hoeing the garden, the heat of the afternoon seeped into Rebecca's skin. Eager to say goodbye to her friends, she washed her face and hands, changed clothes and ate a quick lunch. When she arrived at the Eastman mansion, she saw trunks and suitcases setting under the portico.

"Maggie, it's Rebecca." She waited for a reply, but when there was none, she knocked on the door. Finally, Lucy, the colored maid, opened it. "Hello, Miss Rebecca. Maggie be over at Lilly's house."

Rebecca thanked her and ran across the street, her skirt twisting between her legs and slowing her down. Boys had it easy. No skirts to get in the way. As she approached the stately brick house, she heard thunder in the distance.

Lilly and Maggie were directing servants to set suitcases, trunks, and hat boxes in the screened-in porch and didn't see Rebecca standing outside.

Happy to find them, she said, "Hello. Lilly, Maggie, I've come to say goodbye."

Lilly motioned Rebecca inside. "We were afraid we wouldn't have a chance to see you before we left."

"Oh, that would've been terrible!" Rebecca looked at Lilly, then Maggie, trying to hold back tears she felt gathering in her eyes.

Maggie grabbed Rebecca's arms and wrapped them around herself. "Not another word. I'm sad enough. This has been the best summer of my life. I've had so many exciting adventures, thanks to you."

Lilly placed her arms around both of them. "Please tell me you'll write to us, and we'll do the same."

Rebecca smelled the sweet odor of Cashmere Bouquet soap on her skin. Lilly, always a lady.

A flash of lightening startled all three of them. A minute later, drops of rain pelted the metal roof. Soon rainwater began to wash down the sides of the porch and splashed onto the ground. Lilly's mother Sarah called to them. "Come inside, girls. We'll have to wait until the rain stops to load our belongings and start for the train station. And Rebecca, you must stay until it's safe for you to return home."

"Thank you. I left my horse tied under the trees at Maggie's house. I think she'll be all right."

The next hour was an unexpected luxury for Rebecca. Lucy served finger sandwiches, fruit salad, and punch while Lilly's mother and father gathered last-minute items to add to the growing pile of boxes and crates. The girls snuggled together on a large sofa, smothered in soft pillows, laughing and arranging them in a nest. They exchanged addresses and Lilly gave Rebecca a box of fine writing paper and envelopes. Rebecca held the pale pink linen to the light and saw an R embossed on the envelopes.

"These are lovely, Lilly. Thank you. I never had such fancy stationary... perfect to use when I write to you and Maggie."

As soon as the rain abated, Mr. North directed the servants to load the wagons and carriages. "The storm's over. Time to leave for Mifflin—the train leaves in three hours. Come Lilly. Say goodbye to Rebecca. And Maggie, I'm sure your family is looking for you. We'll join them across the street."

Lilly placed her hand in Rebecca's. "I'll be back next summer. Goodbye."

Squeezing her hand and reaching for Maggie's, Rebecca said, "Goodbye, my friends. I'll miss you."

Lilly's eyes riveted on Rebecca's. "Not nearly as much as we'll miss you."

Colored servants helped the women into the carriages. They gathered their full skirts and sat in the back seat under the fringed surrey. "Get," the driver yelled, and the surrey lurched forward.

As the procession of wagons and carriages drove down the lanes to Main Street West, Maggie and Lilly turned in their seats and waved goodbye. Rebecca did the same, her eyes watery until she blinked the cloudiness away. She walked through the wet grass to her horse and hoisted herself up. The saddle on Jenny's back was wet from the rain, but Rebecca didn't care that her skirt got soaked. She was preoccupied with thoughts of Lilly and Maggie. She'd miss her friends and the luxuries their families shared with her. But soon the smell of the meadows after the storm... clean and earthy... reached Rebecca's nose. She took a deep breath and looked around her. Rain made the trees and bushes glisten in the afternoon sun. Butterflies landed on the edges of puddles, their wings opening and closing as though keeping time to a silent song. Birds drank from water that pooled in ruts in the road. She rode through the meadows to the farm, taking in the beauty all around her. Up ahead, the mountains seemed greener, the wet tree trunks blacker. Soon her sadness lifted.

That evening everyone celebrated Wind's recovery around the supper table: Ma and Pop, Grandpa and Grandma Wagner, Rebecca, Gary, and Back So Straight. They ate chicken potpie, pepper cabbage, and applesauce, and talked about the encounter with the copperheads and Wind's heroism.

Filled with the emotions of her day, Rebecca dominated the conversation. She recounted the nice time she had with her friends because of the delay due to the storm. She described the dozens of trunks and boxes the servants packed into wagons and carriages before they left for the train station. When she finished, Gary rolled his eyes and asked for another helping of food.

Rebecca didn't see that her father hardly touched his supper.

But her mother did. "Elwood, what's wrong? You didn't eat much of your favorite meal tonight."

Elwood didn't answer. He sat still, then pushed his plate away. With an unsteady voice he said, "Decided to sell a hundred acres of timber in exchange for money to buy farm equipment and lumber to rebuild the barn."

Everyone sat in stunned silence. Rebecca stared at her father. Desperate. That's what he said about never selling our mountain land.

"Why not just harvest enough trees from our land to build the barn? Or sell Mr. Eastman the trees and keep the land? Jane said

"New wood's too green. Would warp and twist apart. Has to dry. Don't have time to wait till next year."

Rebecca chimed in. "But you could just sell the timber."

"Eastwood wants the trees and the land. Best investment, I guess. Buying cheap land seems to be what these fellas want just now."

Gary stood and roughly pushed his chair away from the table. "I can't believe you're going to sell our timberland."

Rebecca felt her heartbeat in her neck. "Me either, Pop."

Elwood slammed his fork on the table. "I'm desperate, damn it. How do you think I'm going to rebuild the barn and buy new equipment?"

Rebecca flinched. She knew that once her father made up his mind, there was no changing it, but she had to try. "Maybe there's some other way to get the lumber."

Elwood's voice grew harsh. "It's not just the lumber. How about the cultivator… rollers… harrows… our barrel seeder? Hay for the winter… nearly all my tools? They cost money—and I don't have it."

Everyone sat motionless. The only sound was a fly buzzing around the table, landing on food scraps. Mary swatted it with the fly swatter that was kept hanging on a small nail under the table. Still holding the fly swatter in her hand, she said, more forcefully than usual, "Who's… who's going to help you rebuild the barn, Elwood? It's too big a job for you and Gary."

"Don't know. Maybe Gary and I have to work on it after we sell the tobacco, bit by bit, and one of our neighbors can help us lift the heavy beams."

Mary placed the fly swatter back on the nail and turned to her son. "Too bad you can't count on your father. He's gotten so fat and short of breath, he can't do much of anything."

The elder Wagner raised his fist at his wife, got up from the table, and scuttled toward the door. His heavy body waved to and fro with each step as his wooden cane tapped loudly on the pine floorboards and his breath came in loud huffs.

Face and neck red and blotchy, Elwood turned to his mother. "Shouldn't be so hard on him. Man worked hard all his life. Deserves to rest now."

Tears sliding down her cheeks, Mary said, "I deserve a rest, too. I… I've wanted to visit my relatives in Berks County for the past five years… but it looks like that's never going to happen."

Rebecca felt sorry for her grandmother. Words refused to come, but finally she found her voice. "Grandpa. She… didn't mean..."

Joseph interrupted. "No wife of mine calls me names in front of my family. She needs to keep her mouth shut. I'm the man of the family and I don't need her sass."

"Please, Grandpa. Everyone, stop arguing. This was supposed to be a celebration of Wind's recovery but it's turned into a shouting match." Rebecca looked pleadingly at her mother, who had started to clear the table. But Jane turned away and carried the dirty plates to the sink.

Rebecca walked to the window and lifted her eyes upward to Little Round Top Mountain. There would soon be a brown, treeless island surrounded by a sea of green. Now she knew what her father meant when he said he'd have to be desperate before he sold any of his mountain land.

CHAPTER 15

WOODLAND FERNS TURNED RUSTY BROWN AS LATE SUMMER gave way to autumn. Rebecca and Gary's farm chores continued before and after school, and all day Saturdays. Construction on the barn still hadn't started, but harvest was nearly complete now that tobacco was cut and dried in the small tobacco shed. It was one of their few cash crops, although it required a lot of work to grow, cut, and hang upside down to dry. Rebecca's father always worked tobacco into the Wagner farm's regular crop rotations—hay-corn-tobacco-wheat. Hay-corn-tobacco-wheat—and sometimes barley, which kept the soil rich.

Although this year's crop of wheat and corn was robust, until her father hauled the grain to the gristmill in Jericho and paid to have it ground into flour, there wasn't much profit. So he ended up with most of his harvest being exchanged for milling his crop. Even though Rebecca knew he trusted the miller, Elwood had explained to her he always watched the grain as it dribbled from a hopper to be ground by several huge stones. He wanted some large bags of "fine" flour for Jane to cook and bake, but also needed wheat and corn meal to feed the animals.

Last year her father lost eight days waiting for stone dressers to chisel the surfaces of the stones that had dulled from normal wear and tear. That delay that cost him their barley crop when a few days of hard rain flattened it and the stalks got moldy before they could be cut. It seemed like weather always played havoc with their success as farmers, something Rebecca never got used to.

Once the wheat and corn were milled, the tobacco crop was ready to be sold to tobacco companies where it was to be made into cigars. The Wagners were one of legions of farmers whose tobacco grown in the rich central Pennsylvania soil was preferred by companies in Philadelphia and Reading.

More than few years ago, when her grandfather was able to walk without too much difficulty, Rebecca recalled Joseph always insisted on taking the tobacco into town, stopping on his way home to buy hard cider. Back then his blue eyes contrasted his ruddy complexion and his thick moustache was always unruly. She remembered him constantly stretching one side of his fat neck that sat atop his heavy frame like a stack of doughnuts. But she found it hard to picture her grandfather as a much younger, robust man. Now Joseph waddled when he walked to relieve pressure on sore joints worn from years of hard labor as a farmer and bearing too much weight.

While Elwood, Gary, and Rebecca loaded bundles of dried tobacco onto the wagon, Joseph approached. He held himself steady with his cane, his pudgy fist wrapped tightly around the worn handle.

"I'm going to drive the tobacco into town. All I need is a hoist to help me get on the wagon."

Elwood walked between his father and the wagon and faced him. "Not sure that's a good idea."

"Well, I don't care what you say. I'm tired of sitting around doing nothing."

"You're not well enough to drive."

"Like hell, I'm not. You better not argue with me. It could get you in trouble."

Elwood opened his mouth to speak, but changed his mind.

"I'll go with you grandpa," Rebecca said, working her way toward Joseph.

"No, you won't. I'm going alone. Son, Gary, just help me up," he snapped, as he took hold of the metal armrest on the side of the seat. Elwood grabbed him under his remaining arm, while Gary pushed from behind as Joseph pulled himself up. The seat made a swishing sound when he sat down.

"Elwood, don't follow me. I'm warning you. I know enough secrets about you to stop you from meddling." A loud "get" and the wagon jerked forward through the lane and onto the road.

Rebecca followed her father to the empty tobacco shed and sat down next to him against the wall. She watched him prop his elbows in his knees and hold his head in his hands. She was curious about what her grandfather had said. What did her grandpa mean about knowing enough secrets about him to stop him from meddling? Why did Elwood give in so quickly?

Her father held a small piece of brown tobacco leaf between his hands and twisted it. The dried leaf made crackling sounds, then drifted silently onto the floorboards. Elwood brought his hands to his face and sniffed the pungent smell. Finally he said, his voice cracking, "Can't seem to do anything right these days. First… can't make my family understand why I had to sell some mountain land. Then… can't make a profit on our grain, and… now can't keep my Pa from squandering our tobacco money on cider."

Rebecca put her hand on his arm. "Pop, let's go inside. Ma probably has supper on the stove and will be calling us to eat soon. Unless you want to follow grandpa into town, we can't do anything now except wait for him to come home."

Elwood stood up and brushed the small bits of dried tobacco leaves from his overalls. "No use doing that. He's already mad enough to hurt someone."

Later that evening the whole family sat on the porch. They watched the wagon wind its way up the long lane. Nearly four hours had gone by since Joseph had left. Supper was long over and the sun was hiding behind the trees on the mountain in back of the farm.

When the wagon pulled closer to the cabin, Rebecca heard the crackling sound of wheels over the small stones on the lane. She held her breath as Joseph stopped the empty wagon and began to climb out. He grabbed the handle and slid to the ground, landing on unsteady feet. The old man tried to balance himself as he retrieved his cane from underneath the seat, but fell against the wagon. His face was flushed, his eyes half-closed. His family remained in their seats, eyes riveted on Joseph. All except Mary, who quietly stepped off the side of the porch and ran toward the back of the cabin.

"That cider wasn't fit to feed the pigs," Joseph mumbled. He struggled up the steps to the porch, cursing, and limped his way into the cabin.

Rebecca followed him, but ran outside when she saw him grab the shotgun over the fireplace. "Pop, Grandpa has a gun!"

The elder Wagner stumbled out the door and looked around. "Where is she?"

Something in Joseph's voice frightened Elwood as much as the gun in his father's hands. He stood in front of Joseph and raised his arms. "Stop. Put the gun down. You've been drinking. Don't do anything stupid."

But this seemed to anger Joseph even more. He pointed the gun at his son and bellowed, "Get out of my way. Nothing you say or do is going to stop me." He staggered off the porch and managed to shuffle a few steps. "My wife called me names in front of my family. I know she's out here somewhere."

Rebecca grabbed her father's arm. "I'll go find grandma."

Shaking off her arm, Elwood shouted, "No, Rebecca."

"Yes, I'm going." She ran around the other side of the cabin, her eyes scanning the outbuildings. There on the ground at the outside corner of the corncrib she spied a piece of her grandmother's skirt. Rebecca sprinted to Mary and found her sitting with her arms drawn up around her knees. "Grandma, I'm here."

"He's going to shoot me. He's drunk and mad as a hornet! I know he's coming… I hear his breathing."

Joseph's panting sounded like a horse that had been ridden hard. When he rounded the corner of the corncrib, he shuffled from side to side without his cane, then stumbled but didn't fall. The shotgun, a twelve-gauge double barrel, was pointed at Mary, trigger cocked. "Mary, you shamed me in front of my family. Get out of my way, Rebecca."

Heart bounding in her chest, Rebecca feared for her grandmother's life. She took a few steps toward Joseph. "Grandpa… put the gun down. You don't want to do anything… you'll regret."

With trembling hands, Joseph braced himself against the corncrib. He looked at his wife of forty years and dropped to his knees. The gun handle hit the ground, buckshot exploding toward the corncrib.

"Mary," he mumbled, eyes opening widely. That was Joseph's last word as he fell face down like a tree blown over by the wind.

The shocking sound of the shotgun blast echoed in Rebecca's ears. "Grandma, are you hurt?"

Mary shook her head.

Hearing footsteps behind her, Rebecca turned and saw her father and mother running toward the corncrib. Elwood rushed to his father's side and knelt beside him, while Jane threw her arms around her daughter. "What happened? Are you all right?"

"Grandpa fell over and the gun went off. I don't think Grandma's hurt but she's not moving or talking." Her knees buckled as she managed to slide onto the ground. The smell of gunpowder made her retch. She wrapped her arms around her sides to stop her body from shivering. "Please check on Grandma."

"Oh, my girl, are you sure you aren't hurt?"

Rebecca nodded no.

"Stay here. I'll be right back.," said Jane, as she held up her skirt and ran to her mother-in-law, who was still leaning against the side of the corncrib, arms wrapped around her legs. "Mary, have you been hit?"

"No. I don't think so."

"Let me see." Jane scanned the woman's body for blood or holes in her clothing.

"I don't see any wounds. I'll be right back after I help Elwood."

By the time Jane joined her husband, he had turned his father's face to the side. She spoke in a barely audible voice, "Thank God Rebecca's all right and your mother wasn't hit. But… is your father… dead?"

"Don't know… have to roll him over." He shouted to Rebecca, "Come here."

Still shivering, she willed herself to walk.

"Jane, you too. Help me roll him on his back."

Twice they tried to turn him but he was dead weight. Each time he slid back on his stomach. On the third try, his body rolled on his back, one arm thumping on the ground. His face was gray, his lips blue. Rebecca placed her fingers onto the hollow between his wrist and thumb where she thought the pulse should be, remembering how to do it from one of the science books her teacher had loaned her.

She pressed down harder. "I think I feel a pulse, but I'm not sure."

CHAPTER 16

AT THE SOUND OF A GUNSHOT, GARY SPRINTED FROM THE forest back to the farm where Elwood was coming out of the woodshed carrying a heavy wide board.

"Where in tarnation were you? Get the hell over here. Take one end of this board and come with me." The two carried the board to Joseph and laid it beside him.

"What happened?" Gary asked Rebecca, who was sitting on the ground next to her grandfather.

Elwood shouted, "No time for talking. Rebecca, help your brother."

Together they pulled him over on his side enough for Elwood to slide the board partly under the old man's body.

"Now go to the other side and roll him over while I push the board under him."

Once Joseph was centered on the board, Elwood pointed at his son. "Going to carry Grandpa to the cabin. You lift that end, I'll lift this one. Ready? Lift."

Gary staggered under the weight of the heavy man and fell to his knees. He sat back on his legs and rested the board on his thighs. "Damn it! It's too heavy."

Elwood's arms shook trying to hold on to his end of the board. He yelled, "Jane, hurry. Come help me. Rebecca, go help your brother." He waited until the women scrambled into place. "When I'm ready, lift." After taking a deep breath and holding it, he squeezed out, "Lift."

They hoisted the heavy board up to their knees, then mid-thighs. The four inched their way to the cabin, arms strained with the heavy weight, through the front door and into the back bedroom. They set the board on the edge of the bed and slid Joseph, still unconscious, onto the bed.

Staring at Gary, Elwood said, "Take the board back to the shed and get the mare saddled. Going to get Doc Headings. Where's my mother?"

Jane grabbed his arm. "Still outside. Rebecca and I'll fetch her while you go for the doctor."

They found Mary sitting against the corncrib, arms locked in the same position. Jane bent down to her. "Grandma, Joseph's in bed now. Come, let's go inside. We'll help you up."

The three women slowly walked back to the cabin arm in arm, and into the bedroom where Joseph lay still, his breaths slow and barely visible. Jane guided her mother-in-law to the rocking chair, sat her down and covered her legs with a quilt. "Are you sure you're all right?"

Mary nodded and stared out the window.

Afraid to do anything to harm her grandfather, Rebecca sat by his side and tried to discern what to do next. This may be too dire for Back So Straight's medicine. We need to wait for Doctor Headings.

Feeling helpless, Rebecca decided to stay in her grandparents' room anyway, until her father returned. She tried to take Joseph's pulse but wasn't sure what she felt. She remembered there should be sixty-to-ninety beats every minute but her grandfather's seemed to be much slower. It worried her that she could do nothing about Joseph's wheezing, nor comfort her grandma, who sat in her rocking chair and wouldn't speak to anyone. But then it struck her: Mary had almost been shot by the man she had been married to for over forty years.

Later that evening the elder Wagner regained consciousness. He opened his eyes and looked around, a frown drawing his bushy eyebrows together. As soon as Joseph saw his wife sitting across the room, he started to whimper.

Rebecca was confused. Part of her wanted to comfort her grandfather, but she also wanted to support Mary. Nothing made sense. She struggled with her emotions. Compassion for Mary. After all, her husband had tried to shoot her. Pity for Joseph. He may be dying.

CHAPTER 17

ELWOOD ARRIVED AT THE DOCTOR'S OFFICE ONLY TO FIND IT empty. A note on the door read, "Be back tomorrow. Please leave message." After scribbling a brief request for the doctor to come to the Wagner farm as soon as possible, Elwood rode back to the farm.

When Rebecca heard steps on the porch, she opened the door and saw her father was alone. His face was drawn. His feet dragged as he walked into the kitchen and took off his jacket, slinging it over a kitchen chair.

"Pop, why isn't Doctor Headings with you?"

"Was gone. Won't be back till tomorrow." He sipped some coffee and hung his head in his hands.

Jane put her arm around his shoulder, and said, "Please go to bed. Gary already went upstairs… you, too, Rebecca. I'll stay here on the sofa in the parlor in case Joseph or Mary need me."

"Are you sure? I can stay."

"No, you've done enough. I'll call you if there's any change."

The night was long. Rebecca got up and checked on her mother and grandparents. Jane didn't stir when Rebecca tiptoed into the parlor, her mother's body resting on the horsehair fabric of the old sofa. Mary sat up rocking, the floorboards squeaking each time the wrongs on the chair crossed them, but said nothing when Rebecca tapped her shoulder. When Rebecca felt Joseph's pulse, he stirred and moaned in his sleep. At least he was still alive.

A gentle rain greeted the morning. Everyone sat somber-faced at the kitchen table when Dr. Headings knocked on the door, water dripping off his hat and his raincoat, wet with stains around the shoulders.

Greeting him at the front door, Rebecca saw his lined face and slightly bent posture. Must have had a short night, too.

When he entered the kitchen, Elwood shook the doctor's hand. "Glad you could come, Doc. Take off your coat and hat. Joseph's in the back bedroom. Rebecca, show him the way."

Still sitting in the rocking chair staring out the window, Mary didn't move when they entered the room. Joseph was sleeping, but he stirred when the doctor spoke to him.

"Wake up, Mr. Wagner. I'm here to take a look at you."

After blinking a few times and clearing his throat, Joseph opened his eyes. Dr. Headings observed his breathing for a minute or two. Opening up Joseph's shirt, he moved the stethoscope around his chest and on his neck. "How are you feeling?"

The old man grunted, "Like hell."

Dr. Headings pulled the quilt from Joseph's body. "Let me see your legs and feet.

Hmm… just as I suspected." He pressed on the swollen legs, their skin shiny and tightly stretched over heavy shins. An indentation remained when he released his thumb. Below Joseph's calves, his feet looked like fat sausages.

The old man tried to yank the quilt back over his body, but it fell on the floor. He didn't try to pick it up but pointed to Mary to retrieve it. She got up from her rocking chair, stooped down, and pulled it over his legs.

His eyes darted to the doctor. In a strained and raspy voice, Joseph said, "What do you mean? What's wrong with my legs?"

"I'm afraid you've had a serious heart attack. Your heart is very weak. That's why your legs are so swollen… heart can't pump the blood. It's called heart failure."

Mary turned to the doctor and put her hand on her mouth. She spoke her first words since the gun went off. "Will… he get better?"

"Can't say. He's lucky to be alive. I can give him some digitalis that may help his heart, but the damage has been done." Dr. Heading took a bottle of white pills out of his medical bag, shook some into a small white envelope and wrote on the front: one pill twice a day.

Handing the envelope to Mary, he said, "See to it that he takes these faithfully. But it would help if he would stop eating so much. His heart is working hard enough without all that weight on top of it."

Joseph glared at both of them, and in a stronger voice said, "I'm going to eat what I want. You can't tell me what to do."

"Don't say I didn't warn you. Rebecca, come help me prop Joseph into a sitting position so he can breathe easier. And I need to listen to his lungs from the back. Joseph… bend your knees and dig your heels into the mattress. When I say now, push with your legs. Rebecca, go to his other side, take your arm and put it under his armpit and grab his shoulder just like I'm doing. When I say now, pull him up and forward. Now." Rebecca pulled with all her might and Joseph slid into position. After Dr. Headings moved the stethoscope around Joseph's back, he said, "Mary, slip a pillow under his upper back to keep him upright."

Once Joseph was sitting up, Mary silently walked out of the room and sat at the kitchen table with her son and Jane, but Rebecca remained behind. She searched the doctor's eyes before motioning for him to walk with her to a corner of the room away from Joseph's listening ears.

"I'm not sure I should be telling you this, but my grandfather was drunk and went after my grandmother with a shotgun before he fell over."

Doc Headings shook his head. "That explains why he had a heart attack. Strain on the heart. Your grandmother wasn't hurt, was she?"

"No, but she had the scare of her life." Rebecca could still feel her grandmother's body shaking.

"Keep your eye on your grandmother. She may get in trouble after experiencing a shock like that."

Rebecca tried to hang on to every word Dr. Headings spoke. "I will. But what do you mean by 'get in trouble'?"

"Well, she was almost shot from what you told me. That's as much shock as a heart attack."

"But what about my grandfather? What exactly does a heart attack and heart failure mean?"

"Hmm. You seem to have lots of questions. Would you like to read about heart conditions in one of my medical books? You won't understand most of it, but you're welcome to borrow it for a short time."

Rebecca's eyes flew open wide. "Yes, thank you. I would like that."

"Now let's go talk to your folks." Turning to Joseph, he said, "I'll be back next week." Dr. Headings followed Rebecca into the kitchen where Elwood, Jane, and Mary sat drinking coffee.

"Mr. Wagner may rally after he has some rest and thinks about what happened and why. In a week or two, it would be good for him to sit outside on the porch for a little while, get some fresh air and a change of scenery. Sit him in a kitchen chair and carry him, but it will take at least two or more very strong men to do this."

That night when Elwood and Jane went to bed, they lay in each other's arms talking quietly. Elwood said, "Don't know how my father could shoot my mother. Been drinking, but… never did anything like this before. If Rebecca hadn't been here to stop him, God only knows what would have happened."

Jane didn't reply for a long while. Then she said, "I know how hard this must be. You love both your parents and when an awful thing like this happens, it shatters your faith in them." She laid her head on his chest and wrapped her arm around his muscled body.

"Always the one to say the right thing, Jane. What would I do without you?"

"You'd be sad, but you'd do just fine. Except for cooking. You can't even make coffee." She chuckled and squeezed his chest. "We'll do what needs to be done to care for your folks, taking it one day at a time."

"But the biggest burden will be on you."

Yawning and turning on her side away from her husband, she whispered, "No need to worry about that right now. Let's go to sleep. I have to get up early tomorrow morning and start gathering things to take care of your folks." She had no more than finished her sentence when her eyes closed and she slipped into a deep sleep. Elwood laid awake listening to his wife's breathing. He whispered to her. "Wish I could be a better husband. Temper gets the best of me more times than I care to admit. Know one thing: don't think I'd last long if something happened to you."

CHAPTER 18

"GRANDPA, TRY TO ROLL OVER ON YOUR SIDE. THE BOOK DR. Headings gave me said you can get a sore rear-end if you stay on your back all the time," Rebecca repeated for the third day in a row.

"I don't give a damn what that book says. I like to lay this way."

Turning toward her grandmother, Rebecca hoped Mary would agree. But Mary looked away and said nothing.

Not wanting to give up trying to help Joseph avoid another problem, Rebecca said, "We'll see what the doc has to say about this next time he comes... probably next week."

The Wagner women took care of Joseph around the clock. Bathing. Changing his clothes and his bed linen. It took all three of them to help him shimmy from the bed to the potty chair they loaned from a neighbor. Mary had the brunt of the responsibility, mostly because of her husband's insistence that only she could hold the Ball jar for him to urinate in. Rebecca was glad to be relieved of that chore and suspected her Ma was too. She made it a point to help take care of her grandfather when she wasn't in school. But her frustration grew every time she tried to get him to move or help himself. It was true he became slightly short of breath when he exerted himself, but she didn't know if he was being belligerent or just plain lazy.

Out of desperation, she said, "Grandpa needs to do something besides lay in that bed or sit in a chair. The medical book I've been reading suggested moving his arms and legs might keep him from getting weaker." Mary shrugged her shoulders. Jane frowned and rubbed her temples. "We don't want to do anything to hurt him, or make his heart work harder. I think it's best to just let him be until Dr. Headings comes back."

Rebecca hoped her mother was right. But she knew her grandfather and grandmother often complained about feeling stiff and weak when they got up in the morning. And that sitting in one place made her grandfather's legs swell, even before he had his heart attack; now they were more swollen than ever.

Since her grandfather's collapse, there was even less time for Rebecca to write to Maggie and Lilly or forage in the woods with Back So Straight. Take care of Grandpa, do farm chores, study her school lessons. Then sleep, eat, and do it again. She felt guilty and resentful. Seventeen years old and stuck.

A week after Joseph's heart attack, Dr. Headings drove his buggy down the lane to the farm. Above him, the leaves in the forests were a mosaic of gold, crimson, orange and yellow tucked into dark green folds of pines and hemlocks. Rows of drying field corn lined the road.

He knocked on the door but didn't wait for an answer before opening it and standing on the threshold. "Hello, folks. How about a hot cup of coffee?"

Jane took her apron off and reached for a mug on the shelf. "So good to see you. It's getting to feel a lot like frost, isn't it? Sit down and warm up."

Wrapping his hands around the coffee mug, and taking a few a sips, Doc Headings waited before he spoke. "Sure is. Now… what's happened since I was here last time?"

"Well, Joseph's still about the same," Jane answered. "We're trying to take good care of him, but he tries our patience sometimes." She poured more coffee into Dr. Heading's cup. He nodded and smiled. "You have your hands full with that one. How about his breathing?"

"I'm not sure. Rebecca may be able to tell you better. Glad you're here on a Saturday so she can explain. She's been watching him closely. But you know Rebecca has her school work and chores to do, too."

"Let's see what she has to say."

Jane walked with him to the back bedroom. Rebecca was trying to put a pillow behind Joseph's head but stopped when she saw them.

"What the hell are you waiting for? I need a pillow," Joseph bellowed.

"Hold on. What's going on here?" Dr. Headings said. He plopped his medical bag on the edge of the bed and frowned.

"Nothing, Doc. Can't seem to get comfortable."

"Let me check your heart before we talk about that. Jane, help Rebecca sit him up. Take his arms and pull him forward, and Mary, come put the pillow behind his lower back so I can listen to his heart."

"Now. Everyone, pull."

Joseph grunted as the women sat him up as far as his stomach would allow, while Mary stuffed a goose down pillow under his lower back so the doctor was able to move his stethoscope. "Now take out the pillow and let him lay back while I listen to his chest." He repeated his movements, first under Joseph's breasts, then below his collarbones.

"Your heart is no better or no worse than last week. Are you moving around and letting folks get you out of bed on a chair?"

"Doc, it's too damn hard to get out of bed. Don't even like to lie on my side. Makes me breathe too hard."

The doctor shook his head and put his hands on his hips. "I'm telling you what will happen if you don't. First, you'll get so weak you won't be able to do anything. Second, your feet and legs will blow up like a cow's stomach after eating green alfalfa. If I were you, I'd stop being so belligerent. Try to help yourself instead of expecting these women to wait on you all day and night."

Joseph grew quiet. Then he whimpered.

Not sympathetic at Joseph's remorse, Rebecca took Mary's hand. "Dr. Headings, would you mind examining grandma now? She's been under a lot of strain."

"Of course not. Mary, sit down on that rocking chair and let me take a look at you."

The doctor felt Mary's pulse and listened to her heart. "Have you been eating and drinking water?"

"Most of the time. But I get very tired."

Dr. Headings put his stethoscope in his bag and turned to Jane and Rebecca. "I know you're all working hard but, if possible, make sure Mary eats her meals and drinks water regularly—and has an hour each day when she can rest."

Inhaling her breath and holding it a short time before letting it out, Jane said, "We'll try our best. But I'm sure Mary will be all right."

But Dr. Headings' frown and the firm set of his jawline didn't escape Rebecca's eyes.

CHAPTER 19

IN HER SMALL CABIN, BACK SO STRAIGHT LIFTED THE SMALL baskets of herbs from the rafters. She took a pinch of red particles and pale green leaf matter of the centaury plant and sprinkled them into a small pan of water. After heating it on the woodstove, she stirred the tincture and strained it into a wooden bowl. This time the Indian woman made a tonic to heal from the inside. She hoped it would make Mary want to eat again.

Next she reached into a basket and gathered a handful of wild mint. She crushed the leaves in her hands and brought them to her face. She inhaled the pungent, sweet odor into her nose. The Indian shaman brewed a strong mint tea to heal a broken spirit. She hoped it would make Mary want to live again.

It depended on which heart prevailed.

CHAPTER 20

"GRANDMA, WOULD YOU TEACH ME HOW TO QUILT? I'VE always admired the beautiful quilt you have on your bed."

"I'll teach you another day, maybe next month, but not now. I'm just too tired."

Rebecca tugged on her lower lip. She climbed down onto the floor next to Mary who was sitting in her rocking chair, staring out the bedroom window like she still did when not tending to her husband. The young woman studied her grandmother, who was becoming thinner and weaker every day. It was like watching her fade away. Mary's hair lost its shine, and she didn't seem to care much about anything. Even the heavy stockings she wore all year round sagged at her ankles, and her shawls had loose fringes hanging from the edges.

"I'll be back, grandma. But if grandpa wakes up from his nap, come fetch me to help you."

"All right… but I can take care of him. Go do something for yourself."

The young woman nodded, but intended to return shortly anyway. She went out in the yard where her mother was hanging up wash and picked up a pillowcase to secure with clothespins. "Ma, are you as worried about grandma as I am? You haven't said much about her getting so thin."

Jane finished placing a pair of overalls on the line and blew on her cold hands. "She… yes, she does look thinner. I didn't say anything to you because I didn't want you to worry."

"But I'm worried. Shouldn't she see the doctor again?"

"No, I don't think so. Doc Headings just wanted her to rest more. Grandma will find her way again in her own time."

"Ma, don't you see how she just sits and stares out the window? I asked her to teach me how to quilt but she said she's too tired."

"Mary will come around when she's ready."

Rebecca was puzzled by her mother's answers. But then she recalled how her mother believed that Gary would also become less belligerent when he got older. That hadn't happened, at least so far, and neither was Mary getting better.

"I hope you're right." Far from satisfied with her mother's reassurance, Rebecca crossed the yard and walked the well-worn path to Back So Straight's cabin. She tapped on the door but there was no answer. In the distance she heard twigs snap and saw Wind bounding toward her. Wrapping her arms around the dog while he licked her face, they romped together in the leaves—Rebecca forgetting about her grandmother for a few moments. Together she and the dog walked to where Back So Straight was digging tubers from the wet ground near a spring.

"Hello, my child. Are you looking for me?"

"Yes. May we talk?"

"Let us go to my cabin so I can cook these in water. And it is getting a little chilly. Ten moons have gone by already this year, and I hear the geese flying south."

Wind followed them and lay down under the table. Nearby, the two women sat on the fur-covered bench in front of the fireplace. A small fire was still burning and giving off the sweet aroma of birch trees. Rebecca inhaled the scent, remembering its fragrance from early summer when they cooked its bark to make birch beer.

After Back So Straight placed the tubers in a kettle on the woodstove, she reached under the table to stroke her dog's head. "When you are ready, you may tell me about your need to talk."

Thinking it would be best to just dive right in, Rebecca said, "As you probably know, my grandfather nearly shot my grandmother when he was drunk. Ever since then she barely eats anything and just sits staring out the windows. I don't know what to do to help her. I asked Ma but she thinks my grandmother will come out of her shell in her own time."

"Yes, I heard the gun and shouting. But it is not my place to interfere."

"What should I do about my grandmother?"

"What do you think, my child?"

"I don't know. She looks so sad and thin." Rebecca scanned the bundles of herbs hanging from the rafters. "Do you have any herbs or tonic I could give her to bring back her appetite?"

"Yes, I do. Centaury. Wild mint. I will give my remedies to her, but your medicine man is powerful. He may give her other medicine."

Rebecca persisted. "But you are a healer, too. My pop's leg and Gary's arms are much better because of your poultices and salves."

"There are some ailments that are meant to teach us lessons... if we pause to learn from them."

Rebecca swallowed. Back So Straight's seemingly harsh answer made her feel defensive. "How can that be true?"

"Your grandmother has suffered a very deep wound in her heart. Now she is two-hearted. The man whom she thought loved her... the father of her children... has betrayed her. Sometimes when the spirit is crushed, there is nothing that can be done to heal it. Your grandmother may be afraid to come back to her previous life. It would be too painful. The Great Spirit, Earth Mother, may be calling to her. It is hard to say, but you must be ready for this possibility. You are a young woman... learning to be a healer. I have seen how you care for your family. It is good."

Rebecca was still skeptical. "But nothing I do is helping them."

"You cannot be sure of this. You have given them a great gift. Your love. You treat them with tenderness. You are patient with them. You do not flinch when they have bad odors or rebuke you. You seek ways to make them feel better. They both know these truths."

Tears welled up in Rebecca's eyes. She tried to blink them away, but they spilled out and ran down her face and onto her lap. Her chin quivered. She hadn't cried since the near shooting of her grandmother, and now it seemed that there was no stopping the torrent. Her sobbing echoed through the small room. Wind came to Rebecca and put her nose on the young woman's knee. She reached down and stroked the dog's head.

Once Rebecca gained her composure, she stared into the fire that had burned down to a few flickers of orange and blue flames. "I'm scared grandma will die if I don't do anything."

Back So Straight moved closer and put her arms around Rebecca, drawing the young woman to her bosom. Rebecca's body melted. They sat quietly until Back So Straight gently released her.

"Sit with her. Do not make any demands. There is no need to speak or do. Just be."

"Then I'm doing what she's doing—nothing."

The Indian healer shook her head. "This is not the truth. You are together in spirit. Do not think of this as nothing."

"I'll try." Rebecca said, looking at the tubers floating in the pan of water, their knobby protrusions poking through the surface. She took a deep breath and smelled their earthy odor. That was her. Floating. Trying to keep her head above water.

Back So Straight lifted Rebecca's chin and faced her young friend. "Do not let your worry make this sorrow more powerful than it already is. In many moons, it is possible life may give you sorrow greater than this."

CHAPTER 21

THE FIRST SNOWFALL CAME EARLY. JUST A FEW WEEKS before, the grass and weeds had turned brown after an early first frost, so little remained in the fields for the horses to graze. Rebecca was worried her father hadn't rebuilt the barn yet but she knew better than to ask him about his plans to start construction. He was busy doing most of the farm work now that Howard wasn't there to help.

The women finally finished canning vegetables, fruits, and meats for the winter. They stacked the jars in the cold cellar, lining the shelves held in place by sturdy posts made from lumber selectively cut from trees in their wood stand. Perishable food and milk was stored in the springhouse, a small stone building built over the spring that fed the creek on the border of the yard. The cool running water coming out of the earth kept their eggs, milk, cheese, apples, and other foods cold in the summer and from freezing in the winter. But since butchering was done last December, the smoke house was nearly empty. A few hams and several slabs of bacon were left, but sausage and scrapple were long gone.

Rebecca and her brother continued to do farm chores before walking to school, which meant they had to get up before daylight every morning except Saturday and Sunday. They didn't need to be awakened by the wind-up clock in the hallway, because as soon as the sun began to show its first brilliant rays skimming across the meadow, the noise from the sawmill a few miles away announced the beginning of a new day. Rebecca thought it wasn't fair that Gary didn't have to help take care of Grandpa Wagner, but her complaints fell on deaf ears.

Just three months into the new school year, brother and sister were already very different students. Gary planned on quitting school in two weeks when he turned sixteen. He admitted that reading was a bore unless subjects were about forests and wildlife. Her telling him how unfortunate he was—just three years earlier there was no mandatory school attendance—did nothing to change his mind about being stuck at school, just like she was stuck on the farm.

Rebecca liked to write stories and essays, but hardly had time to devote to it. Outside of the occasional letters she managed to write to Maggie and Lilly that described farm life, she also thought her day-to-day experiences uninteresting compared to her more refined friends. Rebecca had a few school friends in McAlisterville, but most of them were, like her, busy helping on the family farm. The only time she saw friends outside school was at Grange dances and church activities, including an occasional hayride.

Although her quest for learning began long before she met Maggie and Lilly, their interest in graduating from high school and plans to go to college inspired her. Her teacher, John Carney, recognized Rebecca's interest in learning, particularly science. When he discovered she had read nearly every book in their small school library, he loaned his personal books to her. But Dr. Headings' medical books interested Rebecca the most. Sometimes she read long into the night, so exhausted that the next day she could barely get up in time to collect the eggs from the chicken coop before breakfast—her most hated chore. Not only did some of the chickens peck her hands when she reached into their nests, the shells were often streaked with fresh manure. Cleaning them added to the drudgery.

One morning after a particularly late night of reading, Rebecca slid out of bed, pulled on her coat and boots, and headed out to the chicken coop to gather eggs. The day was overcast. A fine drizzle was falling, adding to the dread she already felt at having to go into the smelly henhouse. She only took a few steps into the yard when she heard a ruckus coming from the back of the coop. Hurrying to see what was making the birds upset, she was greeted by squawking chickens scattering around the fenced-in pen.

Approaching carefully, she realized the eggs were unattended in their nests. Her eyes scanned the perimeter and rested on a dark shadow in the far corner.

Moving closer, the shadow began to move. Then it slithered down a wooden post—a very big black snake with its mouth stretched around an egg.

"Shoo, you varmint," Rebecca shouted, backing up to give the snake room to crawl out. With the heavy egg clamped in its jaw, the snake could barely move. While Rebecca kept her distance, it slowly undulated across the rough wooden floor through the open door, under the wire fence, and into the weeds. Lucky snake. Heavy with its burden but now free to do what it wants.

After collecting the remaining eggs and washing them at the hand pump in the front yard, Rebecca returned to the cabin. "Ma, you'll never guess what happened in the chicken coop this morning. A black snake was after the eggs."

Gary sauntered into the kitchen dressed in his long underwear—his hair looking like a rat's nest. "So what? Black snakes are good to have around. We can spare a few eggs."

Rebecca swatted him on the arm. "You weren't there to see it. Had to be six feet long."

"It's a wonder you got up early enough to hunt the eggs. You always have your head in one of those medical books half-way through the night."

Elwood heard voices in the kitchen and yelled from upstairs. "Don't go anywhere today, Gary. We're figuring out how much lumber we'll need to build the new barn."

Rebecca stiffened. Not another argument.

Gary rolled his eyes and said under his breath, "I can't believe he's finally going to do this. Might as well get it over with. That freak dusting of snow the night before last must have convinced him."

"Don't make it any harder than it already is. Why can't you just do what Pop says for a change?" Rebecca's voice was soft and pleading.

"Listen. I'll help him with the measuring but don't expect me to go with him to mark off the hundred acres of our land to give to Eastman."

Rebecca sighed deeply. "He isn't giving it to Eastman. He's selling it for money to build the barn and buy farm equipment."

"Yeah, that's what he says. Suppose he has another reason for selling our land?"

Elwood hurried down the steps and joined Gary at the table. He forked a slab of ham and put it on his plate. "Hurry up and eat some breakfast. Eastman gave me more time to let him know how much lumber we need, so we're going to walk off the perimeter of the barn foundation this morning."

Gary pushed his bowl of oatmeal away and stared at his father. "What do you mean by walk off the perimeter?"

"Need to get an idea of how much lumber we need to build the barn. Didn't you hear me the first time?" Elwood slammed his fork on the table.

"You didn't say anything about lumber."

"Yes, I did. But even if I didn't, anybody with common sense could figure out what I meant. Use your head."

Gary narrowed his eyes, his voice getting loud. "I can't read your mind. You expect me to know what you want me to do without explaining it."

"If you'd pay attention to what's going on around here, you'd know what needs to be done." Red blotches appeared on Elwood's neck. "Now finish your breakfast and get the lead out of your rear end."

Hating the conflict, Rebecca said, "I'll help you measure, Pop, if Gary takes care of Grandpa in my place."

"No. Your job is to help your mother and grandmother."

"But—that's not fair."

"Fair or not, that's how it is."

Gary grabbed a jacket and slipped on boots near the back door. "Never mind. I'm on my way."

Rebecca stomped her foot on the floor. Once she calmed down, she had to admit she felt guilty not wanting to help her mother and grandmother take care of Joseph. It wasn't that she didn't love him. She just wasn't able to figure out if her anger was because her father relegated her to women's work or if he thought she wasn't capable of measuring and calculating as well as men could. Or why men had a choice and women didn't.

The two men hurriedly approached the barn. Pointing to the corner, Elwood said, "Start here and walk long steps on the perimeter. Go slowly so you can count the number of steps you take. Step's about yard's length."

Gary shot a stern look to his father and hopped onto the wall. He stomped along the top calling off the number of steps until he returned to the starting point. "Thirty-six."

"You sure?"

"Do you want me to do this or not?"

Elwood ignored his son's comment and handed him the device that held the string and loose blue chalk powder. "Now go inside the foundation with me—we'll use the chalk line to mark off the location of the studs for the interior walls. Need to be sixteen inches on center."

Once the strings were held taunt on the ground, Elwood snapped the blue lines to mark off each interior wall on the dirt floor. He carefully measured the length of each blue line and recorded the totals on a ledger he borrowed from one of the neighbors. Then he used the perimeter measurements to calculate the amount of lumber needed for the second floor. Elwood carefully added up the number of board feet by multiplying the thickness of each board, times the width and length in inches, and divided it by one hundred forty-four.

He also had to calculate the lumber needed for roof rafters and boards, plus bundles of shingles for a 6:12 roof pitch. Some of the neighboring barns had higher roofs, but Elwood didn't want anyone getting hurt trying to put shingles on a steep roof.

Gary stood waiting for his father to add up the columns in the ledger. He kicked the stone foundation and spit on the ground. Finally, he laid down on the wall and pulled his hat over his eyes.

"What the hell do you think you're doing? Taking a nap? Need to go to Eastman to talk about our woods and agree on which acreage I'm willing to sell."

"No, we're not. You are. I'm not going with you. You made that deal without talking to any of us so you can finish it yourself."

Elwood bristled, his voice rising. "Look here, Gary. You think I wanted to sell? We already went over this."

Gary got up and stretched to his full height—at age sixteen, almost as tall as his father—his fists clenched at his side. He stood motionless while his father turned his back and walked away, boots thudding on the hard ground. After a brief moment the young man did the same, in the opposite direction.

It was nearly noon when Elwood arrived at the manicured yard surrounding the Eastman mansion. He tied his horse to the post out front and knocked on the door. While he waited, he turned around and studied the stone wall surrounding the house. Each stone was laid to ensure the wall was the same height, just like the foundation of his barn.

The sound of the door opening startled him from his thoughts.

"Hello, Mr. Wagner. Surprised to see you." Hugh motioned for him to come into the house.

After wiping his boots on the doormat, Elwood stepped into the handsomely decorated mansion. Brussels tufted pile carpet covered the main rooms, except the hallways that were made of parquet flooring. His eyes followed Mr. Eastman into a formal dining room where a servant was clearing away lunch.

"Now. What can I do for you?" asked Mr. Eastman.

Elwood's eyes darted from the colored man to his host. Not knowing what to say, he impulsively held out a piece of ledger paper. "Here's what I think it'll cost to rebuild my barn and buy new tools and equipment. Ready to sell some of my woodland for the cash to do it." Elwood paused. Red blotches rose on his neck. "If we can settle on where the boundaries will be set. We agreed on one hundred acres."

Studying the paper for a moment, Hugh said, "I'll need to look more closely at these figures later, but I'm free now to look at your land if that suits you."

Elwood cleared his throat and swallowed. He felt like he was being manipulated but powerless to do anything about it. "All right. Let's get it over with," Elwood said, his words sounding more enthusiastic than he felt.

He followed Eastman across the street to his neighbor's barn where the lumber baron kept his horses, and together they set out for Little Round Top on the same path he and Rebecca had taken earlier that year. The two men rode through the foothills and up the steeper side of the mountain, carefully following the switchback path through dense trees and around rocks. Elwood led the way with Hugh following behind. Several times Elwood had to stop to let him catch up. What he didn't see was Eastman guiding his horse into dense patches of hemlock and pine and quickly returning to the path.

When they reached the summit, the two men dismounted and tied their horses to a mountain laurel bush. Pointing ahead of him, Elwood said, "Was thinking of this ridge. 'Bout a hundred acres, more or less."

Hugh shaded his eyes with his hand and looked across the mountainside. "I think that land we passed on our way up here is what I'm interested in."

Squinting and scanning the treetops, Elwood said, "Mean that heavily-wooded knob a little way down from here? But that land has my biggest trees."

"Sorry, but that's what I'm interested in buying. According the paper you gave me, you'll need $3,000 to build your barn and buy new equipment."

"But the timber on that land is worth more than that, not to mention the land itself."

Eastman peered at Elwood with squinted eyes but did not respond.

"You're a hard businessman, Hugh." Elwood kicked his boot against a rock. "Gave you my word and now I have to live with it."

"I'm sure once your barn is up and you can move your horses and hay back in, you'll be glad you made this decision." He reached in his pocket and jiggled some coins.

Elwood swept his eyes over the trees again and rubbed his hand over his heart. "Hope you're right."

CHAPTER 22

THE CALL TO HELP ELWOOD WAGNER REBUILD HIS BARN came at the November Grange meeting. All the Grange leader had to do was tell members that Wagner was ready to rebuild and all were invited. That's how it worked in Juniata County. Neighbors helping neighbors.

At daybreak on an unusually warm, sunny Saturday morning, wagonloads of lumber and other building materials snaked their way down the dirt road to the Wagner farm. Following the lumber wagons came more wagons loaded with over two dozen men, women, building tools, baskets of food, and picnic tables. Some were Grange members, some from neighboring farms, some church friends, and a few total strangers.

Once everyone was ready to begin, the men placed four by ten-inch planks on the stone foundation and anchored them, making sure they were level. Two by ten boards were fastened to larger planks to frame the outer perimeters of the barn. One by one the walls formed the exterior frame of the barn. Hammers pounded new round nails into the seasoned lumber, their hammering echoing down the valley. The odor of sawdust was carried along with the wind.

Aproned women carried baskets of food onto the porch and into the cabin where kettles awaited to cook ham with red new potatoes and green beans, and vegetable soup. Pans of corn bread batter followed, ready to bake.

Pies and cakes were set up on the porch and covered with tablecloths to keep the insects from tasting them, particularly yellow jackets, who were attracted by their sweetness.

Rebecca helped in the kitchen, but then slipped away to see how the building was progressing. In her haste to rush to the barn, she opened the door and bumped into a young man she had never met before. He bowed slightly, and said, "So sorry. I was just about to ask about the white horses in the back field. Won't be too long till they'll need this barn."

"Yes, you're right. Thank you for coming to help us."

"Glad to. Well, I'll better get back to work."

Such nice manners, thought Rebecca. Handsome, too.

Gathering her skirts, Rebecca ran to the partially constructed barn and went inside.

"Hey, what are you doing here? You're supposed to be helping the women cook. This is man's work. You'll get hurt," Gary said.

Her lips flattened in anger. "Since when are you worried about me getting hurt? You never seemed to care about me when I did your barn work while you were out traipsing in the woods."

"Well, we have to know what we're doing when we measure and cut."

A nearby man who was lifting a long, heavy board yelled, "Yeah, if you want to be useful, get me a drink of water."

Rebecca suspected it was futile to argue. She went to the pump to fill a bucket but wasn't pleased to be relegated to carrying water. When she handed him the bucket, he didn't thank her. "I can measure and calculate with the best of them. Where in the Bible does it say women can't think?"

The man looked wide-eyed at Rebecca and threw a ladle of water onto the ground. Rebecca grabbed the bucket and walked away. Next time he could fetch his own water.

By noon the sides of the barn were up and the joists set for the second floor. When Jane rang the bell for lunch, the workers went to the water pump to wash their hands. Bonnet-covered women dipped spoons into deep kettles of hot food and ladled heaping spoonful's onto plates for the hungry men. After the men were fed, Rebecca walked to the partly built barn, still disappointed she couldn't help with the construction. Why was this different from helping her father and brother repair the pigpen or put a fence around the chicken yard? Maybe because there weren't any other men around to disapprove.

Following the construction of the second story, a mid-afternoon break was called. When no one was paying attention, she sneaked into the barn. It smelled of freshly cut lumber. A crooked floorboard caught her attention. Taking a hammer that had been left on the floor, she pounded the partially sunk nail into the wood.

One of the men entered the barn where Rebecca was kneeling. "What're you doing? You're supposed to be working in the kitchen."

Hammer poised in her hand, she said, "I'm fixing this board because it wasn't hammered down all the way." She defiantly kept hammering until the nail disappeared and the board straightened.

"That's not for you to decide. Women don't know construction."

Rebecca slapped the hammer in the palm of her free hand. "I know enough to see a nail head and a crooked board."

The man shrugged his shoulders and walked away, mumbling, "Darn women. Next thing we know they'll be wearing trousers and telling us what to do."

Rebecca smiled.

CHAPTER 23

SHE STOOD ON THE SIDE OF LITTLE ROUND TOP AND LOOKED up, imagining the whole mountain and the sister Shade Mountains treeless like this newly barren patch at her feet. She listened. The silence deafened her.

Back So Straight shaded her eyes with her hand. No shade, only Father Sun. Her heart nearly stopped.

The overstory trees. Gone. More than a hundred species since her ancestors lived here.

The understory trees. Gone. More than dozens of native species since her ancestors walked these hills.

Her basket was empty. Plants and shrubs. Gone. The ones her tribe's healers used for medicine.

She looked for feathers. Birds that once nested here. Gone. More than 400 species. Warblers, thrushes, hummingbirds, woodpeckers, wrens, swallows, tanagers, finches, swifts, vireos, jays, crows, ravens, larks, nuthatches, waxwings, blackbirds, sparrows, mockingbirds, creepers, cuckoos, thrashers, creepers, gnatcatchers, larks.

She searched the sky. It was empty. Raptors that once hunted here. Gone. Hawks, owls, eagles, falcons, kites, vultures.

She scanned the forest floor for animal droppings. Mammals that once nursed their young here. Gone. Bears, deer, red and gray foxes, bobcats, beavers, squirrels, rabbits, coyotes, chipmunks, opossums, weasels, badgers, porcupines, raccoons, hedgehogs, skunks, chipmunks, wood rats, minks, ermines, muskrats, bats, mice, voles.

She walked where bogs once dotted the level low spots. Amphibians. Gone. Salamanders, skinks, frogs, toads.

She stumbled over tree trunks. Reptiles. Gone. Snakes, lizards, turtles, tortoises.

Back So Straight sank to her knees and wept.

CHAPTER 24

TIMBER! LUMBERMEN SAWED THROUGH EACH TREE WITH their two-man saw, back and forth until they reached the middle of the trunk. Then a wedge was pounded into the opposite side and the saw withdrawn. Finally, the giant tree cracked as it fell with a noise that sounded like thunder. Pine and hemlock trees over one hundred and fifty feet tall fell by the hundreds.

The lumbermen ran for their lives, shouting and jumping over branches. Shards of branches broke away or clung to trunks as the giant trees fell against their unsuspecting neighbors. Hardwoods. Oak: black, pin, post, scarlet, white, red, bur. Hickory: shellbark, mockernut, red, butternut. American chestnut. Maple: red, sugar. Their leafless winter trunks shook the earth with each blow.

A crew of ten men worked their way across the one hundred acres now owned by Hugh Eastman, leaving a path of tree stumps. Piles of branches, some four feet deep clung to the slopes. Sweeping back and forth, the seasoned lumbermen cleared all that grew on the lush mountainside. What wasn't cut down succumbed to the falling giants, horses' hooves or wagon tracks. Seedlings, plants, ferns, wildflowers, moss, mushrooms—all ground into the forest floor, a mangled mass of life, trampled and forgotten.

Trees were hitched to horses that dragged them to a staging area where the bark was stripped from the giant hemlock trees and loaded on wagons. White pine and hardwood trees were cut into lengths and piled on the ground. Roads were cut into the mountainsides to make way for horse-drawn wagons that delivered the trees to sawmills at the bottom of the mountain or delivered to barges on the Juniata River and then on to the Susquehanna River.

A cluster of three men gathered at the edge of the clearing. Gunther, his thick muscles spanning his shirt sleeves, pointed to nearby trees. "I'm thinking of cutting a few more acres."

A second man, older with a slight limp, looked out over the forest. "Why would you want to do that? We're finished cutting."

Gunther tugged his empty pants pockets inside out. "This is why."

The second man spoke again. "But the boss said to cut only what was marked off."

"Who's going to tell if we move the marker a bit? We'll cut the trees in the middle and let the ones around the perimeter stand. That way no one will see the missing trees unless they're right on top of them. Let's send the crew home and come back Saturday. We can cut those big guys down in a day or two. No one here to stop us."

The third man, quiet until now, looked up at the canopy. He stroked his dark beard and put his hands in the pockets of the wool jacket that spanned his broad shoulders. "We'll have to work like hell to get these trees down in two days. I know a few other men who'd like to get some extra money, and I'll get my boys to work the horses and wagons."

The second man limped toward the others. "What if we get caught?"

Gunther laughed and slapped the other two on the back. "Not a chance. Wagner will be busy building his barn. Most of his neighbors too. They won't be coming up here Saturday, and on Sunday, they'll all be in church. After that, it'll be too late."

It was exactly that—too late.

Elwood slammed the cabin door as he returned from checking the land he sold to Eastman. "Damn it. There's a swath of trees next to it with nothing but stumps. Markers were moved."

"What do you mean, Pop?" Rebecca dropped the towels she was folding and stared at her father.

"For crying out loud, they're gone. Question is, who cut them?"

Still confused, Rebecca said, "What trees are you talking about? Shall I fetch Ma? She'll want to hear about this."

Ignoring the question, Elwood poured himself a cup of coffee and sat at the kitchen table. Lowering his head to his hands, he said, "Just when I thought things were getting straightened out… new barn… new equipment, this has to happen."

"I thought you sold a hundred acres to Mr. Eastman."

"Don't mean those acres. Couple hundred trees next to it on our land were cut too."

"Isn't that against the law?"

"Yeah. But who did it? Looked around. No trace of anything. Just tree stumps and branches strewn everywhere. Looked like whoever did it was in a hurry. Even if I find out, how could I prove it?"

Rebecca pitied her father. She wasn't the only one feeling stuck.

CHAPTER 25

On a sunny, crisp February day, Dr. Headings rode to the Wagner farm to check on Joseph and Mary. Huge, fluffy, white clouds contrasted the sapphire blue sky. The sun was low on the horizon, shining dappled light through the trees, giving the snow that still covered the ground a shimmering glow.

But some of the lower elevations were brown: fields, meadows, weeds, ferns, barnyard, and dirt roads, although snow hugged the hills and forest floors. Deer tracks crisscrossed the fields, like games of tic-tac-toe. Small tracks of woodland animals could be seen peppering the snow mounds.

As Dr. Headings pulled his creaky old buckboard to a stop in front of the cabin, Jane and Rebecca stepped onto the porch. Grabbing the handle on the seat, he slowly eased himself to the ground and reached in the back seat for his medical bag.

"So good to see you this morning, Dr. Headings," Jane called.

"Well, hello ladies. I thought I'd pay a visit to some of my patients since the weather's nice. Any change in Joseph? For that matter, how's Mary?"

Rebecca answered, "Sorry to say Grandpa's getting more contrary as the days go on. My grandma's not so good either."

"Come in and have some coffee," Jane said, "and rest a little." After placing a mug on the table and pouring steaming black liquid into it, she swept a few crumbs from a chair with her hand.

Sipping from the coffee-stained mug and eating his last bite of pie, Elwood paused and said, "Hello, Doc. Glad you could come by."

The older man tilted his head toward the bedroom. "What's your read on things since I was here last?"

"Not so good. The women are able to get Joseph out of bed just long enough to put the potty-chair in back of him. Had been using the jar to pee, but now wants to stand up to do that, too. Come on, have some pie."

Dr. Headings laughed—his eyes crinkling toward his temples—recalling there was nothing pretentious about Elwood Wagner. "Thanks, but I'll wait for my pie until after I examine your father and mother."

"Before you do that… need to tell you. Gives the women a hard time. Cantankerous. Maybe we can get him out on the porch a bit today for a change. Been a long time since that was possible."

Dr. Headings nodded. He opened the bedroom door and tried to stifle a gasp. There sat Joseph in bed, eating a heaping plate of ham, eggs, and fried potatoes. The old man looked fatter than a pregnant cow, the mound of his belly rising above the quilt. He balanced the tin blue plate on his stomach with one hand and held a large serving fork in the other.

Mary sat in a small rocking chair near the window. She was motionless, her face slack. Her eyes looked past the doctor and through the window into the woods beyond.

"Well, let me take a look at you, Joseph."

"Have some breakfast first, Doc." Joseph pointed toward the plate of food tottering on his belly. His color was ruddy but his deep-set eyes were alert. "I feel pretty good, but my legs don't want to cooperate—and I can't breathe very well."

"Mary, take his plate. I need to listen to his heart and lungs."

She slowly walked to the bed and lifted the plate from his stomach.

Dr. Headings said, "Sit up, Joseph. I'll help you this time but you have to help yourself more." He placed his arm behind Joseph and pushed him forward so he could listen with his stethoscope, moving the instrument around Joseph's back.

"Hurry up, doc, I can't sit up much longer."

"You can sit back. Mr. Wagner, your heart is not any worse than the last time I listened." He pointed to the plate of food Mary was still holding. "I see you're well-fed. Let me take a look at your legs." Pulling down the quilt, he stared at Joseph's lower body and saw the enormous swollen legs, even more swollen than the last time he had checked. The skin looked ready to split open.

"Are your legs always this large? Your face and eyelids seem puffy, too."

"What is it doc? My legs always feel tight and achy. But I can't see them unless they give me a mirror or I sit way up like this. My legs don't hurt, just feel stiff."

"Mary, will you please ask Rebecca to join me?"

Rebecca came into the room and stood next to Dr. Headings. "I think the medical book I loaned to you may have covered this problem. Let me explain what's going on." He pressed his thumb into the swelling in Joseph's lower leg. Then he lifted it but the indentation in Joseph's legs remained. "This is called pitting edema... a clear sign of heart failure. Do you remember reading about this?"

"Yes, I do. Should we prop his legs up?"

"You can, it may help... but not too much considering how weak his heart is."

Joseph pulled the quilt up over his legs. "No need for you to use those fancy words. Just tell me what they mean."

"It means your heart is not pumping very well. As I told you before, it may help if you cut back on your eating. Your heart has enough work to do without your extra weight on top of it."

"I get cranky when I'm hungry, so let me be. I already told you I'm going to do what I damn well please."

Rebecca looked at the doctor and shook her head. She wanted to say something but caught herself, unsure whether it was in her place.

"All right, Joseph. Don't say I didn't warn you." Grabbing his medical bag and turning around, Dr. Headings added, "I'm going to talk to your wife now."

"Fine with me, Doc. All she does is sit around. Might as well be here by myself."

Trying to control her rage, Rebecca felt bile rise up in her throat. "Grandpa, you should be ashamed of yourself! Grandma takes care of you night and day. She gets you food. She empties your potty bucket. She washes your dirty clothes and bed, and when you have an accident, she cleans up your shit. In case you haven't noticed, she's sick. Can't you see what she's been through? Haven't you noticed how thin she is? Why can't you think of her instead of yourself?"

Joseph gripped the sides of the bed, his eyes bulging as he stared at Rebecca, then Dr. Headings, who shook his head but said nothing.

Unsure what to do next, Rebecca quickly crossed the room to where her grandmother had retreated. Her heart pounded and her breaths came in rapid succession. "Grandma, please let Dr. Headings have a look at you."

Dr. Headings walked to where the two women were standing. Mary's back was stooped and her shoulder blades protruded through her worn sweater. Then he gently took her hand and sat her down in the rocking chair.

"Mary, I'd like to listen to your heart and lungs." The doctor gently placed his instrument against her chest in several places, glancing at Rebecca and nodding slightly. "Your heart is okay, but it looks as if you've lost weight—and you're very pale. Are you eating enough?"

Mary looked up at the doctor and said, "I think so, but nothing tastes good anymore."

"I don't want you to skip meals no matter what your husband needs you to do. I also want you to let someone else take care of your husband for an hour each day while you rest. Can you do that?"

"I'll try, but everyone has their own work to do."

Still shaking from her outburst, Rebecca took her grandmother's bony hand and patted it. "Grandma, I'll hurry home from school. Don't worry. We'll all help more. Let's go into the kitchen and have some pie. Dr. Headings has waited long enough."

Mary nodded as they filed into the kitchen, leaving Joseph, his jaw locked in defiance. Rebecca hoped her mother and father hadn't heard her outburst, but she could tell by the frown on their faces they had heard every word. Her reprieve came when Jane shoved a plate in the doctor's hand. "Dr. Headings, it's time for pie," and continued to prattle. "Have you ever eaten a milk tart? I make them whenever I have some left-over pie dough. It just takes milk, butter, flour, and brown sugar. Would you like to try it?"

The doctor sniffed the air and smiled. "It still smells warm from the oven. Thank you. I'll take another cup of coffee, too."

"Of course. There's enough for everyone. You too, Mary."

But Mary's attention was on Rebecca. They locked eyes. A faint smile broke against the corners of Mary's mouth and tears escaped her eyes. The room was quiet except for forks scraping against blue enamel plates and coffee being poured into thick mugs.

After finishing his pie and coffee, Dr. Headings pulled a medical book from his black bag. "Rebecca, would you like to borrow another of my medical books?"

"Yes, thank you. I'll give you the one I just finished. I find these fascinating. The last one you gave me had me awake reading till all hours of the night. If you're sure you can spare a new one for a little while, I'll give it back to you the next time you come." But she was still reeling from the way she had spoken to her grandfather. Grateful for Mary's smile but still trying to suppress her lingering anger and shame over her outburst, Rebecca said, "Please leave the book on the table. I'm sorry, but I need to excuse myself."

The young woman ran outside, slamming the cabin door behind her. It had started to rain, a cold penetrating rain that could easily turn to sleet as the day progressed. She stood on the porch until she started to shiver. The words she had shouted at her grandfather rang in her ears. Maybe she should have kept quiet instead of scolding her grandpa. What if Dr. Headings thought she acted unbecoming of a young woman?

Ignoring the cold drizzle, she ran to Back So Straight's cabin and burst inside. Wind rose from her blanket under the table. She raised her head and locked eyes with Rebecca. Then the dog turned to Back So Straight. The Indian woman nodded. The dog snuggled next to Rebecca and placed her muzzle under Rebecca's hand as though she was waiting to be petted.

Back So Straight sat on a wooden rocking chair near the fire and continued to sew a piece of rawhide around the top of a moccasin. She usually waited for Rebecca to speak before asking why she came to visit. But this time the dog's reaction to the young woman was unusual.

"What is the trouble, my child?" Back So Straight motioned for Rebecca to sit on the bench near the fire.

"Not sure where to begin," Rebecca blurted. "Dr. Headings came to see grandpa and grandma this morning. While he was examining Joseph, my grandfather accused Mary of doing nothing for him—just sitting around."

Back So Straight raised her eyebrows but waited for Rebecca to continue.

"I swore. Said… you know, the other word for manure."

Back So Straight cocked her head to one side. "Do you mean shit?"

Rebecca's eyes grew wide. She stared at the Indian woman and saw a smile break across her face. Soon Back So Straight chortled in a belly laugh that shook her body, the beads in her shirt rocking back and forth. Rebecca laughed too, not only at hearing the Indian woman say shit, but also at the absurdity of trying to avoid the word.

The two women laughed until they were breathless. When they exhausted themselves, they sat for a moment until their bodies relaxed.

Finally, Back So Straight's expression changed and she said in a somber voice, "Did you speak the truth?"

"Yes, I told him he should be ashamed of himself—that Mary cleaned up his shit and he didn't think of anyone but himself—in front of Dr. Headings!"

A small smile crept up one side of Back So Straight's face. "Did he correct you?"

"No. He stayed for pie and coffee and gave me another medical book to read."

"Do you know why he did this?"

Rebecca pondered her question. "I'm not sure."

"Maybe he thought you were justified in defending your grandmother."

"I hope so."

They sat quietly while the fire made soft, sizzling sounds and sent orange sparks up the chimney. Back So Straight moved next to Rebecca on the bench. Wind put her chin on Rebecca's lap while she stroked the dog's head.

Dreading the scolding she anticipated from her father or mother, Rebecca stared at the fire. Doubts about the sharp rebuke she gave her grandpa played in her mind. After all, she was only a young woman and had no right to speak her mind. Or did she? Finally, she swung her feet onto the bench and laid her head on a Back So Straight's lap. Closing her eyes, she imagined the scene playing in her mind... Joseph rebuking her grandmother... Mary's bony hand... Dr. Headings' kindness... until she drifted off to sleep. A dream of the trees... the screeching sound of a saw... a bloody arm... played in her head. The splayed fingers moved. The hairs on the severed arm stood straight up like trees in the forest, only to be cut down with giant two-man saws.

CHAPTER 26

A COOL APRIL SPRING FINALLY ARRIVED, BUT IT CAME IN FITS and starts. The first signs were early May Apples beginning to sprout their banana tree-size leaves in the moist woods, floating just above the forest floor. Ferns pushed through the leaf beds. Spring warblers trilled their songs as they darted in the tree canopy, its leaves bright as the new moss below. At dusk tiny frogs called their high-pitched peeps to each other from the bogs and wetlands. Bullfrogs laid their milky masses of eggs in the edges of vernal ponds. It was Rebecca's favorite time of the year, almost as if God had created everything for the first time. Everything was new and wet and smelled clean.

At least on the remaining forests her father owned, as well as a few neighbors to the west and north.

As soon as frost was no longer a threat to tender leaves and stalks, the women started to plant their garden. Lettuce, peas, onion sets, then later several types of beans, squash, turnips, sweet potatoes, beets, and peppers. Some of the vegetables had been started from seeds in a cold frame, a small wooden enclosure with an old window over top that warmed the inside and kept the tender plants from freezing. Built years ago by Rebecca's grandfather, the window was fastened with iron hinges to make it easy to uncover when the plants were safe to replant in the garden. Jane had already grown tender lettuce in the protective structure in early March when the temperature was close to freezing, and had harvested it all spring to be eaten with hot bacon dressing and hard-boiled eggs.

Later, pumpkins and sweet corn, in addition to tomato plants grown from last year's seeds were planted and surrounded with a mixture of manure and hay. Rebecca hoped the planting was soon finished because it was only a short time until Lilly and Maggie would be coming to McAlisterville again for the summer. She had written to them but didn't tell them about her grandfather's violence or her outburst afterwards. She wasn't sure how they would react since none of their letters included stories of their grandparents, or for that matter any struggles that kept them from reaching their dreams. Maybe when she got to know them better, she would consider telling them about her family and her struggles to assert herself.

However, late that April, a letter came from Maggie, one that Rebecca found not only fascinating, but caused her to think about the world outside McAlisterville.

Dear Rebecca,

I cannot wait to come to McAlisterville this summer and see you again. My studies are going well. I am growing ever more interested in the natural world and pleased that Bryn Mawr is one of the few colleges to offer science classes to women (my favorite is science laboratory in the new Dalton Hall). I love them because they remind me of you and the times we found interesting flora and fauna in your mountains. However, my interest in women's place in the world has also been heightened because of the lively discussions that ensue in our liberal arts classes. Most of my classmates are serious scholars. Although I would much prefer simple skirts and blouses (and no corsets), we are required to wear caps and gowns to distinguish us from other female seminaries and academic institutions. What a gross encumbrance to running and playing basketball, my dear. You would die if you had to wear them!

My heroine at Bryn Mawr is our dean and second president, M. Casey Thomas. I read that even at age 14, she wrote in her diary: "How unjust, how narrow-minded, how utterly incomprehensible (sic) to deny that women ought to be educated & worse than all to deny that they have equal powers of mind. If I ever live to grow up, my one aim & concentrated (sic) purpose shall be & is to show that a woman can learn, can reason, can compete with men in the grand fields of literature and science... that a woman can be a woman & a true one without having all their time engrossed by the dress and society." Can you imagine such boldness and courage at that tender age? I was still a naïve girl whose only rebellion was against wearing ribbons and petticoats!

I also learned quite recently, to my surprise, that Iroquois women (isn't your mentor Back So Straight Iroquois?) actually influenced my other heroines, namely American feminists like Matilda Jocelyn Gage, Elizabeth Cady Stanton, and Lucretia Mott. These suffragists read newspapers and other correspondence about activities by Iroquois women, and were impressed that Iroquois women, as well as white women, could go unprotected in the reservations while searching for plants without fear of insults or violence from men, and that the men would actually help them.

I can understand why the suffragists were impressed that Iroquois women were more liberated that we white women, even when it came to egalitarian matters. My favorite, Elizabeth Cady Stanton, bravely advocated for divorce laws that would allow women to leave a loveless or abusive marriage. I read in an 1890 speech, she informed the National Council of Women that Iroquois women had domestic authority and could insist an abusive husband leave, but she retained authority over their children. Can you imagine white men agreeing to such arrangements? Or even allowing women to express their wishes to be autonomous and think for themselves?

I have decided I am not going to marry unless my husband agrees to total equality. Of course, I will probably not marry at all. My goal is to work in the tenement houses near the port of Philadelphia and help poor women achieve control over the number of children they have, and join the suffragists in their quest for the same rights for women that men now enjoy.

Mother and father do not know about my plans, but I am not deterred. I want to do something to make it easier for women of all ethnic backgrounds to rise above their oppression by white men who view women as possessions and servants.

You have inspired me, Rebecca. You are intelligent and brave. You already know so much about the human body from the medical books you read and I know you will do something meaningful with your life.

Please consider your future and join me in the quest for knowledge and autonomy.

Until we meet again, I am unquestionably your friend and admirer,

Maggie Eastman

Post Script: Are there any colleges near McAlisterville?

CHAPTER 27

REBECCA READ AND REREAD THE LETTER FROM MAGGIE, mulling over every line. In just a few months, she would see her friends again and was curious to find out if her friends had grown taller since last summer like she had. Her body shape had also changed from nearly straight to curvy, seemingly overnight. Jane scurried to sew new dresses, full skirts and high-necked blouses and warned Rebecca to dress decently.

She was a woman now, with a narrow waist to accent her chest and hips, despite the clothes that were designed to minimize them. Her already long legs seemed to stretch even longer. And her tan skin had darkened into a rich bronze from the summer sun. The young men in her school and from town noticed her shapely figure too, sometimes making rude comments to her behind her back. She made a mental note to ask Maggie and Lilly if city boys were as rude as boys in the country.

There were changes in her grandmother, too. Mary took patches of half-finished squares out of a trunk and laid them on the kitchen table. "Rebecca, would you like to help me finish these patches for the quilt I'm sewing while Grandpa takes a nap?"

"Sure, but you'll have to help me learn how to make tiny stitches like you do."

"Watch how I just catch the fabric through the batting with the needle. Push it through to the back and then through the front again."

Practicing over and over, Rebecca didn't quite master what her grandmother taught her. Fortunately, Mary never scolded her even though she sewed patch after patch with uneven stitches. Finally, her grandmother excused her. That was fine with Rebecca. Now she had more time to read medical books from Dr. Headings. She was fascinated by the illustrations of anatomy and the various body systems, particularly the reproductive system. Her mother hadn't told her much about her monthly bleed, and even less about how one became pregnant. Once again, she was thankful Back So Straight carefully explained the bleeding and said it was a blessing. According to her customs, Rebecca was no longer a girl, but a woman.

The drawings of male organs were a curious site to Rebecca. She certainly knew how male animals looked, but her father and brother never walked around naked. She watched farm animals mate, curious how even the male chickens managed to mount hens despite their feathery bottoms. It made her laugh when a female animal ran away from a suitor, leaving his organ awkwardly hanging from his underside.

Most fascinating to Rebecca was the section of the book that outlined the circulatory system. Now she understood why Dr. Headings pressed his finger down on the swelling in grandpa's legs: to check for fluid under his skin. And he listened to Joseph's chest for wheezes and squeaks and other signs of pneumonia.

Rebecca yearned to read more, but studying her school work, taking care of her grandfather and doing farm chores took up almost all her time. Sometimes she read by lantern late at night. Thankfully, school ended mid-May and she was rewarded by a straight-A report card.

Graduation was held on a sunny Friday. Only six girls and ten boys received their diploma. The whole family attended the ceremony, except Gary who wasn't interested in anything academic. Rebecca resisted offers to work as a "nurse" companion to wealthy families, although she didn't know what her future would be if she didn't find some sort of paid work. Having to take care of an elderly, possibly cantankerous person wasn't something she looked forward to. She already had two jobs: farm chores and taking care of her grandfather. Doing those tasks day after day for the rest of her life did not appeal to her. The idea of further schooling stuck in the back of her mind, recently made stronger by Maggie's letter. But what and where still eluded her.

Late that month, on an overcast, sultry day, the Tuscarora Valley Railroad train pulled into the station. Elwood and Rebecca made the trip to Mifflin, even though it took over two hours by wagon. She was eager to see her girlfriends again and her father told her he wanted to speak to Mr. Eastman about the barn agreement.

The first one to step off the train, Maggie had grown taller and a bit slimmer, although she still had a baby face and chubby cheeks. Rebecca ran to embrace her. Maggie laughed and lifted Rebecca off the platform with a bear hug. Next off the train was Lilly, gloved hands holding a parasol. Her perfect hair was arranged in curls piled high on her head and tied with yellow ribbon. "Rebecca! It's good to see you again. Let me take a good look at you. Oh, you've grown even lovelier than I remember." Then she turned to Rebecca's father. "I beg your pardon—hello, Mr. Wagner."

"Good to see you again, Lilly. Did you and your family have a good trip from Philadelphia?"

"Yes, it was tolerable, despite the heat and humidity. We were able to have a lovely picnic on board, complete with lemonade."

Elwood stood far back from the adults stepping onto the platform who were followed by servants carrying suitcases and large trunks. The caretakers of their homes and lumber company foremen stood in line waiting with wagons and fancy buckboards to take the two families and their belongings to their beautiful summer homes. Each item was unloaded from the train and carefully placed in wagons, along with baskets of food left over from their on-board picnic. Colored servants carried hat boxes and cartons of books, following close behind the girls. Rebecca studied the procession, in awe of the spectacle and curious about what was in the trunks and suitcases.

Her father waited in the background. She suspected by the somber look on his face he was thinking about asking Mr. Eastman some questions about the trees that were cut on Wagner land. As though Elwood could read her mind, he approached Eastman, but Hugh only walked past and hoisted himself up in his buggy. Rebecca's loyalty was torn between her Pop and Maggie's father. She wanted to say something to comfort her father but didn't know what. So she said nothing.

The ride back to the farm took Elwood and Rebecca past the mansions. Colored servants were sweeping the porches and cutting flowers. Rebecca's father turned to look at one house, then the other. "Three of our cabins could fit inside one of those houses. Can't imagine the lumber it took to build them."

Once again, she felt conflicted. She loved spending time in that mansion and wondered if her father had been right to want to question Mr. Eastman about the lost trees on Wagner land.

When they reached the farm they rode directly into the barn. Gary and his friend Jake walked in a few minutes later. They had shotguns slung over their shoulders and mud on their boots. Friends since primary school, Jake was a year older and already a head taller than Gary. Both spent their growing up years exploring the mountains and hunting and fishing.

"Hey sister, where were you? Your horse's all lathered up," asked Gary.

"Pop and I went to Mifflin to meet the Eastmans and the Norths. They're here for the summer again."

"Did those silly, spoiled friends of yours come back too? They look like they would faint if a grasshopper jumped on them."

Gary's friend, Jake, slapped his back, and they both laughed.

But Rebecca refused to get defensive. "Go outside and do something useful. You're just jealous because they're rich."

Gary continued teasing. "So what? Their Pops make their money cutting the trees. If you ask me, you're all spoiled brats."

"What's going on here?" Elwood came from behind hay bales carrying a saddle and hoisted it over the stall. "Gary… you're supposed to be working in the garden with your mother."

"Yeah, while Rebecca goes riding with you all over the place. If she gets to have fun, so do I." Gary stormed out of the barn, nearly tripping over a shovel. Jake followed.

Elwood took off the horse's blanket and sat down on a bale of hay. He ran his fingers through his hair and hung his head. Rebecca sat down beside him. "Are you upset, Pa?"

Her father waited a long time before answering. "Can't really say. Tried to talk to Eastman but got nowhere. And now your brother irritates me. Forgave him for throwing the knife—but nothing's changed. Unless Gary stops challenging me, he'll have to leave the farm. Your old man will have to go it alone."

CHAPTER 28

STANDING AT THE EDGE OF THE CREEK, GARY PULLED A STAKE with a "W" painted on the side out of the ground. It was loose, nearly falling over. He said to his friend Jake, "I had these pounded well into the creek bed. Wonder what… or who loosened it."

"Heck if I know. Are there any gouges on it?" Jake answered.

"Nope. Someone might have messed with it… tried to pull it out."

A twig snapped nearby, and Gary saw out of a slither of his eye a man's elbow retracting from behind a tree. Gary yelled, "Hey, what are you doing back there?"

"Nothing. Just wondering who put these markers in the creek."

"Well, come out where we can see you."

A large, fleshy man with thick arms and legs emerged from the edge of the forest. His mass of curly hair, the color of coffee with a little cream, was so thick it framed his lion-sized head like a mane. Deep-set eyes peeped out under hairy eyebrows. A thick mustache added to his already menacing appearance.

Gary said, "What the hell are you doing hiding?"

"This stake was loose and I was trying to put it back, but… but then I heard someone coming." He pulled the stake out, but instead of handing the stake to Gary, the man reached around him and handed it to Jake. Gary caught a glimpse of his hand and saw the index finger on his right hand was missing above the knuckle. "How'd you get your finger chopped off?"

"I got too close to a saw blade," he lied. The truth was, Gary learned later, he got it caught in an animal trap.

Jake climbed down from his horse and showed the piece of wood to Gary, who moved closer to the large man and pointed a finger. "Listen, see this W? This stake is mine. I put it here to mark my traps."

"So what? I'm Gunther Troutman. I work for Eastman. He owns a big lumber company."

Gary thought… great. Another Eastman lackey. "Listen, I don't care who you are or who you work for. Just remember, Lost Creek is mine. Set your traps somewhere else." He lied. Gunther didn't know no one owned the creek. Gary didn't want anyone to trap the creek except Jake and himself.

Gunther sneered. "Hey… my mistake. I'll know better next time."

"There'd better not be a next time."

Gunther nodded, his sneer revealing tobacco-stained teeth. "So, where are you boys going? Do you know of any other good spots to set traps?"

Gary's eyebrows drew together, showing his annoyance at being called a boy. "None that I want to show you. Why don't you go downstream?"

"Nah, already looked there. Mind if I tag along while you check your other posts?"

Gary looked at Jake but his friend just shrugged his shoulders. "Suit yourself. Only stay out of our way."

The two young men mounted their horses and began to pick their way along the edges of the creek. Gunther ran behind them trying to keep up. After a quarter of a mile or so, the three men came upon a trap that hadn't been taken out of the creek at the end of trapping season last spring. An unusual animal was caught in it, still alive and struggling to free itself. The creature had partially chewed off its left front paw. As they got closer, Jake bent down to look more closely. "I've seen one of these before when I was hunting in Canada with my uncle. It's a fisher. Looks like a weasel but it's bigger. Don't see too many in Pennsylvania. Too warm."

Covered with blood, the fisher's mottled summer fur was still visible. As the men approached the animal, it hissed and bared its teeth. Gunther grabbed a stick and poked at it. It whirled around trying to avoid the jabs from the stick, and as it did, the animal raked its bleeding paw further through the trap's jagged teeth.

"Stop that, Gunther. Put the stick down." Gary loaded his shotgun and pointed it at the screaming animal.

Gunther kept aggravating the fisher. "Don't waste a bullet. It's going to die anyway and its fur isn't worth anything."

"I said stop poking and I mean it," Gary repeated, this time louder.

Jake grabbed the stick out of Gunther's hand. "Just put the poor thing out of its misery."

Gary pulled the trigger, putting a single shot to the head of the writhing animal. "Done."

Gunther held his palms up. "Like I said, waste of a good bullet, if you ask me."

Jake carefully opened the trap and propped it open with a stick so the trap wouldn't snap shut while he pulled out the fisher's mangled body. He took the animal by the tail and placed it in a pile of leaves, covering its body with rocks. "Let's get going, Gary. I've had enough."

Gunther shrugged and smiled. "I'd best be getting back to the mill. I'm supposed to be learning how to run it."

Gary snapped, "Oh yeah? Can't imagine you running anything."

"Looks like you can't run anything either. Else your father's barn wouldn't have burned down."

Gary pointed the gun at Gunther. "Let my Pop out of this. Get going before I take this gun and whack you."

Gunther backed up and started to walk away. Holding both arms up, a broad sneer crossed his face. "No harm done. Just forget about it."

"Don't worry. I won't forget."

"We'll see about that," Gunther growled under his breath as he walked into a thick stand of trees.

Gary narrowed his eyes. “That man’s trouble.”

“You’re right,” said Jake. “Glad he’s gone. Are you game if we check the rest of the creek?”

“Yeah, let’s go.”

They mounted their horses again and rode to the top of Little Round Top, checking the spring that fed Tennis Run, the small creek that eventually ran past the Wagner farm and into Lost Creek. Gary reached down into the cold, bubbling water and cupped his hand to get a drink. Jake tapped him on the shoulder and pointed down the mountain. “What’s that bald spot down the west side of the mountain? I thought your Pop owned that land.”

Gary looked down and ground his boot in the dirt. “I hate to tell you—my Pop sold it to that Eastman fella who owns the lumber company. He sold it for lumber to build our barn and buy the farm equipment we lost in the fire.”

Jake’s eyes grew large. “Never thought I’d see the day your Pop would do that.”

“Neither did I. Didn’t have any say in it.”

Taking his hat off and wiping his forehead, Jake said. “I think I’d better be getting home. It’s getting late and my uncle’s probably waiting for me to eat supper.”

“Me, too. See you soon.” Gary watched his friend walk away. He almost stopped him, wanting to explain how he felt about losing acreage and a prime stand of timber on land he hoped to own someday, but changed his mind when Jake disappeared out of view. He stood still, his eyes searching the mountains surrounding Little Round Top. His stomach churned. Checkerboard patches of bare ground peppered the landscape. Large swaths of evergreen trees were gone. He turned his horse toward the valley below and slowly made his way down the mountain. When he came upon tall trees standing like sentinels guarding the land, he clicked his horse into a gallop. Before Gary realized where he was going, he crossed the foothills and found himself near the mansions outside town.

As the stone house came into view, he heard a soulful, haunting sound. It grew louder as he approached the stone wall surrounding the large mansion.

Gary pulled the reins to a stop at the edge of the yard. He stood mesmerized as the resonance echoed through the trees. He got off his horse and walked toward the sound. Stopping when he neared the house, he closed his eyes and listened. Soon the music ended and Gary opened his eyes to see a young man with long, wavy, reddish brown hair tossed about his face walking toward him. The man was tall and slender, with long arms and fingers. A violin and bow hung from his left hand.

"Are you looking for someone?"

"No. Sorry to disturb you."

"That's okay. I was just practicing."

Gary pointed to the instrument. "Is that a fiddle?"

Smiling, the man held the violin up to his chin. "No, it's a violin. They're the same musical instrument, just played differently. Here, let me show you." The bow danced over the strings as he played a chorus of *Turkey in the Straw.*

"How'd you do that? Don't your fingers hurt?"

"They used to when I was little."

"How long have you been playing?"

David tucked the violin under his arm. "Close to ten years. I started when I was seven… begged my father to take lessons after he and my mother took me to the symphony. My father wasn't too happy about it."

"My father isn't too keen on me hunting and fishing either. I'd rather be out in the woods, not digging in the ground." Gary ground the toe of his boot in the dirt.

"Well, my father thinks I should follow his footsteps in the lumber business, but I'm not the least bit interested."

"That makes two of us. Thanks for showing me your fiddle. Guess I'd better get going."

"If you want, I'll ask the maid to get us something to eat. Do you like coconut cake?"

"Can't say I ever ate it."

David walked to the door of the portico and said something to the person inside. In a few minutes, a colored maid brought a tray with two pieces of cake and a pitcher of lemonade into the yard. David motioned for her to go to the gazebo while the young men followed.

They sat down and ate their cake in silence. Finally, David asked, "What were you doing in the mountains before you came here?"

"I was with my friend Jake—we were checking my animal traps."

"What kind of animals do you trap?

Gary was pleasantly surprised the young man seemed interested in trapping. "Muskrat, beaver, mink, and occasionally, we find ermine."

"Does your friend go with you?"

"Yeah, he had to go home but I don't think he'd be interested in hearing a violin."

David placed his empty plate on the small table in the middle of the gazebo and stood up. "I've got to go inside now."

Gary handed him the dish and studied the young man's face. "Thanks for the cake." He was different from Jake and his other friends—more interesting. "Well, I guess I'd better get home, too."

"If you're not out somewhere with your friend—what's his name…?"

"Jake."

"I didn't catch your name either. Mine's David Eastman. Maybe you could come over again sometime and I could go with you into the woods. I must admit I don't know much about trees."

"Name's Gary Wagner. I know a lot about trees, but I don't know what kind of wood your violin is made of."

David handed his violin to Gary. "I'm not sure about this wood, but my father paid a lot of money for it. I'll ask him when he gets home from the mill."

Fixing his eyes on the grain of the wood, Gary ran his fingers along the belly. It felt as smooth as glass. "All right. I'll see you around. Maybe I'll come back next week and we can take a hike to a cave up on Little Round Top."

Gary walked back to where his horse was tied. Home from the mill? David's old man was Eastman. He bought our mountain land.

CHAPTER 29

REBECCA HURRIED THROUGH HER CHORES SO SHE COULD walk to her friend's house before it became too warm. Following the path off the dirt road, she entered the manicured lawn surrounding the Eastman's' great stone house. When she knocked on the door, no one answered. She suspected Maggie might be across the street at Lilly's house. As she walked across Main Street and neared the brick mansion, she heard laughter coming from the backyard. Greeting her when Rebecca rounded the corner, were white tents with picnic tables underneath, and colored servants carrying baskets of food. Large coolers with blocks of ice lined the backyard near the house. Young people were playing croquet and badminton. Rebecca had never seen families play games and picnic together in the middle of the day… but also in the middle of the week. Most families in McAlisterville and nearby towns worked long hours farming nearly every day or in family businesses.

"What a nice surprise. Mother, Rebecca's here," said Lilly, as soon as she realized that Rebecca was standing at the edge of the yard.

"Come join us, Rebecca." Mrs. North took her hand and led her toward a grassy area where boys were hitting wooden balls through metal hoops.

"Miss Wagner, I don't know if you remember them from last summer, but this is my son Charles, and," pointing to the young men across from him, "these are Maggie's brothers, David and Carlton." Rebecca felt herself blush, hoping they didn't notice her homemade cotton day dress and scuffed shoes.

Charles came forward and bowed. "I'm pleased to meet you, Miss Wagner."

"Thank you," she answered, trying to remember her manners.

Before she could collect her thoughts, Maggie's brother David approached her with his hand extended. "Hello, Miss Wagner. I remember mother and father telling me about your trek up the mountain with my sister and Lilly to pick berries."

Smiling nervously and feeling her cheeks flush in embarrassment, Rebecca blurted, "That's something I'd prefer to forget." Shifting her attention to the boy who was walking toward her, she tried to ignore the perspiration running down her back and beading up under her nose.

"I'm Carlton," the gangly adolescent boy-man squeaked. "Nice to meet you."

Before Rebecca could answer, he turned around and ran to pick up his croquet mallet lying in the grass. The other boys quickly followed. She was relieved when Maggie took her hand and led her to the side of the yard where Lilly and she had been playing badminton. A net was strung between two wooden poles and narrow ropes held them in place with stakes on either side. Maggie picked up her racquet and slammed the birdie over the net to where Lilly was waiting. The two girls played for a few volleys, then Maggie gave her racquet to Rebecca. She swung and missed the first few swings.

Rebecca's chin dropped to her chest. "It looks like I'm not too good at this game. Let me try to hit the birdie to you, Lilly. Maybe I'll get the idea of it better."

She tossed the birdie in the air and hit it with her strong arm. It sailed high over the net, far beyond the edge of the yard where Lilly was waiting. They all burst out laughing.

The next try went better. Rebecca swung the racquet and hit the birdie directly to Lilly. "I got it." She volleyed the birdie in a perfect arch over the net to Rebecca, who gently returned the birdie.

"Oops." Lilly swung and missed, her white dress twirling around her legs. In perfect form, she swooped down, picked up the birdie and sent it back to Rebecca.

After a while, Rebecca forgot all about her dress and shoes. The three young women laughed and played until they were breathless, only stopping when they heard a voice announce, "Food is being served."

They sat down under the white tent with its banners flying in the breeze. Tables were covered with blue and white Irish linen tablecloths and napkins to match. Servants dressed in starched black and white uniforms served them, smiling but saying nothing. Silver trays of food—*hors d'oeuvres* of olives, fried oysters wrapped in bacon, assorted nuts, sandwiches with cream cheese and cucumbers, glazed figs topped with mascarpone, and fresh fruit were served first. Then beer-battered fried chicken, herbed German potato salad, roasted corn on the cob, asparagus cradled in flaky dough, and cheese soufflé.

Deserts were served next: fudge, coconut cake, lemon meringue pie, and homemade ice cream. Rebecca tasted bits of everything, eating until she felt like she would burst. As she stared at the scene around her, she pressed a piece of ice against the roof of her mouth, savoring the feel of the cold pieces against her tongue and cheeks. Maggie and Lilly had everything. Pretty clothes. No chores. Servants. Their lives were so easy compared to hers. But the things she envied most—were their private schools and bright future that included college.

Her thoughts were interrupted when Lilly's brother Charles approached her.

"Would you like to play croquet?"

Feeling unsure of herself, Rebecca hesitated. "If… if you'll teach me. I have never played before."

"It's not hard. I'll put you on my team and show you as we go along. Our balls have red stripes. Watch where I direct the ball when I hit it." Charles struck the wooden ball, sending it through the hoop at the first stake. When it was Rebecca's turn, he showed her where to hold the mallet. He leaned over her and placed his hands over hers. "Now let me help you." Rebecca was nervous. Her hands sweated underneath his. They both swung, slamming the red striped ball through the hoop where it struck a ball with green stripes that belonged to the other team. It rolled several feet away from its original place.

"Hey, that's our ball," protested the other boys.

Lilly and Maggie watched from the sidelines and edged her on. "Rebecca, that was a perfect shot," said Maggie.

"Just beginner's luck," shouted Rebecca, not knowing if she should keep trying to compete with the boys on the other team. But the longer the game went on, the stronger her competitive spirit came alive, especially with her friends cheering her on. Each time she hit the wooden ball, it went exactly where she wanted it to go. Charles declared, "We're the winners," as the red ball went through the last set of three hoops.

The three girls hugged in triumph and danced in a circle, their dresses flying and feet skipping in the air.

Their opponents shook their heads in disbelief. But Charles smiled and shrugged his shoulders. "Come on, guys, let's go down to the pond."

After Rebecca and her friends finally caught their breath, they walked to the back porch for a cool glass of lemonade. "I feel sweaty and messy," Maggie said, as she flopped down on a wicker chair. "Feels good."

When they finally settled down, Rebecca held up her hand. "I almost forgot. I came over to your house today to ask if you would like to go with me next week to see a cave up on Little Round Top Mountain."

Maggie's eyes widened. "I've never seen a cave before. Is it dangerous?"

"No, it's interesting. Sometimes I find animal bones and pieces of fur."

"But what if there are animals in the cave?"

"I've never seen any, and I've been there lots of times." Rebecca hoped she didn't sound like she was bragging.

"Okay, I'll go if Lilly goes."

Seeing Lilly's hesitance, Rebecca tried to be persuasive. "It'll be fun, I promise. What do you say, Lilly?"

"All right. What shall we take along?"

"Just water and some lunch. Wear boots and old clothing. Come to the farm and we'll leave from there. How about Tuesday morning about nine? Tell your parents we'll be careful. After all, we're a year older now." But the memory of the snakes in the berry patch tempered her confidence.

CHAPTER 30

THE DAY DAWNED BRIGHT AND SUNNY. WHITE, FLUFFY clouds drifted through a perfect azure sky. Maggie and Lilly arrived in a surrey driven by one of the men who had served the picnic last week. He helped them down from the seat and handed them two small satchels of food and canteens of water, each one with a strap to carry it across their backs. "Miss Lilly, Miss Maggie, I come by at four o'clock—take you on home."

"Thank you, Edward. We'll be ready." Maggie grabbed Lilly's arm, then Rebecca's. "Let's go. I can't wait to see what a cave looks like."

"Just a moment. I must tell my mother we're leaving. Please come on the porch while I find her." In her haste, Rebecca left the front door half-open. Jane was helping her mother-in-law get Joseph onto the potty chair, in plain view of Maggie and Lilly. There he sat, his pants down below his knees.

Realizing what had just happened, Rebecca quickly closed the door. "I'm sorry you had to see that." Her face flushed with embarrassment.

Lilly and Maggie looked at each other, then away from the cabin. Rebecca tried to explain. "My grandfather needs to use a potty chair since he can't walk to the outhouse."

"Do you mean like a baby?" questioned Lilly.

Rebecca smiled at her friend's innocence. "Sort of. We have to help him get up and walk a few steps and slide the potty chair against him to make sure it's in the right place."

"Does that mean someone must be here all the time in case he has to… you know… go?" asked Maggie.

"Yes. I try to help whenever I can but my mother and grandmother do most of the work taking care of him."

Jane heard their voices and walked out of the bedroom, making certain she closed the door. "Girls, are you ready to head up the mountain?"

Relieved her mother changed the conversation, Rebecca said, "Yes, we are. We'll be back by four."

"Have a good time, girls. Rebecca, you're in charge of your friends, so be careful." Jane made sure the girls were out of hearing distance before she crossed the yard and went into the barn where Elwood and her son were cleaning animal stalls. Gary stopped shoveling as soon as he saw his mother. "What's going on, Ma?"

"Your sister and her friends left a few minutes ago to climb up to the cave. I want you to follow them in a little while. They went up the way you and Rebecca usually go."

"Why? Don't you think Rebecca can take care of herself and her friends?"

"No, I just know how eager she is to show her friends how brave she is. Sometimes that gets her in trouble."

"Well, have to agree with you about that," said Gary.

Elwood stopped shoveling manure and frowned at his wife. "Need him to stay here and help me."

"I know, but I'm worried about the girls being up there alone. Just in case they need help," said Jane.

"What can happen? They're grown women and there's three of them."

"Please, Elwood." Jane pleaded. When her husband said nothing, she nodded to her son.

"I'm going, Ma, as soon as I finish these last few shovels full."

The forests were lush and dense. There had been just the right amount of rain and sunshine to keep them vibrant, their new growth evident in the emerald green tips of the hemlocks and white pines. Tiny, bright golden mushrooms sprouted from the forest floor, pushing their way through the carpet of leaves. A centipede crawled over a group of spongy orange pods. Nearby, larger flesh-colored mushrooms paled in comparison to their bright cousins.

Rebecca led her friends on the path that zigzagged up the mountain. She smelled the earthy loam and pine trees, and pointed to the mushrooms growing under a mammoth hemlock, its branches drooping to the damp understory.

As soon as Maggie spied the spongy growths, she questioned Rebecca as she pulled a pale one out of the moist ground. "Are these mushrooms good to eat?"

"I'm not sure, so don't eat it. My Indian friend knows about the mushrooms but I can't remember if this one is poisonous or not."

Maggie nodded. She threw the mushroom on the ground and smashed it with her boot.

They climbed the switchback trail a little further until they heard the sound of water. A creek appeared around a bend of the trail, its water running white where it tumbled over boulders and dead trees. Further downstream, small tree limbs were stacked like toothpick spanning the water and forming frothy waterfalls. Huge hemlock trees stood guard over the creek, their lacy branches forming a canopy over the water. The creek bed was lined with rocks and a brown ribbon of wet mud where matted leaves left their spongy pillows, dotted here and there with deer and raccoon tracks. Moss blanketed most of the gray, green, and black rocks, slippery and still.

Drops of perspiration dripped off Rebecca's forehead and ran down her nose. She stopped near the creek and looked at Maggie and Lilly. Their faces were red and flushed. Lilly wiped her face with a handkerchief but Maggie wiped her forehead with her sleeve.

Rebecca took the bait. "Let's sit down and dangle our feet in the water to cool off. Here's a good spot."

The girls took off their boots and socks, giggling with delight as they felt the cold water trickle over their toes. Small brook trout darted under sloping rocks. But bright color caught Rebecca's eye. She spied a corn snake, half-submerged under a small earthen overhang in the creek bed. "Look! Over there," Rebecca whispered. "Shhhh. It won't hurt you. It's a harmless corn snake, I promise. Let's see what it's looking for."

Lilly and Maggie jerked their feet out of the water and watched silently. Their bodies were stiff with fear but they didn't make a sound. The snake was motionless, while a fish swam closer. It struck the trout and returned to its hiding place where it slowly worked its victim head first through an opened mouth and down its throat. The bulge in its belly, showing its black, gold, white, and red bands of color, moved downward as it stretched to make room for its prey.

Although Rebecca knew the snake was harmless, she was not eager to frighten her friends again. She quietly stood up and motioned her friends to back away from the creek. Still watching the snake, they dried their feet with their skirts and pulled on their boots. When they were a safe distance from the creek, Maggie and Lilly began talking at the same time. Maggie said, "Mercy. I never saw anything like that. How did that snake swallow a fish without chewing it?"

Lilly joined in. "How did you know the snake wasn't poisonous? Weren't you afraid? All I could think of was what happened last summer."

"I knew the snake wasn't poisonous because I recognized the colored bands and circles around its body. It didn't have a triangular-shaped head either, as poisonous snakes do. All snakes have jaws that open like a hinge and allow them to swallow their pray whole."

The young women listened intensely, never taking their eyes off Rebecca.

Excited by their interest, she told them about another harmless snake. "I saw a black snake take a chicken egg out of our chicken coop. The egg looked like it was stuck in its throat but the big black snake got away before I could see it work its way down its body." Rebecca was pleased her friends seemed in awe of her.

As they walked along the creek again, Rebecca answered more questions. She realized that despite being a farmer's daughter in a small town like McAlisterville, she was smart in her own way.

The climb became more difficult as more large hemlock trees, tall and lush, spread their great arms over the ground below. Tiny pinecones hung from the branches, forming clusters like hundreds of grapes.

On the high slopes of the creek lay huge boulders that looked as though they had been tossed about like pebbles skipped across a pond. Dozens of these silent, gray sentinels, setting in groups of seven or eight, appeared before them, some larger than others. The creek split into two channels with a sandy gravel island between them upon which large piles of dead trees, leaves and branches formed a barrier. A family of beavers took advantage of the easy source of trees to build a dam.

A huge tulip poplar lay on the ground near the dam, its roots clinging to the black earth. Deep under the root mass, a black bear had carved out a den, long abandoned when spring spread her warmth like a great quilt covering the forest floor.

The girls chatted happily as they passed by one wonder after another. Sometimes Rebecca would point out things she recognized. She felt important... more confident... more aware of things her friends didn't understand.

Maggie stopped suddenly and pointed to the ground. "Look! What are these beautiful white things, Rebecca? You can almost see through them." Small, delicate, transparent flowers sprouted beneath lacy, green ferns. Their trumpet-shaped heads had an orchid-like flower drooping from the tops of their stems, with tiny brown spots on their sides. Two small "ears" covered the flowers, giving them the appearance of a horse's head.

"They're called Indian Pipes. They grow in wet areas under the trees. My Indian friend told me that her people considered them sacred." Rebecca felt like she was seeing the wonders of the woods through her friends' eyes. One after another, she described plants and wildlife to Lilly and Maggie when they discovered things in the forest.

Lilly stopped walking and took Rebecca's arm. "Rebecca, you know so much about the woods and the animals. You're lucky to have grown up here."

Her face lit up. "I guess I am." She pondered Lilly's compliment for a few minutes. Maybe she was right. However, self-doubt blurred the glow she felt just a moment ago. "But you know things I don't know, too."

Nodding, Lilly's smile reached the corner of her eyes. "Maybe, but you are so smart."

As they walked around a large, gray boulder, a familiar landmark for Rebecca, she craned to see the dark opening in the rocks. It was nearly hidden by overhanging roots and branches. They cautiously approached. Rebecca listened for sounds. Hearing nothing, she stuck a long stick inside the black cleft in the moss-covered boulders. After she took a few steps into the cave, Rebecca motioned for her friends to follow. The damp air made them shiver.

The girls stepped over a few pebbles and small objects on the ground that they could feel under their boots but couldn't see. Rebecca stopped and listened again. "This is a far as we can go." Just as she was turning around, a roar echoed against the walls that shook the ground beneath them. They grabbed each other. Their screams reverberated through the dark chamber.

"What's that?" Maggie whispered.

"I don't know," Rebecca whispered back. Her heart was pounding in her temples.

Another roar shattered the silent cave, sounding more guttural than the first. The girls clung to each other, shaking, and afraid to move. As they stood frozen in the darkness, they heard footsteps coming toward them. A large man with a mane of curly hair appeared, silhouetted against the streaks of light from the mouth of the cave.

"Who's this?" the man asked, a sneer on his face, barely visible in the dim light.

Rebecca's knees were shaking but she wanted to be strong for her friends. "Never mind. Who are you—and why did you scare us like that?"

Before he answered, they heard another voice from the front of the cave. "Rebecca, are you alright?"

"Gary? Is that you? There's a man inside the cave."

"What's going on here? Come out where I can see you."

"It's me. Gunther. I didn't do anything. Just having a little fun."

"I know who you are. Rebecca, all of you, come out."

Gunther walked past Gary on his way out of the cave, followed by the girls. Rebecca hugged her brother. "I'm so glad to see you." Pointing, she said, "That man acted like a wild animal—scared the wits out of us. No telling what else he would have done if you hadn't come."

"This is the second time I have caught you messing around something you shouldn't have. You owe these ladies an apology."

"Yeah, says who? You can't tell me what to do."

Rebecca strode up to him, feeling stronger now that her brother was there. "You have no right to scare me and my friends."

"These girls know me. I wouldn't have done them any harm."

Maggie pointed at Gunther. "I've seen you a few times at our house."

"Yeah, I work for Eastman. He's sort of my uncle."

"What do you mean? My father's your uncle? I've never even heard him mention you."

"Well, not exactly. My old man and Eastman worked together in Williamsport. When he died, Eastman took me on as a hired hand to work in his sawmill. I call him Uncle. Doesn't say otherwise either."

"We don't care who you work for. You were rude. Now, excuse us. We want to go home." Rebecca wanted to protect her friends against any threat this man may pose, whether or not he worked for Maggie's father.

"That's right." Gary stood between the girls and Gunther, spreading his arms out at his side. "Let them pass. And stay away from them from now on."

"Just try to stop me."

CHAPTER 31

GLAD HER FRIENDS RETURNED HOME WITHOUT ANY FURTHER threat from Gunther, that night Rebecca remembered with fondness the pride she felt being able to identify and explain the wonders of the forests. For the first time in her life, she felt intelligent and competent. Maybe the next time she took her friends into the mountains, she would teach them about the plants and trees Back So Straight taught her to use as medicine.

But until then, Rebecca took advantage of a lull in the farm work to spread a quilt under a large willow tree near the creek. She sat down and opened a medical book Dr. Headings had loaned her on his last visit to check her grandparents. Photographs and illustrations helped her learn the terms for organs, blood vessels, muscles and bones. She tried to pronounce and memorize their names, saying them out loud. Often she referred to the glossary of terms in the back of the book. Just as she turned the page, a horse whinnied in the distance. Coming down the lane toward the farm were Lilly and Maggie riding in the family surrey. She waved and ran to greet them. "To what do I owe this surprise?"

"We have something for you." Maggie looked at Lilly with a wide grin on her face. "Promise you'll keep it. We want to thank you for teaching us about the forests and wildlife. We found it in a catalogue and asked my mother to send it from Philadelphia. May we stay while you open the package?"

"Of course. Let's go into the cabin." Rebecca felt less guarded about her friends seeing the cabin—really a farmhouse as it was made of logs—ever since their trip to the cave.

The colored driver helped the girls down from the surrey before he climbed back on the front seat, waving as he drove away. "Be back before dark to pick you up."

Jane was sitting on the porch shelling peas into a blue and white enamel pan when she saw the girls walking up to the cabin. "Hello girls."

"Ma. Maggie and Lilly brought me a present!"

"That's wonderful, girls. How nice of you to surprise Rebecca."

The three girls walked into the cabin and sat on a bench while Rebecca carefully loosened the paper and folded it carefully as though she wanted to prolong the moment of anticipation. Inside the box was a beautiful long, white dress with a high neckline and elbow-length puffy sleeves, just like the one Rebecca saw in the Macy's ad when she and her friends paged through a catalogue a few weeks ago. White lace surrounded the bodice and hem of the dress—all nestled in soft tissue paper. A sheer petticoat was hidden in the second layer. In the corner of the box was a black ribbon with a cameo pinned to it. Rebecca looked at the dress for a long time.

There was a quiet lull in the conversation. Finally, Jane said, "Girls, the dress is lovely. I'm sure Rebecca will look beautiful in it." But Rebecca caught a brief glimpse of sadness in her mother's eyes.

"Stand up and hold the dress up to your shoulders," said Maggie. "I think it's a perfect fit. Please try it on. The cameo is a gift from my mother and father."

"All right." Rebecca climbed up the stairs to the loft, fighting back tears. She wasn't sure she was crying because the dress was so beautiful or because she knew her mother would never be able to afford to buy her a dress like that. She wanted to keep the dress but didn't want to hurt her mother.

When lifting the white dress and petticoat out of the box, Rebecca felt the smoothness of the fabric, soft and silky in her hands. The petticoat made a soft crinkling noise when she moved. After she undressed, she fit the dress over her head, down over her breasts, and let it fall to her feet. Her tan skin and her nearly black hair against the whiteness of the dress was striking. For the first time in her life, she felt beautiful.

She stood before the stairway and took the first step. All eyes followed Rebecca's tall form drift down the stairway, but it was Jane who responded first. She took her daughter's hands in hers and said softly, "You look beautiful."

Rebecca kissed her mother on the cheek and turned to her friends. "Thank you so very much. I'd be lying if I said I didn't love the dress. I just feel it is too extravagant for a farm girl."

"What do you mean, it's too extravagant for a farm girl? I don't understand," Lilly said, her voice tentative and soft.

Maggie chimed in. "You're smarter than any girl I know. Besides, you're our best friend."

"I just don't know what I've done to deserve it."

"My dear daughter," Jane said, "It's not a matter of deserving it. Maggie and Lilly love you and want to show it. Enough of this nonsense."

"All right. Thank you. And please give my thanks to your parents too."

After Rebecca changed back into her old dress, the young women walked down to the small creek that meandered through the front yard. They sat down on the quilted blanket where they first saw Rebecca when they arrived at the farm.

"What kind of book is this?" Lilly asked when she accidentally sat on the hard cover.

"It's one of the medical books our family doctor loaned to me. Want to look at it?"

Lilly gently paged through the thick book, stopping where she found a drawing of the internal female reproductive organs. "Why is the womb called the uterus in this book? And the monthly bleeding called menses or menstruation?"

"These are medical words doctors use. Most of them have a Latin origin."

"Oh. We study Latin." Maggie and Lilly looked carefully at every detail and tried to interpret each drawing and description. Finally, Lilly asked, "What did your mothers tell you about your monthly bleed? Mine only told me a little—how I was to use these clean cloths to put inside my chemise. She told me it would come every month for about five days."

Maggie face turned red. "My first bleed happened nearly two years ago. I was mortified. It happened in school. I saw the dark blood in my panties when I wiped myself. Luckily my teacher had some cotton pads in her desk drawer. My mother didn't tell me it would hurt. The first day of my bleed, I still have these cramps in my belly right above my… you know… where the hair is. Rebecca, what did your mother tell you?"

"She didn't. I think she was ashamed to talk to me about it because her mother hadn't told her either. The first day she had her first monthly, she thought she was bleeding to death. When my Indian friend saw me hanging cloths on the wash line, she asked my mother if she could teach me about becoming a woman."

"Did your mother agree?"

"Yes. I think she was actually relieved. Back So Straight told me that in her tribe, women told these things to their daughters just as they had been told by their mothers. Having your first bleed was a rite of passage. It meant that one had become a woman and was ready to marry."

Maggie face wrinkled up. "Marry when she was that young?"

"Yes, it was expected of them."

"Your Indian friend seems very fascinating. She must be very wise. Who is she? Has she always lived with you?"

"Her name is Back So Straight. She lives alone in the small cabin on the edge of the farm near the forest. I go to her when I need advice. But she pretty much keeps to herself."

Lilly laid her hand against her breastbone. "Why doesn't she go into town or talk to us?"

"She would speak to us if I asked her. I think she knows that some people don't like Indians. But we love her and learn a lot from her about herbs and healing."

Maggie nodded and smiled. "Tell me more about what she taught you."

"She also told me a lot about her people and how in some tribes the women were respected as leaders and healers."

Lilly said, "That's amazing. What did she tell you about their monthlies?"

"She explained that all the women would go into a special hut during the heaviest days of their bleeding, since most women tended to have their monthlies—or moons as they called it—together. They would talk to other women about female matters and share stories. Sometimes they would weave or paint."

Despite the frowns on their faces, Rebecca continued. "My Indian friend placed me outside of a ring of stones, where she built a small fire. She sprinkled sage on the fire on each of the four sides representing north, south, east, and west. I can still smell the sweet, pungent odor of the herb."

"What happened next?" Maggie asked, as she moved closer to Rebecca.

"She laid her hands on my head and when she let go, she walked around the circle, carrying a small pouch around her neck, singing something in her Iroquois language she learned from another ancient healer."

Lilly moved next to Rebecca's other side. "What did it sound like?"

"She taught me the chant. I think I can remember the words. Let me see. 'May the Great Ake:weh Mother Spirit give you peace… may you open your heart to her… may you be aware of the Great Ake:weh Mother Spirit within you.'" Rebecca paused and closed her eyes before resuming. "May the Great Ake:weh Mother Spirit heal you." Rebecca struggled to remember the last part, but finally continued. "And may your medicine heal others."

Maggie and Lilly sat still, their eyes glued to Rebecca, who was enjoying the attention of her city friends.

"What does that mean?" Lilly asked.

"I'm not positive… but Back So Straight told me I would someday be a healer."

CHAPTER 32

LATE SUMMER, WHEN DAYLIGHT LENGTHENED AND THE grains turned light brown and gold, was harvest time for the whole Wagner family. They cut hay and oats with hand scythes and sickles, working from dawn to dusk, stopping only to eat quick meals. This year, the days were longer and the work harder without the farmhand to help them.

Tiny oat lice were released that made them scratch where the little buggers landed on their moist arms and necks. Dust from harvesting the grain, mixed with sweat that dripped off their faces and down their arms, created brown streaks that dried in the hot sun. Broad-brimmed straw hats kept the sun from turning the skin on their face to leather.

Evenings, after taking a bath in the galvanized tub, Rebecca went upstairs to rest and cool off. Her new, white dress hung from a wooden hanger on a peg in her room, covered with a clean sheet to keep it from getting dusty. Every night before going to bed, she pulled the sheet off, wondering when and where she would wear such a fancy dress.

After the last of the field corn was cut and arranged in teepee-like piles, Gary handed Rebecca a flyer. The slight smile on his face told her he was up to something sinister. "Look at this, Rebecca. Grange is having a dance. Wouldn't you like to go with Gunther?"

Rebecca made a gagging noise. "Stop chiding me. I wouldn't go with him if he was the last man on Earth."

"Don't you want to wear your white dress?"

She shook her head vigorously. "Not for that man who enjoys intimidating women."

"How about going with me? I'm a lot better looking than him."

Rebecca studied her brother for a minute. "Why not? As long as you take a bath. And no taking Jake with us." Gary liked to show off when his friend was around. She didn't want to endure a whole night of posturing.

"Aww, come on. Jake's my friend. You're just afraid he'll ask you to dance."

There was some truth to that last statement. "I can't help it if I'm fussy."

"You think you're too good for Jake, and for that matter every other boy in McAlisterville."

"That's enough, Gary. I'll put up with you for one night so I can wear my white dress."

The dance was held Saturday night at the Grange hall. Men from town and nearby farms played fiddles and guitars and one old gentleman strummed a banjo. Their renditions of Civil War songs, ballads, and camp songs kept folks dancing and tapping their feet. Farm tables were filled with homemade pies—shoofly, Montgomery, apple, cherry, pumpkin. Plates of cookies—sugar, molasses, raisin, spritz, and snicker doodles. Along with the traditional pork and sauerkraut were ham and sweet potatoes, chicken pot pie, pepper cabbage, and cucumbers with onions and cream. Kegs of birch and root beer stood on hay bales near a wheel barrel filled with wooden-handled mugs.

All eyes were on Rebecca when she and her brother arrived shortly after the dance began. Her brown skin contrasted the brightness of her dress. Shiny black hair with chestnut highlights pulled back from her face with a herringbone barrette and piled in curls on top of her head added to her beauty. Rebecca took a deep breath and leaned into her brother. They slowly walked toward the food tables and stood in line. As they shuffled closer to the heavily-laden tables, people started talking to them, asking about their grandparents and the new barn. Rebecca felt herself relax. The band took a break and the pianist started to play the banjo, making it easier to make small talk with folks around them. By the time they reached the food table they were ravenous.

Gary helped Rebecca find two seats at the edge of the dance floor, and held her plate while she arranged her dress. As he handed the plate to her, she saw Gunther coming towards them, carrying food in each hand—his eyes staring at her as he made his way through the crowd. Gunther usually wore flannel shirts and overalls but tonight he had on a pair of dark trousers and a dress shirt with a string tie.

"Howdy, Miss Rebecca. Fancy meeting you here with your brother. I thought a girl like you could find your own beau."

She ignored him, pretending to concentrate on eating the plate of food balanced on her lap.

"Cat got your tongue?"

"Leave her alone," Gary growled, his face puckered with anger.

Gunther's nostrils flared as he made a huffing sound. "Sure, but watch your animal traps."

"And you better watch your ass."

Gunther mumbled under his breath and turned around, his large frame leaving a shadow across Rebecca as the lanterns strung on the rafters gave off bright light.

"Good riddance," Gary said.

When they finished eating the band started playing, *She'll Be Coming Round the Mountain When She Comes,* the banjo player stomping his foot to the music. Rebecca glanced up and saw a man she never saw before approach. He had sandy-colored hair and a broad smile. "Hello. Ben Siebert. May I please have this dance?"

His eyes were kind... hazel with a gold rim around the iris. They held steady as he studied her face. He was tall, with long, lean legs and cowboy boots. As he smiled, she saw small dimples on both sides of his mouth. Rebecca placed her empty plate under her chair, stood up, and offered her hand. "Yes, you may have this dance. My name's Rebecca Wagner." The manners she learned from Lilly and Maggie gave her confidence. “It’s a pleasure to meet you, Mr. Siebert.”

“Actually, I think we already met. At the barn raising. We nearly collided in front of the farmhouse.”

“Oh, yes. I remember. How nice it was of you to help us.”

He led her to the dance floor and stood before her. She felt his hand on her back. Not sure what to do next, she laughed. “I haven’t had very much practice dancing, but I’ll try to follow your footsteps.”

“Me neither.”

When he moved, Rebecca moved with him, keeping her steps light. She looked down, placing her feet next to his, swaying slightly as he stepped back and forth and side to side. The scent of his body reached her nose—soap and leather, and she liked it.

“Where are you from, Mr. Siebert?

“Please call me Ben. I grew up in Port Royal but moved to Mifflinburg several years ago. My folks own the carriage factory. We make anything that can be pulled by a horse.” He smiled broadly, showing his straight, white teeth.

Rebecca lifted her head slightly so she could look at his face. She felt excitement clear down to her toes. Maybe it was the dress making her feel new and pretty, or maybe it was the way he looked at her with a smile that crinkled the corners of his eyes.

“I’ve lived on that farm all my life—just finished my last year in school. Most of the time I’m helping on the farm or taking care of my grandfather.”

“Do you know the Eastmans who live in the big stone house on West Main road? We built a square-top surrey for them.”

“I’ve actually ridden in that surrey. It’s very handsome.”

His eyes grew large, his eyebrows lifting on his forehead. “Well, isn’t that something? Then you must have seen the yellow fringe around the top. My mother makes them by hand. We like having her and my sisters work in the shop with us—especially when they bring us cakes or pies to eat at lunchtime.”

Neither Ben nor Rebecca had noticed the music had stopped playing. They stood there talking until Gary walked up to them. "So, who's this dancing with my sister?"

"This is Ben…" She searched for his last name but in her excitement couldn't remember it.

Reaching out his hand, Ben said, "Siebert."

Her brother did the same. "Oh, yeah. You came to the barn raising. I remember seeing you there but we didn't actually meet. You from around here?"

"Yes. I live about eight miles from here in Mifflinburg."

Gary nodded and began to grill him. Where did he work? What did he do?

Rebecca stood fascinated by what she saw, her eyes switching from one man to the other. She was surprised her usually shy brother actually initiated a conversation. But Ben fascinated her. She wished he would ask her to dance with him again.

The answer to her wish came as soon as the band started playing. Ben turned his attention away from Gary and faced Rebecca with a slight bow. "May I please have another dance, Rebecca?" She marveled at his lightheartedness. Most men she knew seldom smiled.

Her heart beat loudly in her chest. "Of course. I'd be happy to dance with you again."

The second dance was easier. More fun. She and Ben found their rhythm. But when the dance was over, Ben said, "Will you please excuse me? I'll be right back."

Disappointed he left, she returned to her chair and tried to relax against the hard back. Her face was flushed and her heart was racing. Maybe it was because she had danced… or maybe because of the handsome man she had just met. She closed her eyes and waited.

When she opened them, Gunther stood in front of her. He nodded and said in his most polite voice, "Well…hello again, Rebecca. You sure look… nice. I… I might have come off as a little… rude… earlier. I… well…'pologize.

And I'm sorry I… scared you and your friends up there at the cave. Don't mean nothin'. I… guess I was just showin' off in front of pretty girls. Hope you don't have no hard feelings."

Rebecca's heart pounded in her chest, this time because of fear. "I appreciate your apology, Gunther."

"Does that mean I may have the next dance?"

Rebecca's breath caught in her throat. "My friend will be coming back soon."

"The dance'll be over by then."

Rebecca didn't want to dance with Gunther but found herself unable to say no, imagining him losing his temper if she refused. She reluctantly stood up. He took her arm and led her toward an empty corner of the dance floor. The music was lively. She had to be careful to keep her feet away from his boots. As the dance continued, he spun her around roughly. He was perspiring and breathing heavily, his breath smelling like onions and tobacco. On the last turn while she had her back to the wall, he put his hand on her buttock and squeezed. Her first reaction was shock. Then anger. She lifted her fist and punched his face with all her strength.

Gunther stood motionless in front of her. Blood gushed from his nose, down his chin and dripped onto his shirt.

"You bitch!"

The music stopped suddenly and the hall became silent. Rebecca watched in terror as he glared at her. But a second later, she felt a brief moment of compassion and took a step closer to him. She may have broken his nose. At least it looked that way.

Gunther licked the blood off his lips and raised his fists. Rebecca backed away, her stomach suddenly churning with nausea. Then he dropped his hands and wiped his face on his sleeve. But as soon as he finished, the blood reappeared.

People stood in clusters; the murmur of whispering grew louder. Then they opened a path as Ben pushed his way through to where Rebecca and

Gunther were standing. He gently took Rebecca by the arm. "What's going on here? Rebecca, are you all right?"

She stared at him, blinking rapidly, not able to speak.

Gunther pointed his finger. "Damn woman, broke my nose. And for no reason. She's crazy… that's what's going on." Looking around, he said to the wide-eyed folks near him, "You were here. You saw what happened. We were just dancing and she hauled off and hit me."

Rebecca's hand was throbbing but she refused to give in to the pain. "That's a lie! He groped me."

"No, I didn't. You made that up because you didn't want to dance with me. You're the one who's lying, you stuck up brat."

Rebecca felt like she was kicked in the ribs. Maligned and embarrassed. She wrapped her arms around her midsection and turned to Ben with a look of terror on her face.

Ben moved close to Gunther, peering into his bloody face. "You need to leave. Now."

A woman standing near him gave Gunther a handkerchief to wipe his nose but the cloth soon turned bright red. He stormed out of the building. Dodging a group of men gathered under a cluster of trees, he spotted Gary and pushed his way toward him.

"Your sister did this to me. Don't think I'm going to forget it, either."

"Oh yeah? If you ever hurt her, you'd better watch out. I'll be looking for you."

Gunther mumbled something about traps and stomped to the fence where his horse was tied. But before he swung into the saddle, he retched, then vomited.

The man standing next to Gary said, "Serves him right. That man's a liar. No telling who gave him that bloody nose. Good chance he deserved it. Let's go inside and see what fella finally let him have it."

Gary led the way as the men filed inside the Grange hall but stopped when he spotted a crowd of people at the far end of the room. He elbowed his way inside. When he saw his sister sitting on a chair with Ben holding her hand, he knelt in front of her.

"Rebecca, are you hurt?"

She shook her head no.

"Are you the one who gave Gunther a bloody nose?"

"I punched him in the face because he squeezed my… my hiney." Rebecca took her hand out of Ben's and showed it to her brother.

Gary stood up and pounded his fist into his other hand. "That does it. Next time I see him, I'll break his arm."

The embarrassment and shame she felt matched the pain in her hand. People she knew gave her nods and patted her shoulders. But others whispered and pointed fingers.

Rebecca wanted to disappear.

Ben said, "Did he hurt you anywhere else?"

She felt tears gather in her eyes. "No, just my pride." Rebecca looked at Ben, then her brother. "We were dancing and Gunther grabbed my hiney while my back was to the wall."

"Gary, who is that guy?" Ben asked.

"Works at the Mill. Acts like some big shot because Eastman helped him after his Pop died." Gary sat on the other side of his sister and ran his fingers over her swollen knuckles. "You really clobbered him."

She still couldn't believe she actually hit Gunther. She knew he'd want revenge for shaming him in front of everyone. Just when she was having a good time with Ben. Rebecca wondered what he thought of her now.

"It's been nice meeting you, Ben. Thank you for teaching me how to dance. I need to go home. My hand hurts."

"You're welcome. I'm sorry you had to go through this terrible humiliation tonight. And I hope your hand recovers by tomorrow, but don't be surprised if it takes a few days."

Rebecca was moved by his kindness. How can he be so thoughtful after she made a spectacle of herself? "Thank you for your concern."

"Of course." Ben glanced at Gary before he spoke, but then turned his attention to Rebecca. "May I come calling on you sometime soon? How about next Saturday evening? We could take a ride in my surrey. Gary, would you mind?"

"It's fine with me, but my sister doesn't need my permission. She has a mind of her own."

Rebecca's heart was pounding and she felt her cheeks flush. She couldn't believe Ben wanted to see her after what happened. Maybe her white dress had something to do with it. She swallowed hard. "Yes. I'd like that very much."

CHAPTER 33

BEN CAME TO THE FARM TO SEE REBECCA THE FOLLOWING Saturday evening, and whenever his work would allow and she was able to break away from her chores. Sometimes he came in a surrey or buckboard, but always with a handful of wildflowers or a candy bar. Because of their obligations, most of the time they could only get away to take walks or go on a nearby picnic. But once in a while, they went to Grange dances or hayrides together. They didn't see Gunther, but were careful to make sure he wasn't nearby.

It soon became clear to Rebecca that she was becoming fond of this young man—and she wasn't sure where her heart was leading her. She felt pulled. Part of her wanted to be with him and yet she knew if they became serious about each other, her wish to be independent and find her own way would suffer.

To make matters worse, her mother and father encouraged Ben to come to the farm whenever he could. Jane always asked Ben to stay for lunch or supper. After a while, Rebecca teased him about whether he came to see her or eat her mother's cooking. She often sent him home with a pie or a jar of applesauce.

Pleased Rebecca was seeing a man who worked with his father in their carriage business, Elwood admitted to her that it would probably never happen with his own son.

But Gary was guarded when it came to his sister and Ben. He sometimes showed up mysteriously when they were out together, making up some excuse. Their relationship soon became a source of tension between them.

"Why don't you mind your own business, Gary," Rebecca said, when Gary followed them inside Zarker's store.

"I'm not minding your business."

"Then why do you happen to be here at Zarker's store at the same time we're here?"

"Talk to her. She's being ridiculous," Gary said, looking at Ben.

Ben smiled and took Rebecca's arm, but his eyes scanned the back of the store where he heard laughter. "He's just being protective. Rebecca, take your brother outside and show him the new bridle on my horse. He's been looking enviously at it for weeks now. Maybe I'll make one for him. I'll be right along. I just want to make sure Gunther's not here."

The laughter got louder. Ben walked behind shelving where hand tools were displayed and stopped to listen.

A man with a raspy voice said, "Did you 'ins hear about that young Wagner woman slugging a man at the Grange?"

Another answered, "Yeah, it was that Gunther fella who got punched in the nose. He works for that rich lumberman… Eastman, I think is his name. Heard the young fella's a bastard, but Eastman took him in."

"You don't say? So who's the father?" Their voices softened. Ben leaned closer, peeking around the corner but could only see one gossiper, his suspenders bulging over a round potbelly.

"Rumor has it he's some farmer from around here, but nobody seems to know who."

"Well, I'll be darned. Thought that loudmouth Gunther came here recently from Williamsport. Right around the time those big houses were built at the edge of town."

Ben turned, retrieved his boots from the counter, and quietly left the store only to be confronted by Rebecca's brother. "You'd better be getting back to the farm. Bad storm's coming. Look at the sky. I'll see you later."

After stashing the boots underneath the seat, Ben climbed in his surrey next to Rebecca. Soon the wind blew dime-sized raindrops against their skin. His horse whinnied, shaking his head. "Come on, Rebecca, your brother's right. Looks pretty dark for the middle of the day."

Scanning the black clouds, Rebecca grew concerned they wouldn't be able to make it to the farm. The wind blew gusts against the surrey, shaking it to and fro. "Ben, I've never seen a storm like this. Please hurry."

Although he seldom took a switch to the horse, he clicked and hit the horse's back. The surrey lurched forward, yellow water-soaked fringes swaying and dripping. Another strong wind blew leaves and branches onto the road and rain seeped in the sides of the surrey. Ben got out and released the rolls of canvas on both sides and tied their strings to metal hooks. At least they were somewhat protected from the sting of raindrops blowing against their skin.

Rebecca pulled her shawl over her head. Raindrops sounded like hammers as they plummeted the surrey. She smelled the rain-drenched air, thick and heavy. Her pulse quickened, beating with each raindrop that pounded the surrey on every side. Frightened and worried, she screamed at Ben, "I'm scared. Should we go back into the store?"

Before Ben answered, loud cracks of thunder deafened her ears. Seconds later, lightning struck a tree ahead of them. The tall chestnut crashed onto the road, spreading branches in every direction and vibrating the ground beneath them. The horse bucked and rose onto his hind legs. When the stallion twisted to get away, it broke loose and the surrey overturned, trapping them underneath.

"Ben! Ben...

"Rebecca, are you all right? Can you crawl out?"

"I... I don't think I can... my dress is caught on the metal hooks."

"Try tearing it off."

"No, I can't. My arms can't reach down that far... not enough room. And I can't shimmy from side to side."

"I'm trapped too... can't get my legs from under the seat. Can't even move them." I hope... someone has to pull the surrey upright."

Torrents of rain pounded the earth, blowing in waves and filling the underside of the surrey where it poured off the sides. Sheets of rain blew in from one direction, then another. Muddy water ran beneath their trapped bodies, soaking their clothes. Thunder and lightning bolts shook the ground.

Rebecca shivered and tried to hold her head out of the puddle forming beneath her. "Ben, what if nobody finds us?"

"I'll keep trying to free my legs and come help you. Don't give up."

They laid trapped under the surrey as the storm raged around them. Flashes of lightning lit up the dirt road as far as they could see. Thunder followed, cracking through rain that continued to pelt the overturned carriage.

"Ben. Can you hear me?"

There was no answer… just the rumbling of thunder and the roar of rain. Rebecca laid on her back in the cold, muddy water and tried again to free her skirt from the hooks that held her captive. She stretched her arm until her shoulder felt like it was separating from her body. Then she tried to move her hips where her skirt was caught, and feel for the hooks with her fingertips. But all she felt was mud. It was no use. There still wasn't enough room.

She laid her arm back down in the cold water. Her neck was sore from holding her head out of the puddle that continued to deepen. Water crept up to her ears and filled them, making it hard to hear. She thought about drowning… wondering what it would feel like.

Then she thought she heard a muffled voice from under the surrey. Legs. Something about Ben's legs. Please God, help us.

Rebecca shivered so hard her whole body shook. She couldn't hold her head up any longer. She screamed, her voice sounding like it was under water. Help! Help! Somebody. Anybody. Help!

CHAPTER 34

"REBECCA, ARE YOU IN THERE?"

The voice sounded far in the distance. Rebecca turned her head to listen. Water seeped into her ear. She tried to answer but her throat felt raspy from screaming.

Shouting over the thunderous rain, Gary leaned under the surrey. "It's me, Gary. Don't try to move. Where's Ben?"

"He... he's under the surrey somewhere. I think his legs may be hurt."

Gary ran to the other side. "Ben, can you hear me?"

A bolt of lightning hit nearby, the sound reverberating against the ground. Gary laid flat in the mud. He pulled his hat lower on his head and tried to look in the narrow opening between the surrey and the road. "Ben, it's Gary. I'll get you out."

He waited for a reply. But when there was none, he shimmied under the carriage. Ben was laying on his stomach, legs wedged beneath the undercarriage.

"Ben. Can you move at all?"

Ben lifted his head as far as he could. "Gary... can't feel legs... can't pull them out."

"I'm going to rope the surrey to my horse and pull the damn thing up." Gary tightened his jacket around his neck. Mud stuck to his boots making the road slippery and his steps slow. The rain blowing in his eyes made it difficult to see where to attach the rope. His hands slipped when he tried to tie a knot. After a second try, he kneeled beside the upside-down surrey and shouted, "Rebecca, can you hear me?" The rain slowed but still fell steadily. He listened for a moment.

"Gary… please… hurry. I'm… so cold… and the puddle under me… getting deeper."

"Hang on." Gary tied the other end of the rope to the horn on the horse's saddle. Then he put his hands on either side of the bridle, coaxing the mare to take a few steps back. "Back girl. More. Back up."

The tethered rope strained taunt as an arrow. Slowly the surrey lifted, then fell upright with a crash. The wheels splashed water into Gary's boots. "Damn it." He loosened the rope from the saddle in case the horse bolted.

When the surrey lifted, Rebecca's skirt tore off her body, which was half submerged in brown water. She gasped from the shock of the cold air.

"Hold tight. I'll help you." Gary lifted his sister up and sat her against the side of the surrey. Then he took a rolled blanket from under the tarp on his horse and spread it over her body and placed the tarp on top.

Ben could only see shapes through the sheets of rain and he could only hear voices faintly, but he felt the weight lifted off his legs. "Gary… is that you? Where are you? Is Rebecca all right?"

"Yes. She's okay. Now let's get you out of this mess." Gary rolled Ben over onto his back. Can you stand if I help you?"

"I don't know. My legs are totally numb. I can't feel them at all. I'll try my best but I don't think I can get up."

Gary stood behind him a lifted Ben under the arms.

"Take it easy. I can't feel my legs."

"Hell, Ben, I'm trying the best I can."

Gary dragged him next to Rebecca. She tried to make room for Ben under the blanket but her arms were stiff. "Ben, what happened to your legs?"

"They got caught under the bench... pinned me down until I lost feeling in them. I'm... He tried to continue but the words stuck in his throat. "I'm so sorry I couldn't help you."

Before Rebecca could answer, Gary yelled to them. "Stay here while I get help."

"No, it's too dangerous out there. Come in here with us," Ben shouted.

Gary shimmied beside his sister. The three of them sat under the blanket and tarp while the storm continued its fury. A blast of wind pounded against nearby trees, gusts matching the thunder echoing across the nearby mountain ridges. Small trees uprooted by the storm blew past them, tumbling until they caught on fence posts or against buildings. The cool wind made them huddle together to keep warm. Ben put his arm around Rebecca, trying to calm her shivering. No one said anything for a long time. Finally, the wind wore itself out and the rain turned to a gentle shower. Gary threw off his side of the mostly wet, heavy blanket and looked around. The roof of Zarker's store hung on the edge of the rafters. Pieces of wrought iron fence had been scattered against the building next to it. Mud and debris covered buildings, their windows blown out.

Rebecca lifted her face. Her brother stood before her and Ben. His favorite hat was missing. His long hair was matted in wet swirls around his head and his clothes were barely visible under the mud. But his smile shone brightly in his dirty face. "Don't want me following you, huh?"

CHAPTER 35

When Doc Headings finished examining Ben, he said, "Looks like the nerves in your legs were affected by the weight of the seat. Probably compressed them against the muscles and femurs. I think they'll recover, but I can't be sure. Only time and rest will tell. Good the rain stopped so we were able to get you into my office and into some dry clothing."

Rebecca excused herself and went to the linen closet to grab a sheet. She wrapped it around her torso and raced to the examination room where Dr. Headings was testing Ben's legs. He took a small hammer with a soft end and tapped it on Ben's kneecaps. "Can you feel this?" Ben's leg did not jerk forward.

"No."

"How about this?"

"I'm sorry. No."

"Just what I suspected. I think it's the nerves. I hope they'll respond when the swelling in your legs goes down. But I can't be sure."

"Shall we take him to the farm? It's far too long to take him home to Mifflinburg." Rebecca also knew her parents would make room for him, probably put a day bed in the parlor.

Ben pleaded with his eyes. "No. I'm not going to impose. Dr. Headings, may I stay here until I improve enough to go home?"

"I suppose so… I'll have to make one of my exam rooms ready first. Rebecca, please come help me."

He led her through the hallway into a small cramped room with shelves filled with medical supplies. A kerosene lamp with metal goose-neck reflector stood in the corner next to the examination table. Dr. Heading pulled sheets and a thick blanket out of a cabinet and asked Rebecca to make a bed of sorts, knowing the hard table would make a poor sleeping surface—but it would have to do.

When they were finished, the doctor asked Rebecca to sit down. "You must be prepared in case his legs are permanently damaged. There's no telling what will happen when nerves are involved. Thankfully, I'm reasonably certain there's no broken bones to complicate matters. We could make the trip to Harrisburg Hospital but that would mean at least eight hours of a bumpy wagon ride."

Rebecca willed herself to stop shaking. She was still cold to the core despite the warm sheet, made worse by her fear that Ben would never regain use of his legs. But she put on a brave front—as much for herself as it was to convince Dr. Headings she was all right.

Finally, she felt calm enough to talk. "Do you think Ben will be able to walk again?"

"I'm not sure. If the nerves are just inflamed from the trauma, they will eventually heal. But if the damage is severe, he may not. Tomorrow I'll send word to his parents about the accident."

Pausing to let his words sink in, Rebecca pulled the sheet tighter around her body and held the ends tightly. Suppose he's not able to walk again. How will he work? What will become of us? She didn't want to give away her thoughts just yet, so she nodded and pretended to be in control of her emotions. But inside, she was beside herself with worry. Ben would never have gotten injured if he hadn't gone with her to Zarker's store.

For the next few days and nights, Dr. Headings moved Ben's legs several times a day, bending them at the knees and rotating his ankles. "Do you feel me touching you?"

Ben said, "Not really. Maybe just a slight pressure sensation."

"Well, that's a good sign. Do you mind if Rebecca helps me—if she is willing—and if you two of you can overlook any embarrassment? I still have patients to see and house calls to make."

Not wanting to be too eager to respond, he said, "I assume you'll show her how to do what's necessary."

"Of course. I observed her taking care of her grandfather and she is more than capable."

Rebecca was eager to help take care of Ben and pleased that Dr. Headings had confidence in her ability. Trouble was, she had more than enough responsibility at the farm to keep her busy. But, thanks to Mary's newfound energy, Rebecca was able to go into town each day between chores.

And there was the issue of embarrassment. After all, she was a young woman and would be handling the legs of a man whom she had only met three or four months ago. But if Doc Headings thought it was acceptable, so did she. That meant there was no reason to ask permission from her parents under the circumstances, even though it may have seemed to others, a reason to disapprove. And gossip.

The first time Rebecca worked with Ben to exercise his legs, she did feel a bit awkward. "Well, Ben, here goes. Let's start with knee bends." She was surprised how muscular his legs were. She was used to heavy legs—her grandfather's legs were large and swollen—but muscles were a different story.

"How does that feel? Am I too rough?"

"Are you kidding? Feels good. I also feel where you have your hand in back of my knee. It feels strange… like a slight tingling."

"I'll tell the doctor when he comes back. I think that's a good sign." Her heart seemed to beat faster than usual. She wasn't sure it was from exertion or excitement.

That's the way it went for the rest of the week. More exercises. More feeling in Ben's legs and feet. They fell into a rhythm. Bend knees. Straighten legs. Rotate ankles and bend feet and toes. With each passing day, the sensation in Ben's legs improved, but weakness persisted.

Dr. Headings suggested massaging the muscles might improve circulation and help strengthen them. Ben was able to do some of this himself, but Rebecca was asked to knead the muscles in his calves where they were difficult for him to reach. Bending and moving Ben's legs was one thing, but massaging his legs was another. Stroking his legs. Feeling the hair on his skin. She felt self-conscious and rattled.

The next day, she tried a trick Back So Straight had taught her. She asked a farmer who kept honeybees to give her a piece of honeycomb that had been drained of honey. Then she added warm water to wash it, followed by melting the wax in the honeycomb over a double boiler. Once strained through a fine sieve, the raw beeswax was a perfect lubricant to help her hands slide over Ben's skin and prevent it from drying out. But it did nothing to quell the uneasiness she felt stroking his legs.

She was relieved he became stronger after another week of exercises and massage. Relieved because she no longer had to feel his muscular legs every day. But sad at the same time, because Dr. Headings planned on sending him home to continue the exercises there. He was now able to take a few small steps as long as Rebecca held on to his belt. They managed to inject some humor into his therapy, thanks to the newly-found fondness between them. While they spent time together, their friendship deepened and their ease with each other became obvious to both of them. She considered the possibility that she loved this man. However, there was that small nagging question in the back of her mind: what would she have done if Ben didn't recover? Would she stick by him if he were permanently paralyzed from the waist down?

CHAPTER 36

A WEEK AFTER THE STORM, LILLY SAT ON THE WIDE PORCH daydreaming about the time she and Rebecca went to the cave. She could hear the screams and feel the terror all over again. After a few moments, thoughts about the Indian pipes, the cold creek water rushing over her feet, and the smell of the pine trees tempered her memories.

She swatted a fly that landed on her arm and looked out over the yard to the meadow where horses were grazing, their tails sweeping back and forth. She saw chimney swifts dart up and down above the horses as they plucked insects in midair. Thoughts of Rebecca entered her mind. If it weren't for Rebecca, she would never have paid attention or known the name of that split-tailed, cigar-shaped bird that came to Pennsylvania every spring.

Her mother sat down beside her, waving a beautiful fan that blew wisps of hair from her face. "What are you doing, Lilly? You've been sitting here ever since I went upstairs to fetch my long-lost fan."

"I'm just thinking about Rebecca, mother."

"You're very fond of her, aren't you?"

Lilly nodded. "Yes. She's different from my friends in the city."

"How's that?"

"She knows a lot about animals and trees—and she reads these medical books a doctor loans to her. When we're together, she teaches me things . . .

fascinating things I never knew about. Maybe I'll walk over to the farm and see her. Would that be all right?"

"Yes, go ahead. It's quite a walk, though. Just be careful. Say hello to her and her family."

Lilly followed the dirt road along the fields until it wound into the foothills, where it became narrower and covered with a canopy of towering trees. As she meandered along the still wet footpath, watching and listening, a large black and white bird with a red crescent on its head caught her eye as it flew through the trees. She was almost sure it was a pileated woodpecker—Rebecca told her that because of its size and coloring, it was easy to spot.

A dark bog appeared on her left, filled by the recent downpour. On their walks in the woods, Rebecca had shown her and Maggie salamanders, frogs, tadpoles, turtles, and newts that lived in these shallow, basin-shaped pools scattered throughout the forest. Had Rebecca not taught her about the wildlife that lived in the bogs and ponds, Lilly would have been frightened by the frogs that squeaked a warning noise and jumped into the water as she passed by.

The path became dim as she walked under the trees. The coolness of the air felt crisp against her face. She touched the huge sloping branches of hemlock trees that were so heavy they looked like giant green arms embracing the forest floor.

As she inhaled deeply, the smell of evergreens and damp earth filled her nose. Lilly's home in Philadelphia smelled different, and there were streets everywhere. Some trees grew in the city, but there weren't any mountains. Most of the forests had been stripped to make room for houses and factories. The nearby Schuylkill River turned brown from the runoff of the factories, so she wasn't allowed to go near it anymore. But here in Juniata County, the water was clear and most of the forests remained standing.

Lost in the wonders of the forest, Lilly didn't hear the man walking behind her until he darted in front of her. He looked familiar but she didn't recognize him until he spoke. Her heart pounded in her chest and her legs started to shake. "Let me pass."

"Don't tell me you're by yourself?"

"You're the man who wouldn't let us get out of the cave. Rebecca's brother warned you not to bother us again."

"Looks like Rebecca and her brother aren't here to protect you, are they?"

"Leave me alone. I know who you are—you work for Mr. Eastman. I'll tell my father if you hurt me. He's a lawyer."

"Is that so? I think I'll teach you a lesson about being a tattletale."

Lilly screamed and ran, dodging rocks and jumping over underbrush. But her dress and petticoats made it impossible to outrun the man behind her. Tree branches scratched her arms as she stumbled over a fallen tree and lost one of her shoes. Gunther tackled her and threw himself on top of her. Her stomach hit a rock and forced the air out of her lungs.

"I can't breathe. Let me go! You're hurting me."

"You're just like Rebecca and most other women—think you're too good for me." Gunther rolled Lilly onto her back and lifted up her dress. She tried to wiggle free, but he sat on top of her and grabbed one of her arms, then the other, and held them above her head. When she started to scream again, he released one of them but put his hand over her mouth. He quickly opened his belt and unzipped his pants. Lilly realized what he was about to do and closed her eyes. Her body froze with terror. The birds stopped singing. She heard the soft whisper of the wind blowing through the trees and felt a breeze against her naked legs… followed by an eerie silence. The forest became a soundless witness to what was about to happen.

Gunther tore her chemise and slid his knee between her legs. She heard him huff and strain in his efforts to hold his hand over her mouth and pull down his trousers. Finally, he released her other arm. "If you scream, I'll kill you." He looked down at her slim body and pale skin. "You have this coming."

He thrust into her small body, mercilessly pounding his flesh into hers. Lilly felt searing pain as he tore her open and continued to grunt on top of her. When he finished, he wiped the blood on his manhood with her dress. Then he whispered in her ear. "If you tell anyone… I'll kill Rebecca."

The dense forest stole the sound of Lilly's sobbing. Tears traced brown streaks on her dirty face. She shivered and pulled her dress over her legs. She tried to move but the pain between her legs felt like a knife was cutting her inside. After a few moments, she tried again. Lilly slowly rolled on her side. The blood on her legs and dress made her gag, then retch. Gathering all her strength and courage, she got on her hands and knees, and remained there for a few minutes. After taking a deep breath, she rose to her feet. Blood oozed down her legs and into her remaining shoe. Sobbing and shivering again, she lost her balance and fell against a tree.

The pain startled her, but she tried again. This time, Lilly was able to complete a few steps until she had to rest. The walk back home came in starts and stops, until she saw the dirt road leading to her house.

Lilly staggered forward but stopped when she saw Lucy hanging up laundry.

She waited until the maid went into the washhouse. Blood was still seeping down her legs. She wiped it away with her dress, and walked-ran as best as she could to the door that led onto the vestibule. Taking off her remaining shoe and tucking it under her armpit, Lilly struggled to open the heavy door. She listened intensely. When hearing no one, she slipped inside, looking both ways.

The stairway looked so far away. She could barely lift herself up each step. The pain in her groin made her dizzy. At the top of the stairs, her mother Sarah called out from her bedroom. "Is that you Lilly?"

Blood rushed to her head and she felt her heart pulse at her temples. Terrified she would be seen, Lilly tried to think how she could answer without creating suspicion.

"Lilly, did you hear me? Are you there?"

"Y… Yes, mother. I'm home. I… I just needed to go to the bathroom… my monthly started." She quickly closed the door behind her and stood clutching the handle. Thank God for the indoor toilet. Lilly washed her hands, then her face and arms. Taking off her bloody dress and chemise, she gently washed her legs and feet. When she tried to wash between her legs, the pain was more than she could bear. Lilly stifled a moan and tried not to cry.

She reached into the wooden box tucked in the back of the toilet and took out cotton pads that had been sewn together to use when she had her monthly. She gently placed them between her legs, hoping her mother would think she was having her monthly bleed when Lucy washed and hung the cloths to dry. Every time she touched her womanly parts, pain coursed through her pelvis.

After dressing in a clean nightgown, she stuffed her bloody clothes and shoe in a pillow case from the linen closet. Lilly looked in the mirror and gasped when she saw leaves and twigs in her hair. She brushed vigorously to remove them, sweeping them into the pillowcase.

Glancing up at the mirror again, she opened her eyes and surveyed her face. Her eyes were puffy—red orbs set in her pale face. She began to cry again. She felt humiliated and weak, and afraid that someone would find out and blame her. Looking down in shame, she saw her arms were scratched and one of her fingernails was broken deep into the flesh. Tears pooled in her eyes but she blinked them back before opening the door wide enough to sneak into her bedroom. Lilly closed the door and hid the pillowcase under bed. She slid under the covers, pulling them up to her chin and tucking her hands underneath.

Lilly strained to listen for footsteps, but instead heard a knock on the door. "Lilly, dear, may I come in?"

The young woman wasn't sure she could hide from her mother any longer, so she spoke as bravely as she could. "Yes, come in."

"Are you not feeling well?"

"I… I just got… my… monthly this afternoon and I have cramps. I think I'll feel better if… I rest."

CHAPTER 37

"LUCY, GO UPSTAIRS AND TELL LILLY IT'S DINNER TIME." Minutes later, the maid came into the dining room. "Miss Lilly sleeping."

Sarah frowned and turned to her husband. Before she could speak, he said, "Let her sleep. You told me she walked to Rebecca's farm today and went straight to bed when she came home. Maybe she's tired. She's not used to walking that far."

"I guess you're right, Peter. If she wakes up later, Lucy can reheat dinner."

That evening when Lilly didn't come downstairs, her mother went to check on her. Sarah crept into the darkened bedroom to Lilly's bed. Laying her hand on her daughter's forehead, she whispered, "Are you all right, Lilly?"

"Yes… I am, but I still have cramps."

"Aren't you hungry?"

Lilly swallowed the lump in her throat. "Th… thanks, but no."

"This is not like you. Shall I send for Dr. Headings?"

"No! I mean, no. I don't need a doctor just for my monthly."

"All right, my dear. But come for me if you need something. Good night."

The next morning Sarah got up early and went downstairs to tell Lucy to bake scones for breakfast, Lilly's favorite. Her husband sat down at his usual chair and pulled out the newspaper. Without putting the paper down, he asked, "Where's Lilly today?"

Sarah answered, "I'm giving her a few more minutes. If she doesn't come down after she smells the scones baking, I'll go up and wake her."

Lilly's brothers Charles and Carlton joined the breakfast table and saw the empty chair. Carlton asked in his squeaky voice, "Isn't Lilly eating breakfast today? That's fine with me. I get to eat her scones."

"No, you don't." Charles, ever the gentleman, argued with his brother. "They're not for you, greedy. They're for our sister."

"Excuse me," Sarah interrupted, her loud voice showing her annoyance that her husband kept his face buried in the newspaper. "I'm going upstairs to check on our daughter."

She knocked on the door. When here was no answer she peeked inside and saw Lilly was awake.

"Good morning, my dear. We missed you at breakfast. Are you all right?"

When Lilly didn't answer, Sarah sat on the bed next to her and looked at her daughter's pale face. "What are these scratches from? Did you hurt yourself yesterday?" Lilly turned her back to her mother and stared ahead.

"Lilly, what's the matter? I'm speaking to you. Why won't you answer me?"

When Lilly remained silent, her mother kneeled on the floor beside the bed. "Darling, what is going on? You can tell me, no matter what it is." When Lilly refused to answer, Sarah ran downstairs to look for the footman.

"I see Mr. North has left for the mill. Please go find him and bring him home—immediately."

While her mother was gone, Lilly quickly changed the bloody cloths and put the dirty ones in the pillowcase. She just made it back to bed when her mother came rushing into her room. "Do you hurt somewhere? Are you ill?" She felt Lilly's forehead but the girl quickly lifted her mother's hand from her face. "You don't have a fever as far as I can tell. Let me feel your belly. Does it hurt?" Lilly pulled the quilt over her head and refused to let her mother touch her.

"I'm sending for Doctor Headings as soon as her father gets here," Sarah called down the stairway to Lucy. "Let me know as soon as my husband arrives." In the meantime, she sat on a rocking chair near her daughter's bed. Lilly turned her head away. Nothing Sarah said or did made her daughter respond.

Her father had no more success getting his daughter to talk than her mother. "She won't talk to me either. I'm as perplexed as you are. What could possibly have happened to her? I'm riding into town for the doctor."

After he finished seeing a room full of patients, Dr. Headings arrived later that afternoon. He thoroughly questioned Mr. and Mrs. North about Lilly's behavior. Then he said, "I'd like to speak to Lilly alone, please."

"Of course. Let me take you upstairs. We're terribly worried," Sarah said.

Doc Headings gently knocked on Lilly's door. When there was no answer, he walked in and pulled a chair close to her bed. "Lilly, I'm Dr. Headings—the doctor who loans medical books to your friend Rebecca. Your mother and father told me you are close to her."

He waited a moment before continuing. "I'm here to help you, but you must tell me what's troubling you."

Lilly turned away from him, bed covers pulled tightly around her neck.

"Are you hurt?"

There was no response.

"At least let me take your temperature and check your blood pressure."

Lilly grabbed her pillow and held it in front of her body.

"I won't touch you if you don't want me to." Using a near whisper voice, he leaned toward her. "Lilly, if you don't talk to us, we can't help you. Your mother said you walked to the Wagner farm yesterday and have been upset ever since. Did something happen?"

The young woman sobbed into the pillow but did not answer.

Dr. Headings quietly stepped outside, leaving the door ajar. Although he spoke in hushed tones, Lilly overheard every word he said to her mother and father. "She won't let me examine her and she won't answer any of my questions. Tell me once again when she first started acting this way."

Explaining a second time, Sarah said, "Lilly had just come home from visiting Rebecca Wagner. When I heard her come upstairs, I asked her if she was all right. She told me she was, but had her monthly and cramps. She went right to bed… didn't eat dinner or come downstairs for breakfast this morning. She wouldn't speak to me or her father, and refuses to be touched."

Dr. Headings thought for a moment. "Lilly is in shock. Something or someone has greatly upset or frightened her. I've seen such a reaction before when people witness a gruesome accident or are terrified about an impending danger. This happens more than I'd like to admit—especially in the lumber camps."

Reaching for his wife's hand, Peter said, "But if she won't tell us, we can't make her."

"I suggest that you wait a day or two and see what happens. Give her time. Meanwhile, be patient with her and don't force her to speak. Offer her food but don't insist that she eat. Just make sure she has water. I'll check in with her day after tomorrow. Until then, it may be helpful to ask Rebecca what may have happened."

"That's a good idea," said Sarah. "Peter, please ride over to the Wagner farm and talk to Rebecca. I know she'll tell us if there was trouble when they were together yesterday. Surely Rebecca wouldn't let anyone frighten Lilly."

"Rebecca, Mr. North is here to speak to you. I asked him to come in but he wanted to wait on the porch," Jane said from the kitchen.

"Tell him I'll be right there." She had been helping her grandmother bathe her grandfather. Rebecca hurried to wash her hands, curious about why Lilly's father wanted to speak to her. "Hello, Mr. North. Is Lilly with you?"

"No. As a matter of fact, that's why I'm here. Lilly isn't well. Ever since yesterday when she came to visit you, she won't come out of her room or speak to us."

Rebecca's inhaled a quick breath. "I'm sorry, but Lilly never came to the farm yesterday. I was here all day."

"Strange. That's what she told us. Something must have upset her. I never saw Lilly act like this."

"What can I do to help, Mr. North? Do you want me to talk to her?"

"Yes, can you come with me now?"

Rebecca turned to her mother, who had joined her daughter on the porch. "Ma, Lilly isn't well. Mr. North asked me to come with him to see her."

"I'm sorry about Lilly. You must be very concerned. Of course Rebecca can come," said Jane.

Hugh North pushed the horse into a full trot while the surrey bounced over the stones and ruts in the dirt road. Rebecca tried to ask questions but the sound of the rushing carriage made it difficult to hear, so she prayed instead.

When they arrived, Sarah was waiting. "Rebecca. I'm glad you're here. Please go upstairs to Lilly's room. I told her you were coming."

Rebecca opened the door a crack. "Lilly, may I come in?" There was no answer. She blinked her eyes. It was dark in the room except for small slits of light that filtered in the sides of dark green window shades. When she neared Lilly's bed, the outline of her friend's body was nearly invisible… as though Lilly had melted into the mattress. She was curled up around her blankets like a butterfly in a cocoon. The sight of her friend caught Rebecca's breath. She held it for a second or two and slowly released it in a deep sigh. Lilly. Dear Lilly. What could possibly have made her so unresponsive?

"May I sit next to you on the bed?" Rebecca waited for an answer. The quietness in the room crept into every corner.

The young woman moved slightly away from the edge.

"May I lay next to you?"

Lilly moved ever so slightly again.

Sliding onto the bed, Rebecca whispered in Lilly's ear. "I don't know what happened to you yesterday when you were supposed to come to visit me. Can you tell me?"

Instead of answering, Lilly broke out in violent sobs that shook the bed. Rebecca couldn't resist touching her friend on the shoulder. The girl flinched but didn't move away. "Lilly, please talk to me. I promise I won't tell anyone if you don't want me to."

The bed trembled as her friend took violent breaths between sobs. When Lilly raised her head and reached under her pillow for a handkerchief, Rebecca caught a faint glimpse of her face and started to cry. It was the same look her grandmother had after she was almost shot by her husband. She reached for Lilly, who froze but did not push her away. Rebecca slowly put her arms around her friend and felt Lilly melt in her arms. She held her close while they cried together.

They lay like that until Rebecca composed herself. She turned to Lilly and took her face in her hands. "I love you. No matter what happened, I will always be your friend."

Lilly's mouth opened in a silent sob.

CHAPTER 38

REBECCA WENT TO VISIT LILLY EVERY TIME SHE COULD BREAK away from taking care of her grandfather and working on the farm. She talked to her friend as though she was a little child—stories about the farm animals, her walks in the mountains, her time with Back So Straight. Once in a while, she read her pages from the medical books Dr. Headings brought to the farm when he came to see the elder Wagners. Sometimes Lilly would nod but her eyes stared ahead.

When Rebecca came at mealtime, Sarah insisted she eat with Lilly, who remained mostly in bed except for a few times a day when she sat in a cushioned chair by the window. Lilly pushed the food around on her plate, taking a few bites but leaving most untouched. Several times, Rebecca brought her food from the farm—chicken potpie with saffron broth, and apple dumplings fresh from the oven. Lilly feigned interest, eating only enough to be polite.

There was little time for Rebecca to see Ben or read her medical books now that she was spending her free time with Lilly. She resented having to take care of her grandfather. Sometimes Rebecca would return home only to find her mother and grandmother waiting for her to lift and bathe the old man. She found herself stumbling into bed, numb with worry about Lilly, and exhausted from working daybreak to sunset.

Rebecca's only respite came from her brief visits to Back So Straight. They sat on the log by her cabin and watched the birds flit under the mountain laurel and then fly to the hemlock trees, where they pecked seeds from small pinecones. She found comfort when Wind rested her nose on her lap while she rubbed the dog's neck and behind her ears. But there never seemed to be enough time to get to the heart of things. While they were together, her mentor sat quietly and said very little.

It was as though Rebecca couldn't concentrate on anything else. Lilly was on her mind before she went to bed and when she woke up in the morning. In an attempt to find time to ask Back So Straight for her advice, she got up before dawn and walked by lantern light to the Indian woman's cabin. Before she knocked on the door, she heard Wind growl. "Back So Straight, it's me." When the door opened, Rebecca was surprised to see the Indian woman fully dressed. Wind poked her nose out the door and sniffed Rebecca's hand.

"What is it, my child?"

"I have to get back to help with grandpa, but I need to talk to you about my friend, Lilly. Something terrible happened to her."

Back So Straight nodded and motioned for Rebecca to come inside.

They sat side by side on the bench near the fire. Rebecca smelled sassafras tea heating in a small pan over the fire. After taking a deep breath, she blurted the whole story.

"Lilly was supposed to walk to the farm about a week ago but never came. Now she stays in her room and doesn't talk and hardly eats anything. Her mother and father—and Dr. Headings—tried to get her to tell what happened, and so did I. She just cries and lays curled up in her bed."

Back So Straight sat quietly for what seemed to Rebecca a long time. "What do her eyes reveal?"

After thinking for a moment, Rebecca said, "She won't look at me. Stares ahead."

The Indian woman grew quiet again. "This is a sign of great sorrow. So deep it travels to the heart where it remains. Sometimes sorrow and fear walk together."

"But if she won't tell anyone why she's sad or frightened, we can't help her."

Rebecca sat forward on her elbows and studied the fire.

Back So Straight poured two mugs of tea and added raw honey before giving one to Rebecca and sipping the other.

"Thank you." She drank a few swallows, letting the flavor linger in her mouth. "I remember you told me that I couldn't do anything to help my grandmother when she wouldn't talk much or join the family. But this is different."

"How is that?"

"Grandma had almost been shot—and she's old. I don't know of anyone who would hurt Lilly. Besides, whatever happened, she's young and has her whole life ahead of her."

"It is not up to you to decide about Lilly's life. That is her path."

"You keep talking about one's path, Back So Straight. I don't know exactly what you mean. Can't we help someone else's path?"

"We can't walk it for them, only with them. Instead of seeing the broken parts, see the light within them. Then you must set them free."

Rebecca tried to understand. Sometimes Back So Straight's advice made no sense at all.

CHAPTER 39

THE INDIAN'S WORDS HAUNTED REBECCA. MAYBE SHE shouldn't try to persuade Lilly to speak. Maybe her friend had suffered a terrible scare like grandma. One thing became clearer since her time with Back So Straight: Lilly would speak when she was ready. Not before.

Two weeks before the Norths' return to Philadelphia, Rebecca visited her friend but didn't ask anything of her. Instead, she told her about her talk with Back So Straight, how she advised Rebecca to see the light in her friend… and to let Lilly find her own way in her own time.

Lilly looked at her friend and nodded. Then she took her hand. They sat quietly until Rebecca had to leave. For the first time since the day Lilly's father came to the farm to ask for Rebecca's help, she felt at peace. She leaned down and kissed Lilly's forehead.

"Goodbye, dear Lilly."

On her way out of the house, Rebecca called out to Mr. North who was sitting at his desk in the parlor. "I must go now. I'll be back another time to say goodbye to all of you before you leave for Philadelphia."

"Wait one moment, please." He got up and walked briskly to Rebecca. She suspected he wanted to talk to her about Lilly, but the broad smile on his face spoke of something else.

"I've been talking to Dr. Headings about you. We've watched you take care of your grandfather and Lilly. He told me you also helped a young man recover from an injury. He said there is a school of nurses' training at Johns Hopkins Hospital that is looking for young women of character who are hard-working and good with sick people. We want you to apply if you're interested. However, the school is in Baltimore, Maryland."

Rebecca's forehead wrinkled in surprise. She cocked her head to the side and searched Mr. North's eyes. "Um… Mr. North, I don't know what to say. Of course, I… I'm interested in going to school again. But I'm not sure I can."

"Dr. Heading is willing to recommend you to the new head of the school at Johns Hopkins Hospital."

"I'm afraid my father can't afford this, Mr. North. We're farmers and don't have money to waste on schooling, especially for a girl."

"Be that as it may, I'm willing to pay for your travel and expenses if you agree to go and do your best. However, time is critical. It's already late summer, but if we act soon, we can meet the deadline."

"I have to go home and talk to my parents. I don't know if they can spare me from working on the farm and taking care of my grandfather. And what about Lilly?"

Ignoring the question about Lilly, he answered, "Let me take you home. We can talk more about this with your mother and father."

Mr. North drove his fancy surrey to the Wagner farm, its yellow fringes shaking like birch tree leaves in the fall wind as the wheels traveled over ruts in the dirt roads. He pushed the horse to a fast trot. Rebecca's mind tumbled as fast as the horse's hoofs beat the ground, thinking how things could change in an instant. Something that didn't exist just a few minutes ago. How could this be possible? How far away was Baltimore? What about travel to Baltimore and back? She was lost in her thoughts and didn't realize they reached the farm until she saw the barn ahead.

Elwood was piercing a bale of hay with a hook, signaling Gary to pull the rope on a hoist that lifted the hay to the barn's second story. He looked up as the hay bale reached the opening where Gary grabbed it and pulled it inside.

As soon as the surrey came to a halt, Rebecca ran to the barn where her father stood still peering at his son.

"Pop, Mr. North is here to speak to you and Ma. Can you come in the cabin, please?" Elwood walked over to their guest and shook his hand. "How are you, Peter?"

"I'm doing well, thank you. Sorry to interrupt your work, but I want to talk to you about your daughter."

"Something wrong, Mr. North?"

"Nothing of the sort. I'd like to talk to you and Jane at the same time. Do you mind?"

"Not at all. Rebecca, go tell your Ma we have company."

Once they were all settled in the front room, Hugh carefully explained the reason for his visit. "I'm here to speak to you about the opportunity Rebecca has to attend a training school for nurses. Dr. Headings and I have been observing how she cares for senior Mr. Wagner and Lilly. She works hard and has a good head on her shoulders."

"Where is this nursing school?" Jane responded.

"In Baltimore, Maryland. It's affiliated with a very good hospital—Johns Hopkins."

"That's quite far from here. How would she get there?"

"By train. It will be about a three-hour ride."

Elwood sat front on his chair and looked directly at Mr. North. "Nope. She's needed right here on the farm. If she wants to take care of people, she can work for families around here."

"I'm sure she could. But this is different. She would become a trained nurse capable of caring for patients in a hospital, and earn higher wages than nurses who work in a private home."

"Can't pay for her to go to nurses' school—or travel. Books cost a lot of money, too. Money I don't have."

Peter North glanced at Rebecca and smiled. "That won't be necessary, Mr. Wagner. I am offering to pay her expenses."

"Why? Already had to sell some of my mountain land just to replace my barn and tools. Can't take the chance of owing more debt. Not a chance."

"Mr. Wagner, I'm not asking you to repay me. Your daughter is exceptional. She deserves to go to school, just like my Lilly."

Rebecca's heart beat in her throat and she almost forgot to breathe. Nursing school. Baltimore. Trains. Leaving the farm. Ben.

"What do you think of all this, Rebecca? Is that something you want to do instead of staying here?" asked Jane.

"I… I didn't even know there were nurses' schools. Yes, I think want to go, but I don't know if I'm smart enough." Turning to Mr. North, she asked, "How long does it take to be a trained nurse?"

"Dr. Headings looked into it—he said it was a three-year course."

"Three years?" Jane looked at Rebecca, the frown on her face deepening. "Why don't I get some coffee while you tell us more, Mr. North." Rebecca knew her mother was stalling for time to think.

Elwood spoke up after Jane left the room. "Why would you want to sponsor my daughter to go to nurses' training? Told you… can't pay you back."

"That won't be necessary. My wife and I have grown very fond of your daughter, and according to Dr. Headings, she deserves a chance to do this. He told me that she has been studying his medical books for several years and shows a keen interest in learning more."

"I know she's smart. But… need some time to think about this."

"I can appreciate this is a big decision. Dr. Headings will help Rebecca fill out the papers and send them to the hospital, but time is of utmost importance. The application is due in two weeks."

Rebecca spent the rest of that day and the next in a state of disbelief. Her usual pattern of farm chores and helping take care of her grandfather did nothing to clear her head. She felt like she was dreaming. Leave the farm. Her mother and father… Back So Straight. Live in a city. Her heart told her maybe this was her chance to be like Maggie and Lilly. Someone with more than a high school diploma. Get away from the arguments between her father and brother. But what about Ben? And the mountains? Everything she knew and loved?

But most of all, she needed to talk to her mother… to let her know how much she dreamed of going further in school... to find out what she's made of. And ask for Jane's advice before making a final decision. After all, her mother—and Back So Straight—knew her best.

As if Jane read her mind, the following day, her mother knocked on her door late at night. "May I come in? I saw your light under the door."

"Yes, Ma. I can't sleep either."

"I guess you know what I want to talk to you about. Tell me what you're thinking. Have you made a decision?"

"I feel pulled. Part of me wants to go to nurses' training but I hate leaving you and the farm. I know I'm needed here." Rebecca held perfectly still in anticipation of her mother's response.

"Yes, you are. But that's not a good enough reason. We'll miss you but we'll adjust. I've always sensed that you wanted a different life. One that gave you a chance to help people. Something other than what you have here on the farm."

Rebecca averted her eyes, guilt building until she couldn't hold it in any longer. "I don't want you to think I'm not happy here. You and Pop have given me everything I ever needed and loved me despite my longing to leave."

"If you don't take this opportunity to follow your dreams, you may regret it. So think long and hard before making up your mind. I speak from experience when I say one has to do what they think is right even though it may be difficult." Jane wiped a tear from her eye and took Rebecca's hand. "Go. Apply to this school. Find your own life, Rebecca."

"I'll try."

CHAPTER 40

DR. HEADINGS CAME TO THE FARM SEVERAL DAYS AFTER MR. North spoke to Rebecca and her parents. The sun was low in the late summer sky; not even a slight breeze stirred in the heavy air. The silhouette of the mountains in back of the Wagner barn appeared as dark green knuckles against the sky overhead. He pulled up to the cabin in his old buckboard and wiped his face with a white handkerchief.

Elwood slammed his ax through a piece of firewood, sending the pieces flying to the ground. He laid down his tool and said, "Nice to see you, Doc."

"Hello there. Pretty sticky this evening, isn't it?" Without waiting for an answer, he got right to the reason for his visit. "I'm here to speak to Rebecca."

"Imagine it's about that nurses' school thing."

Dr. Headings nodded. "Yes. Once I talk to her, I'll want to meet with you and Jane, too."

"Go on in. She's in the kitchen."

Rebecca stood by the dry sink washing dishes when the doctor walked up the steps to the porch.

"May I come in?"

"Please." She pulled out a chair at the kitchen table. She hoped the anxiety she felt didn't show on her face.

He sat down and pulled papers out of his black bag. "Rebecca, I have your application here for you to sign if you want to pursue the offer Peter North and I made. Have you and your mother and father reached a decision?"

Rebecca swallowed hard. "Dr. Headings, I'll be honest with you. I'm flattered you have confidence in me. I want to go but I'm afraid I'm still not sure I can leave the farm and move to a big city."

"Let me get right to the point. I have all the confidence in the world that you're smart enough to succeed. The rest is a matter of determination. If you think you can do it, you will."

"But what about my family? They need me."

"They'll manage without you and be proud of you, Rebecca. We all will. Now let's fill out this application together. I have no doubt you'll be accepted. I'll let you know as soon as I hear." Dr. Headings handed the application to Rebecca.

But she made no move to reach for the papers. Finally she turned to face her mother. "Do you still think I should apply?"

After taking off her apron and sitting down at the kitchen table, Jane said, "My daughter. Remember what we talked about last night? If you want to study nursing at this school and Dr. Headings thinks you should go, then don't let your worry about us hold you back. If you want to go… go."

Rebecca studied the expression on her mother's face. A slight smile. Steady brown eyes looking directly at her. Ma. Always the one who tried to make things work, no matter her own sacrifice.

Rebecca reached for the application. But her hand was trembling.

CHAPTER 41

THE FOG IN HER MIND WORSENED EVERY DAY. SHE VACILlated between wanting to be accepted at the Johns Hopkins Hospital Training School for Nurses and hoping she wouldn't be. Then the decision would be made for her.

It didn't help that Ben had completely recovered from the accident with the surrey and came to the farm regularly. More than once Rebecca tried to tell him about her decision to apply to nursing school, but lost her courage after he pitched in to help her in the garden or muck the stalls. Or kissed her. Or told her she was pretty.

Time and time again, she gave in to her doubts, only to change her mind when thinking about the opportunity that had been given to her. Did Mr. North and Dr. Headings really believe she was intelligent enough to be accepted? Or even graduate? Then why didn't she?

About a week after she filled out the application, she heard a wagon approach the farm. Her heart beat fast thinking it was Doc Headings to tell her if she had been accepted or not. But the closer it came, the large man's silhouette made it unlikely to be him. It turned out to be a neighbor asking for her father.

She directed him to the toolshed where Elwood was repairing a broken ax handle. Not wanting to appear nosy, she skirted around the side of the shed and pulled weeds from a flowerbed. Soon she heard the man raise his voice. "Listen, you can do what you want. But I'm telling you I'm going to sell my woodland. Eastman is paying me top price. I'm getting old and can't manage the farm work anymore and my sons think I should sell."

A familiar voice answered, "Look up. See those scattered openings in the mountains, including the ones on my land? Think they look bad? Wait till you see all the Shade Mountains bare. I only sold my hundred acres because I lost my barn and everything in it last year."

"Yeah, I know. But the lumber camps and mills are giving men jobs."

The argument continued. But Rebecca couldn't stand to hear any more. Maybe she should go away. Maybe if she made something of herself she could help her father avoid having to sell more of their mountain land. Maybe if she were more educated she could convince Mr. Eastman to stop building more lumber camps and take his business somewhere else.

But then the reality of a woman expressing her opinion about something she knew little about hit her. It wouldn't matter even if she had a nursing school diploma. Besides, she hadn't found out if she was accepted, or for that matter, if she wanted to go.

The sun was high overhead, locusts singing their long, whirring call of late August. Dust clouded the air behind Dr. Headings' buckboard as he pulled into Wagner's lane and stopped in front of the log cabin. It was his second trip in a little over a week. No one was there to greet him so he walked onto the porch and knocked on the screen door.

When no one answered, he shouted, "Hello. It's Doc Headings. I came to the farm to tell Rebecca she was accepted at the Johns Hopkins Training School for Nurses."

Jane came to the door carrying an armload of dirty sheets and towels. "Oh, my goodness. Just a minute. We're changing Joseph's bed. Come in. Are you here to see Rebecca?"

"Yes. But while I'm here, I'll check on grandpa and grandma Wagner. Is Rebecca with them?"

"Yes. Just go into the back bedroom."

Rebecca and her grandmother were washing Joseph's back when Dr. Headings approached the two women. "Might as well check your heart while you're sitting up, Joseph." He moved his stethoscope around the old man's back, then his chest. "Sounds the same. Not good, but no worse."

Joseph ignored Dr. Heading's remark, and when the doctor tried to pull the sheet away from his legs, the old man grabbed and pulled them back up.

"All right, Mr. Wagner, I won't fight you. I came to see Rebecca, anyway."

He took Rebecca by the elbow and led them into the kitchen. "Jane, do you mind fetching Elwood? I want to talk to both of you—and your daughter."

Rebecca set tumblers on the table and poured meadow tea, her heart pounding in her throat. When all were seated, Dr. Headings began. "Rebecca has been accepted as a student at Johns Hopkins Training School for Nurses. I know this is a difficult decision for all of you, but it's one that can change her life for years to come. Not many young women have this opportunity. Peter North is still willing to pay for her travel and other expenses." He paused and took a drink of tea. "And I was able to vouch for her good character and intelligence. We both believe she is capable of completing the studies and rigorous training, after which she will be a graduate of one of the finest nursing schools in the country."

"When would she have to leave for this school?" Jane asked.

"By the end of the month. Nine days from now." Doc Headings cleared his throat and took a long drag of tea.

"What do you think, Rebecca?" asked Jane, her arms folded across her chest.

"That's not much time to get ready."

"The question is... do you want to go, Rebecca? The rest is not important."

Rebecca searched her mother's eyes and nodded.

Smiling, Jane said. "Elwood, we want her to go, don't we?"

His silence answered for him. He stared straight ahead. But he didn't forbid her from going.

Rebecca began to gather her clothes and lay them on the trunk at the foot of her bed. A list of personal items sat on her dresser. Hairbrush. Hairpins. Block of homemade soap. Tube of Crème Dentifrice. Toothbrush. Mum deodorant. Pencils. Tablet. All her and Jane's egg money gone just to buy these few things.

She checked off the list and glanced out the window to where Back So Straight sat on the log by her cabin. Panic ran down Rebecca's spine. She sat on her bed and tried to imagine her life in Baltimore without her mentor. No one to listen to her… no one who truly understood her.

She hesitated to tell her mentor she was soon going away and didn't know when she would come home again. She squared her shoulders and took a deep breath before she joined Back So Straight on the tree bench where they had spent many hours together. She'd miss this bench and the one by the fire. But more than that, she'd miss the one who was teaching her to be a healer.

They sat quietly for a few moments, looking out into the woods. Rebecca took Back So Straight's brown hand in hers and traced the blue veins that bulged through her skin. Then Back So Straight did the same thing. Rebecca's skin was also light brown, but smooth and the veins barely visible. This was a simple ritual they sometimes did before either of them spoke.

Finally gathering her courage, Rebecca said, "Back So Straight, I have something important to tell you." Her mouth was dry as the field corn in the meadow. "I have a chance to study nursing at a big city in Maryland. Dr. Headings and Mr. North recommended me to the head of the school. I'll become a nurse who takes care of sick people and helps to heal them. I'll be studying there for three years."

Back So Straight pressed her free hand on her breastbone. Then she grasped the beads on her blouse, rolling them between her thumb and index finger. In a little while, she spoke in a voice barely above a whisper, "I have known you would become a healer. It is time to learn your people's medicine. It will be hard. You will face many strange things in this big city." Then the Indian woman removed a little rawhide pouch from around her neck. Rebecca recognized it as the same one she carried when Wind was close to death. After retrieving a black stone from the pouch, Back So Straight placed it in Rebecca's hand. The stone was smooth and flat, slightly larger than a Morgan silver dollar. On the front was an intricate carving of a young woman with a baby. She was beautiful—a singular braid hanging down one shoulder, a blanket draped over the other. Beads were sewn on the collar and she wore a beaded necklace. Many bracelets circled each wrist. Her hands were large and one had rings on two fingers. The baby was swaddled in light cloth and strapped in a papoose lying across its mother's lap—dark eyes alert and mouth slightly open.

But it was the Indian woman's face in the carving that commanded attention. Wide-open eyes looked straight ahead. Her gaze was steady and resolute… haunting but beautiful. Rebecca studied the carving and smiled. Then she turned the stone over and held it close to her eyes. A carving of a magnificent tree with branches and a furrowed trunk appeared in repose. She ran her fingers over the carved surface again and again as though mesmerized by some power she didn't understand.

"What does this mean?

"The tree remembers."

CHAPTER 42

HOW WAS SHE WAS GOING TO TELL BEN SHE WAS LEAVING for Baltimore in four days? Her own doubts could fill a milking can, but convincing him to wait for her would spill them over the top. She knew he was a wonderful, decent man. He hadn't talked about marriage yet, but she knew he'd be a good husband someday. But would he wait three years for her?

Her answer came two days later when Ben arrived at the farm. He sprinted onto the porch and tapped on the door. Rebecca answered, her apron splattered with red beet juice and her hair sticking to her face sweaty from steam escaping from the boiling kettle on the stove.

"Ben, you're early. Come in." She wiped her hands on a towel hanging by the sink and tucked a loose strand of hair under the cloth that held her hair back from her face.

"I know I'm early but I have something special planned for us today."

Rebecca froze. It would be hard enough to tell him… she hoped he wouldn't make it more difficult.

Ben continued. "I'd like to take you to meet my mother and father. The buckboard is all packed with a basket of food so we can picnic on the way home."

"All right. But there is something important I need to talk to you about."

"What can be more important than meeting my folks? They hear me talk about you all the time."

The happiness in his face softened her resolve. "Give me a minute." Calling to her mother in grandpa Wagner's bedroom, "Ma, may I go with Ben? The beets are cooked and cooling. We can pickle them when I get back."

"Go ahead. Your grandmother and I can manage… hello, Ben. Sorry I can't come talk to you right now."

"That's fine, Mrs. Wagner. We'll be leaving now. I want Rebecca to meet my mother and father. Give my best to grandpa and grandma Wagner."

Ben chatted all the way to Mifflinburg. The new wagon he just delivered to a merchant in Oakland Mills. Trouble with a sewing machine. His sister getting married. Rebecca sat quietly trying to decide when and where to give Ben the bad news. He was happier than she'd ever seen him and didn't realize he was doing all the talking.

When they reached the buggy shop, Ben helped Rebecca's from the buckboard and gave her a kiss on the cheek. She could hardly keep from blurting out that she would be leaving for Baltimore in a few days.

His hand was firm as he led her into the buggy shop. She took a deep breath. The air was filled with the smell of leather and wood. Ben smelled much like this the first time she met him.

All the workers, including his father, mother, and two sisters, stopped what they were doing. Ben's father gave Rebecca a stern look and said, "'Bout time we met you. I'm George, Ben's father."

"So nice to meet you, Mr. Siebert."

Ben's mother reached out and shook Rebecca's hand. "We're glad to finally meet you, Rebecca. Ben has told us so much about you. Please call me Irene." Her handshake was strong as a man's—and her fingers red with small cuts and dried blood.

Rebecca masked her surprise by keeping her eyes on the woman's face. "Me, too. Ben brags about how you work as a family to make these buggies and carriages. I have seen one in particular that you made for Mr. Hugh Eastman."

Ben's father shook his head up and down and smiled. "That one's a beauty. Would you like me to show you around the shop?"

"Of course."

Before she could answer, Ben said, "Maybe for a short time, but we have to leave soon. I promised Rebecca I'd take her on a picnic."

"What's your hurry?"

"She needs to get back to the farm to help take care of her grandfather."

Rebecca looked blankly at Ben and wondered what he was up to. Then she saw the tiny smile on his face and decided to go along with his lie. Besides, she wanted time to tell him about Baltimore.

Ben's father took Rebecca through the buggy shop, explaining the types of buggies they made. Open buckboards. Two-person buggies with roofs. Fancy, high-wheeled carriages.

Piles of lumber lined the sides of the room. Vices to hold tires. Tables of tools. Racks of leather hides. A large, stone fireplace to heat the building.

Rebecca nodded politely but her mind was on Ben. Finally, he tapped his father on the shoulder. "Thank you for showing her the shop, but we must be going now."

"Won't you please stay for lunch? We stop working midday and I have some vegetable soup and fresh bread nearly ready," said Irene. Ben's mother looked expectantly at her son and Rebecca.

'I would love to, but—"

Since Ben had already lied about her having to return to the farm, she didn't know what to say.

It was an awkward moment, but Irene graciously acquiesced. "Well, we hope you come back again when we can spend more time together."

"I would like that." Rebecca curtsied slightly. "It was a pleasure meeting you. I hope you can come by the farm when you're out for a ride or delivering one of your handsome carriages."

As they started for home, Ben took Rebecca's hand, the other hand holding the reigns of the buckboard. About half way back to the farm, they stopped by a clearing in the trees and spread a blanket on the ground. Ben grabbed the picnic basket from the back of the buckboard and placed cornbread, butter, pickles, and two bananas on the blanket.

Rebecca laughed despite the regret she felt at having to decline Hanna's invitation and the heavy weight on her mind. She liked Ben's family, particularly his mother. She reminded her of Jane—warm, asking people to stay for a meal, inviting them back again.

Ben grabbed her by the waist and held her close. "This isn't funny. I managed to get this food together all by myself—with the help of a merchant I delivered a fancy buckboard to yesterday. Hence, the bananas."

His pride in the picnic melted her heart. She avoided eye contact and broke away from his arms. "Come on, let's sit down and start eating."

She remained quiet, hardly touching the food, while Ben talked between bites about the new carriage he had just delivered to a blacksmith in Port Royal. "You wouldn't believe the number of carriages we sold recently. Seems everyone wants bigger, better, newer wagons… buckboards… buggies. Business is good, I'm proud to say."

There's more to this conversation. Ben seldom brags about anything. She was right. Ben gathered Rebecca in his arms and kissed her. She was caught off guard by his passion. When he kissed her again, she felt herself respond. Her breasts pressed against him when she put her arm around his neck and her hand behind his head. A fluttering sensation ran down her abdomen and into her groin.

When they broke apart, Ben took her hand. "Rebecca, the reason I needed you to finally meet my parents is because I love you."

The sound of his words sobered her. She blinked several times before speaking. "I… I love you too."

"I want to marry you and settle down… raise a family."

She swallowed, not sure how to respond. "I want this too, but it may be on hold for a few years."

"What do you mean—on hold?"

"Ben, I wanted to tell you before we went to meet your folks. I'm going to nursing school in Baltimore. I leave in two days." After she said it, the reality of her commitment made her question her decision.

He drew back as though he had been struck. "How long will you be gone?"

"Three years. But I think I can come home for a short while every year."

"What? Three years? Why didn't you tell me about this before?" His voice was loud and angry.

Startled by his tone, she became defensive. "I didn't know about it until about two weeks ago. There was so much up in the air... I didn't want to say anything until I was sure I was going. Dr. Headings recommended me and my friend Lilly's father is paying for my expenses."

Ben grabbed her arms. His voice cracked. "I'll miss you, Rebecca. Three years is a long time."

Rebecca's resolve slipped away. "Please, Ben. I… I know I've disappointed you. But don't make this any harder than it already is."

"It sounds like you already made up your mind. I won't stand in your way."

Her voice took on a pleading tone "Don't you understand? If I don't try, I'll never know if I can do it."

Ben's shoulders slumped forward. He sat still for a few moments, then gathered the picnic food in the blanket and threw it in the buckboard. "Come, let's go to the farm."

Trying not to cry, Rebecca made a valiant effort to hold back tears. But when they drove past Zarker's store on the way back to the farm, her mind flashed back to the day they got caught in the storm—when they lay helpless underneath the surrey. She felt that same helplessness again. But this time it was self-inflicted. Tears spilled out, along with a sob.

By the time they reached the farm, Rebecca composed herself. As soon as the buckboard came to a stop, she turned to Ben and kissed him.

He stiffened. "I hope you do well, but I'm angry you didn't include me in your plans."

"I'm so sorry, Ben."

Her plans? No one was more uncertain about her plans than she was.

CHAPTER 43

THE REMAINING TWO DAYS ON THE FARM WERE A FLURRY OF activities: packing, filling out the remaining papers for nursing school, and figuring out the train schedule. Rebecca spent one evening in Dr. Heading's office asking questions. What exactly did nurses do? Where did they live? Who were their teachers? Would her studies be difficult?

Unfortunately, he wasn't able to answer her questions, as he hadn't ever spoken to the head of the Johns Hopkins Training School for Nurses in person. The only information he had was that the school was seeking young women of character who were intelligent, healthy, and had good stamina. But he read in one of his medical journals that in some nursing schools, girls from farms were especially desirable to become nurses because they were accustomed to odors and hard work.

Rebecca hadn't said goodbye to Lilly or Maggie yet. She dreaded it. But saying goodbye to her friends couldn't be near as hard as saying goodbye to Back So Straight and Ben.

Sunday after church was the only free time she had until she left for Baltimore the next day. After changing out of her church clothes, she walked the worn path to the mansions outside town.

When she knocked on the front door of the stone house, David came to the door.

Maggie's brother stood looking at her as if he couldn't remember who she was. "Who's at the door?" Maggie pushed her brother aside to see for herself. "David, are you blind? Rebecca, come in."

Rebecca smiled. Seemed like Maggie and her brother has spats like she and Gary did. "Thank you. Can we talk? I have something to tell you."

"What is it?" Pointing to the parlor, she said, "Sit down and tell me. Is it Lilly?"

"I'm going to Johns Hopkins Training School for Nurses tomorrow, and I came to say goodbye. I'll be living in Baltimore for the next three years."

Maggie hugged her fiercely. "I can't believe it. You'll be so good at taking care of people… but I will miss you terribly. Summers won't be the same around here without you."

"I know. I'm scared, to tell you the truth. But as I told you, I want to do something besides get married and keep house."

"But what about your beau? I thought you were serious about him."

Rebecca sighed. "I know. He's very upset. I don't know what will happen to us."

"Well, I think it's wonderful. One of my friends from Philadelphia is going to study nursing at the Pennsylvania Hospital. And I'm going to Bryn Mawr soon."

"I'm sorry but I have to go now… must say goodbye to Lilly too. Please write to me. I'll do the same and send you my address once I know it. Bye, Maggie. I love you."

They hugged, each holding on a long time. Rebecca half ran-walked across the street to the North mansion. Sarah North was reading on the sun porch when Rebecca approached the backyard. "Rebecca, it's nice of you to come. I was hoping we'd see you before you left."

"I couldn't possibly leave without saying goodbye to Lilly and speaking to Mr. North one more time. Is he home?"

"No, he isn't. He went to see Dr. Headings about a specialist in Boston who may be able to help Lilly. But he left this package in case he missed you."

Mrs. North handed a large sealed brown envelope to her with her name on it and 'Peter North' on the back. "You are not to open it until you get home."

"Please give him my sincere thank you. Now, would it be all right if I went upstairs to Lilly?"

"Yes, certainly. She's awake. Already had breakfast."

Rebecca climbed the steps, trying to rehearse what she would say to her friend. She dreaded telling Lilly she was going away for three years and may not see again her for a long while. It wasn't fair that she was starting a new life and Lilly was still suffering.

Her friend sat in a beautiful, velvet chaise staring out the window, but looked up at Rebecca when she walked in the room. Her face was drawn and pale, much like the last time Rebecca saw her. Her nightgown hung loosely around her thin frame.

"Hello, Lilly." Rebecca sat on a small, cushioned bench beside the chaise. "How are you today?"

Lilly gave a slight shrug.

"I have to tell you something, but it's hard for me to say. I'm soon going away to nurses' training school in Baltimore. Your father has made it possible and I'm very grateful to him—and your family—for including me in your lives."

Lilly sat still as an oak tree on a windless day. Her eyes riveted on Rebecca, jaw clenched, and a fierce expression on her face. Rebecca was unsure of her friend's response, so she sat quietly, listening to the ticking of the clock on Lilly's dresser.

"It's going to be hard to start a new life away from my home. I feel guilty about leaving you and going to nurses' training school when you're still sick."

The slap across Rebecca's face echoed against the plaster walls.

CHAPTER 44

The horse strained at the sound of Rebecca's voice. Git. Now. Snot escaped from the filly's nose and flew into the wind. As Jenny neared the path to the farm, she heaved, her breaths coming in loud snorts. The horse was not accustomed to running this fast and hard, but obeyed her rider without hesitation.

Tree branches grazed Rebecca's legs but went unnoticed. A flurry of thoughts raced through Rebecca's mind as fast as the horse was galloping. Anger. Hurt. Confusion. Why did Lilly strike her?

When Jenny stumbled slightly over a loose rock, Rebecca realized she was taking out her feelings on her horse and slowed down to a trot. She reached up and felt the cheek where Lilly slapped her. It still stung. But not as badly as her heart.

She couldn't remember what she said to Lilly… or her mother… before she left their house. Something about needing to get ready for her trip to Baltimore. Had to get home right away. That she would write after she was settled in. Thank Mr. North for the envelope.

As soon as reached the farm, she guided Jenny into the barn, hoping no one was there. She was in no mood to explain anything… the foam on her horse's flanks, her bad mood, her wanting to be alone.

That evening after a quiet supper, she sat down on her bed and opened the envelope from Mr. North. Inside was a ticket to Baltimore, a small cardboard fan, a map of downtown streets with streetcar stops marked in red ink, and two crisp twenty-dollar bills.

Tears slid from underneath her eyelids. Poor Lilly. She should be going to school, not me. No wonder she's angry. Her father should be sending her to school… and instead he's sending me.

Jane came into her room and sat on the bed next to her daughter. "Honey, you've been very quiet this whole evening. I suppose you're nervous about going away."

"Yes, I am," she said, turning away so her mother wouldn't see her red eyes. But not soon enough.

"Oh, you've been crying. Are you upset about leaving the farm?"

Not wanting to reveal what had happened earlier that day, Rebecca lied. "No, just a little jittery… not sure I'm doing the right thing. It was hard saying goodbye to everyone, especially Ben. He didn't take it well."

"That's understandable. He's very fond of you… and he's probably worried you'll be gone so long."

"Back So Straight, too. She gave me this beautiful stone to take with me."

"Yes, I've seen it before. She often carries it in her little bag of fetishes." Jane grew quiet and had a faraway look in her eyes. Then she said, "Here, let me help you pack. There's a lot to remember… make sure you have your papers."

Rebecca began to arrange her clothing and toiletries on top of her suitcase, ready to pack inside early the next day. Gathering her papers and placing the black stone from Back So Straight in her small drawstring purse, she continued to act as if nothing had happened earlier that day. However, inside, her stomach was churning.

Maybe she was making the biggest mistake of her life. But all was in place. There was no turning back now.

CHAPTER 45

BALTIMORE WAS UNLIKE ANYTHING REBECCA COULD POSSIbly have imagined. More people than she had ever seen milled about. Rows of beautiful brownstone houses. Carriages, wagons, and surreys crisscrossed the cobblestone streets. Pedestrians maneuvered around all types of horse-drawn vehicles. One young boy barely missed reaching the other side of the street when a Hansom cab pulled by a gigantic colored man crossed in front of him.

The four-passenger public carriage in which Rebecca rode was old and slow. Curls of peeling paint drooped down the wooden frame. A man in dirty clothing, his face unshaven and pock-marked, sat next to her. As the carriage jolted around the corner, he leaned against her. She smelled his body and tried to move away, but she was already crammed against the door. She patted the hem of her skirt to see if the money Hugh North gave to her was still where she had sewn it.

Rebecca turned her head and tried to ignore him. The smell of butter and salt contrasted the man's body odor. She stretched her head through the side of the carriage to find its source. Parked along the street was a Popcorn Wagon, its canvas sides rolled up to show a stuffed clown who cranked a small glass cylinder of peanuts.

She thought of Ben... his finely made carriages and surreys... his sturdily made wagons. Then his smile, his smell of leather and soap.

A flash of color brought her back, when a bright red wagon pulled alongside the carriage. Bold golden letters reading 'Eastern Estate Tea Company' matched its gold-painted wheels. *A whole wagon, just for tea.*

The carriage continued through the streets until it reached a busy intersection and turned left, almost hitting a small ornate carriage that looked like the front half had been cut away. It was empty, allowing Rebecca to glimpse inside at the diamond pleated burgundy walls and leather seats. *Ben could fashion a carriage exactly like this.*

Her thoughts were jarred by a screeching noise so loud she held her hands over her ears. She saw streetcars moving on metal tracks, wires attached to their roofs. Passengers sat on benches facing the street and stood on the back platform. Rebecca marveled that there weren't any horses pulling it.

The ride through Baltimore seemed endless. Despite the interesting things she saw, she was hot and tired. Looking ahead, she saw massive gray buildings with smokestacks belching dark, thick smoke. Intersecting the main streets were narrow alleys with little, unpainted wooden houses—colored people standing on the sidewalks and sitting on the steps leading up to their porches.

In this part of the city, the streets had rotting garbage—banana peels, oyster shells, tin cans, putrid drainage filled the gutters. Piles of horse manure were everywhere. Rebecca gagged at the stench, holding a handkerchief under her nose.

After the carriage rolled on, the air grew less nauseating. Here there were hucksters selling fish, clams, crabs, and oysters. Others sold melons, peaches, tomatoes, and corn. Shops selling everything Maggie and Lilly told her about in Philadelphia: fancy furniture, shoes, medicines, delicate baked goods, and confections. Barber shops, restaurants, and law offices.

Rebecca closed her eyes, half drifting into sleep. She had been riding in the rickety wagon for over an hour. Sweat rolled down her neck and the back of her high-collared blouse. Baltimore was loud and stinky. She missed the farm already.

The sudden stop of the carriage jolted her awake. "Here we are Miss. Johns Hopkins Hospital Nurses' Building."

"Are you sure this is the right place?"

"Yes, Ma'am. Brought a few other young women here this mornin'."

Rebecca felt slightly reassured. "No turning back now."

"No, Ma'am. Guess there ain't."

The driver opened the door and Rebecca climbed over the man seated next to her, holding her breath and moving carefully to avoid bumping his legs. As she stood hesitating, the driver gave her one last look. Rebecca returned his stare, thinking maybe she should get back in the carriage and go home to McAlisterville. A moment later the carriage pulled away.

Rebecca looked up at the massive four-story brick building. She counted the chimneys: eight. In the center of the roof was another smaller story with a tall multi-roofed copula.

She took a deep breath before climbing the steps to the front landing. She knocked on the massive, ornately carved door. No one answered. A feeling of dread came over her. Maybe she was too late. Maybe this was the wrong building after all. Just as she reached up to knock a second time, the door opened wide. A slight woman in a high-necked black dress with a small, white collar stood smiling at her. She wore a white gauze cap over the top of her brown hair that was pulled back into a loose chignon.

"Good afternoon. Are you Miss Wagner?" Rebecca nodded but before she could answer, the woman continued. "I've been expecting you. I'm Adelaide Nutting. Please come in. Let me show you to your room. Your roommates are already here."

Rebecca followed her through a large, carpeted room with an enormous chandelier that held ten white globes on the end of upward-curved arms. A fireplace adorned with a large framed mirror took up part of one wall, while ceiling to floor windows graced the opposite one. Wicker chairs, rockers, and sofas provided ample seating for about a dozen people.

She took it all in. This room was a lot like Maggie's and Lilly's parlors, only bigger. Sure didn't look like a school.

When Miss Nutting led her down the stairs to the ground level, they passed room after room of young women sitting on beds or at desks laughing and chatting. Finally, they reached the last room at the back of the hall. Miss Nutting knocked on the closed door.

She tapped her fingers on the doorframe while she waited, and leaned toward the door as though she were listening for footsteps. "Ladies, your roommate is here."

The door opened quickly. "Hello, Miss Nutting. Is this Rebecca?"

"Yes, it is."

A petite woman with blond, curly hair grabbed Rebecca's suitcase. "I'm Gracie. Please come on in." Rebecca immediately thought of Lilly. Gracie was shorter but had the same clear skin and delicate, slim frame.

"Thank you," Rebecca said. But her eyes never left Gracie. Her wasp-like waist made Rebecca feel like a giant. However, her hair made up for the woman's diminutive frame. Tiny, golden-yellow ringlets framed her flawless face despite having her hair pulled back into a chignon. But most endearing were the small dimples that dotted her cheeks on either side of her mouth when she smiled.

Miss Nutting interrupted her thoughts. "Miss Wagner, should you need something, come to me immediately." Then she looked into the room, and said, "Ladies, after you've all had a chance to get acquainted, report to the dining room for dinner at six o'clock sharp."

Taking Rebecca's hand, Gracie led her further into the very large, beautifully furnished room. Ornately carved dressers flanked four beds, two on each side of the room. They all had mirrors: two dressers with small, oval mirrors on each side, and two dressers with mirrors so large they spanned the length of the top. Small plants sat on top of some, while photographs adorned the others.

She put Rebecca's suitcase on the floor next to a bed. "This is yours, Rebecca. Mine is next to it. And this dresser is empty and so is your desk. But before you unpack, I would like you to meet your roommates."

A large, buxom woman about Rebecca's age walked toward her. She wore a beautiful midnight blue dress embroidered with silver thread around the hem and sleeves. "Bertha Perkins from Annapolis. Glad to meet you."

Rebecca curtsied slightly and smiled, but her tongue was glued to the roof of her dry mouth. She hadn't had a glass of water since morning. She glanced around the room, eyeing a woman sitting on a bed with a pillow on her lap.

"The best is always saved for last. My name is Maude Driscoll, from Washington D.C. The capital, you know." She stretched her long frame and yawned.

Thinking it rude that Maude would insinuate that she wouldn't know Washington D.C. was the capital, Rebecca nevertheless walked across the shiny chestnut floor to greet her. "Nice to meet you."

It was a challenge to remember her roommates' names. But she did her best: Grace is the graceful one. Bertha is quiet. Maude is haughty. Rebecca wondered if they were as scared as she was. She lifted her suitcase onto the bed and placed her clothing in the dresser. The only personal touch was an embroidered bureau scarf her mother had made for her, and the black stone from Back So Straight. She wasn't sure where to put the stone, so she tucked it under the scarf. She'd have to find a place to hide it later. Then Rebecca placed the box of writing paper Lilly had given her, three pencils, and a wind-up clock on her desk. She turned toward the other desks and dressers. Hers was the only one nearly bare.

Gracie pulled the chair away from her desk, sat down and faced Rebecca. "Where are you from?"

"I'm from McAlisterville, a small town in the middle of Pennsylvania... but I live on a farm near the mountains." Strange. She had never had to tell anyone where McAlisterville was. "How about you?"

"I was born in Ontario, Canada. Whew. This heat in Baltimore is something I'll have to get used to." She swept her hand over her forehead and giggled.

Rebecca was certain she was going to like Gracie a lot. "Is Ontario far away from here?"

"I think it is. The trip here took a few days. And the further south we traveled the hotter it got."

Feeling guilty she only had to travel half a day, Rebecca said, "It's good it's not winter though. There must be a lot of snow in Canada."

Gracie nodded.

After a time when no one spoke, the woman who boasted she was from Washington D.C. got up from her bed and stood before Rebecca and Gracie. "Well, it's hot in Washington D.C. too. But one time I got to see President McKinley when he passed by in a new automobile."

Rebecca studied this thin woman with protruding front teeth. Pencil-straight black hair as coarse as burlap was tied with a bow in the back of her head. She had pockmarks on her cheeks—Rebecca suspected Maude had suffered from a disease of some sort that left her scarred. Poor Maude. She was the homeliest girl Rebecca had have ever seen. Maybe that's why she was a braggart.

When none of the roommates responded to Maude, Gracie jumped up from her chair and pointed to the clock on her dresser. "Oh, my. We'd better get going to the dining room. It's nearly six o'clock."

The dining room was lovely. Linen tablecloths and vases of fresh flowers graced the tables. Water in tall, clear glasses. The four roommates sat at a table with 3 other nursing students while two other tables also held seven students each.

The room grew quiet as soon as Miss Nutting stood up from where she had been seated with several other nurses dressed in white uniforms and gauzy nursing caps. "Good evening. I'm Miss Nutting, superintendent of nurses and principal of the training school. It is my pleasure to welcome you to the class of 1901. This is an important day for all of us—you because of your decision to become trained nurses, and for us—because we have the privilege of teaching you to become the noblest of all women. Now let us give thanks for God's blessings."

She waited until the room was completely quiet. "Dear Lord: we come before you in humility and gratitude. Thank you for the safe travel of these young women and their commitment to become trained nurses. Now we give thanks for this abundant food. May it nourish our bodies and souls for your honor. Amen."

Dinner was bland but plentiful: baked fish, boiled potatoes with parsley and butter, and collard greens. Applesauce with cinnamon on top for dessert. Rebecca gulped a whole glass of water as soon the prayer was over. It was warm and had no taste. Not like the cold water from the pump in the kitchen. She was so hungry she ate everything on her plate, even though the collard greens looked like the green slime at the edge of the farm pond. What she wouldn't give for some chicken potpie, homemade bread with her mother's apple butter, and a dish of sweet-sour pepper cabbage.

After dinner, Miss Nutting took a spoon and tapped it against a glass. "Students, you are free the rest of the evening to settle in and get to know your classmates. Tomorrow you are required to report to the classroom adjacent to the dining room at six a.m. to receive your uniforms and begin orientation. Good night."

Rebecca went downstairs to her room. She wanted some time alone to write a letter to Ben while her roommates lingered in the dining room.

Dear Ben,

I have safely arrived in Baltimore. There are many tall buildings and the houses are right next to each other. It is noisy from the trolleys and carriages that fill the streets. The nurses' home where I live is bigger and fancier than any building in McAlisterville. I have a room on the lower floor with three other students. They seem nice but it feels strange to undress in front of them. There are 21 students in my class who live in rooms down the hall from me. I hope to meet all of them soon. There are so many hospital buildings. I do not know if I will ever be able to find my way from one to the other. Tomorrow we receive our uniforms. I am very excited to wear one. I already miss the mountains and my horse. But most of all, I miss you. I know how disappointed you are that I came here. I hope you will find it in your heart to forgive me. It was the most difficult decision I ever had to make. Please don't forget about me. I must go now. I am required to go to bed soon. Give my best wishes to your family.

Love,

Rebecca

P.S. Will you please go to the farm on one of your trips nearby and tell my folks I am fine and will write as soon as I have a free moment?

Rebecca's roommates returned later that evening but by then Rebecca was lying on her bed pretending to be asleep. At nine o'clock, Miss Nutting knocked on the door. "Lamps out, ladies."

Rebecca tossed and turned in her lumpy bed, trying not to wake her roommates. She was intimidated by the confidence her roommates seemed to have, especially Maude. Her chin quivered as she tried not to cry, but tears slid out of the corners of her eyes as her hands held the starched sheet tight up to her chin. She wanted to cover herself despite the heat in the room. Sleep finally came just as streaks of sunlight peeped through the edges of the window shades.

That morning Rebecca and her roommates awakened to the sound of Bertha's alarm clock. She felt awkward dressing in front of strangers but tried facing the wall when she pulled on her chemise. She wore a simple, woven, white blouse and black skirt in contrast to the puffy-sleeved, white dresses Gracie and Bertha wore. Maude wore a plain blouse but her skirt was rich brown cotton brocade.

The four young women walked into the dining hall, joining the other students in their class who also lived on the lower floor of the nurses' home. Miss Nutting and several other women were already seated at a table set in an alcove formed by a large bay window. An ornate tea service sat in the middle, its sliver patina visible from across the room.

Rebecca was barely awake but she managed to eat a bowl of oatmeal with brown sugar. Seated next to her, Bertha ate some white pasty-looking mush that Rebecca thought looked like lumpy flour and water gravy. "What's that you're eating Bertha?"

"Grits. Would you like to try some?"

Rebecca shuddered. "No, thank you."

Soon Miss Nutting rose and said, "Good morning, students. Today you will receive an outline of your studies for this first year. However, the first six months before you start to work on the wards is a probation period after which, if you are successful in maintaining a good academic standing, you will receive a nurses' cap. I will explain more about that at a later time. The remaining six months will combine work in the hospital for a minimum of eight hours in addition to two hours devoted to lectures, classes, and study."

Rebecca had been paying close attention to Miss Nutting when Gracie tapped her arm and whispered, "Ten hours every day?" Rebecca shrugged. A stern look from Miss Nutting quickly ended the conversation.

The principal then distributed a circular that listed the educational program for the first year:

Practical teaching and training in medical, surgical, and gynecological free wards. Demonstrations and classes in practical work weekly.

Class work:

Elementary Material Medica;

Anatomy, physiology and hygiene;

Cookery and dietetics, practice and theory.

Then Miss Nutting called out each student's name and asked them to line up to receive their uniforms already laid on tables according to size. She stood behind the first table with a tablet perched on her arm. "You are to select one uniform of your size and when you are finished, I will issue two more uniforms to you."

Rebecca, Gracie, Bertha, and Maude selected a size and climbed down the stairs to their room to try on their selection. Turning her back to the other students, Rebecca let the long sleeved, light blue cotton dress fall over her hips. She smoothed out the folds, and hoped she had selected the right size. It felt stiff but not too loose or tight. When she turned around, she saw Bertha struggling to pull her dress over her shoulders.

"Let me help you."

"It seems to be a little tight."

"No need to force it… I'll go up and get you the next size."

By the time Rebecca returned, Grace and Maude were fastening their starched white apron with wide straps that crossed in the front and buttoned in the back. They each helped position the fabric so it covered their blue dresses. Bertha slipped the larger uniform over her head and it fell into place. She glanced over at Rebecca and smiled. Then the two women helped each other slide their arms through the apron's holes and fasten the four buttons.

Maude twirled around and stood with her hands on her hips. "How do I look?"

Not sure how to answer, Rebecca said, "Just fine. Now let's go upstairs before Miss Nutting misses us."

Maude gave her a sidewise look, but started to walk toward the stairway. Rebecca followed and watched Maude from the back, wondering if she looked like Maude—clean and crisp—a real student nurse. She wished her mother and Back So Straight could see her in her new uniform, but by the time Rebecca walked into the hall, her collar felt scratchy around her neck and she had already begun to perspire.

The other student nurses were waiting when Rebecca and her roommates returned to the assembly hall. Miss Nutting's frown and sideward look troubled Rebecca, but she was glad she helped Bertha avoid embarrassment.

"Ladies, please come forward to claim your remaining two uniforms. When you have done so, return to your seats."

Rebecca quickly gathered her uniforms. As she turned to walk to her chair, she saw shelves at the back of the room that held black shoes arranged by size. Next to them were bins of heavy black stockings and chiffon bags filled with hairnets. A round table near the door held white starched caps. They looked like small maharaja's hats from one of her history books.

The principal said, "You may now a select a pair of shoes to try on. When you have found your correct fit, you may take a second pair, three pairs of stockings, and a bag of hairnets." Miss Nutting waited until all twenty-six students returned to their chairs. "Now you will take your belongings to your rooms. In fifteen minutes, come to the parlor. We will then go on a tour of the hospital buildings and grounds."

Students were divided into two groups. Rebecca was glad Gracie, Bertha, and Maude were in her group. The tour started with a walk down a manicured street with trees and shrubs planted on expansive green stretches of lawn. Large, red brick buildings with blue sandstone and molded terra-cotta stood near each other, some with elevated bridges above the corridors that connected them. Nurses and patients, some in beds, sat or laid in the sunshine on the bridges.

When they reached the main hospital and walked into the five-story domed rotunda, Rebecca gasped. In the middle of the black-and-white tiled floor stood a nearly 20-foot-tall statue of Christ. A wide-open stairway that led to a balconied second story was nearly obscured by the statue. Gaslights hung on some of the walls; others stood on large wooden pedestals. Dark wood panels lined the bottom third of the white walls.

Their shoes made clicking noises as the student nurses and their guides walked across the tile floor and up the steps. Gracie took Rebecca's hand as they entered the Octagon Ward. Beds were lined up along the walls. A wide-open area in the middle allowed ample space for workers and equipment. Many windows brightened the room and limited the need for gas lighting during the daytime.

Bertha approached the nurse who was guiding students on the tour of hospital wards. "Why are these rooms shaped like an octagon? Seems to be an extravagant use of space."

"Because the octagon shape avoids corners where dirt and dust and insects can harbor diseases. Our housekeepers find these rooms easy and efficient to clean."

Leaning toward Rebecca, Bertha asked, "Do you really think that makes a difference?"

"I don't know. I'm just a farm girl."

One by one they visited the common wards. Some were large enough to hold 20 beds or more—lined up like slices of bread. Each bed had a tall metal headboard. Radiators provided central heating. Gaslight sconces hung on the walls between two beds and rocking chairs rested in the middle section of the wards.

Rebecca whispered to Bertha, "Not much privacy here, is there?"

"Sure isn't. I wonder what the patients do when they're bathed? And what about when they have to, you know… have to go?"

Rebecca recalled hearing Back So Straight say 'shit' and tried not to laugh. But it was impossible. She held her hand over her mouth but a giggle escaped.

"What's so funny?" asked Bertha.

"Do you mean shit?"

The two of them burst into peals of laughter, causing Maude to look sideways at them and make a shushing sound. Then their guide pointed her finger and shook her head. Rebecca regretted her behavior. She knew she would have to act more refined from then on.

The student nurses continued their tour of sixteen buildings, all arranged around an open courtyard: Administration, two private wards, four regular wards, an isolation ward, an amphitheater, bathhouse, kitchen, laundry, dispensary, apothecary, pathology, and a stable.

By the time they returned to their rooms, they had covered nearly the entire 13-acre property. Rebecca was grateful she was used to walking but questioned how she would ever find her way around the campus.

A late lunch was served in the dining room. In keeping with their lowly estate, probationers were assigned to tables near the door. She was surprised to see nurses who worked on the wards eating there too. Their white uniforms and nurses' caps made them stand out in contrast to the blue dresses with white apron uniforms students wore.

Rebecca was too nervous to eat. She picked at the green peas and beef resting in weak gravy. Her mind swam with names of wards and buildings... and names of classmates and teachers. And that didn't include names of second- and third-year students she hadn't met yet.

Miss Nutting dismissed the first-year students and encouraged them to explore the nurses' building: library, parlor, bathrooms, kitchen, sitting rooms. Rebecca walked through the rooms as though she was in a trance. So fancy. So many books. Fireplaces in every room. But, except for a few of her classmates, no nurses or doctors.

CHAPTER 46

HER OTHER CLASSMATES ALSO LIVED FOUR TO A ROOM. A FEW were from Canada like Gracie; others from Massachusetts, New York, Nebraska, and Kentucky. Several students had been working as a 'special' nurse to wealthy families. Rebecca later learned that some graduates of the school of nursing had come from Germany and West India. Many had stayed on to become head nurses and supervisors. Others were private duty nurses of the highest caliber. Rebecca was shocked to learn that at age eighteen, all members of her class were older than her, the oldest being 26. Despite their differences in age, Rebecca soon learned to know several women within a short time. Mary Elizabeth Brown lived across the hall from Rebecca and sometimes asked her to go to the dining room at dinnertime. Another classmate, Carolyn Conrad Van Blarcom admired Rebecca's long, dark hair and styled it in a twist on top of her head. Rebecca liked her because her name was interesting. But as far as she knew, none admitted to coming from a farm.

With each passing day, classes increased in content and complexity. Rebecca quickly found out that the relatively easy pace of the first week was an exception. Students were up at six, went to breakfast, then classroom instruction began at seven. Rebecca and her roommates worked, studied, slept, and ate together like sisters in a Catholic convent.

Maude was always the last one to go to breakfast and was often already in their room at the end of the day. She was the mysterious one—told vague story after story of her beaus at home, and hinted she already had a male friend at the hospital, going against strict rules designed to protect the virtue and character of its young charges.

Soon after school started, soap and shampoo disappeared from their room, and Gracie was missing a pearl brooch given to her by her grandmother. None of them could prove Maude was the culprit but they all suspected her. Just to be on the safe side, Rebecca hid her money and the black carved stone Back So Straight had given her under her mattress.

Rebecca was closest to Bertha, whose quiet and studious demeanor made her different from her other roommates. She had beautiful clothes that she hung on wooden clothes hangers suspended from the hooks on the wall near her bed. Her shoes were lined up beneath them in perfect order. Rebecca admired her self-confidence and determination. Although Bertha came from privilege, she never spoke condescendingly or flaunted her family's wealth. Sadly, she confided in Rebecca that she really wanted to be a doctor, not a nurse. But her father, who was a physician, didn't believe that women should become doctors, even though Johns Hopkins School of Medicine was the first to admit women several years ago.

They studied together, but it soon became evident that the farm girl from McAlisterville knew more than Bertha, or for that matter, any of her classmates. Medical terms and their Latin origin, especially anatomy and physiology rolled off her tongue. However, she soon realized her knowledge only made her feel more at odds with the expectation that she refrain from thinking on her own. Despite the valiant efforts of Miss Nutting and a few of her instructors, Rebecca feared she was there to become nothing more than a free laborer in the wards, maid, and loyal and subordinate handmaiden to physicians.

She had no way of knowing that the Johns Hopkins Training School for Nurses demanded higher standards of achievement from its nurses in training than any other school; and that she had entered a program with stiff admission requirements that had just increased the term of study from two to three years. Dr. Heading's endorsement and her own academic and moral standing gave her the advantage she needed to be accepted.

Rebecca learned to admire and respect her instructors: especially Mary Adelaide Nutting, Elsie Mildred Lawler, and Anna Wolf. But for now, the daily routine of classroom instruction, lectures by physicians, and studying late into the evening left little time to speculate what lay ahead.

She was shocked when she learned that in the early years of nursing, student nurses were placed on duty in the wards as soon as they arrived—no prior instruction or practice. The thought of being thrust into a twenty-eight-bed ward and left to sink or swim left Rebecca grateful that such a practice no longer existed… but left her with lingering misgivings about her decision to become a nurse.

The biggest surprise for Rebecca was the requirement that students learn cookery and dietetics practice and theory. Emphasis was on the processes of cooking and the different ways of applying heat, such as making proper toast and poaching eggs. Their laboratory was a fully equipped kitchen with gas stoves. She learned the goal of dietary practice was to train nurses who could prepare nutritious food while doing private duty nursing both in the hospital and in private homes, and monitor the food intake of patients. Students were required to follow specific recipes designed for patients with various diseases and digestive conditions.

Rebecca found her classroom studies in dietetics to be a most boring and unnecessary waste of time. Surely other students had learned to cook at home. She was taught cooking at an early age using a wood-fired cook stove. But despite her failure to see the importance of cookery and dietetics, she copied the recipes in her notebook and carefully followed them as she was told. She never knew there were so many recipes for gruels: arrowroot, oatmeal with rolled grain, imperial granum, flour, cracker, and farina. Or drinks such as eggnog, toast water, whine whey, or milk punch. Or flaxseed lemonade, barley water, or apple tea. The gruel made her glad she never had to do more than taste them. And none of the drinks tasted half as good as meadow tea or cold water from the kitchen pump on the farm.

After a particularly tedious day listening to lectures and working in the dietary kitchen, Rebecca went to the library to look up recipes for patients with heart disease. Her mind wondered back to the farm… her ma… her grandfather. She raced downstairs to her room and grabbed a piece of writing paper Lilly had given her, a pen, and an inkwell before returning to the library.

Dear Ma,

Please forgive me for not writing sooner. I hope you are doing fine and that Ben told you I am doing well like I asked him to. So much has happened since I came here. I live in a beautiful nurses' building with three roommates. There are 21 other students in my class. My uniform is light blue cotton with a white apron, black shoes, and hosiery. I wish you could see me wear it.

Last week we started long hours of classes and practical work. Some days we are taught to cook special foods so that we know how to prepare food for our patients. I can't believe I have to learn how to make toast and poached eggs!

We are also being taught how to make hospital beds and bathe patients. I learned to wash them all over (not their private parts). Then we roll them over and wash their backs. Next we pull out the dirty sheet before making that half of the bed with a clean sheet. Then whole process is repeated on the other side. I wish I had known how do this instead of trying to lift grandpa or convince him to sit up. The corners of the sheet must be mitered. I'll show you and grandma how to do that sometime.

The hospital is a large red brick building with lots of windows and an octagon-shaped end on one side. There are many buildings surrounding it such as a laundry and a repair shop. I don't know my way around yet. I'm glad there are trees and flowers and a lot of grass, but I miss the woods and your cooking.

Please read this letter to the rest of the family and Back So Straight and tell them I love them.

Your loving daughter,

Rebecca.

That night Rebecca dreamed of the farm. She pictured the stall where her horse Jenny should have been but wasn't. She smelled manure. The tree bench near Back So Straight's cabin sat empty. All was quiet. Too quiet. No sounds of gears, belts, and saws.

Then she saw it again—the severed arm lying in the sawdust.

She awakened to the sound of her voice. "Nooooooo!"

When she opened her eyes, Gracie was leaning over her. "Rebecca, wake up. You were screaming." Rebecca opened her eyes but struggled to see in the darkened room. "Oh… Gracie.

"I… I had a nightmare. Something… I haven't thought about… in a long time." She gulped at the air but only shallow, rapid breaths seeped into her lungs. After forcing herself to take a deep breath, she felt her heart stop racing.

"Please go back to sleep. I'm fine now."

"All right… if you're sure." Gracie pulled the blanket up to Rebecca's shoulders and crawled into her own bed. "Good night."

Another severed arm.

CHAPTER 47

THE NURSING CURRICULUM SOON ACCELERATED IN COMPLEXity and difficulty. Long days spent in hands-on practical nursing, lectures, study, and tests rivaled the endless days on the farm. Rebecca struggled to stay awake through lecture after lecture. First, the diseases of the digestive system by Dr. McCrae. He was very knowledgeable, but he spoke rapidly and the amount of information overwhelmed her.

Rebecca's favorite subject followed: the circulatory system. Dr. Barker outlined the entire network of arteries and veins, and the coronary-lung circulation. He required students to trace the blood as it left the arteries in the heart until it entered again through the veins.

One physician spoke about how newly discovered X-ray revolutionized their ability to diagnose diseases and injuries, especially of the bones. When he demonstrated the machine, Rebecca and her classmates were captivated. Patients had to hold very still for a long time—sometimes an hour or more, but when they were finished, the cloudy gray and black images showed bones, tumors, and the location of bullets in every part of the body.

When Rebecca studied the digestive system, she remembered the remedies Back So Straight would use when one of the family had an upset stomach or diarrhea. Fresh yarrow juice mixed with water was her favorite tonic for nausea or indigestion. Sometimes the Indian woman boiled sumac leaves into a strong liquor and gave it to whoever suffered from too many trips to the outhouse. She was curious to learn if the medicines she was about to learn about in Materia Medica were made from plants.

Next came lecture in pathology by Dr. Flexner, and the immune system by Dr. Welch. Rebecca took copious notes. She hung on every word. Terms for organs and their functions triggered her memory from reading from Dr. Headings' medical books.

Bertha and Gracie asked Rebecca to study with them, Rebecca often serving as a tutor while reviewing her notes. Soon she excelled in classroom work and examinations. But underlying her success in the classroom was a nagging fear of slipping behind her classmates who seemed to learn more quickly and study less. Each evening, Rebecca studied with Bertha or went to the library where it was quiet, then stumbled into bed exhausted.

Maude kept mostly to herself, preferring to sit on her bed to study alone. Rebecca tried to include her but became impatient when Maude curtly declined. But there were times when Rebecca caught her listening to her roommates reviewing their studies. After repeated offers to include her, Rebecca gave up trying. Still, there was a part of her that felt sorry for Maude.

But something wasn't right. Sometimes her soap went missing from its soap dish, later to be found wrapped in a hankie lying under Maude's bed. Bertha complained about her Mum deodorant disappearing from her dresser top. Gracie never did find the brooch her grandmother gave her. Just to be on the safe side, Rebecca searched under her mattress. The little pouch was there, but the purse was gone.

That evening after they returned from the wards and finished studying, Bertha and Rebecca confronted Maude. "Listen, we're roommates. We all have to live together, but we have reason to believe you've been stealing from us. Things are missing or borrowed without our permission."

A blush spread across Maude's cheeks. "I don't know what you're talking about. I may have used your soap or… but I didn't steal anything."

Rebecca moved closer to Maude until she stood face to face with her before she spoke. "I don't believe you. I had a small purse with money in it hidden under my mattress and it's gone."

"That doesn't mean I took it. Maybe you forgot where you put it."

Gently moving Rebecca aside, Bertha said, "No, she didn't. When I went to use my deodorant, I couldn't find it. And there it was, on your dresser."

"That's not the same as stealing. I just borrowed it." But her voice quivered.

Gracie joined Bertha and Rebecca and pulled herself up to her tallest height. "My grandmother's brooch is still missing and I know exactly where I had it."

Before Maude had a chance to answer, Rebecca scooted across the room and lifted Maude's mattress. Nothing. Then she went to the other side and did the same. There near the middle was a small towel folded around a slight bulge. She grabbed it and shook the contents onto the bed. Her purse and the brooch dropped out. She looked inside the purse; all the money was still there.

All eyes turned to Maude who stepped back and said, "You're all rich. You have everything you need. I don't. You can't blame me for wanting what you have."

The bile in Rebecca's throat rose just like it did when she scolded her grandfather. "That's not true. If you needed anything, I'm sure we would have been willing to share. You're a thief. And now you're a liar. I should report you to Miss Nutting."

Maude's already pale face turned white as she crumpled onto her bed. She broke into sobs. After a few minutes, she said in a cracked voice, "I'm sorry I stole your things. Please don't report me. I'll never do it again. I promise. Please."

Ever the softie, Gracie's soft voice broke the tension in the room. "I forgive you. At least I have my grandmother's brooch back."

But Rebecca was still angry. "I won't report you this time. But if we find anything else missing, I'll go straight to Miss Nutting."

"And I'll go with her," Bertha said, her arms across her chest.

CHAPTER 48

PRACTICAL TEACHING AND TRAINING IN THE MEDICAL, SURgical, and gynecological free wards were Rebecca's favorites. She loved hands-on learning. There was an order in which every task had to be completed. But sometimes head nurses in the wards had their own way of doing things and expected students to conform. Do this, then this. Do not ever deviate from the procedure, even if there was a better, easier, or more logical way. Be demure. Obedient. There was a right way and that was the only way she had to learn.

However, sometimes their teachings and demonstrations were not in line with her textbook: *Nursing: Its Principles and Practices*. When she questioned the differences, she was admonished to do as she was told.

Miss Nutting tried her best to minimize the confusion. Once she figured out what was causing the differences in procedures and expectations, she hired only graduates from Johns Hopkins Training School for Nurses to fill leadership positions. After these disputes were over, Rebecca's appetite to learn more blossomed. She questioned. She wanted more "why" and less "how".

Life in the nurses' home gave her a reprieve from the tedium of lectures, study, practice, and memorization of body systems and their functions. Some evenings, if there was time after studying, Rebecca and some of her classmates would gather around a piano and sing. Or they played games such as Snakes and Ladders or checkers. Occasionally their teachers hosted informal parties. On one such evening, Miss Nutting and her colleagues gathered a dozen or so students around the fireplace. They told stories about Isabel Hampton, who founded the nursing school.

Miss Nutting surprised everyone by standing up in the middle of the conversation and laying her hand against her breastbone. The room grew hushed. With a fixed gaze on the young women nearby, she spoke in soft tones. "Isabel Hampton Robb, as she is now called since she married five years ago, was and remains my heroine."

Who could possibly gain the adoration of the director of the entire school and hospital? Rebecca didn't move, her eyes transfixed on Miss Nutting.

The head of the school continued. "Miss Hampton Robb knew Florence Nightingale and formulated her vision of this school after her. I studied nursing under Miss Hampton Robb's tutelage and hope to join her in establishing her next vision . . . the Nurses' Associated Alumnae of this country and Canada."

Bertha slowly slid from her chair and stood up. "What exactly does that entail, Miss Nutting?"

"She envisions this organization to be a means for graduates to keep in touch with one another and share information to build the practice and status of all nurses. This is a bold step, one that has implications for all of you."

Tapping Rebecca's arm, Bertha whispered, "We are in the midst of something great, Rebecca, just you wait and see."

Rebecca's pulse quickened as she held up her hand to speak. Her knees shook under her uniform. "All I know is that we work hard, study relentlessly, and do what we're told. Sometimes my head hurts just from thinking and trying to remember everything I learned."

Miss Nutting gave a weak smile.

A classmate sitting nearby turned to Rebecca. "I agree. Remember me? I'm Elizabeth Griffin. I sat behind you in Dr. McCray's' lecture. You're just tired. We all are. I think being a graduate of this school is a very prestigious honor. Before we know it we won't be probationers anymore."

Just as Rebecca started to answer, Elizabeth tapped her on the shoulder. She looked up and saw Miss Nutting and her colleague Elsie Lawler walking toward her.

Rebecca felt her stomach clench. Oh no. They must have heard her complain. She stood up, her eyes staring in disbelief. "I meant no disrespect, Miss Nutting."

A smile crept up the corners of Miss Nutting's mouth. "No offence taken, Miss Wagner. Miss Griffin, I assume you know Miss Wagner?"

"No, I… actually just met her this evening."

"Well, she's a very good student. I like her inquisitiveness and spunk. Seems she was highly recommended by a doctor in Pennsylvania. I'm glad I took him at his word. I'm sure she won't disappoint me."

Rebecca held her stomach again and bent forward slightly. "I'll try my best not to disappoint you, Miss Nutting."

CHAPTER 49

BALTIMORE GREW GRAY AND GLOOMY AFTER ALL THE TREES were bare, their branches reaching out, forming their fingers into long, black gloves. It rained for days at a time, the gutters overflowing with bits of manure, sticks, and newspaper. Even the grassy areas throughout the hospital grounds were brown and muddy. In the evening, Rebecca and her roommates studied, their lamps burning until Miss Nutting called her usual "lanterns out." But mornings, when the alarm clock went off at 5:30, all Rebecca wanted was to roll over and go back to sleep. Only Bertha's gentle tap on her shoulder saved her from being tardy, a failing that Rebecca wanted to avoid, especially after Miss Nutting's statement about having confidence in her.

Rebecca looked for a letter from Ben, but each passing day she was disappointed. So when a letter arrived, she nearly fell down the steps racing to her room. Her fingers shook as she tore it open.

Dear Rebecca,

I am writing to tell you how sorry I am that I did not answer your letter until now. Your leaving was such a shock to me that I was not sure if I could ever forgive you for not including me in your plans. I have come to realize what a wonderful opportunity this is for you, even though it means we have to delay our marriage. I hope I can wait for you and I hope you still want to marry me when you finish nurses' training.

Every time I pass by the Grange hall where we met or ride past the meadows where we picnicked and took walks together, I remember how I felt when I was with you. But it is very difficult to be here alone while you are in Baltimore. I see other young men and women together, some with babies and small children and I think this could be you and me.

Please write back. I need to know if you still care about me.

With love,

Ben

Her pulse pounded in her temples. He still loves me. She tucked the letter under the embroidered cover on her desk and went to the library to study. She was more determined than ever to do what she set out to do: study. Do well. Return to Ben.

Practical Nursing became her passion. She took detailed notes of mixtures for baths, and poultices. Two precise recipes were as follows:

Bath: 30 gallons equals one-half bathtub. Poultice: Bran to soften skin; Linseed oil; mustard. Put bran, linseed oil, and mustard in a bag to create a mustard poultice. Never place next to skin.

Another recipe was given for treatment of constipation, called eliminate:

Three oz. liquid soap to one quart water; three small glasses; one small black nozzle; olive oil. After enema given, rinse nozzle in cold water. Wash in warm soap and water. All oil removed and rectal tubes boiled.

Rebecca thought it would be much easier to just give the patient dandelion root tea. That's what Ma and Back So Straight always made for anyone in the family who couldn't go.

One evening after the mandatory two hours of study, Rebecca told Bertha about her experience giving her first eliminate. Seems the tubing separated from the container and sprayed her uniform and drenched the patient. She had to go back to her room and put on a clean uniform before finishing her work. They both laughed about it until their sides hurt. Rebecca's spirits lifted slightly after that. But she hoped Miss Nutting didn't find out about her clumsiness.

Equally challenging for Rebecca was the treatment of cantharides. Great care had to be taken to memorize and practice before nursing students were allowed to treat blisters.

To make sure she remembered correctly, she took out a small notebook she kept in her apron pocket. There in her own handwriting were the instructions:

> *Clean and scrub. Cut plaster round. Take Vaseline or olive oil and apply to parts. Wrap lightly to allow room for blister. Leave on for 6 to 8 hours.*

Her first patient with blisters was a little boy about 10 years old who was burned by lantern oil. She gathered all her materials together and began to scrub a large blister. The little boy screamed. His pleas for her to stop must have reached the ears of the head nurse. She took Rebecca aside and scolded her for hurting the child. Rebecca's chin quivered. She wished Back So Straight were there to put some Slippery Elm salve on the blister. But she knew she had made another mistake. First the eliminate tubing. Now she was too rough when taking care of the little boy. She looked down at her trembling hands. How many mistakes can she make before she would be asked to leave?

CHAPTER 50

THAT EVENING, AFTER A QUICK DINNER AND SEVERAL HOURS of study, Rebecca felt lost and afraid she wasn't measuring up to her instructor's expectations. She made mistake after mistake. She was so tired. And her self-confidence was at its lowest point yet. She tried to steal time to write letters to Ben and her family, but exhaustion often got the best of her.

But tonight, discouraged and lonely, she finally took time to write to her mother.

Dear Ma,

It has been a long winter so far. The streets and buildings in Baltimore are covered with dirty snow from the gritty dirt that settles from smoke-stacks and streetcars. I miss the bright snow that covers the meadows and mountains back home and the trees that surround our farm. But most of all, I miss my family and Back So Straight. I think of you so often, especially when I take care of patients your age and wonder if you are well.

I like my roommates, but one of them tries my patience. We all work so hard and then have to study until Miss Nutting announces lamps out. Maybe that is why my spirits are low. Sometimes I wish I were home sleeping in my bed that smells like fresh air-dried sheets and covered with one of grandma's quilts. I can almost smell the cabin's pine logs and fried bacon that always found its way up the stairs to my room every morning. The hospital wards sometimes smell worse than the manure we spread on the fields.

Today I took care of a boy who was burned. If Back So Straight were here, we'd put slippery elm and witch hazel on the blisters like we did for Gary. But here, we use different medicines. I truthfully don't think they work better.

I don't mean to worry you, but I'm terribly homesick. Sometimes I think I made a mistake by coming to this training school.

I wonder if the mountains are still being logged and if our neighbors have sold any more of their woodland. I worry about Lilly, too. Have you heard anything about her? Is she able to speak yet?

Have you planted any seeds in the cold frame yet? You always have a green thumb when it comes to gardening. Flowers and vegetables thrive under your care. I must admit, I don't miss canning, though I do like to eat what we put up. The food here is not near as tasty as on the farm and some of it is strange. For example, a white tasteless breakfast food called grits seems to be popular and a vegetable called collard greens ends up slimy on my plate. But there is an abundance of fish and we often have cornbread, which I love. What I wouldn't give for some chicken pot pie and apple dumplings.

I hope we are granted some time off soon so I can come home. It seems like a lifetime ago since I saw all of you. I miss Ben, too, and wonder if he misses me. I will write again as soon as I can.

Love,

Rebecca

When Rebecca read the letter before sealing it in an envelope, she became even more homesick. She tried not to cry, but there was no stopping the tears that had built up over the past months. Soon she cried herself to sleep, only to wake up the next morning feeling drained and with a headache.

She forced herself out of bed and grabbed breakfast before hurrying to the mailbox on her way to the hospital. But before she dropped the letter inside, she had second thoughts. No sense to worry her mother. Just as she decided to tear up the letter, a robin flew nearby. Maybe she should send it.

Rebecca slid the letter through the opening. Now if she could just hold on until Miss Nutting announced their first vacation in almost a year. But that was months away. She doubted she would make it.

CHAPTER 51

WINTER'S SNOW TURNED TO SLUSH… THEN ICE. THE TREES surrounding the hospital buildings sparkled in the sun and dripped their icy water onto the grass sleeping below layers of dirty gray mounds that used to be white. Paths had been cleared between the main hospital, the apothecary, laundry, nurses' home, and other buildings, but as soon as they were shoveled by scores of colored men in heavy coats, more snow filled them up.

Finally, Baltimore slowly awakened to spring. Patches of mud mixed with green grass gave the expanses of land surrounding the city a checkerboard appearance. Trees, once bare and black, sprouted tiny buds, some red, some brown, some nearly invisible.

Rebecca began to think she would make it through the next months now that winter was over. At least she hoped so.

She began to walk between buildings, even though she had to walk too quickly to identify the birds she heard in the nearby trees and bushes. Now and then the fragrance from a magnolia tree made her smile. She must tell Back So Straight about this tree. Not as beautiful as the red bud trees at the edge of the woods, but its cup shaped flowers made her nose happy.

Her next clinical assignment was a large men's medical ward. Rebecca had just finished attending a series of lectures by the Physician-in-Chief, Dr.

William Osler, on diseases and illness such as diabetes, stroke, and urinary obstruction. She took careful notes and reviewed them over and over.

There was nearly one quarter colored men in this ward, their bodies emaciated and their faces sad. Some had open ulcers on their legs. Others coughed violently from pneumonia and tuberculosis. Rebecca and her classmates were instructed to be especially careful to vigorously wash their hands in soap and water or chlorinated lime before every patient contact.

Rebecca tried to remember the facts she learned in Dr. Osler's lectures and the ones that followed about cleanliness, procedures for cleaning wounds, and policies about bathing men. This was especially important to protect the propriety of females and insure their good reputations were upheld.

One day when Rebecca was particularly busy taking care of twenty patients, she heard a man call "nurse". When she walked over to his bed, he became confused and tossed his sheet off his body, exposing his erection. Rebecca covered her mouth with the palm of her hand and drew back. Oh, my God. Was that what they look like? She had seen animal's organs but nothing prepared her for that moment.

Rebecca picked up the sheet and covered the patient. His erection created a small mountain in the middle of the cloth. She squeezed her eyes shut. But then her curiosity won and she opened them again, staring at the sheet. Another student working at the end of the ward approached her. "Go with me into the linen closet a moment."

The young women filed into the closet and stood staring at one another. Finally, Rebecca started to giggle. She held her hand over her mouth but laughter bubbled out the sides of her mouth. The other student nurse tried to stifle her giggles but instead she snorted loudly. That made the two of them laugh even harder. Sounds of their fun seeped under the bottom of the closet door.

A loud knock startled them out of their merriment. Miss Nutting opened the door and stood before them, hands on her hips. "What is going on here? Sober up and get back to your patients."

Rebecca felt like someone had just thrown ice water on her face. She drew in a breath and focused her eyes straight ahead. Then she took the other student's arm and led her out of the closet. Miss Nutting's lips pressed into a straight line but she said nothing. After watching the students return to their duties, she walked away.

Rebecca was beside herself with guilt. Another incident on her record. But she couldn't shake the image of the naked man and the bulge in the sheet. Every time she cared for a male patient that day, it surfaced again and again. Although she did nothing wrong and was able to laugh at her lack of decorum, she felt like her innocence had been violated. Finally, the tortuous day ended and she hurried back to her room.

That night after study hours, Rebecca pondered the events of the day. Who can I tell about this without embarrassment? Bertha's too serious and Gracie would faint. It has to be Maggie.

After her roommates were asleep, Rebecca lit the lamp on her desk and turned it down low so she could see to write.

Dear Maggie,

Hello from Baltimore. Please forgive me for not writing sooner. I have so little opportunity to write letters, but I will try to do better in the future. Oh, so much time has gone by since we went on adventures together. I long for those times again. You are probably finishing up your first year at Bryn Mawr and I am nearing the end of the most difficult year of my life. I never dreamed nursing school would be so demanding of my body, heart, and soul. My heart yearns for simpler times. But here I am and I must persevere. I have made new friends and my fondness for them grows, but no one can compare with you and Lilly. Please give her my best as I am still concerned about her well-being. There are a few dinners and socials here, but I long for time spent with you both.

I am engaged in vigorous study nearly all the time. I just finished a course of lectures on diphtheria, amoebic dysentery, malarial fever, tuberculosis, and leprosy. Alas, a second-year student was expelled because she refused to care for a patient with leprosy. I do not know what I will do if faced with that situation. I have already misbehaved several times and been scolded by the head of the school. But I have managed to excel in my examinations and written assignments, thanks in large part to the medical books Dr. Headings loaned to me.

Next month we will learn about the anatomy of the urinary system and diseases that occur in the kidneys and bladder. We will also have to analyze urine samples. That will be nasty, worse than emptying our family's chamber pots at the farmhouse. At least I knew whose eliminate it was.

Now about the real reason I am writing. Today a very embarrassing and shocking thing happened to me. I was called to the bedside of a man when he threw off his sheet and revealed himself to me. Oh, Maggie, I tried to close my eyes but my curiosity got the best of me. Then worse things happened. When I placed the sheet back on him, his organ stood straight up! I could see the bulge it made in the middle of the sheet. I wanted to disappear into the walls. Then another student nurse saw what happened and pulled me into the linen closet where we proceeded to have an uncontrollable fit of laughter. Soon my director of nursing found us in the linen closet and scolded us. I was mortified and so ashamed.

Maggie, his organs were purple and very unsightly. I cannot imagine an organ that big fitting inside a woman. Please tell me it is not possible. But it must be. Or there would be no children, including us. I assume the process is similar to mating of the pigs and other animals on the farm, and I did see our stallion's organ when he bred our mare, but that seemed different.

I wish we had talked about these things when we looked at the medical books together. I would have been better prepared for what I saw. But somehow the pictures didn't seem real and they were not in color. I feel so naïve and unworldly. But I had never seen a naked man before. I remember helping to diaper my brother as a baby but I never saw him naked when he got older.

I pray you are not angry with me when you read this letter. Please write back as I am in your debt for allowing me to write about such delicate matters. I hope to be able to come to McAlisterville for a visit this summer and that we can resume our friendship.

Until then, I am most affectionately yours,

Rebecca

CHAPTER 52

THE HEAT IN BALTIMORE NEARLY MADE REBECCA SICK TO HER stomach. The odors of sweaty bodies, open wounds, excrement, and disinfectants permeated the ward's still air. Lectures in the nurses' home gave a respite from the odors but not the relentless hot temperatures. Her heavy cotton uniform, apron, and black hosiery added to her discomfort. Sweat dripped off her nose and ran down her back. Her black stockings clung to her legs. As soon as she wiped perspiration away from her face, it formed again and again. Even nights made her feel like she was suffocating in her basement room. Bertha and Gracie moved their beds nearer the window but Maude's was already in front of the other one. When Rebecca tried to convince her to move her bed aside, Maude told her told she wanted to have quick access to the window in case of fire.

Each morning when Rebecca dressed for work, she patted Johnson's baby powder, a gift from Bertha's mother, onto her body, hoping she would avoid chaffing between her sweaty legs and starched uniform. She recalled the heat last September when she first received her cotton uniforms, aprons, and stockings. But this was her first full summer in Baltimore and it was proving to be hotter than working in the fields on the farm.

By August, she saw that her uniforms were loose around the waist and arms. Her weight had plummeted from hard work—walking, lifting, shoving, and carrying heavy buckets.

On a particularly hot day, Rebecca was working in a large ward, helping lift an overweight patient. As she stepped back from the bed, the room started spinning. She heard a loud ringing in her ears and saw flashes of light. Then everything went blank.

She felt cool air when she woke up. A nurse was waving a paper fan over her face. When she finally focused her eyes, she saw a very tall man with bright blond hair and a gentle smile staring down at her. He was holding her hand taking her pulse.

"Welcome back, Miss. I'm Dr. Morgan. You fainted. Did you hurt yourself when you fell?"

Her voice wavered. "No, thank you. I…" but truthfully she didn't know.

"Are you sure?"

Rebecca blinked rapidly and shook her head. "I'm… quite all right, thank you." She tried to sit up but started to fall back down. "I'm so sorry. Let me try again. May… may I get up now?"

"Yes, of course. Let me help you." He put his arm in back of her shoulders and carefully lifted her into a sitting position. Then he held out his hands to grasp hers and pulled her from the floor. "Will someone get a glass of water for the young lady?"

"Thank you."

"I think you should go back to your room for the rest of the day. I'll speak to Miss Nutting."

"I do… feel a little weak, I must admit. Thank you again. You've been very kind."

"What is your name?"

"Rebecca Wagner." Her stomach churned and growled.

"I've seen you in the wards before."

"Yes, I've been working in this ward for several weeks now." She felt beads of perspiration slide down the side of her face and wiped them with her hand.

"Are you a first-year student?"

Wonder why he's asking. "Yes, I start my second year in about a month."

He leaned in close and looked directly at her face. "Are you feeling better?"

"Yes. I must get back to work."

The head nurse handed the glass of water to Dr. Morgan who gave it to Rebecca. "Nothing doing. First you must drink this and agree to go to your room and rest." He waited for her to drink it.

She closed her eyes and gulped down the water. A small amount dribbled down her chin and she and wiped it with her sleeve. "Thank you."

Dr. Morgan smiled. "I will speak to Miss Nutting as soon as I can. Meanwhile, go to your room, drink more water, and rest." Then he walked away.

Until they started to walk away, Rebecca was unaware of the small crowd of nurses, orderlies, and housekeepers that had gathered around her. The nurse who brought the water approached her. "You sure chose a handsome one to come to your rescue."

Excitement about the upcoming two-week vacation made the last of the summer heat more tolerable. Rebecca and her classmates eagerly awaited their final grades so they could begin making plans to return home. But they had to wait until Miss Nutting posted the scores of their tests on a blackboard in the main classroom. Unfortunately, some would not be returning. Already two students needed to drop out because of health problems. Rebecca had recovered from her fainting spell, but she became more aware of the hazards of not staying hydrated and working around contagious diseases. She was relieved that Miss Nutting showed nothing but kindness after the fainting episode and allowed her to rest the remainder of that day.

Rebecca scored the highest grades in all subjects but pharmacology. Bertha was a close second. Surprisingly, Gracie and Maude were neck in neck with average grades. All would be returning to start their second year.

Home. Rebecca could hardly believe she was going home, however brief her stay.

The whole family except grandma Wagner was there at the train station when she arrived. Even Jenny nickered when the wagon pulled in. Jane ran to her daughter and stopped short of grabbing her in a bear hug. "You are so thin. Are you well?"

Rebecca extended her arms. "Of course, Ma. Just a little skinnier." They hugged, holding on to each other for a long time.

Her father came forward and opened his arms. "Glad to see you, daughter." She walked into his embrace.

But Gary stayed a distance away. "Well, sister, you finally decided to come home."

"Yes, I did. Aren't you glad to see me?" She looked at her brother, and then her Pa. Not much changed between the two of them. Can't even stand next to each other.

Gary sided up to his sister, and said, "Well, put it this way. While you were gone, I got to ride Jenny and there was more to eat." He spit and ground the moist circle into the ground with his boot.

Despite managing a smile, Rebecca felt hollow inside. Glad to be home but aware of the family tension that surfaced so soon after she returned. She wondered if this was a foretaste of how Ben would react to her after being away for so long.

The ride to the farm was like a well-remembered dream. Patches of bare mountains but larger than a year ago. Ribbons of fields with ripening corn, barley, tobacco, hay, and wheat. Farms with copulas resting on red roofs. Silos reaching to the clouds. Wash hanging on lines between barns and houses.

Then they passed the stone and brick mansions. People were sitting on the gazebo but when Rebecca waved, no one waved back. She hoped they hadn't forgotten her.

When they reached the edge of McAlisterville, the scene changed. Shops with buggies tied in front. Carriages weaving their way down Main Valley

Road. Children and dogs ducking out of the way. The school sitting empty and still. Dr. Headings house on the corner with buggies tied out front.

They turned the corner and headed back the lane to the Wagner farm. The barn showed its new raw-wood sides. She was glad to see the outbuildings had a fresh coat of whitewash and the fences were in good repair. Animals grazed in the nearby fields and a whiff of manure reached Rebecca's nose. Even that smelled better than the hot, odiferous wards.

Scanning her eyes toward the cabin, Rebecca said, "Pa, did you buy a new buckboard?"

"Did no such thing." He broke out in a broad smile.

"Ben! It's Ben. Hurry."

Elwood clicked the horse and drove near the porch where Ben was standing against a post. As soon as Rebecca jumped down from the wagon, he ran and picked her up. She wrapped her arms around his neck and laid her head on his shoulder.

"Can't you two do that somewhere else? It's embarrassing," said Gary, in his soupiest voice.

The two huggers ignored him but Elwood slapped the back of Gary's head. "None of your business. Leave them alone."

Brotherly teasing didn't bother Rebecca but she knew Jane didn't like it. "Why don't you come in the cabin? Your grandmother and Back So Straight are waiting for you."

As soon as they walked inside, the Indian woman called her dog. Wind let out a whelp and ran through the door. She stopped when she saw Ben and turned toward Back So Straight, who nodded. Once the dog sniffed Ben, she trotted to Rebecca and rolled on her back. Rebecca rubbed the dog's belly—a little slice of heaven.

Rebecca reached for Back So Straight. "My mentor. I missed you. Many a time I wanted to tell my teachers about your remedies and what you taught me about the trees and plants. But I couldn't. They already had the required classes and demonstrations planned and didn't ask us what we already knew."

"I am pleased you are learning about other medicine. It is good. Then you know the best of mine and the best of another's."

Rebecca formed a steeple with her hands and pressed them to her lips. "I know. Thank you."

"I will leave now with Wind. You must spend time with your family and this man whose heart is yours."

Quietly approaching Rebecca, Grandma Mary reached for her hand. "I am so glad to see you, my grandchild. I have missed you."

"Me, too. Last winter I longed for one of your quilts on my bed. Especially when I needed to snuggle with something from home."

"Too bad you can't take one with you when you go back."

"I would if I could manage to carry it on the train. I'm afraid it would be too heavy."

"Well, they'll be waiting for you when you return. Now why don't you two go out on the porch while us old folks start cooking supper?" She winked at Rebecca and gave her a slight nod.

Rebecca took Ben's hand and led him outside. "Do you want to take a walk?"

A smile lit up Ben's face. He tucked a strand of hair behind Rebecca's ear and said, "I thought you'd never ask. Let's walk down to the creek."

When they were away a short distance, Ben pulled her to him. "You look so pretty. May I kiss you?"

She stood on her tiptoes and stretched her face toward his. He reached down and wrapped his arms tightly around her back as he pressed his lips to hers, gently at first, then strong and hungry. After they kissed again, he studied her face, drawing his eyebrows together. "You can't know how much I've missed you, Rebecca. You hardly ever wrote to me. I thought you forgot about me."

Rebecca bit her bottom lip. "I know. That was wrong of me. I have no excuse except that I was overwhelmed so much of the time… so confused about the way we parted… I didn't know if I you would ever want to see me again."

"Then we both made mistakes. I'm sorry for what I put you through." He reached for her hand and kissed the back of it. "I know I may not measure up to some of the educated people you met in Baltimore, but I work hard and make a good living."

"What's this all about? I'm not sure I understand what you're trying to tell me."

"I'm just saying that you'll be able to talk about medical things... I only know about carriages and buggies."

"I don't know anything about carriages and buggies either. And I'm only home for two weeks. Let's not waste our time arguing." She slid her hand around the back of his neck and pulled him toward her. When she nibbled his lip instead of kissing him, he laughed hard, showing his straight, white teeth. Just like when they first met. He still smelled like leather and soap.

"Come on. I'll race you to the creek." Rebecca took off, running as fast as she could. A short time later, Ben overtook her. "Darn skirts. Men have it much easier. Someday I'm going to wear trousers so I can run faster."

Ben laughed again. "I'm afraid you're bold enough to do that. Just don't be seen in McAlisterville if you do. Tongues will wag."

Rebecca and Ben sat by the creek and talked until it was nearly suppertime. When they returned to the cabin, two plates with sandwiches made from homemade bread, summer bologna, sliced tomatoes, and mayonnaise were waiting for them on the kitchen table. All was quiet except for the sound of occasional laughter.

"I must go now. It'll soon get dark and I have a long ride ahead of me. May I see you again before you leave?" Ben voice grew softer with each word.

"You better come by if you know what's good for you," Rebecca teased. "I must see Maggie and Lilly, too, but please come to see me as often as you can."

Ben exhaled as if relieved. "I'll come to the farm this Sunday. Let's go for a ride in one of my new surries through Bunkertown... then to Evandale and out my neck of the woods. Maybe even venture to Selinsgrove."

"I can't wait. I'll pack a picnic lunch." Rebecca gave Ben a peck on the cheek and walked him to his surrey. After a long goodbye kiss, he slowly rode away, looking back over his shoulder now and then and waving.

Before Rebecca went upstairs to unpacked her suitcase, she headed to the water pump. Nothing tasted as good. The tin cup quickly formed dew on the outside as she savored each mouthful. She sat at the kitchen table and looked at the surroundings. The wood stove. The dry sink. The mason jars sitting on the windowsill. The kitchen chairs with their chestnut spokes. The sweet odor of pine logs. This is home. And now she had Ben again.

Jane walked in from the parlor and sat next to her. She poured them each a glass of meadow tea. Rebecca nodded and drank the entire glassful.

"Tell me, Rebecca, what is it like in Baltimore at nurses' school? Are you doing all right? We hardly heard from you at all."

"I know, Ma. I'm sorry about that. We had so many lectures and dozens of demonstrations on how to do things. There were no deviations, not skipping steps. We had to memorize each step and if we didn't accomplish that way of doing things, we had to start all over again."

"Back So Straight and I always taught you to do things the easiest and most efficiently, and if you discovered a better way, we tried it. If it worked, we adopted it for our own."

"I remember. I much prefer to experiment and not be forced to do things a certain way just because they were always done that way."

Jane looked down at her hands.

"It's all right, Ma. I learned how to adjust and accept the way that was expected of me. I only got in trouble a few times when I found a situation to be funny and I shouldn't have. But I only have myself to blame. I'm sorry if my letters worried you. I was so down in the dumps."

"I can only imagine how hard it must have been for you to be away for so long. But enough. Let's go outside where it's cooler."

The rest of the evening was spent on the front porch with Rebecca asking questions about the forest. Did Pop tell you how many new acres were being cut by Mr. Eastman's crew? What farmers worked for him in the lumber camps and sawmills? Were people still getting hurt?

Her mother answered as best as she could but finally said, "You'd better ask your Pop these questions, not me. He keeps himself pretty tight-lipped these days, ever since he sold some of our woodland to Mr. Eastman."

Finally, Rebecca stood up and excused herself. She had a headache and wanted nothing more than to go to bed in her own bed in her own room. That night she looked out the window at the hemlock tree. It seemed to have grown even bigger the year she was away. The moon sneaked behind the lacy branches and cast shadows on her bedroom walls. Soon whip-poor-wills began their relentless calls back and forth from the tree to some unknown mate across the meadow. She sniffed the clean sheets and folded the bed quilt to the bottom of the bed. Wouldn't be needed this hot summer night. Rebecca was glad to be home. But there was also a sadness she couldn't explain. Then she remembered. In just two weeks she had return to Baltimore.

CHAPTER 53

REBECCA SLEPT UNTIL MID-MORNING THE NEXT DAY. WHEN she woke up, the sun was beaming in her window and the crows were chatting loudly. She instinctively listened for the din of the sawmill. She was surprised she slept through the noise of the screeching and whining of the blades and pulleys. They reached their pitch intermittently—the loud grinding echoing through the valley when a log was pulled into their path. Thank God she didn't dream about the severed arm last night.

The smell of bacon lured her downstairs. Jane was alone in the kitchen. "Good morning, Rebecca."

"Morning, Ma. Where is everyone?"

Gesturing toward the barn, Jane said, "Your Pa is trying to figure out how to add a piece on to the barn for a tractor."

"Yes, you wrote to me about that. Where are Gary and Grandma?"

"Gary went over to David's house and grandma is in her room crocheting."

While they ate breakfast, she studied her mother. Sweat streaking down her face. Lines under her eyes and around her mouth made her look tired. Gray hair peeped out from the widow's peak on her forehead. Maybe this is how I'll look in about twenty years.

Each day brought the routine of farm life back to Rebecca. Hunt the eggs. Hang wash on the line. Feed the pigs. Hoe the weeds in the garden and pick vegetables. Can as much as possible for winter. Some evenings the family sat on the porch or under the apple tree and drank meadow tea till the gnats drove them inside. On Sunday, they went to the church. Rebecca enjoyed the attention she received from members who hadn't seen her in a year.

Ben and Rebecca took long walks. But tension built when they tried to figure out what Rebecca would do when she finished nursing school. Ben insisted they would settle down and raise a family as soon as she returned to McAlisterville. Rebecca tried to explain her desire to first practice nursing somewhere, somehow. Often times they argued until Ben left in anger.

Two nights before Rebecca had to return to Baltimore, they took a long carriage ride. Evening was warm, but a breeze made it pleasant. The sun drifted behind the foothills, leaving streaks of light glowing between the trees. Ben pulled the carriage under a tall Chestnut tree and lifted Rebecca out of the seat. Then he put his arms around her and hugged her to him. "Rebecca, I will miss you. I don't know if I can wait two more years for you."

"I'll miss you too, Ben. But I don't have any choice but to continue my studies to be a nurse."

"Yes, you do. You told me you already learned more that you ever thought possible. Quit now and stay home."

Rebecca lifted her chin and broke away from his arms. "We've... talked about this before. I don't want to quit. Dr. Headings and Mr. North would be very disappointed if I did. I can't do it."

"Well, I'll be the one who's disappointed if you don't."

She clinched her hands and dug her fingernails in her palms. "Please, don't make me chose between you and nursing. Give me another year and we'll be clearer about what to do."

"Then what? You'll go back for another year? How does that change things?"

"Well, I'll only have another year to finish and then we can be together again."

"Another year. I'm the one who's waiting. That's all I seem to do. Wait for you."

"Ben, let's not argue. I only have a short time until I have to go back. Please. Try to understand. I must do this."

He let out a long sigh. "A lot can happen in two years. I just hope there's room for me in your life by then."

"I promise there will be." But inside she felt torn. She loved him, but the more he held her back, the more she struggled to be free.

The few remaining days of Rebecca's stay at home were filled with a blur of emotions—joy of being home with her family but sadness and confusion about what happened between her and Ben. And there was just enough time to see Maggie and Lilly again.

She decided to visit Maggie first. It felt good to ride Jenny so she took her time riding the familiar path through the woods and meadows. The smell of late summer was in the air… heavy and humid. Flying grasshoppers alighted when her horse nearly stepped on them. Not even a slight breeze moved the leaves on the trees.

When she reached the stone mansion, Rebecca found her friend sitting in the gazebo and thought back to the first time she saw the copper-haired girl over a year ago. Maggie spotted her and ran across the yard between the small pine trees, her full skirt blown around her legs. "Rebecca, I was wondering if you would be home this summer."

"Yes, I have another day before I must go back. It's wonderful to see you." As soon as Rebecca got off her horse, they hugged each other for a long time despite their sticky arms.

Her friend had grown taller and the fullness around her chin was replaced by a firm jawline. Freckles still covered her cheeks and her nose. They sat on cushioned benches facing each other. Rebecca smiled when her friend wiped the beads of perspiration under nose with her sleeve. Just like she did when picking raspberries last year.

"So, how are you?"

"I'm doing well. But Lilly isn't. Our families traveled here together for the summer about two months ago. Lilly's still not speaking. She only let me see her a few times for a short while. I miss her. She's thinner than ever and looks away when I talk to her."

"I'm so sorry. Do you think she'll see me?"

"I believe so. She always talked about you before she got sick."

That same feeling of helplessness took Rebecca by surprise. "I'll give it a try."

Maggie reached for Rebecca's hand. "First let's talk about us. We have a lot of catching up to do."

They talked through most of the afternoon—sharing school stories and funny things that happened with their new friends. Maggie described her involvement in the women's suffrage movement. She was particularly adamant about the sacrifices famous women like Susan B. Anthony and Elizabeth Stanton made to gain the right for women to vote. "You should see us, Rebecca. Like I told you in my letter, students at Bryn Mawr held rallies led by the National American Woman Suffrage Association. We sold newspapers and raised money."

Rebecca listened, her eyes wide with fascination that women could gather and demand their right to vote and hold public office. But she wanted to tell Maggie about her struggles, too. "You have no idea what women are expected to do as student and graduate nurses. We have to defer to physicians, give them our seats, respond when they bark orders at us, and act demure when they tell us we don't know what we're doing."

"Oh, dear. When I graduate, I am going to do something to change the status of women. I'm not sure what, but we must stick together."

"Me too. But I don't think many people in McAlisterville even know about the movement to obtain women's right to vote."

"My father and mother have been talking about it but they don't agree. My mother and Mrs. North are well aware of the poor conditions women in Philadelphia live in, especially immigrant women. But they aren't sure how they feel about women holding public office."

Rebecca shook her head. "I don't know any woman who has been a judge or state legislator or even a local township official. They're all men as far as I know."

"Well, let's pay attention to what's going on in Harrisburg after we get out of school, and take a train to a rally in Philadelphia, maybe Pittsburg. I have a feeling change will come in the big cities before it comes to small towns like McAlisterville."

"Let's write to each other Maggie. But don't expect regular letters from me. I'll write when I can but I have very little free time."

Maggie hugged Rebecca and patted her on the back. "I'll write—I have more time than you do. But I'll look forward to your letters, no matter how many times you write."

"Thank you, Maggie. You are a true friend. I have to go now to say good-bye to Lilly."

A sense of dread spread over her as she guided her horse into a slow walk across the street. Lilly's mother Sarah stood in the front yard cutting flowers, but stopped when Rebecca tied her horse to the post in the driveway. "Hello, Rebecca. It's wonderful to see you."

"It's good to see you again, too, Mrs. North. Is Lilly here?"

"I'll let you see for yourself. Go around the house to the back porch. She's sitting out there watching the birds."

When Lilly saw Rebecca approach, she acted startled, putting her hand up to her throat. She was thin and her face drawn.

Trying to be casual but nervous inside, Rebecca said, "Hello, Lilly. I can't tell you how glad I am to see you!" Lilly didn't answer but kept her eyes riveted on Rebecca's face.

"I just came from Maggie's house. We talked about school and things… I asked her if she thought you would be up to having a visitor. Is it okay if I sit with you for a while?"

Lilly nodded slightly before looking down. Her arms rested in her lap with her small hands tensely gripping each other.

"I've finished my first year of nursing school, thanks to your father and Dr. Headings. It's been very hard. We work and study ten hours or more a day. Most of the patients are poor and have all kinds of sickness and diseases."

Lilly looked up briefly before turning her head to stare past Rebecca into the yard. She sat motionless while her friend continued to talk. After a lull in Rebecca's stories, Lilly frowned.

"Am I saying too much about my school?"

Lilly shook her head no.

"I'm sorry I didn't' write... but I want you to know I'm not angry with you. In fact I thought about you often and hoped you were doing better."

But there was no response.

Out in the yard, the whirr of a cicada broke the silence.

Lilly averted Rebecca's eyes but she took Rebecca's hand and kissed it. Tears ran down her face and onto her lap. She sat staring at their locked hands.

A baby's cry came from the upstairs window. Rebecca gave Lilly a puzzled look, her eyes moving to the opened window with white curtains blowing in and out with the breeze. When she looked back down, there was a terrified expression on Lilly's face as the front bodice of her dress became wet with two dark circles. She darted into the house, slamming the door behind her.

Rebecca leaned back in her chair and sat motionless until her heart stopped pounding. Once she gained control of her emotions, she stood up and stared up at the window. Sarah North walked onto the porch and stood next to her. "Please stay and sit down. You have probably figured out the baby is Lilly's. But I ask you to keep it to yourself. Do not tell anyone, even your mother or father."

"Of course."

"Last year when we returned to Philadelphia, we sent her to every expert we could find. She would not let any of them examine her, nor could they persuade her to speak. We even sent her to a hospital in New England so doctors in the field of mental conditions could treat her. She was there three months when they contacted us to tell us she was four months pregnant."

Rebecca swallowed, her eyes welling with tears, but she blinked them back.

Mrs. North paused and took a deep breath. "We were shocked, of course, and brought her home. She was probably raped, but since she won't speak, we have no idea who did this to her. Lilly's baby was born in May. She's a beautiful girl with curly blond hair. At first, Lilly wouldn't even hold or feed her so we bound Lilly's breasts and fed her baby with canned milk. She still leaks now and then when she hears the baby cry. We don't know who the father is—that remains locked in Lilly's heart."

Stunned by what she had just heard, Rebecca's chin quivered and she felt a heaviness in her chest. "Mrs. North, I am so sorry Lilly has gone through this horrible experience. You and the whole family must be upset, too. Should I go to Lilly and the baby, or would that upset her even more?"

"No, my dear, I think it's best if you leave her alone for now. She cries so much of the time. None of her friends in Philadelphia, including Maggie, or her schoolmates know. They think she went abroad for a year and assume the baby is mine." Sarah dabbed her eyes with her handkerchief. "We hoped she would eventually talk when we came here this summer. I know you're very close. Maybe she'll trust you enough to confide in you."

"I hope so, but I must soon return to Baltimore. Please write to me if there is anything I can do to help."

Sarah North gently hugged Rebecca and gave her a brief kiss on the cheek.

Since Rebecca needed time to process what had happened to her friend, she decided to ride home the long way through the foot of the mountains, stopping to sit under a stand of large white pines. A blue jay objected to her presence, squawking loudly as it flew from a tree to the ground in front of her. In contrast, she heard the "chip-per" of a scarlet tanager. She tried to see it but the bird was seldom found in the lower branches of the trees. Not unlike Lilly, seen but not heard.

There was a warm breeze blowing the scent of pine through the woods. She felt herself finally relax, melting into the soft pine needles. She could see movement through the underbrush. It was a roughed grouse, walking out of the green undercover onto a small ridge, followed by a row of chicks. A squirrel approached the chicks tentatively, then aggressively. Mother grouse spread her wings and thumped them on the ground. She chased the squirrel into the brush and quickly came back to her chicks. A male ruffed grouse stood several yards away strutting and puffing up his tail and neck feathers. He appeared to be unconcerned about his chicks as he watched his mate protect his offspring.

Maybe females are stronger after all, especially when it comes to protecting their babies.

But what about when a female can't protect herself?

CHAPTER 54

JUST AS REBECCA WAS PACKING HER SUITCASE, GARY BOUND up the stairs to her bedroom. "You have a letter from Baltimore. Maybe you have a secret admirer. It has a return address:

Dr. Christopher Morgan

Johns Hopkins Hospital

Broadway Street

Baltimore Maryland."

Her mouth fell open but she quickly composed herself and grabbed the envelope. "Get out of here and stop minding my business."

Chuckles bounced off the walls as Gary hopped down the stairs two at a time.

Moving her clothes aside and flopping down on her bed, Rebecca stared at the envelope. Indeed the letter was from Dr. Morgan. Her first thought was that she was being dismissed from nursing school. But when she opened the letter, she looked at the signature first. Christopher Morgan, MD. Her thoughts swirled so quickly she had to take a few deep breaths before reading the letter.

Dear Miss Wagner,

I took the liberty of asking Miss Nutting for your address because I have been concerned about your welfare. Thankfully, you, along with your classmates were given a well-deserved two-week hiatus from nurses' training. I hope you have recovered from your fatigue and are now ready to return to your studies.

It is for that very reason I am suggesting that you may want to receive extra tutoring as you begin your junior year. According to Miss Nutting you are already an excellent student having received prior knowledge from your local physician. I inquired as to your upcoming lectures and would be happy to instruct you further in those given by the following physicians: Dr. Barker—Hygiene (Chemistry of the air, water, disinfection and personal hygiene); and Dr. Futcher—Histology, The Skeleton, and The Glandular System. Also, I spoke to Dr. Livingood. He will be teaching The Physiology of The Circulatory System, The Respiratory System, and The Excretory System. Later your second year, Dr. Camac- is scheduled to teach Materia Medica—medicines and their methods of administration, classifications of drugs, drugs that act on the respiratory, circulatory and excretory systems, and poisons. These subjects are tedious but I am confident that with my help, you will excel. Finally, Dr. Flexner will conduct lectures in Bacteriology and Pathology. I have had the privilege of learning from these doctors and would like to review your notes, as you are able.

Please accept my invitation to call on you so we can discuss my proposal.

Yours sincerely,

Christopher Morgan

Rebecca's gritted her teeth. She was baffled and frightened. What does he mean, call on me?

It was peak harvest time and rain was threatening to flatten the grain that had to be cut, but Gary insisted on taking Rebecca to the train station.

She knew he was probably trying to get out of doing farm work, but Rebecca still thought it strange that Gary was adamant about driving the wagon. They loaded her suitcase and a small satchel with her lunch and tickets in the wagon, while the rest of her family stood nearby. Rebecca hugged her mother, father, and grandmother, and climbed on board. They all spoke at once. "Goodbye." She felt sorry for her mother, who stood with her shoulders slumped and her face pale.

Jane said, "I'll miss you, Rebecca. God be with you and keep you safe."

"I'll miss you too, Ma."

Back So Straight lingered alongside the barn. She placed her hand over her heart, then held it up, palm facing out.

Feeling empty and sad, Rebecca felt her throat constrict. She mouthed goodbye, determined not to cry. "Go, Gary, before I change my mind."

As the wagon drove down the lane, she focused on the sound the wheels made on the dirt road… wheels crunching on rocks and thumping through uneven ground. She turned and waved when they passed the new barn. "Go slowly, Gary. I want to look at the everything one last time." She silently said goodbye to the trees. Then the mountains. And goodbye Ben—just for now, she hoped.

Neither of them spoke until the wagon entered Main Valley Road and passed the last house in McAlisterville. Then Gary said, "I have… to… talk to you."

"What is it? Trouble with our Pa again?"

He shook his head. "No, not this time. It's something else. But first, you must promise not to say a word to anyone."

"I won't. But why so secretive?"

Gary put the reigns of the horse into one hand and wiped his forehead with the other. "I… don't know if I can talk about it."

"Listen. I've seen lots of blood and gore and all sorts of filth and misery. Nothing you tell me will shock me."

Still keeping his eyes on the road ahead, Gary clicked the horse when it slowed. Finally, he said in a low, soft voice, "David and I have been writing to each other all winter. Well, a month ago I received this letter from him—but I'm not sure what it means."

"Do you want me to read it?"

"No. He actually wrote what I think is a poem for me. A poem! What the hell do I know about poetry? I'm not very good at this sort of thing."

Rebecca frowned, not knowing what to think about a man writing a poem to another man.

"I'll... I'll read it to you, but don't be upset."

"I'll try, but you're being mysterious."

He leaned forward and pulled the wrinkled paper out of his pants' pocket. His voice was shaky as he read:

As I sit here in my room and turn down the lamp, the dark moves in.

Is Gary looking at the same stars I see and does he see our sin?

What wonder fills my heart and empties it into the sky above!

My head whirls in confusion and turmoil

But I am mindful only of thoughts of love.

Despite taking a few deep breaths to calm her churning stomach, Rebecca felt slightly nauseated. He was right—she was shocked. She looked at Gary's face for signs of his feelings, but his face was expressionless.

"What is he trying to tell you?"

Gary didn't answer for a long time. He started to cry but quickly composed himself. "I don't know. Should I talk to him and make sure I understand what he means?"

"Do you have feelings for him?"

"I think so. I can't tell him about my feelings in case I'm wrong. I'm scared. You must think I am a pervert. Pop and Ma will disown me. Jake will shoot me. He's already angry that I don't spend more time with him."

Rebecca's tried not to reveal her fear. "Gary, are you telling me that you and David...? I don't... understand... but I won't betray you. My nursing books talk about attraction for someone of the same sex… it's described as a type of mental illness." But she felt confused. Was he mentally ill?

Gary took both reigns and yelled 'git'. The horse tore into a gallop, creating a long cloud of dust behind them.

"Stop. You're going too fast. I want to talk to you." Rebecca grabbed the reigns and pulled them back. Her suitcase and satchel slammed against the back of the wagon. The horse slowed but foam covered her flanks. "I'll stick by you but this can never come out in the open. People will gossip and judge you. Maybe even our family will disown you—and his."

Her brother slumped into the bench.

She turned toward him and took a deep breath, thinking about the times he defended her against Gunther and rescued her and Ben when they were trapped under the surrey. Despite her misgivings about the relationship between her brother and David, she couldn't abandon him. In a gentle, soft voice, she said, "I don't know how to help you. But I want you to know you can always come to me. Just think long and hard about you and David. Perhaps the best thing you can do is get over this idea of love and not see each other ever again."

The tears that Gary managed to hold back spilled to the surface. Rebecca stopped the wagon and put her arm around him. He jerked away and wiped his nose with his sleeve.

Rebecca drove the wagon the rest of the way to Mifflintown. Neither of them spoke. But Rebecca still had more questions than answers. What will happen if Gary and David continue to care for each other? Or if they're seen… kissing or something else?

The shock of that possibility made her nauseated again.

When they reached the train station, Gary retrieved her belongings and carried them to the walkway.

Rebecca pushed her fears aside and touched her brother on the shoulder. This time he didn't pull away. "Goodbye, Gary. I still care about you. You're my brother."

CHAPTER 55

"I'M SO GLAD TO SEE YOU, REBECCA. DID YOU HAVE A NICE vacation?" Bertha stood in front of the door to their room, took Rebecca's suitcase, and hugged her.

"Yes, I did but it was over too soon."

Gracie said, "I didn't want to come back to school, but then I changed my mind. I didn't want to waste the whole year I already spent working so hard to pass."

Sitting at her desk with her back turned, Maude kept her face in the book she was reading. "Not me. I couldn't wait to return. I missed working in the wards with the doctors."

The next morning the day began with lectures by Dr. Barker. Rebecca remembered that name from Dr. Morgan's letter. She took careful notes but he spoke so fast she had difficulty keeping up. "Chemistry of the air: The influence of its various constituents on the animal body... the alterations on the surrounding atmosphere through respiration... the pollution of the air from various sources."

Each week the lectures became more numerous and difficult. The only ones she found easier were "Anatomy and Physiology" by Dr. Futcher, thanks to Dr. Headings' medical books. Rebecca thought about the letter from Dr. Morgan and his offer to help her and wondered when he would contact her.

Rebecca's training also required her to learn housekeeping skills first, even though head nurses and supervisors made it very clear her future depended on separating herself from the hospital's domestics. Students were instructed to use tact and firmness in dealing with orderlies and maids, and not become too familiar with them—in contrast to the way she saw the Norths and the Eastmans treat their hired help.

Practice. Practice more: how to make beds with hospital corners and no wrinkles—with sheets that were starched and difficult to keep tucked in under the thin mattress. How to wash instruments: use hot water and lye soap that made her hands red and raw, rinse with scalding water and wrap them in clean muslin. How to turn a patient using a sheet: un-tuck the sheet and draw the patient toward you, then hold the patient while you tuck a pillow under the back and shoulders to keep him or her from rolling back. How to bathe a woman: modesty is paramount; make sure all body parts are covered except the one you are washing. How to bathe a man: be especially careful to avoid all suggestion of impropriety. Wash all body parts except genitals and buttocks; then instruct patient to wash those himself or call an orderly to finish. Never, never touch male genitalia.

The days melted into a mix of work, study, eat, and sleep, one after another. The numbing struggle to remember rules, procedures, protocols, and body systems fed her growing fear she would make a mistake and be dismissed. Coupled with self-doubt was her overwhelming homesickness. Rebecca was starved for her family, for Back So Straight, for the farm, and when she thought about Ben, the idea of two years ahead of her before she could even think about marrying him seemed like thirty. After days of relentless fatigue, she admitted to herself that she must have been crazy for thinking she wanted to do something besides become a wife and take care of a house and family.

But a sense of obligation to Mr. North sobered her. How could she disappoint him? And Dr. Headings. They believed in her. She had to keep trying no matter how homesick she was or how mind-and body-numbing her days were. Quitting was not possible.

Her first opportunity to write home came early fall after a week of blistering heat. Rebecca retreated to the library and opened a window where the breeze gave her new hope.

Dear Ma,

It was hard to return to nurses' training but I knew I had to try. Please forgive me for not writing very much. I work long days at the hospital but I will try to do better in the future. There is so much I want to tell you. First, I am faring well, but I feel the load of caring for the patients getting heavier every day. The weather is finally cooler after weeks of stifling heat caused me to perspire profusely in my starched uniform. My roommates and I get along, all except one who continues to try my patience. Right now I am learning to make perfectly smooth beds, make bandages, and wash instruments. I do more cleaning than I did on the farm, including mucking the stalls. My studies are difficult, but my roommate Bertha and I do our schoolwork together and help each other memorize the information. I wish there was more study of anatomy and physiology. It comes easier because of what I learned from Dr. Headings' medical books. Please tell him I send my gratitude for trusting me with his precious volumes. Sometimes we students seem to be evaluated more on the tidiness of the room than the care of our patients. I think it should be the other way around. But I have learned, after much struggle, to be quiet and follow the rules. Doctors give orders and we follow them, no questions allowed. Not at all like Dr. Headings. I am trying to adjust to the food but sorely miss your cooking. It hasn't gotten any better this year. Most of it is mushy as cornmeal or tastes like slop we fed to the pigs. What I would give for some scrapple and summer bologna, shoofly pie, and a glass of your meadow tea, I cannot say. I miss the woods and the mountains. There are some trees here, mainly chestnut, and colorful birds, but the crows are very noisy. They remind me of the ones that sat on the hemlock tree by my bedroom window. Every time I hear them talk to each other, I think about the farm. I even miss the smell of manure! Everything in the hospital still smells like bodies or disinfectants. I try to remember the smell of bacon and pine logs in the cabin when I wake up in the morning, but the sweetness is not here. When I close my eyes at night, I imagine opening my bedroom window and seeing the moon behind the hemlock tree and sniffing the leafy ground after a rain. How is Back So Straight? I miss her, too. I wish I could talk to her about the herbs and leaves she uses instead of the strong medicines that sometimes make the patients sicker. Be sure to tell her.

I must go now. My eyes are heavy and I will have to rise again in only a few hours.

Love,

Rebecca

Weeks passed. October, then early November. More daily cleaning. More instructions on conduct and character. More lessons on cleanliness and order, how to keep a proper linen closet, and how to write nurses' notes. And most importantly, how to obey doctors.

Each time Rebecca saw a doctor walk into the nurses' station, she was required to stand up and offer him her stool. This rule was not to be violated. It wasn't unusual for Rebecca to give up her seat so often she fell behind in her charting, making it necessary for her to explain to her superiors why she needed more time.

She soon settled into a routine: work, eat, sleep. Repeat. She worked harder than she ever did on the farm. She was assigned to care for children with polio, mumps, measles, diphtheria, whooping cough, dog bites, and accidents that gave them bruises, burns, and abrasions. And old people with strokes… immigrants who spoke Italian, Russian, Swedish, Irish brogue,

German… colored folks with fear in their eyes. Most were poor people… people nobody wanted.

Some of the doctors were rude and authoritarian. One particular doctor demanded that Rebecca drop what she was doing and get bandages or other supplies for him. He insisted she worked too slowly and singled her out whenever he saw her in the wards. No matter how hard Rebecca tried, she couldn't please him. On one particularly busy day after placing dirty bedsheets down a laundry chute he stood in front of her, his hands on his hips and his face nearly up against hers.

"You're mulatto, aren't you?"

"What do you mean?"

"Sure you do. You're part colored, aren't you?"

"No. I'm not. I grew up on a farm in the middle of Pennsylvania. I never even saw a colored person." But then she thought of the servants at the mansions back in McAlisterville. She quickly walked toward the end of the ward.

He followed her down the hallway and spun her around. Putting his arms on either side of her shoulders, he trapped her against the wall. "Yes, you are. At least you don't have big lips."

"I have work to do." She tried to duck underneath his arms but he pressed himself against her.

"Let me go."

"Why should I?"

"I don't want to make trouble."

Sneering, he leaned close to her and whispered in her ear. "You're already trouble."

"Please, let me go."

"Maybe this time." He walked several steps away before turning around and smiling.

Miss Nutting appeared around the corner. "Is something the matter, Miss Wagner?"

Rebecca stifled a gasp, terrified she had been seen with a doctor standing questionably close to her. "No, Miss Nutting. I… I'm fine."

"Something went on here, I'm sure of it. I'll let it go this time. But it better not happen again, Miss Wagner. Now, get on with your work and stop dawdling."

"Yes, Ma'am." Rebecca hurried to the linen closet and shut the door. Her hands shook and she fought back tears. Another Gunther Drupp. She wondered if Miss Nutting heard what Dr. Ames had said. Or what he did. But she didn't dare to ask.

"I don't know how to act around him. You know the doctor I mean… he's very short and has a full beard… and he smells like tobacco smoke."

Gracie pulled herself up to her full height and pointed a finger at Rebecca. "I know who he is. One time he brushed against my breasts on purpose when I was carrying a bucket of water. Sneered at me and laughed."

"He did?"

Bertha took her apron off and plopped on her bed. Her eyes darted toward Rebecca. "That's disgusting. I'd ask my father to talk to him but I doubt he would agree. One doctor telling another doctor what to do and what not to do… that would be unheard of. You could report him to Miss Nutting, you know."

"Do you think anyone will believe me instead of Dr. Ames? I'll be punished, not him."

"There's nothing we can do about this," said Gracie.

Bertha frowned. "But we can look out for each other if he's around."

They all agreed except Maude. "I can't do that, Rebecca."

"Why?"

"I don't want to get on the bad side of him or any of the doctors."

Rebecca chewed on her lip and looked directly at Maude. "Maybe someday a doctor will do something to humiliate you."

She said in a very subdued voice, "That's better than being ignored."

Rebecca felt the weight of Maude's confession fall on her shoulders. Surely Maude knows she's homely, skinny, and has crooked teeth… and she must know others see her imperfections and judge her unworthy of their attention. Rebecca decided she would not be one of them.

CHAPTER 56

REBECCA TRIED HER BEST TO AVOID DR. AMES WHENEVER she could. But sometimes he snickered when he passed her in the wards, or mumbled something under his breath. She felt helpless to do anything to stop him from harassing her. When one of her coworkers was nearby, he treated her with indifference. But when no one was around, he bumped her shoulder and called her 'Mulatto'.

She felt powerless. His belittling undermined her confidence and made her unsure of whether she was worthy of belonging in the school. Rebecca questioned what made him accuse her of being part colored. Sure her skin was slightly browner than most women, but no one had ever commented about it. After all, she was a farm girl… a mountain girl, and spent lots of time outside in the sun.

But he was relentless, subjecting Rebecca to slight after slight, always when he found her away from patients or other nurses. She was grateful the majority of doctors treated her fairly, or simply ignored her unless they needed her help. Maude was wrong. Being ignored was better than being harassed.

Several weeks after the incident with Dr. Ames, Rebecca, and Bertha sat in the library studying when another student walked into the room, and said, "Miss Wagner, you have a visitor."

Rebecca turned her head to the side and frowned. "Who could be visiting me? I don't know anybody in Baltimore."

The student broke out in a big smile and motioned for her to come. "Well, he must know you."

There in the living room stood a tall, handsome man, his body tilting toward Rebecca as she drew nearer. "Hello, Miss Wagner. Do you remember me?"

"I'm not sure. Are you the doctor who helped me when I…? I fainted?"

"Yes. I also wrote to you a few months ago about your academic progress."

Rebecca's cheeks flushed red. "I did receive your letter. Thank you."

A slow, deep smile spread across his face. "I hope you don't think it too bold of me, but I came by today to ask you if you would like to go for a carriage ride while we discuss my proposal."

The student standing nearby giggled.

"Excuse me, Miss, but I wish to speak to Miss Wagner alone."

"Oh, yes. I'm sorry." She slowly walked away, looking over her shoulder as she left the room.

"Now. Where were we? I was asking if you would like to go for a ride with me to talk about your studies."

Rebecca was at a loss for words. She stood wide-eyed, staring at the handsome man before she gained her composure. "I… I guess that would be acceptable."

"Very good. My carriage is just outside. "

"One moment, please. I must go to my room and get a coat. Shall I bring my books along?"

"No, not this time. I want to discuss things further before we delve into your studies."

Rebecca smoothed her dress and nodded, but as she walked to the library, she wondered if she should bring them anyway. No, she decided, better to wait.

Astounded and nervous, Rebecca said to Bertha, "You are never going to believe who has asked me to take a carriage ride. Dr. Morgan."

Her roommate's hand flew up to her mouth. "Oh, my. Are you going to go with him?"

"I told him yes. Do you think I should?"

"Of course. He's a resident doctor."

"But are we allowed?"

"I don't know any rules as long as you're back by curfew."

Rebecca sighed deeply. "I'm going to take my books to our room and get my coat. Then I'm leaving. Please don't say anything about this, although another student saw me with Dr. Morgan."

"Don't worry. Tongues will wag no matter what we do to avoid them. Go and have a nice time."

The doctor's face brightened when Rebecca returned to the living room. He extended his arm, and said, "May I?"

Hoping he wouldn't feel her trembling, she put her arm through his. He took her hand and helped her onto the carriage seat. Oh, my. This carriage was just like the one Ben's family made except for the yellow paint.

Dr. Morgan covered her legs, then his own, with a finely woven plaid wool blanket. "Are you warm enough? The sun has warmed the air a little, but I don't want you to be chilled."

She stroked the fine wool of the blanket, and said, "Actually, I love the outdoors and don't get a chance to enjoy it very often."

"That's good, because I do too." He clicked the horse and looked ahead. "Miss Wagner, would you like me to show you some of the unique buildings near here? There is also an iconic church I would like you to see. It sports the most beautiful gothic architecture in the city and can be seen for miles around."

"That would be lovely. I only got to see Baltimore on my way to and from school and the few blocks surrounding the hospital buildings."

"Well, we'll see to that."

She turned away from him and pretended to look at the passing scenery. What could he possibly mean by we'll see to that?

The horse trotted slowly down McElderry Street, then to Jefferson and made a right turn onto Orleans.

Rebecca looked from side to side and up at the nearby buildings. The breeze was cool but refreshing. She gazed at houses and shops and people walking in the streets, then at the horse, a handsome chestnut gelding with a white patches on his rump that looked like puffy clouds. For a moment, she imagined herself riding Jenny.

"What are you thinking, Miss Wagner?"

Startled by his voice, she said, "Oh… I was just remembering something." She wasn't ready to reveal her thoughts. "Some of these homes and buildings are beautiful."

"Yes, they are. One of my favorites is the Norman-Gothic Mount Vernon Place Methodist Church. My father knows the architects Dixon and Carson. It's actually not too far from my family home in Mount Vernon Place."

The carriage passed the towering structure. Rebecca couldn't take her eyes off the spiraling towers and arched entrances to the multi-roofed building that occupied an entire city block. Further on, they rode past the Enoch Pratt Central Library on Carriage Street. After they passed the main structure, Rebecca turned her head and stared at the massive buildings until they reached the end of the block. When she looked back at Dr. Morgan, he was smiling.

"I'm glad you are enjoying yourself, Miss Wagner."

Rebecca smiled back. But she was uncertain about what to say. She had never seen buildings like these and didn't want to appear unsophisticated about architecture or libraries, or churches for that matter.

"Would you like to stop at the park? We can walk a little bit to keep warm."

Relieved he didn't ask her anything about city structures, she said, "Yes, that would be fine."

Dr. Morgan drove the carriage at a fast clip until they approached an area with footpaths under large chestnut and oak trees. A few held on to rusty-colored leaves, but most were bare.

"Let me help you down." The doctor took Rebecca's hand and steadied her as she stepped down from the carriage. "Your hands are cold. Here put on my gloves." Before she could protest, he stripped his gloves and placed them one a time on her hands. They were made of soft tan rawhide and lined with rabbit fur. "Now, doesn't that feel better?"

She opened and closed her fingers and felt the soft fur against her hands. "They feel wonderful. Thank you for your kindness. But now your hands will be cold instead of mine."

"I can put them in my pockets." He lifted up the flaps of his long, wool, camel-colored coat and stuck his hands inside, leaving his thumbs resting on the edges of the openings.

They walked along the dirt path with browned shrubs and plants on either side until they came to a small pond. Rebecca bent down to look in the water and saw her reflection along with Dr. Morgan's. He's such a handsome man. And so kind. She wished she could dip her hand in the water just like she would if she were at the farm.

"Do you think there are fish in here?"

"There are. Some sort of small fish with a flat body and bluish-colored sides."

"They sound like bluegills. We have them at the farm pond. And some bass… they feed on the bluegills."

Dr. Morgan turned to Rebecca, his eyes open wide. "So, you come from a farm?"

She drew back from the water and hesitated before answering. "Yes, Dr. Morgan. We… grow crops and… have some animals. But we also own about 700 acres of wooded mountain land, too." She didn't want to tell him they raised pigs and chickens. "And we have two horses, one of which is mine."

The doctor stood closer, his eyes searching her face. "Please… call me Christopher. And may I call you Rebecca?"

"Of course. I'm getting a little cold. Could we walk now?"

Christopher nodded and held out his arm. "I guess you're wondering why I asked you to spend the afternoon with me."

"Well, you did mention in your letter that you wanted to tutor me in the sciences. I do pretty well in all of them except Materia Medica. I have to work hard to remember the classifications and all the drugs in each. Dr. Camac is very thorough but I have trouble with the dosages and weights."

Dr. Morgan smiled widely, his grin reaching up to his blue eyes. "Interesting you should say that. Dr. Camac taught me too. He's tough but fair. I'm willing to go over your notes the next time we meet." Christopher took her gloved hand and held it in his. "Would you be free next Sunday?"

Rebecca felt a tingling down her spine, the same sensation she felt when she met Ben. "I… guess that would be all right. Shall I bring my notes from every lecture or just the ones I don't quite understand? For example, drugs that work on the circulatory system. Like Digitalis."

"That would be a good start." He released her hand and brought his cold ones to his mouth, blew on them, and rubbed them together. "It's getting colder. Would it be acceptable for you to go with me for some hot cocoa?"

"I would love that." She was also getting hungry but was too shy to say so. After they walked back to the carriage, Christopher took hold of her elbow and guided her onto the seat. As soon as she was seated, he took the blanket and covered her legs. Then he took another matching blanket and draped it over her shoulders. When his arm touched her back, he paused, and looked across at her face. The doctor grinned widely, leaving his arm linger a moment before he withdrew it and grabbed the reins. He clicked the horse into a trot.

Rebecca felt a sense of wonder. Did he treat everyone with such courtesy and care? A blanket across her legs and shoulders. Asking about her preferences.

The ride through town gave Rebecca another chance to look at downtown Baltimore and the people who lived there—men in heavy coats and top hats, and women in sleek coats cinched in at the waist with matching bonnets. The horse trotted swiftly along street after street. She snuggled under the blankets and tucked her gloved hands underneath.

When the carriage neared Orleans Street, Christopher said, "I know this delightful little French pastry shop near the hospital. They serve delicious hot cocoa, cream puffs—and their specialty is soda cracker pie. Will you allow me to indulge you before we return?"

Rebecca didn't want appear too eager, even though she was cold and starved. "Well, if you insist, it does sound nice."

They entered the small door with a bell tied to the curtain. Christopher greeted the small woman behind a case of pastries. She came around to the front and seated them at an intricately made metal table with tiny matching chairs. White crocheted doilies covered the tabletop.

Dr. Morgan ordered a sample plate of pastries, a small soda cracker pie and two cups of hot chocolate with miniature marshmallows floating on top. "Do try as many as you would like." He blew on his hands and wrapped them around the dainty cup. Rebecca marveled at his long, slender fingers with perfectly groomed fingernails.

She and Christopher sat tasting the pastries and sipping from their dainty cups until the plate was nearly empty. "These are truly delicious."

After the doctor cut the pie, he placed a small piece on Rebecca's plate. She took a bite, savoring the sweet-salty taste. "This is my favorite. Much lighter than our pies at the farm."

"I would like to know more about your life on the farm, Rebecca. If you will allow, I will come to call again next Sunday at about two. Bring your notes from Dr. Camac and we can review them right here. The proprietress is a friend of mine and won't mind us sitting here for a few hours."

Rebecca was speechless. She pressed her fingers to her lips.

"Does that mean no?" Christopher cocked his head and frowned.

"No. I mean yes."

CHAPTER 57

BERTHA WAS WAITING IN THEIR ROOM WHEN REBECCA arrived back at the nurses' home. "Well, hello. How was your time with the doctor?"

Gracie chimed in, "Yes, tell us all about it."

Rebecca took off her coat and flopped on her bed. "It was wonderful. He took me on a carriage ride to see all kinds of beautiful buildings… and then we took a walk in a park… and then we had hot cocoa and pastries… and then… "Then what?" Bertha grinned and bent her head forward, her eyes opened wide.

"He asked me to go to the pastry shop again next Sunday. We're going to study my Material Medica notes from Dr. Camac."

Bertha looked at Gracie and they both burst out laughing.

"That's the truth. It really is."

Gracie laughed again, so hard she snorted.

Rebecca couldn't help but chortle too. She got up and hugged them, squeezing her eyes shut and patting them on the back. When she opened them, she said, "I see Maude's not here. Where is she, Bertha?"

"We don't know. She never came to dinner."

"That's not the first time. I wonder where she goes?" said Gracie.

Rebecca answered, “Well, let’s not worry. At least she stopped stealing our belongings. Right now we need to study for tomorrow’s lectures.”

The three student nurses lay on the beds, stomach down and facing each other, and took turns reading aloud. At nine o’clock, Miss Nutting knocked on their door and said, “Lights out, ladies.”

Bertha whispered, “Maude’s not here yet. What should we do?”

“I don’t know. Maybe we should tell Miss Nutting,” Rebecca answered.

“No, let’s go to bed. Maybe she went home or something happened we don’t know about. I’m tired and need my sleep.” Bertha quietly changed into her nightgown, washed her face, placed her uniform on her chair for the next day and crawled into bed. Gracie did the same. But Rebecca lay sleepless on her bed thinking about Christopher and their afternoon together. Then her thoughts turned to Ben. What would he think about her studying with Dr. Morgan? And going to a pastry shop? And him asking her to do it again?

After about an hour or two, she got ready for bed and drifted off to sleep. But she bolted up in bed when she heard Gracie whisper. “Shhhh. Do you hear that noise?”

A soft tapping sound came from the window near Maude’s bed. Rebecca got up and placed her forehead against the glass. “It’s Maude.”

Maude mouthed, “Open.”

Not sure what to do, Rebecca unlatched the lock and slid the bottom sash open. Maude crawled through and quickly closed it. Her jersey blouse was unbuttoned at the neck and her skirt wrinkled. She smoothed back her black hair and rubbed her hand over her lips.

“Where were you?” Rebecca asked.

“None of your business. Just out.”

Bertha trudged up to Maude, and said, “Yes, it is our business. You broke curfew and might have gotten us all in trouble.”

“If you must know, I was out with Dr. Kent.”

“What do you mean by out?”

“Having fun.”

“Do you expect us to believe that?”

"Why wouldn't you?"

"You haven't been honest with us before."

Maude crossed her arms over her chest and stepped back. "I was a guest in his room in the doctor's quarters, if you must know."

"What were you doing in his room?"

"That's between Dr. Kent and me."

Rebecca stomped her foot on the floor. "Listen to me, Maude. First you stole from us and lied when we caught you. Now you expect us to let you sneak around without any consequence?"

"But… I… we…"

"What? Did you… sleep with him?"

"That's… that's none of your business."

"You did, didn't you? You're not even engaged! We should tell Miss Nutting."

Maude collapsed on her bed. "Please don't. You don't know what it's like to be homely. Men look at you and then turn away. I want to be attractive to someone… even if it means what you think it means." She sobbed into her pillow and curled up like a small child.

It was true. Rebecca had never experienced rejection in that way. Sure some boys and men made rude remarks behind her back, but they were usually about her being smart or stuck-up. Others stared at her breasts or rear-end when they thought she wasn't looking. But as far as she could tell, no man ever turned away from her.

Maybe this poor, unattractive girl just wanted to be loved.

CHAPTER 58

NEARLY EVERY SUNDAY WAS A REPEAT OF THEIR FIRST ONE, blankets and all, only now Dr. Morgan took her directly to the pastry shop. Again, the proprietress showed them to a small private table near the back of the store. When Christopher ordered a plate of pastries, along with small finger sandwiches, hot cocoa, and soda cracker pie, the lady smiled and nodded.

While waiting for their treats, Rebecca showed him her notes from Materia Medica. He nodded and commented about the thoroughness and accuracy of her notes, and occasionally added a brief suggestion on how to convert measurements into the metric system.

They paused now and then between pages to sip cocoa and eat. After an hour or two, Christopher stopped eating and commenting. Rebecca looked up from her notebook and saw that he was staring at her. She bit her lip before gathering the courage to speak. "Is there something wrong with my computations, Christopher?"

"No, they're all correct. But there's something I must tell you."

She drew back and sat on the edge of her chair. "What is it?"

He smiled widely. "I really didn't want to review your notes. You are perfectly capable of doing this work without my help. The reason I wrote to you last summer is because I wanted to see you and didn't want to take the chance you would refuse."

Rebecca felt the blood rush to her face and hoped he wouldn't see her blush. "But that was months ago."

"I know. But I was very involved in my residency training with Dr. Osler and had to put that first. Now I have the time and want to spend it with you."

Rebecca grew very still but her heart pulsed in her chest. "I… I don't know what to say. I enjoy your company…"

"That's all I need you to say. Please forgive me for not being entirely forward with my intentions. I hope you'll consider me a suitor. I know we have limited time as we pursue our training but it would be my great pleasure to see you again and as much as I can."

Guilt became her constant companion. Rebecca looked forward to their excursions together, more than she dared to admit. Her feelings for Ben were still strong but faded a little each time Christopher and she were together. The question that loomed foremost in her mind was this: should she tell Christopher about Ben and vice versa?

So she decided to wait until she had the answer.

Sundays became their regular day together. Christopher and Rebecca went to the library, and the one after that to an organ concert at the Mount Vernon Place Methodist Church. The weather was cold, so Christopher hired a driver to take them from place to place in a closed carriage. They sat close together under thick woolen blankets to keep warm. Rebecca loved it when he put his arm around her and drew her close. Afterwards, on the drive back to the nurses' residence they talked about challenging medical diagnoses and new treatments. They told funny stories about patients that made them laugh until their sides hurt.

Later, as she lay in bed, Rebecca thought about Christopher, this handsome, worldly, exciting man. Then Ben. Wonderful, kind, sweet Ben. Was it possible to love two men at the same time?

A week later, Rebecca finished her work on the ward and went to her mailbox. She was surprised to find a letter and a small card. Her breath caught in her chest as she read the letter's return address: Ben Siebert, Main Street, Mifflinburg, Pennsylvania. Then she looked at the card: Dorothea Susan Morgan, Mount Vernon Place, Baltimore Maryland.

She ran to the parlor and sat on a wicker chair. Her hands fumbled with the envelopes. Which to open first? She opened the letter from Ben.

Dearest Rebecca,

I went to the farm last week on my way to deliver a new wagon. Like usual, your Ma asked me to stay for lunch. It was the best ham with new potatoes and green beans I ever tasted. After I ate until my stomach hurt, I took a walk to the front meadow. I remember sitting there with you and talking about everything we hoped to do before we grew old. I can still see you sitting there, your hair blowing in the wind, stray strands sneaking out the sides of your bonnet touching your checks, your hand trying to brush them out of your eyes.

I drove the wagon on the roads near your farm and through McAlisterville, remembering the places we walked together. I saw the big tree where we had our picnics, and thought about the time I kissed you for the first time. Everything here reminds me of you. I miss you more than you can imagine. I don't know if I can stand being away from you much longer. Even my work in the carriage shop doesn't keep my mind occupied. It always comes back to you, Rebecca. I wait for your letters every day. I know you are busy so I am trying to be patient. I hope you are doing well in your studies, but I wish you were here instead of in Baltimore.

Love,

Ben

Rebecca glanced around the room as if searching for wisdom. She blinked rapidly to stall the tears that formed under her eyelids. Should she tell him about Christopher? But no answers came. Only silence—and a hollow feeling in the pit of her stomach.

The second fancy envelope contrasted the plain envelope from Ben's letter. Rebecca carefully broke the wax seal beneath the letters DSM on the flap, not sure what she would find inside and pulled out two notes. The top one was a small piece of paper with the following:

Rebecca, enclosed is an invitation to our families' Thanksgiving dinner. Our coachman will pick you up at eleven thirty. Please wear a formal dress.

I look forward to spending the holiday with you.

Fondly,

Christopher

The second note was heavier and made of ivory-colored linen paper with fine fringes on the edges.

Rebecca Wagner

Your presence as a guest of our son, Doctor Christopher A. Morgan II, is requested for dinner at President McKinley's newly declared Thanksgiving Day to take place at 793 Mount Vernon Place, Baltimore, Maryland on Thursday, November 30, 1899 at the home of Doctor Christopher A. Morgan I and Dorothea Susan Morgan at Twelve O'clock Noon.

Your acceptance is eagerly anticipated.

Dorothea Susan Morgan

Rebecca wasn't sure she wanted to accept this unexpected invitation. Christopher had told her his father was a physician and her mother an important member of the hospital auxiliary. She wondered if her table manners were good enough and whether she spoke enough proper English to hold an intelligent conversation. But finally, her fondness for Christopher and sense of curiosity convinced her to go.

She planned to wear the white dress Lilly and Maggie had given her. It was her only dress fancy enough to wear to such an occasion. To make it more fashionable, she added some ecru lace and pink bows around the neck and bodice. She had seen a dress almost like it at the organ concert several weeks ago. The dress fit her perfectly now that she had gained back the weight she had lost earlier in the year.

Rebecca pulled the dress off the wooden hanger and held it up to her body. She smiled, remembering the day her friends Lilly and Maggie had given it to her and the day she wore it to the Grange Hall and met Ben. She felt guilty about accepting the invitation and wearing the white dress, but she wanted to look her best, not like the farm girl she really was.

CHAPTER 59

On Thanksgiving Day, a large, handsome coach with leather seats pulled up to the nurses' residence. Rebecca greeted a footman when he came to the door. He walked her to the coach. An arm reached the door handle from inside the coach and threw it open. A familiar voice greeted her. "Rebecca. Happy Thanksgiving."

"Christopher! I'm glad I don't have to travel to your home alone."

"I wanted to surprise you. Carter, please help her in the coach."

Rebecca lifter her dress and coat and sat beside him. He took her hand and squeezed it. "Glad to see you have gloves on."

"I borrowed them from my roommate. She has beautiful clothes."

"Her father's a doctor, isn't he?"

"Yes. She told me she wanted to be a doctor too, but her father doesn't believe women should be physicians." Rebecca immediately regretted telling Christopher about Bertha, not sure what he would think of the idea of women doctors.

"Well, I suppose that would be possible if she would apply to Johns Hopkins. Her father may be able to sway the hospital board to accept her."

Rebecca recoiled at his remark. "She's smart enough to be accepted on her own. Anyway, she's almost half way through her nursing studies and is right behind me in class standing."

Christopher laughed. "I don't doubt that in the least if she's half as bright as you are."

Rebecca relaxed and settled back in her seat. They talked about their families.

Christopher told her about going to private schools and that he always wanted to be a doctor like his father. That he had a younger brother who was a bit rebellious growing up and they weren't particularly close. But when Rebecca asked him if he had courted other women, he laughed and said, "None worthy of mentioning, until you."

Not sure if that was a compliment or a way of avoiding the question, she hoped he would have asked her the same question. Trouble was, she didn't know if she would have answered it, just like he refused to do.

After an awkward silence, Christopher squeezed her hand, and said, "Now let's talk about Thanksgiving dinner. This is new for all of us. I must warn you, my mother and father can be intimidating. Don't let that fool you. They're very nice people who happen to have grown up with privilege."

Rebecca frowned. "How about you, Christopher? It appears as though you've grown up with privilege."

He looked at her with wide-open eyes. "I guess I have, but I hope you won't hold that against me."

"Of course not. You've been nothing but kind to me. I just feel uncomfortable around people who are arrogant or mean because of their wealth or position."

Christopher's face wrinkled up. Then it softened. "You're amazing, Rebecca. You're so innocent but worldly at the same time… always sticking up for what you believe in. I admire that about you."

She smiled. But her mind was on Dr. Ames and his remark about her being a mulatto.

The coach rode up a slight hill before lurching to a stop. The footman opened the door. Christopher took her hand and led her between a row of holly bushes that formed a curved pathway. A colored butler opened the front door of a large Victorian mansion and showed them to the drawing room where

Christopher's mother and father were seated holding gold-rimmed stemmed glasses filled with red wine.

"Good afternoon, mother and father. May I present Miss Rebecca Wagner from Pennsylvania? Rebecca, I want you to meet my mother Mrs. Dorothea Morgan and my father Dr. Christopher Morgan the second."

Rebecca curtsied slightly. "I'm very pleased to meet you, Dr. and Mrs. Morgan. It's so kind of you to include me in your Thanksgiving celebration."

"Not at all. Please be seated," Mrs. Morgan said, as she motioned Rebecca to sit on a very small, straight, velvet chair. Rebecca glanced around the room, her eyes sweeping past the paisley wallpaper and windows covered with dark green tapestry curtains tied back with silk tassels. Shelves on two sides of the fireplace were lined with figurines, vases, and sculptures. Large potted plants sat in front of each long window. Wide crown moldings, chair railing, and trim around the doors and windows shined with glossy wood grain. Rebecca tried to stay calm but she felt her pulse in her temples. She had never seen anything this opulent in her life.

Finally, Christopher's father spoke. "Miss Wagner, where in Pennsylvania do you come from?"

"A small town called McAlisterville, about 60 miles northwest of the capital, Harrisburg. I grew up on a farm along with my younger brother."

"How did you get accepted at Johns Hopkins? My son told me you are a second-year nursing student."

Her heart beat even faster. "Yes… I… a physician and an attorney recommended and sponsored me."

"You are a very fortunate woman, my dear. I hope you are proving worthy of their generosity?"

"I am, sir, I… I can assure you," trying to stay composed and looking directly at the elder Dr. Morgan.

Christopher said, "Rebecca is an outstanding nurse, father. My colleagues agree."

Rebecca thought Christopher seemed nervous as he spoke, not the easy, relaxed person he was with her.

The room grew quiet but not for long.

"Well, well, big brother. Whom do we have here?"

"Rebecca, I'd like you to meet Michael, my brother. Michael, this is Miss Rebecca Wagner."

The young man bowed slightly as he greeted his brother's new companion. "Pleased to meet you, Miss Wagner. Glad you could join us for Thanksgiving." He was shorter than Christopher, but had the same light hair and blue eyes. His arms filled out his shirt and his legs showed muscles beneath his trousers when he sat down opposite Rebecca. He casually crossed his legs and stared at her for a longer time than Rebecca thought was polite.

"Nice to make your acquaintance, Mr. Morgan." Rebecca remembered Christopher saying that when he met a gentleman at the library, and thought she would say it when she met someone new. She had hardly finished her response when the butler announced that dinner was served.

Throughout dinner, Christopher's mother peppered her with questions. "So you are in your second year in the new nursing school. Exactly what do you do at the hospital?"

"I attend lectures on various medical subjects and work on the wards to assist the doctors in taking care of the patients."

Dorothea Morgan slowly lowered her fork, and turning to Christopher said, "Is that where you met Rebecca?"

"Yes, it is. She was working on the men's medical ward at the time."

Mrs. Morgan's face flushed. "Oh, dear, do you have to do very dirty work on the wards? Doesn't that bother you?"

Rebecca wasn't sure how to answer, but she decided to be honest. "Not usually. The operating room was the hardest. I was raised on a farm, so I'm used to dirty things. Besides, someone has to take care of the patients no matter how difficult it is."

Michael glanced sideways at Rebecca, then turned to his mother and winked. "Mother, it's obvious that Miss Rebecca is dedicated to her work or she wouldn't have chosen her profession."

Mrs. Morgan's face became pinched, her eyes narrowing.

Dr. Morgan looked at his wife, a weak smile on his face. "Now, now, Dorothea, Miss Wagner's probably hungry. Why don't we let her enjoy her food?"

Christopher's mother opened her mouth to say something, but stopped. She did not look up from her plate.

Although the food was exquisitely prepared and served on silver plates with crystal stemware surrounding every setting, Rebecca hardly touched her food. She was too nervous to eat and the Morgans kept asking questions.

"What exactly do you raise on your farm, Miss Wagner?" Christopher's brother asked as he sipped a glass of wine.

"Mostly everything. Wheat, oats, barley and hay, plus a small plot of tobacco. And of course, a large vegetable garden and some fruit trees." By now, Rebecca was tired of pretending to apologize for being brought up on a farm.

Dr. Morgan senior followed. "Do you have any animals?"

"We do. Milk cows, pigs, chickens, and ducks, and two horses."

Christopher turned his attention to his brother. "Michael, how are your studies coming along? Are you applying yourself or doing your best at attending every party you can?"

Michael broke out in a smile. "No need to ask, brother dear."

Rebecca listened as Michael and Christopher bantered back and forth until a colored maid announced dessert was being served. Fancy pastries, chocolate éclairs, lemon tart, candied fruits, and sugared pecans were served on clear pale green plates covered with paper dollies. Hardly anyone ate them except Michael.

Rebecca was relieved when dinner was over. She was tense and exhausted. "I need to be getting back to the hospital, Christopher. Nice to meet you, Michael. Thank you so very much for including me in your family dinner, Dr. and Mrs. Morgan."

"You are very welcome, my dear. Do take care of yourself." Mrs. Morgan smiled, but her cheeks barely moved.

CHAPTER 60

THE DAYS AFTER MEETING CHRISTOPHER'S FAMILY WERE filled with doubts and anxiety. Nights were even worse. Sleep was difficult and fraught with dreams. Dreams of making a mistake when she was with Christopher. Dreams of being tossed aside when he realized how uncultured she was. Yes, he was kind and attentive, but Rebecca realized the contrast in their upbringing. He was cultured and came from a prominent family. Much like Lilly and Maggie. From what she could tell, money was no object. Yes, she was accepted… even welcome in their homes, but this was different. Christopher was a doctor. His father was a doctor. His mother was prominent in the hospital community.

And there were dreams about Ben. Her first love. His tenderness and kindness. He lived nearby in Juniata County. He loved coming to the farm. He loved her, too. Sometime—the sooner the better—Rebecca had to tell Christopher about Ben. But her fear of being rejected stood in her way.

Yet, when Dr. Morgan and Rebecca were alone together, she felt accepted and respected. She realized families were important too. And she had a strong feeling Christopher's family wasn't exactly thrilled their son was spending time with a farm girl from Pennsylvania.

Bertha became Rebecca's go-to. She came from an educated family, and might be able to shed light on the issue. At least Rebecca thought so. So one day after a particularly difficult night sleeping, she decided to ask Bertha to help her. But before she had a chance, Bertha interrupted her.

"Rebecca, there's a letter for you in your mailbox marked 'Important'. We'll have to talk another time."

Disappointed but eager to go to retrieve the letter, Rebecca said, "Thank you, Bertha. Maybe another time we can talk."

She tore through the parlor to the mailboxes. The letter was postmarked December 21, 1899 from Jane Wagner, McAlisterville, Pennsylvania.

She opened it with unsteady hands and unfolded the single page.

Dear Rebecca,

I am sorry to tell you that Grandpa is not expected to live more than a week or so. I don't know if you can be excused to come home but I want you to try. Grandma is not doing well either. She has become skinny and frail. I hope you can ask your supervisor to let you off duty. We need you.

Love,

Ma

Early the next morning, Rebecca went to Miss Nutting's office. She found the nursing leader sitting quietly at her desk with her eyes closed.

She knocked on the open door. "Miss Nutting. I'm sorry to disturb you, but I need to ask you something important."

The head of the school sat up straight, and asked, "What is it, Miss Wagner?"

"I just received a letter telling me my grandfather is close to death and my grandmother isn't well either. Would it be possible for me to go home for a few days?"

Miss Nutting didn't answer for what seemed to Rebecca a long while "I suppose that will be possible, but it will put a burden on the other students and nurses. When would you have to leave?"

"As soon as I can. But I have to get word to my family to pick me up at the station. So the earliest I can leave is two days from now."

"Then go back to work. Prepare your things tonight. I will ask one of the wagon drivers to take you to the train station day after tomorrow. Meet him at the front door at eight o'clock. Now send a letter immediately to make arrangements for someone to pick you up when you reach Pennsylvania."

Rebecca wrote a hasty letter to her father and posted it on her way to the hospital. The remainder of the day she thought about her grandfather and grandmother when she cared for older patients. One sweet older lady even looked like her grandmother. Slight in build, but tall, and threads of silver weaving through her dark hair.

After a long day in the ward, she packed her small wooden and leather suitcase and retrieved her carved stone and money from under her mattress. She carefully sewed them in the hem of her skirt, keeping enough in her small reticule to pay for her round trip to Mifflin.

Heavy snow fell in large flakes the day the carriage driver picked her up at the nurses' residence. The ride to the station took longer than expected because of slippery roads and poor visibility. Rebecca arrived just in time to purchase her ticket. She ran to the train, suitcase and satchel bouncing at her side, and dodged the steam that was escaping from the black engine. Breathless, she sat down on an empty seat just in time for the train to pull away.

Rebecca settled down, taking deep breaths. She pictured her grandfather, his large body still and quiet except for his wheezing. She wished she could have taken care of him instead of the strangers she nursed at the hospital… and saved her grandmother from caring for him just one day and night.

She watched the snow cover the buildings, then the hills and trees, and listened to the clacking of the wheels against the track. She had forgotten how the train swayed from side to side as it lumbered down hills and around curves. The sound of the wheels on the track lulled her to sleep, only rousing when the steward announced the stops.

When she got to the Mifflin station, Gary and her father were waiting for her in the wagon. She ran to them and hugged them close. "How is grandpa?"

Elwood hung his head. "Not good. Glad you're home."

Snow was still falling hard, so they grabbed her suitcase and wrapped her in woolen blankets before she climbed into the back of the wagon. On the ride home, she snuggled against the seat and lifted her face to the sky. She took a long, deep breath. The air smelled different—no factory smog or garbage smell that clung to the streets in Baltimore.

The horse had a string of bells around its neck that jingled in contrast to the silent snow falling on the earth. Rebecca tilted her head back and opened her mouth, letting the snowflakes melt on her tongue. They tasted like spring water from the pump. As they passed through the foothills of the Shade Mountains, she smelled the wood smoke that curled from the chimneys on the farmhouses tucked into the meadows along the road. Her cheeks were stiff from the cold and her hands lost their feeling despite the heavy woolen mittens.

Gary shouted from the front of the wagon, "Are you warm enough?"

"No. I can't stop shivering. Please hurry as fast as you can."

"We can't go any faster. The snow's getting deeper. Hang on. Only a few miles to go."

By the time they reached the farm, the snow reached half way up the wheels of the wagon. Gary retrieved her belongings while Elwood swept the snow from her body and helped her out of the wagon. He took her hand and guided her to the cabin, where Jane stood at the open door.

She hugged Rebecca and took off her daughter's wet coat and mittens. "You must be half frozen. I have chamomile tea ready. Come sit down."

"Thank you, Ma." Rebecca wrapped her hands around the mug and looked around the room. "Where's grandma? Did I get her in time?"

Before Jane could answer, Elwood and her brother burst through the door, stomping the snow off their boots and clothing. Jane placed two mugs on the kitchen table and poured coffee in them. The sad look on her mother's face told the story.

"Ma, is Grandpa dead?"

"Yes, he is, my dear. He died early this morning. Grandma is with him."

Rebecca stopped breathing until she couldn't hold her breath any longer. She felt strange. An eerie calm spread over her as she walked into the back bedroom and stood at her grandmother's side, next to Joseph's body. She slid her hand into Mary's and squeezed it. "I'm here, grandma."

Mary took Rebecca's hand and placed it over her heart. "I'm glad you came." She turned to her granddaughter and the tears that Rebecca knew were just under the surface began to tumble out. Rebecca folded her arms around Mary's thin body and held her until the crying stopped.

"Let's go into the kitchen and have some coffee, Grandma. Then you can tell us what you want to do about Grandpa's burial."

The family sat together talking until later that afternoon. Elwood decided the weather was too difficult to ask Dr. Headings to come to the farm so they closed the door to the back bedroom and let Grandpa's body in the cool room until the next day. Rebecca covered the sofa in the parlor with a soft quilt and tucked Grandma in before she went upstairs to bed.

Rebecca awakened when the sun's light crept toward the horizon. Out her window, the mountains formed a black silhouette against the gray sky. She quickly dressed, tiptoed downstairs and went into the back bedroom. Joseph's skin was iridescent white and his eyes partly open in death's stare. His massive body filled most of the bed but Rebecca sat on a narrow space next to him. "You are at peace, Grandpa, and no more heartache for Grandma."

The snow had stopped falling during the night but had dumped another foot on the ground. Rebecca grabbed the shovel by the back door and shoveled a path to the outhouse and Back So Straight's cabin. When she was finished, she sat on the log bench nearby and watched the sun come up.

Wind pushed the cabin door open with her nose and trotted to Rebecca. Back So Straight followed wrapped in a crimson blanket with black and yellow chevrons woven into it, and high buckskin boots covering her strong, straight legs. "My child, it is wonderful to see you. I am sorry you grandfather departed this life and has now joined his ancestors."

"Yes, I suppose I am too. Especially for my grandmother. She took care of him day and night… and he was not an easy man."

Back So Straight nodded. “Now your grandmother can decide it she wants to join him or remain with her family.”

Rebecca thought for a moment, then asked, “Does she have a choice?”

“Yes, she does. You see, her heart is still two-sided. But the part that died when she was nearly shot is no longer struggling with the part of her that wants to live.”

“I’m not sure I understand, but I hope Grandma is now free of any hurt or confusion.”

The Indian woman smiled, looked directly at her and nodded. Rebecca saw the love in her eyes. She marveled at the women in her life—three strong women to love and guide her—a grandmother who endured an emotionally abusive husband; a mother who kept her family together despite conflict and turmoil; and a mentor who taught her to believe in herself.

CHAPTER 61

"DO YOU THINK WE CAN DIG A GRAVE? THE SOIL IS STILL frozen." Rebecca shoveled snow off the ground at the family cemetery in the back meadow.

"Don't know, but we have to try. Gary, hand me the pick." Elwood took a hard blow to the frozen earth. The pick bounced upwards, leaving a small indentation of tan-colored earth where the tool struck.

Gary grabbed the pick from his father and began to strike the ground, grunting with each blow. Slowly, a small hollow area grew deeper and deeper. When he paused to catch his breath, Elwood took the pick and continued to chip away at the opening. After the hole was about a foot deep, he rested and Rebecca took the tool. She took a deep breath as she raised the tool high above her head and, using the weight of the iron blade and her own body, carved another few inches out of the earth.

The three of them continued to work the ground free of its frozen grip until they reached the frost line. Gary jumped in the hole and shoveled out the ground with a spade.

He hit a rock and his foot flew off the shovel. "Shit."

Rebecca knew her brother's anger would fuel his determination. He kicked the rock aside and jammed his foot onto the top of the shovel, digging with all his might—shovelful after shovelful—and tossing them out of the hole.

One spade-full narrowly missed hitting Rebecca. "Watch where you're throwing that ground."

"Well, don't stand so close. Move away."

Elwood took the pick and blocked the next shovelful as Gary tried to throw it out of hole. Gary stepped out and threw his shovel on the ground. "You always take her side."

Rebecca said, "I'm cold. I'm going inside. I'll make hot cocoa for you after you both settle down," and walked away.

When she reached the cabin, Ben was getting out of a sleigh, his arms full of packages. "Ben!" She ran to him, nearly knocking them out of his hands.

He tossed them on the seat, grabbed her, swung her around, and kissed her on the mouth. "Rebecca, why are you out in the cold? You look half-frozen."

Rebecca's smile disappeared, her enthusiasm tempered by the reality of what she and her family were about to do: bury her grandfather. "My father and brother are trying to prepare a grave. My grandfather died early yesterday morning."

"Let me go help them. Here, take the packages inside and I'll join you as soon as I can."

The three men continued digging until the hole was big enough for the casket Elwood made about a month before. They used the same board that transported Joseph from near the corncrib just a short five months ago to carry him to where the wooden casket lay waiting. They placed his body in the casket and nailed it shut.

Elwood, Gary, and Ben carried the casket to the cemetery and placed it in the hole. A light snow began to fall and the wind picked up, swirling flakes into their faces.

"Gary, go inside and fetch the women."

Rebecca took one arm and her mother, the other, as they led Grandma to the family graveyard, their boots crunching in the newly fallen show. The wind blew hard, making it difficult to see through the white curtain that swirled around them. As soon as they reached the dark hole in which the coffin lay,

Elwood took a small Bible out of his pocket. His hands shook as he turned the pages to Psalms, Chapter 23, and held them in place.

He read, "The Lord is my shepherd. I shall not want. He maketh me… lie down in green pastures. He…" His voice trembled, then was inaudible. Jane put her hand over Elwood's and held it steady. She began reading, "Maketh me lie down in green pastures." Elwood joined her reading the remainder of the verses and finished with, "Surely goodness and mercy will follow me all the days of my life and I will dwell in the house of the Lord forever."

Everyone stood watching the snow fall over Joseph's casket and bracing themselves against the cold and wind when, out of the blowing white, came Back So Straight. She neared the procession, her snowshoes wrapped with rawhide around her feet and leggings, and placed woolen blankets over the women's shoulders. Gary took the shovel and began to cover the casket with ground, now mixed with newly fallen snow. The clumps of frozen earth fell loudly on the top of the wooden casket.

Ben took the shovel from Gary and resumed shoveling dirt into the hole. He pulled his scarf over his face where ice crystals formed on the cloth and his eyes blinked rapidly as the wet snowflakes fell on his face.

"Gary and I can take over now, Ben. Take the women and go inside," said Elwood.

"Come, Ma… Grandma… Back So Straight… let me and Ben go first." Ben took Rebecca's hand and together they led the three women, ducking their heads low into their coats as the snow deepened around them. One by one they shuffled through the cold white until they reached the cabin and ducked inside.

"Do you think we should have asked our neighbors to come to Joseph's burial?" Jane asked no one in particular after they took off their wet coats and sat at the kitchen table.

Mary answered loudly, "No."

"If you want, we can tell our neighbors after the storm is over… and maybe invite a few over for a meal," Jane said, as she put the kettle on the stove. "Rebecca, why don't you and Ben go in the parlor?"

"Mrs. Wagner, I almost forgot. I have more packages on my sleigh and should get them before I forget."

Rebecca grabbed his coat and helped him put it on. "Be careful."

In a little while, Elwood and Gary stumbled into the cabin, bitter cold sweeping in the door with them. Ben followed, his arms loaded with snow-covered boxes. Rebecca helped him dust off the snow and place them on a bench.

The men joined the women at the large farm table while Jane poured hot coffee in white mugs and set a pitcher of cream in the middle. Rebecca opened a tin of sugar cookies and passed it around.

"I'm sorry about Mr. Wagner's passing. I didn't know he died… or that Rebecca would be home. I just wanted to bring these gifts to all of you in time for Christmas," Ben said.

Jane put her hand on Ben's arm. "How thoughtful of you. I'm glad you braved the weather to come all the way out here. You must stay the night. It's too dangerous to try to go back to Mifflinburg."

Rebecca tried to smile but a wave of nausea crept up her throat. Christopher.

Ben smoothed back a lock of his sandy brown hair, wet where it had escaped his hat. "I don't want to be in the way. You've just had a loss. But before I go, I want give you the gifts I brought." He handed Rebecca's father the first package. Elwood hastily opened it and pulled out a beautiful hand-stitched leather bridle. Jane was next. A bolt of fine cotton fabric with small daises printed on it tumbled out of the wrapping when he placed it on her lap.

When Ben approached Gary, Rebecca's brother cocked his head to the side and held out his hand. He shook the foot-long package tied with twine before tearing it open, almost cutting himself on a hunting knife.

Ben turned to Mary, got down on his knee and reached into his pocket for a small package. He placed it in her hand and watched her open a packet of quilting needles. She looked up at Ben and wiped a tear from her eye.

Rebecca bit her lip. She looked at Back So Straight, whose face was expressionless. Ben approached the Indian woman and pulled a roll of strong rawhide rope from a drawstring burlap bag, placing it in her hand. She nodded and smiled.

There was one package left on the bench. Ben retrieved it and sat down beside Rebecca. He handed her a large box wrapped in Baker's Christmas paper with small gold and white calendars in the corner and 'The Golden Year" printed above, along with a black and white winter scene.

"This is for you, Rebecca." The room grew quiet. She slowly opened the wrapping, trying to calm her trembling hands. She peeled back the paper and drew a sharp breath. There among white tissue paper was a red cloak, with black satin frog closings starting at the neck and continuing halfway down the front.

"It's… beautiful." She blinked several times, feeling the fine scarlet wool with her fingers. "It… feels so soft and warm. Thank you." Her sense of guilt overtook her. Nausea returned, saliva drawing together in her mouth.

"Ben… I…"

"Please put it on—I ordered it from New York. It only arrived yesterday because of the snow. I was going to leave it here until you came home this summer but now I don't have to wait."

Rebecca placed the cloak around her shoulders and swallowed hard to push down the burning in her throat. She vowed to tell Christopher about Ben. She wasn't going to deceive him—or Ben, anymore.

CHAPTER 62

BEN LEFT THE WAGNER FARM LATE THAT AFTERNOON, HIS horse pulling his sleigh on snow-covered roads along the open fields with drifts as high as the nearby fence posts. He was halfway to his home when his horse stalled in a deep snowdrift, the sleigh coming to an abrupt stop. Ben tried to kick the snow away from the horse's legs but it was too deep. Snow had packed under the bed of the sleigh, making the runners useless.

He scanned the horizon looking for a barn or farmhouse but saw nothing but white fields and a few stands of bare trees. He pulled a blanket over his shoulders and sat for a few moments. His horse's ears pricked up at the same time he heard a faint sound in the distance. Bells. The sound got louder. He squinted against the glare of the white bend of the road ahead of him.

An enormous gray workhorse pulling a sleigh came toward him, a lone driver in the seat. Ben blinked away tears that had pooled in his eyes from the cold air. Through his blurred vision, he saw Gunther, a broad smile across his ruddy face.

"It's you again. Looks like you're stuck."

Ben's hope of rescue faded. "Hello, Gunther. Yes, I am in a predicament. Could you give me a hand?

"Why should I? You've never done anything for me."

"That may be true. But if the situation were reversed, I'd help you out."

Gunther laughed, his breath looking like steaming puffs of clouds in the air. "I could let you and your horse freeze to death."

Ben tried to think of something that would convince Gunther otherwise. "I'm at your mercy. You wouldn't want a good horse to die, would you?"

A sneer spread across Gunther's broad face. He pulled his knitted hat over his forehead and looked at Ben's horse. "How about I cut the horse loose and let you here?"

When Ben didn't answer, Gunther said, "Maybe I'll do this for Rebecca. She hates me, but when she finds out I saved your ass, she'll change her mind."

Ben tried to think of the right thing to say… something that would placate him. "Thanks, Gunther. I'll be sure to tell her you saved my ass."

"Yeah, you do that. I've got a shovel and some strong rope with me. Just remember, I'm doing this for Rebecca, not you. Now get your ass off your fancy rig and start shoveling."

Gunther and Ben took turns digging the packed snow from around the sleigh and in front of Ben's horse. It was hard, tiring work. They worked together, one with the shovel and one with gloved hands. Sweat ran from their damp faces despite the frigid air. Once they cleared a rough path, Gunther tied the heavy rope to the rigging on Ben's sleigh and made his huge horse pull the impacted sleigh forward. Ben's horse tried to kick loose of the snow, straining and snorting mucous out his nose. After two tries, the struggling animal managed to free his legs and the rig pulled out of the deep snow.

"Now I'm going around you so stay out of my way. Next time don't be so stupid."

"Thanks, Gunther. I appreciate what you did."

Gunther grunted something as he cracked his whip over his horse's rump and squeezed past Ben's horse and sleigh. Ben thought he heard him mumble something about Rebecca but wasn't sure.

Ben's hands and toes lost their feeling but he continued on his way, shivering and cooling down even further from cold air against his perspired skin. His horse showed signs of fatigue, his breaths coming in deep gasps and foam forming on his sides. Ben did his best to avoid snowdrifts along Main Valley

Road. He passed through the villages of Bunkertown and Evendale, but then the road led through the countryside again. Several windblown piles of snow nearly blocked his sleigh again, but he managed to coax the horse through the narrow pathway to Mifflinburg made by another sleigh.

Ben thought maybe Gunther wasn't so bad after all. On the other hand, Gunther manhandled Rebecca that night at the Grange dance. He surely saved his ass and his horse. But Ben wasn't about to tell Rebecca about Gunther pulling him out of a snowdrift. All he cared about was that Gunther left her alone.

CHAPTER 63

REBECCA TRIED TO DRAW ASIDE THE CURTAIN OF SADNESS and guilt, but the look on Ben's face when he gave her the cloak lingered in her mind. She wasn't ready to talk to Back So Straight and the snow was too deep to take a walk in the forest… but perhaps working with the horses would be a good substitute.

On her way through the path, Elwood and Gary shoveled to the barn, she looked up into the mountains and saw the checkered patches of bare ground. Stopping to shake the snow off her boots, she thought about the men who worked in those mountains—the cold wetness—their hands and feet numbed and tingling from cutting the slippery logs and sending them down the mountainsides in snow-lined chutes. She closed her eyes, remembering the severed arm in her dreams, still fresh in her mind after all this time.

"Rebecca, what are you doing standing out here in the cold?" her Pop asked, his breath forming wisps of fog against the frigid air.

"Thought I'd spend some time with the horses before I go back to school."

"Well, don't just stand there daydreaming. Help me shovel the stalls and put clean straw down."

Elwood scooped a shovelful of steaming manure mixed with straw into a wheelbarrow. "Looks like we can get this done and check on the sleigh before we take you to Mifflin tomorrow. Come on, pick up a pitch fork and start spreading straw."

They worked silently, each lost in their own thoughts. Elwood checked the harness hanging on a spike and loosened the buckles that would fit around the horse's rump, while Rebecca placed woolen blankets on the seat.

"Should be all ready for tomorrow, Rebecca. I'm going to take you. Make sure you're up at dawn to give us enough time. Main Valley Road will be tricky."

"I will, Pop. Let's go inside and get warn."

Walking back to the cabin, Rebecca saw her father look at the mountains behind the barn, his eyes scanning back and forth before looking down at the trampled path. Maybe her father felt as guilty about selling his mountain land as she did about not telling Ben about Christopher.

"Pop, what do you think it's like for the woodmen up there in those lumber camps? It's so bitter cold down here... think how cold it must be in the mountains. Do you know what happens to them if they get hurt or sick?"

"Heard Jacob Hafley's brother had to have some fingers cut off when they turned black. But most men up there are looking for ways to earn a living even if it means getting hurt."

Rebecca blew into her mittens. "I feel sorry for them. It looks bleak up there, just dirt paths and piles of dead branches."

Elwood's steps slowed. He kicked the snow and winced when the wind blew it back into his face. "Hate it. Hate how the forests look. Hate how rich and powerful men buy the land and strip the trees. Hate it that some of us have work for them."

Rebecca hadn't give much thought recently to Hugh Eastman and Peter North. But knowing that Mr. North was paying her expenses to attend nursing school muddled her opinion about him and his connection to Mr. Eastman. She leaned against her father and took his arm as they hunched down against the bitter wind and walked to the cabin, their boots crunching and trampling the snow.

The following day just before dawn, Elwood loaded Rebecca's suitcase into the sleigh while she lingered on the porch trying to savor every last minute left to be with her family. Jane, Mary, and Back So Straight huddled together waiting their turn to hug her, but Elwood remained in the back of the wagon, his shoulders slumped against the cold. "Let's get going. Train won't wait if we're late."

Rebecca jumped into the sleigh and looked back at her family. "Wait. Where's Gary?"

Without answering, Elwood snapped the reigns and the sleigh jerked forward, its runners slicing through the deep snow, their blades squeaking. She turned around to see Gary standing beside the barn. Rebecca waved, mouthing the words 'Goodbye, Gary'. He lifted his hand waist high and gave a slight wave. She stared at her brother until hot tears blurred her sight.

CHAPTER 64

REBECCA WALKED DOWN THE HALLWAY TO HER EMPTY ROOM. Her hands were stiff and cold and she lost feeling in her toes. The little stove in the railroad car didn't warm them very much and the cold ride in the public wagon in Baltimore added to her misery. She was relieved her roommates hadn't returned from their shift in the hospital, so she had a chance to unpack and think about her family and Ben. She crawled into bed and curled on her side, hugging her body. Ben. It was as though he was only a dream. Ma, so busy with cooking and cleaning. Pop, worried about the trees but powerless to stop the cutting. Gary, afraid of getting too close to anyone. Grandma, saying nothing. Back So Straight, quiet, her dark eyes seeing everything.

A letter sat on her desk postmarked Philadelphia. She tore it open, hoping to hear something about Lilly and eager to think about something other than her family troubles.

Dear Rebecca,

I hope you are still doing well in nursing school. Thank you for writing, but your letter was too short. I wanted to read more about your adventures with your patients, even though you told me you couldn't reveal their names. I laughed when I read about the first time you had to bathe a man who had a stroke. That must have been weird. Did he have an e---------, you know what I mean? I admire you, working so hard and learning to take care of people who are very sick. I'll bet you see lots of gruesome things. Like the lady who had ulcers on her legs with maggots in them. I would have gagged! What did you do with them? Pull them out? Ugh.

Your story about the doctor who cornered you made me angry. Did he really look like a bearded Napoleon ready to put his hand in your uniform? What a narrow escape before the head of the school saw you. What are you going to do if he does it again?

You asked me to write about Lilly. All I really know is that she was sent away to a hospital for a few months, but when she came home, she still was not speaking. Because Lilly didn't return to college, I only saw her once briefly when our fathers met for business reasons. She looked pale and sad. I just didn't know what to say. I can't imagine what has happened to her. We were best friends but now it feels like I lost her.

I wonder if Ben is writing to you? There was no mention of him in your letter. Maybe you just forgot. I am doing well in school. There are lots of parties and dances this season but I would rather study. One more year of this nonsense and I graduate. I am not ready to come out as a debutant but my mother and father wish I would act more ladylike. If that means giggling and curtsying, forget it. I want to do something more meaningful with my life, like you, Rebecca. I just have to find out what it is. Please write back. I can't wait to see you again next summer.

Yours truly,

Maggie

P.S. Is Ben still your beau?

She read the letter a second time, laughing and feeling sad at the same time. Maggie. She always cheered Rebecca up. But she also made her think. Especially about Ben.

"You're back," Bertha said as she burst in the room. "I'm glad Miss Nutting gave you time to go home. Did your grandfather pass away?"

Rebecca quickly folded the letter and put it in her desk. "Yes. We buried him three days ago." Rebecca forced back tears, not because of grief, but because of guilt. She felt hollow… empty. Hoping to avoid the tears forming in her eyes, she changed the subject. "Where are Maude and Gracie?"

Bertha took her apron off and sat on her bed. "Gracie's very sick with the grippe. She's in the hospital along with four other students and may not be able to come back to nursing school. I don't know where Maude is."

Rebecca closed her eyes and pulled the blankets over her head. Not Gracie. Why couldn't it be Maude?

Bertha continued. "I might as well tell you. Maude has been sneaking out again at night and coming in early in the morning. I don't know how she stays awake during the day. She wore one of your dresses while you were gone. Not your white one. I tried to stop her but she wouldn't listen."

Rebecca bit her upper lip and threw back the covers. "That does it. I'm going to Miss Nutting. Will you go with me?"

"I don't know. Suppose she's asked to leave? Worse yet, suppose someone saw her and thinks it was you?" The young woman wrung her hands together, her voice cracking.

"I can't take that chance. Tomorrow morning before we go on duty, let's go to Miss Nutting's quarters and tell her about Maude." Rebecca sounded a lot more confident than she felt.

"I guess you're right. But we have to be factual. No speculation. Just what we saw and what Maude confessed to doing."

At five o'clock the next morning, Rebecca and Bertha walked to the top floor of the nurses' residence where Miss Nutting and several other nursing instructors lived. Rebecca's heart beat in her throat but she didn't know if it was from climbing the stairs or her nervousness.

She knocked on the door and looked at Bertha with questioning eyes. Footsteps were audible from the hallway. Miss Nutting opened the door and stood squinting at the two fully uniformed student nurses. She was still in her nightgown, her hair flowing down her shoulders and back. With a scratchy voice, she asked, "What is it that brings you to my door at this early hour?"

Rebecca swallowed and said with a shaky voice, "We have something important to discuss with you, Miss Nutting. May we come in?"

"Yes, of course. Let me light another lamp." She lit an ornate gas light just inside above her dining room table and gestured for them to sit down on a large velvet settee. "I assume this is something you are not able to solve yourselves. Or am I wrong?"

To Rebecca's surprise, Bertha took the lead. "We have come to talk to you about our roommate, Maude Driscoll. We have reason to believe she is breaking rules of conduct and we came to report her."

Miss Nutting cocked her head and asked, "Exactly what rules is she breaking?"

"First of all, she has stolen some of our personal belongings. Now she is sneaking out at night and meeting with a doctor in his quarters. She confessed to doing both."

"Those are serious accusations, Miss Wagner. Are you sure?"

Hoping to bolster their case against Maude, Bertha answered instead. "We know they are, but Miss Wagner and I feel obligated to come forward, knowing that our own upright standing is in jeopardy."

Miss Nutting gathered her hair and placed it over the middle of her back. Her face grew stern. "When did these accusations take place?"

"The thefts of our things belongings happened last year but the sneaking out episodes are recent," answered Bertha.

"Why didn't you come to me when you first discovered your items missing, Miss Wagner?"

"Because Miss Driscoll promised to stop stealing… she begged us to not report her. Then she wore my dress while I was in Pennsylvania for my grandfather's burial and secretly met with a doctor at night… I… was afraid she would be discovered wearing my dress." She held her arms close to her body to control her trembling.

"You should have come to see me when you discovered her stealing your things. However, these later accusations are even more serious. I will question Miss Driscoll as soon as possible. Meanwhile, say nothing about this to anyone. You may go now and report to your unit."

After finishing their shift, Rebecca and Bertha returned to their room late afternoon. Maude was packing her suitcase, her face red and streaked with tears. "I hope you're satisfied. I was asked to leave and it's your fault for being a tattletale."

"I'm sorry you're leaving, but you are to blame, not us," Bertha countered. Rebecca and I warned you about getting all of us in trouble, but you didn't listen. Now it's too late."

As convinced as Rebecca was that Maude was reckless in sneaking out at night, seeing her pack her belongings gave her second thoughts about her decision to tell Miss Nutting. "Maybe this is for the best. You sometimes struggled with your studies because you stayed out all night. Once you're back home you may find something is better suited to what you want."

Maude started to cry again. "Well, that's easy for you to say. All I want is to be loved and respected. Don't we all want that?"

"Of course. But there are better ways to get it."

"Don't preach to me, Rebecca. I know you're going out with a doctor, too. So be careful of what you say."

Rebecca felt the blood rushing to her head. How did Maude know? But at least she wasn't sneaking out at night and putting her roommates in danger of having to lie on her behalf.

After snapping her suitcase shut, Maude put on her coat, walked out and slammed the door. The silence was eerie. Maude's words echoed in Rebecca's ears. She was going out with a doctor. And there was a chance Miss Nutting knew about it.

Soon Bertha's words jarred her back to the present. "Come on, Rebecca, let's go to dinner."

But she still was unsure about going to Miss Nutting. A nagging feeling that she and Bertha really did tattle on Maude stuck in her mind. But once they changed their clothes and went to the dining room Rebecca realized there was no turning back. Students surrounded them with questions. As Rebecca and Bertha answered each one, the group grew smaller until everyone left the room except some tables where graduate nurses sat.

"I can't believe everyone knows about Maude. Did Miss Nutting tell them?" Rebecca felt as though she had betrayed one of their own.

"No, didn't you hear Elizabeth say she saw Maude leave a little bit ago with a suitcase in her hand?"

"Ah... no, I didn't." Rebecca pressed her hands against her stomach that had started to churn. She whispered to Bertha, "I'm beginning to think we should have kept quiet. Did we do the right thing?"

"I think so. But now it's just you and me—Gracie is still in the hospital."

Rebecca started to speak but suddenly put her hand across her mouth and mumbled, "I'm… going… to…" Bolting into the bathroom, she vomited into the toilet.

"Are you all right?" Bertha asked, knocking on the door. After a minute or two, she knocked again.

"I'm… feeling better. Give me a minute to wash my face and rinse out my mouth."

"Let's go to our room. You'll feel better if we concentrate on our studies. We have a test on analysis of urine… your favorite subject."

Rebecca's mood lifted somewhat, but it would take more than a little humor to erase her guilt at being responsible for Maude's dismissal. Only time and self-forgiveness would take care of that.

That next day and every day for over a week when Rebecca reported for duty, she faced a completely full ward. Most of the patients were poor or didn't have anyone at home to care for them. Pneumonia, tuberculosis, frostbite, flu, and the usual cancer, cholera, and typhoid fever. Student nurses were the backbone of the hospital, providing hours of uncompensated care. According to Miss Nutting, there had to be implicit obedience as the foundation of their work. Junior students sometimes worked under the leadership of senior students who had been placed in positions of responsibility when their progress and ability warranted it. But like Gracie, some of Rebecca's classmates fell ill under the pressure of work. They were often required to return to work before they completely recovered.

Gracie succumbed to the grippe over three weeks ago and was still in a hospital room with five other students recovering from various illnesses. Other students were not allowed to visit them lest they also become ill. After her fever came down, Gracie was released and made to resume her work and studies. Rebecca and Bertha tried their best to help tutor her and help her with her work on the wards, but she fell ill again and had to leave nursing school. Rebecca grieved over Gracie's departure. She remembered the day she first met Gracie when she opened the door to their room on the day they had all arrived at Johns Hopkins.

Rebecca felt like a slave to the hospital and now one of her own was gone because of it. Only Bertha remained as her support; they made a pledge to help each other get through until summer when they looked forward to having two weeks off.

She was grateful for Sundays when Christopher came to see her, even when the weather made travel difficult. Sometimes Christopher would order the driver to lead the carriage around the nearby streets and they would just hold hands and talk about patients they took care of. Rebecca asked him to explain the whats and whys of treatment protocols, questioning their effectiveness and risks, especially when her nursing instructors told her differently. Her world became narrower and narrower as she focused on her life as a student nurse in Baltimore and less on Ben and McAlisterville. She even thought less frequently about her friend Lilly.

However, in February, a letter from Ben brought her thoughts back to Juniata County.

Dear Rebecca,

It is snowing and bitterly cold here in Mifflinburg. I have not been able to get through the roads for over a week now. I do not like working in the buggy shop near as much as the rest of the family, but I am keenly aware they need me because several of our workers are sick, some with the grippe and one with frostbite in his fingers.

Back in early January I went to McAlisterville shortly after you left to deliver a new wagon. I rode my horse to your farm to say hello to your folks. No one was home except your grandmother but I gave her my best. She told me your Ma and Pop were at a Grange meeting and she did not know where Gary was. The new barn still looks very sturdy. I heard the horses nicker, their heads sticking out the openings of their stalls. I imagined us taking a ride on my sleigh. It is very lonely without you. I miss you very, very much. I question why you have not written. Surely your work cannot be consuming all of your time. I think about you every day and try to imagine what you are doing. Do try to write when your studies and other duties lessen, and tell me about your life in Baltimore.

Love,

Ben

She had to tell him about Christopher. But how? In a letter? That was too cruel. It would have to wait until she was able to tell him in person. She owed him that. But when?

CHAPTER 65

SUNSHINE WARMED THE BUDS ON THE TREES OUTSIDE THE nurses' home, coaxing them from their winter prisons. Burgundy red bumps covered branches on the purple beech near the front of the nurses' home, while tiny weeds poked through the cracks in the cobblestone street. Rebecca savored the walk to and from the hospital, smelling the lilacs and magnolia blossoms coming from the grassy mall between hospital outbuildings.

If it weren't for the coming of spring and outings with Christopher, Rebecca would have been disconsolate over being responsible for Maude's departure, Gracie's departure because of illness—and her turmoil over Ben.

There were also the endless lectures on the importance of loyalty and deference toward physicians. Drill and discipline, as well as character, became the overarching theme of most subjects. Rebecca and Bertha often pretended to pay rapt attention but silently yearned for the lectures to be over.

In contrast, Miss Nutting occasionally followed the lectures with stories of individual nurses who intelligently and courageously elevated the status of nursing by displaying unflinching dedication to patients and adhering to strict moral standards. Once she spoke of having to straddle the line between supporting doctors and placating those who were reluctant to share their authority. She wanted all of her nurses to know that she and her predecessor, Lavina Dock were reformers who were trying to define a role for women in service of humanity. But they had to do it softly and tactfully to balance the equally difficult poles of total deference and outright defiance to accomplish their work. Miss Nutting also tried to persuade nurses to campaign for women's suffrage as part of her effort to raise the status of women. After hearing these lofty statements about the status of nurses being elevated, along with the fight for the right to vote, Rebecca felt conflicted. She wanted to be the kind of nurse who was totally dedicated to her patients but frustrated that she had to defer to doctors and others who were unwilling to recognize the nurses' contribution to the patients they all served.

Several seasoned nurses on the wards told students about their efforts to change the role of nurses from submission and self-sacrifice to independence and individual thinking. But they were the exception. Most nurses, and students that emulated them, remained compliant.

Rebecca didn't know where she fit in. Her work became her sole focus. She obeyed the rules, deferred to those above her and worked hard to gain their approval. She seldom went outside the hospital except for outings with Christopher. He became her confidant, dear friend, and loyal admirer.

She still hadn't answered the letter from Ben. Her guilt about reporting Maude and her inability to tell Ben about Christopher took their toll. More sleepless nights. Days where she thought about nothing but her own insecurity made her more vulnerable to Christopher's kindness and attention. He hadn't invited her to his home since last November, but he asked her to accompany him to social events and restaurants.

One warm spring Sunday, Christopher arrived at the nurses' home in a new, beautiful, navy-blue single-seated buggy. When Rebecca spied the shiny paint and leather seats, she gasped. Just like a buggy Ben made.

Christopher bowed deeply. "So are you are pleased with my surprise?"

"Yes… of course. It's… lovely," she lied, pasting a fake smile on her face.

"I have another surprise for you today." He took her hand and helped her into the handsome vehicle. "We're going to the Chesapeake Bay and then out to my favorite restaurant."

Through the entire buggy ride to the edge of the bay, Rebecca could not take her mind off Ben. She tried to focus on passing carriages and people walking along the streets to no avail.

Christopher leaned against her and placed the reigns in one hand and took her hand with the other. "Is there something bothering you, Rebecca?"

She lied again. "No, I'm probably just tired."

"Then relax and let me take care of you. We'll sit by the water and then we'll go to a wonderful restaurant." He squeezed her hand and gave her a light kiss on the cheek.

Rebecca let her shoulders slump and edged closer to Christopher. It was wonderful to be taken care of instead of taking care of others.

When they reached the steps that led down to the bay, they sat together on the sandy boards. Seagulls flew around them looking for food, some landing close to their feet. Rebecca marveled at their acrobatics and daring fights when they snagged a crab from the shallow water lapping against the shore. She watched Christopher, his face lit up as though he was seeing the bay for the first time, even though it was new to her, not him. She couldn't help but smile at the handsome man beside her, his blond-white hair combed back from a neat part in the middle, his blue eyes contrasting the black of her own. She finally felt calm. Periods of silence didn't seem awkward as they sometimes did when she was around some other men, especially men in authority. Rebecca reached into the greenish brown water and let its coolness slip through her fingers. She brought her hand to her nose. The water smelled fishy.

Christopher broke the silence. "Would you permit me to take you to an exquisitely fancy restaurant for dinner?"

"Actually, I'm famished! But I… have we been there before? Is it more exquisite than the others you've taken me to?"

Once again, his face lit up. "Yes, it is. You are about to experience one of Baltimore's finest."

Rebecca took his arm and looked up at him. "I'm ready if you are."

The restaurant was only a short distance from the Wharf—a Victorian structure that had nets hanging from pink and blue clapboard siding. Dormers with intricate wooden scrolling around the top and halfway down the sides and lamps in each high window graced the slate roof. Anchors were moored in the ground leading up to the painted steps to the wraparound porch. Glancing into the dining room, she saw round tables covered with lace tablecloths, a lighted lantern and small vases of flowers in the middle of each one. A man dressed in a captain's uniform greeted them at the door. After they were seated in a little alcove to the side of the main room, a waiter handed them large parchment menus. Rebecca's eyes grew open in astonishment at the number of items to choose from. Oysters. Blue crabs. Soft-shelled and hard-shelled clams. striped bass, Chesapeake rockfish, bluefish, Spanish mackerel, croakers. Beef with bordelaise sauce. Berger cookies with fudge ganache. Still trying to pronounce the foreign sounding names in her mind, she didn't notice Christopher looking at her with a wide grin.

"Would you like me to order for you?"

She shook her head yes emphatically. "There are so many choices of fish. I've never tasted many of these before. What do you recommend, Dr. Morgan?"

The waiter, dressed in black pants drawn tight at the knees and a white shirt with billowing sleeves, came toward Christopher. "Perhaps you both need more time to decide."

The young doctor said to Rebecca, "I'll order a dozen steamed clams first so you can taste them. Then we'll have some roasted striped bass. They grow quite large in the bay and have a nice, mild flavor. I'm quite sure you'll like them." Then he turned to the waiter. "We'll have a dozen steamed clams with drawn butter, striped bass, roasted fresh root vegetables, corn bread with honey, and a bottle of your finest Sauvignon blanc."

Rebecca studied this man beside her again. His jaw was angular but not sharp. A gently sloping nose sat above his mouth that was slightly upturned in a small smile when he spoke. He was the most handsome man she had ever seen.

While they waited, Christopher talked about the restaurant and how the *maître d'* recognized him from the many times he had dined there in the past. Rebecca wondered with whom he had dined before—fascinated but somewhat intimidated by her lack of experience eating in fancy restaurants. But as soon as the waiter brought plates of clams balanced on his arm covered with a white linen towel, Rebecca forgot about herself. She stared at the odd shells that looked like a larger version of small fresh-water mussels from Lost Creek. "Oh dear, how does one eat such a thing?"

His laughter was like a soft, distant roll of thunder, not too loud but robust and naturally deep. He picked up a clam, dipped it in butter and placed it in his mouth. "Just chew it a few times to get the taste. Like this—and let it slip whole down your throat."

Rebecca's face squished with revulsion.

"No... no. It's an acquired taste. Don't be afraid to try one."

She did exactly that, and actually smiled with delight as she tasted their rubbery flesh. Oh, my goodness. If her mother and father could see her tonight. Eating in a very fancy restaurant with a doctor.

The sound of the wine bottle clinking against her wine glass brought her attention back to the man across the table. "Miss Wagner, may I offer you a glass of white wine? It's my favorite. Just perfect to drink with fish." Rebecca had never tasted any wine except for the dandelion wine her parents made every spring when the dandelion plants were new and tender. She remembered being allowed to drink a small glass before they poured the yellowy liquid into bottles, and the slight dizziness she felt afterwards.

She took a small sip. It was light and smooth. She felt the cool liquid slide all the way to her stomach. When their dinner arrived, she was relaxed and eager to try the enormous plate of food in front of her. Rebecca paused after each bite, pleasure written all over her face.

Christopher watched her eat, and smiled. Conversation stopped while they ate and drank, each of them looking at the other.

"I must admit I've never seen any woman eat as much as you did, Miss Wagner. So many women I know hardly eat anything."

"What exactly do you mean by that, Dr. Morgan?" Rebecca felt a blush come into her cheeks as she studied her dinner companion.

Christopher reached across the table and put his hand on hers. "You just enjoy your food. As I said before, I want to take care of you. Now and for a long time to come."

Rebecca's hand trembled underneath his. "I don't know what to say."

"Say that it's all right with you."

She closed her eyes before answering. What does he mean a long time to come? What about Ben? But she didn't want to ruin the moment.

"I… I'm… all right, Christopher."

CHAPTER 66

THAT SPRING MISS NUTTING GAVE NEW ASSIGNMENTS TO ALL second-year nursing students. Some were to work in each of the children's ward, infectious ward, private wards and dispensary. Class work consisted of care of medical, surgical, and gynecological patients, infectious diseases, analysis of urine, and massage.

Bertha was assigned to a private ward. Rebecca was hoping to be assigned to the same ward to avoid being alone with Dr. Ames, but instead, she was scheduled to rotate to the children's ward. Many little ones were poor or orphans. One particular trying day, she was taking care of a young boy who had been badly burned in a farm accident. The little boy reminded her of Gary. Burns on his arms. Same light brown hair and well-defined eyebrows that lifted up when he spoke. However, he only spoke Pennsylvania Dutch; his family was from one of the "plain" sects that settled in the flatland outside Baltimore. Crying for his momma, the boy looked at Rebecca with pleading eyes. When Rebecca helped the doctor changed his dressings, the little boy screamed in pain so loudly it upset the other children, making them cry when she approached them. She went to bed that night hearing the screams of the children and pictured their tear-stained faces looking up at her from their cribs. But the boy with burns bothered her the most.

The next day Rebecca got up early and wrote a letter to her brother. Sadly, she realized she hadn't done that in a long time.

Dear Gary,

You have been on my mind lately, particularly after taking care of a little boy who was seriously burned, especially on his arms. I remember like it was yesterday how brave you were when Back So Straight and I put slippery elm and witch hazel on your burns. We did that three times a day and you endured it without complaining.

This little boy only speaks Pennsylvania Dutch but I can understand some of it because some of our neighbors at home speak it too. I hope he is brave like you were, because he is in for some difficult days and weeks ahead.

I may not have written to you very much, but I do think of you and what you told me about you and David the day we went to the train station. I am glad you trusted me enough to confide in me. That is an awful thing to hold inside. I think if David is anything like his sister Maggie, he is a good person. And so are you, even though I get angry with you for your stubbornness and bad temper. I care about you and only want you to be happy.

Now about David. You asked me what you should do. This is a serious matter. Although I don't quite understand it, I believe it is too dangerous for you to keep seeing him. There is no future for the both of you together. As harsh as that sounds, I must be honest. I remember telling you all of this before on our wagon ride together, but now I'm saying it again.

I know what it is like to be ridiculed and made to feel inferior. There is at least one doctor here who calls me names and tries to get me expelled. Your situation is even worse. You and David will either have to live a secret life or face the threat of being shunned or even beaten. People you think may stand by you, will turn away. They will not understand and when they see you and David showing any affection, will be repulsed. Honestly, even I find it difficult to understand what you feel toward David but I will try, and I will not reject or betray you. You are my brother and I will always love you.

Perhaps you can find something to do to occupy your mind and heart and give you strength to avoid David as much as you can. I know your love for the mountains and how upset you are about the trees being cut. I am too. But think about what you can do to stop it. Perhaps the forestry school you told me about will introduce you to people who share your passion about saving them. I know you don't like school but you are as smart as I am and I believe you are strong and capable of doing anything you put your mind to.

Now I must go. My patients need me. Especially that poor little boy. I hope I can take care of him like I took care of you two years ago. Too bad I don't have the trees and plants to make healing medicine for him.

I hope you are doing well and I look forward to my return to the farm in several months for a short break in my training.

Your loving sister,

Rebecca

On the way to the hospital Rebecca thought about Gary and David and the possible similarities between their situation and hers. She loved Ben but received a letter from a doctor whom she later learned wanted to be her suitor. Was she wrong for being curious and excited about that? He was interesting, and they had a love of medicine in common. He made her feel attractive and important. Maybe David made her brother feel interesting and important too. Was that so wrong?

Maybe it wasn't. But she mailed the letter anyway.

When Rebecca arrived at the children's ward, the little boy's mother was there visiting her son. She wore a shawl over her long, plain, dark dress, a white apron held to her shoulders and back with straight pins. Rebecca watched the boy cling to his mother despite the burns on his arms.

Talking slowly and enunciating each word in English, Rebecca asked, "Would- you- be- willing- to-leave- your- shawl- here- for- your- boy? He- cries- for- you. It- may- comfort- him- to- have- something- of- yours."

The little boy's mother said, "Ya," and gave her shawl to her son, who placed it under his nose, sniffing in and out. That night he slept for the first time since he came to the hospital and clung to it day and night.

Rebecca's supervisor questioned where she got the idea to give the boy his mother's shawl. Rebecca smiled. "I thought about what it would be like to be a child alone in a strange place, especially if I couldn't speak their language, and how smelling and feeling something familiar would be comforting."

"That shows you're thinking about your patient's well-being. Well done."

Rebecca appreciated the praise, but her ideas were not always welcomed. Some doctors became angry when she questioned them or made suggestions, and senior nurses resented Rebecca because she didn't always follow the rules or knew more than they did. Despite their disapproval, her determination to do her best was above anyone's opinion of her. Her mother and Back So Straight had taught her well.

But near the end of her practice in the pediatric ward, she was assigned to children with diphtheria. Terrified she would get the disease, she was told to wrap a cotton cloth across her face and wash her hands with carbolic soap after touching a child, bed linens, and any other equipment she used to care for the children. Linens had to be placed in drawstring laundry bags to be taken by the housekeepers directly to the laundry house.

Rebecca learned in her infectious disease course that Hopkins physicians, always on the cutting edge of medicine, recently began using antitoxin they learned about from Dr. William Park, a biologist from New York.

However, the disease ravaged the city, especially the poorest neighborhoods. Despite the use of the antitoxin, each day at least one child died from the disease that began with a sore throat, fever, and a cough. Parents waited too long to bring their children to the hospital, thinking they were just getting a cold. But the poor little ones quickly developed purulent nasal discharge, swollen neck, and difficulty breathing. Often the bacteria affected their heart and nervous system, making it nearly impossible for them to survive.

After a particularly hard day, a little four-year-old girl in her care died of diphtheria. It was Rebecca's job to administer post-mortem care. She was careful to tie a cloth across her nose and mouth when she bathed the girl, put a clean nightgown on her small body, and brushed her fine brown hair. Rebecca arranged a woven blanket over the girl's body, and turned it down to her chest to reveal a clean linen sheet. Finally, she placed her right hand over her left, which was missing fingers due to a birth defect, and rested them on top of her small midsection. The little girl looked like she was sleeping.

Rebecca waited in the ward until the doctor told the parents their child had died. When the mother and father came to see their daughter for the last time, they flung themselves on her body, weeping loudly. Rebecca took them aside and tried her best to comfort them. She lifted her mask so they could see her face. "Your little girl was very brave. She died quietly while I held her and..."

Before she could finish, Dr. Ames strutted into the ward. "You are disturbing the other children. Please be brief." Rebecca quickly put back the mask and hoped Dr. Ames wouldn't recognize her. "Doctor, I'll stay with them for a while until they have a chance to say goodbye to their child. Please give them a little more time."

"Are you questioning my authority? Who do you think you are? I'll report you to Miss Nutting."

Rebecca shook her head sympathetically at the parents, who hurriedly left the room. She followed them into the corridor. "I'm sorry for what happened."

"Thank you for your compassion," the girls' mother said between sobs as she and the girl's father held each other up and shuffled down the hallway.

Several hours later, Rebecca was placing dirty linens in the special drawstring bag in the linen closet when she overheard that same doctor talking to a colleague.

"Do you know Miss Wagner, the student nurse who worked in this ward today?"

"Yes, I know who you mean. The tall one with black hair?"

"That's the one. She was insubordinate with me today, trying to tell me what to do. I ought to have her dismissed. I heard she and Dr. Morgan were seen together. What does he want with a girl like her? She may be smart but she's a troublemaker. And she looks like a mulatto. If it weren't for Dr. Morgan and his family, I would make sure she never practices nursing again, so help me, God."

CHAPTER 67

A MONTH BEFORE THEIR TWO-WEEK VACATION, REBECCA AND Bertha moved to a new room on the first floor of the nurses' home, next to the recently added annex. Rebecca was relieved they would not have additional roommates. One Maude was enough. She was also pleased the windows in her room gave her a welcome view of the trees and grass.

Except for the time spent with Christopher and a few evenings spent in the parlor playing games, her days melted into one another as she worked on the wards, tried to please those who outranked her, and studied notes from daily lectures. Rebecca's classes consisted of practical teaching and training in medical, surgical and gynecological work in free and private wards. Her least favorite subject was medical nursing. Caring for patients with strokes was the most difficult. Many were incontinent and needed their beds changed frequently throughout the day. This also meant hauling water to wash patients and rolling them over to clean their backsides.

Cardiac patients were also difficult, having suffered massive heart attacks and were completely bedridden. Others had circulatory problems that caused their whole bodies to swell. One died while she was bathing him. That day was etched in her memory because her patient had red hair and a mustache like her grandfather. Rebecca recalled how lovingly her grandmother and mother took care of him—and the time she scolded Grandpa for accusing Grandma of doing nothing.

Some days she was assigned to fifty patients. After more than eight hours, her back hurt and she ached all over from lifting and shoving and carrying buckets of water. Her uniforms were stained with body fluids and her own perspiration. She often fell asleep while studying in the evening, too tired to turn the pages of her notebooks.

Even though she wasn't fond of medical nursing, since that day the little girl died in her arms and Dr. Ames complained that she was insubordinate, Rebecca vowed she would never take care of children after she graduated. Although Miss Nutting never disciplined her about the incident, Rebecca still felt the sting of Dr. Ames' disapproval. The list of people who judged her was growing. First Gunther. Then Dr. and Mrs. Morgan. Now Dr. Ames. Maybe it's true. What does Christopher see in her?

"What do you mean you're not the right woman for me? Where did you get that nonsense?" Christopher put his arm around her shoulders and drew her close to him as they rode past city hall and toward one of Baltimore's eight city parks in his shiny blue buggy. Large chestnut trees in full summer green gave shade to summer's hot sun.

Rebecca bit her lip and thought about how she was going to answer without sounding like she was whining. "I might as well tell you. I went against Dr. Ames orders and comforted a mother and father who had just lost their little girl to diphtheria."

Christopher looked at her with a frown on his face. "Did he report you to the senior nurse or Miss Nutting?"

"I don't know. But he did complain about me to another doctor. He said if it wasn't for you, he'd have me dismissed." Rebecca tried to hold back the tears that were pooling in her eyes. She looked away and pretended to cough.

Christopher winced. "That bastard. He's a brilliant doctor but I never did like his arrogance. Try not to worry about him. Be a little more taciturn. If Miss Nutting didn't discipline you, nothing will happen."

"What does that mean? Taciturn? Turn the other cheek?"

He laughed. "No… reticent. Don't give him the satisfaction of a response."

Rebecca watery eyes searched his face. She wasn't sure his response was what she wanted to hear. "Oh. But there's more. He said he doesn't know what you see in me." Sobs wracked her chest. All the hurt and self-doubts rose to the surface and spilled out along with her tears.

He tightened the reigns and stopped the horse under the shade of trees. "Rebecca, you are the most beautiful, interesting, and intelligent woman I've ever met. I'm proud to be seen in public with you. It doesn't matter to me what Dr. Ames or anyone else thinks about you." After taking a white handkerchief out of his pocket and wiping the tears from her face, he leaned forward and tenderly kissed each cheek. Then he wrapped his arms around her and kissed her passionately on the mouth. "My lovely Rebecca, I love you."

He loves me. He thinks I'm interesting and intelligent. But what about everyone else?

"Christopher, you are sure? I'm just a farm girl. I know nothing about your world… your place in Baltimore's society… or what your family thinks of me."

"They'll love you just as much as I do. Just give me a chance to prove it."

Rebecca took her hands and placed them on either side of his face. She looked in his eyes, searching for approval. She saw the love in his eyes.

Christopher smiled broadly, his eyes crinkling in the corners. "Come, let's walk in the park and sit by the pond. I'll race you there."

"When I say so, 'go.'"

He had no sooner said go when a young man on a bicycle nearly ran Rebecca down, stopping within inches of her legs. The bicyclist jumped off and gently laid his roadster on the ground. "Oh, my dear girl. I almost crashed into you. That would have been a disaster. A pretty woman like you." He bowed and swept his arm along his body, his eyes never leaving Rebecca's face. "You must forgive my audacity. Surely a lady like you has it in her heart to overlook my temerity."

Rebecca lifter her hand to her heart and smiled. "Of course. You did not cause me any harm." Audacity? Temerity?

Christopher marched between Rebecca and the young man and raised his hand. "She's quite all right, but next time watch where you race or you'll answer to me."

The bicyclist smiled and stood up his roadster. He examined the white tires and narrow fenders. When he finished, he leaned past Christopher and blew a kiss to Rebecca, who giggled softly. The young man raised his hat in salute as he raced away.

"What was that man thinking? He almost killed you."

Rebecca smiled, her nose wrinkling in delight. "I think you're jealous, Mr. Morgan."

"Me, jealous? That man flirted with you."

"Yes, I think he did. But no harm was done, was it?"

Christopher smiled back. "You're right, Miss Wagner. I confess. But all this commotion has made me hungry. Would you go to the Bay with me? I know a lovely inn I would like to take you to."

An inn?

CHAPTER 68

THE BUGGY BROUGHT THEM TO A BEAUTIFUL NEW INN ON THE waterfront, a Victorian-style building with intricate woodworking around the porch and eaves of the second floor. The handcrafted trim was painted blue and white, while the shingles on the gable ends were bright pink. Lanterns hung on the porch ceilings and posts around the inn, casting golden shadows on the wooden structures.

Rebecca took Christopher's arm as they walked up the steps to the front entrance. The innkeeper greeted them and led them to a small alcove near the back of the dining room where a large window afforded them a view of the water. Low flying birds swooped along the channels and through tall reeds and grasses.

Dinner was her favorite—a dozen clams, roasted blue fish, wild rice, and fresh corn. By this time Rebecca had acquired a taste for seafood, and didn't need coaching to understand the menu. Christopher ordered fine wine. After dinner he whispered to the waiter, "Bring a small vanilla cake to the table and serve us when it comes."

Rebecca looked puzzled but said nothing. In several minutes, a colored waiter with gloved hands carrying a delicately decorated cake arrived at their table. He cut small pieces and placed them on small clear plates covered with paper doilies.

"Happy birthday, Rebecca." Am I correct in saying you are about twenty… twenty-two?"

She made him wait for an answer, playing coy. "Twenty on the nose."

Christopher smiled and said, "Please excuse me. I'll return in a moment."

On his way out of the room, he ordered the waiter to clear the table. When he returned, he placed a large package in front of her.

"Happy Birthday, Rebecca. I hope you like it."

Rebecca slowly opened the box. Inside the layers of white tissue paper was a pale blue lace-trimmed panne dress with attached jabot, tulle, and lace petticoat, and satin bustle.

Her eyes were wide with astonishment. She glanced at the dress and then Christopher. The latest Victorian fashion, no doubt. "Christopher, I don't know how to thank you. It's the most beautiful dress I've ever seen—but where will I wear such a fancy dress?"

"I want you to wear it when I take you to the opera when you return from Pennsylvania. The New York Metropolitan Opera is traveling to Baltimore. Olive Fromstad from Stockholm will be singing *The Song of the Lark.*"

"I've never been to an opera, nor do I know anything about it."

"That's all right. I'll teach you. Miss Fromstad is known for her impassioned portrayal of Richard Wagner's heroines. Who knows, Richard may be a distant relative of yours!" He had a twinkle in his eye, but Rebecca didn't notice. That inner voice of uncertainty about their compatibility kept her from enjoying the moment.

"I doubt that very much. My father's a farmer—probably never heard of opera or Richard Wagner."

"It doesn't matter to me."

"Christopher, I'm afraid I don't know much about your world beyond medicine. You're so worldly compared to me. A pretty dress won't change me into the kind of woman you deserve. Maybe I should give the dress back to you." Just like the dress she should have given back to Lilly and Maggie.

The young doctor frowned. "You'll do no such thing! I'm proud of you, and want to show you to the world. Please allow me to spoil you, give you gifts—take you places you've never been." His eyes riveted on her face.

Rebecca smiled and placed the dress back in its box. When she looked up, he was smiling too. Their eyes found each other. In that instant Rebecca knew she loved this man, not because he gave her gifts but because he was kind, generous, and obviously adored her.

When dinner was over, Christopher took her hands in his. "My dear Rebecca. I love you. I know you love me too. Tell me it's true."

She took a deep breath and closed her eyes. When she opened them, Christopher was leaning forward, his face close to hers.

"Yes, it's true. I do love you."

He lifted her hand to his lips and kissed it. "Rebecca, I'm a twenty-four-year-old man. I need you. Tonight. Please say you'll stay with me here at the inn. No one knows us. We needn't worry about being seen together. I can reserve a suite and register us as Mr. and Mrs. Whoever. Say you will. Please." His pleading eyes searched her face for the slightest hint of approval.

Rebecca sat back in her chair. Her pulse throbbed in her temples. Stay with him overnight. Wouldn't that be doing just what Maude did? Oh my, Bertha. What will she say?

"I… can't. I'm afraid. What if I get caught staying out all night?"

"Isn't there a way into your room other than the front door?"

"Yes, a window is on the same level as the new annex. But I don't think I can risk getting caught. If I do, I'll have to leave nursing school. I've worked so hard—I'm sure you don't want that either."

"You won't get caught. I'll take you back early tomorrow morning. No one will know you were gone except your roommate, and if you ask her not to, she won't tell anyone."

"But suppose she does?"

"I'll tell Miss Nutting you became ill this evening and it was too late to return to the hospital, so I took you to my home."

She bit her lip. "I don't… I don't know Christopher. I have one more year of nurses' training to finish and I'm determined to do so. If I agree to come with you, I know what will happen. We won't be able to resist each other."

"Rebecca, please believe me when I tell you I'm very much in love with you. I'm asking you to trust me. Say you'll come with me. The room is beautiful—there's a fireplace and large window facing the inlet. You'll love it."

Rebecca's mind was racing. He was so handsome and wonderful. They loved each other. Maybe this wasn't so wrong. But what about Ben? She felt nauseated for betraying him all these months, and yet here she was thinking about staying overnight with Christopher.

Her thoughts were interrupted when Christopher touched her arm. "Rebecca, will you come with me?"

She struggled between fear and excitement. All good judgment and reason began to slip away until she admitted to herself: he's asking me to sleep with him. Rebecca was about to say no when she looked in his eyes and saw his expectant face. She hesitated, then nodded slightly.

Christopher registered them as Rebecca nervously waited in the parlor. They walked up the stairs, Christopher steadying her with his arm and carrying the dress box by its cord in the other one as though it was a suitcase. He winked at her when they reached the landing that circled the entrance to the suites.

The heavy ornate walnut door had leaves carved around matching trim. Christopher held the door open and waited until she entered. A large bedroom with an open doorway that led to a bathroom with a claw-footed bathtub, sink, and water closet met her eyes. There was an adjoining sitting room with matching velvet chaise chairs. It was just as Christopher described, only lovelier.

A hand crocheted coverlet swept down to the floor and covered the large poster bed with pillows stacked against the entire headboard. The fire in the fireplace and small gaslights on the tables cast a warm glow. Rebecca walked over to the double windows and looked out over the water. Reeds and cattails stood like tall sentinels along the winding channels of dark water that eventually gave way to the inlet. It was near dusk, and the birds swooped down near the surface of the water to feed on insects.

"Rebecca, please sit down with me near the fire."

She lowered herself to the soft cushions and nervously waited to see what he wanted her to do next. He softly kissed her face, first forehead, then both cheeks, then each lip. His hands ran down her arms and slid to her breasts. Then he kissed her hungrily.

Her breath caught in her throat.

Christopher said, "Please stand up." She nodded and closed her eyes. She felt as if in a trance—numb to the reality of what she was about to do.

He turned her around and unbuttoned each small black button on the back of her dress, slowly at first then as fast as he could. The dress fell to the floor. He unlaced her corset and placed it on the floor next to her dress. When she was naked except for her chemise, he turned her around again and looked at her.

"Rebecca, you are the most beautiful woman I have ever seen. Please let me make you mine."

She felt herself responding to his touch, the fullness in her breasts and groin growing intense. "Christopher, I'm frightened. I've never been with a man. I'm afraid I'll become with child."

He undid his tie and took off his shoes before answering. "I need you to trust me. Do you remember something called Coitus Interruptus? I'll pull away from you so this doesn't happen."

Rebecca took a deep breath. "I know what it means because I read about it. But I'm still not sure about this…"

"Please… trust me."

Rebecca hesitated again. Christopher kissed her firmly on the mouth and teased her lips with his tongue.

"I… I do."

He took off his trousers and walked over to where Rebecca stood, her eyes riveted on his manhood that was erect through his tight drawers. Rebecca couldn't help but stare. She had never seen an aroused man close-up except for the old man in the medical ward who was half-conscious.

Christopher picked her up and carried her to the bed. She quickly went under the coverlet and soft, white linen sheet. He slipped out of his underwear and climbed in beside her. This time it was Rebecca who pulled him close.

She felt his heart beat against her. He responded by kissing her lips one at a time, then slipping his tongue into her mouth. She tasted his mouth—like the wine they had been drinking, sweet and soft.

Christopher stopped kissing her long enough to remove her chemise. Her breasts were firm, her nipples dark and erect. She shuddered as he kissed them.

"Your skin is so smooth and soft. I've tried to imagine what you would look like naked, Rebecca," as he placed his hand on her flat abdomen. Rebecca admitted to herself that she had fantasies about his body too, but never imagined he had so much hair. She even surprised herself as she traced the light strip of hair that grew from his navel to his manhood with her index finger.

He responded by exploring every inch of her body. She closed her eyes and surrendered to the sensations she felt inside and out. Her lack of modesty helped her surrender to him. Perhaps growing up on a farm and seeing naked women as she bathed them took away any shyness she may have had.

Christopher whispered, "Rebecca, I don't want to hurt you. I'll be as gentle as I can, but are you ready for me?"

"Yes, I think I am."

He hovered over her, and looked down at her face. "Good. I can't wait any longer." She felt his manhood touch the soft wetness, then a resistance as her hymen broke. She gasped, then relaxed as the movement of their bodies took over. Rebecca arched her body against his. Their bodies moved together. The slight pain she felt gave way to pleasure.

Christopher suddenly pulled away. "Oh God, I didn't want to do that. I never realized how difficult it would be. Rebecca, are you all right?"

She sighed and pulled the sheet over her naked body. "Yes. Just a little embarrassed." Her groin ached and she felt a sticky wetness between her legs. It had a sweet, starchy smell. Underneath her was a small stain of pinkish blood. Christopher pulled her to him. They lay nestled against each other. He wrapped his arms around her, as her abdomen rested against his manhood. Neither of them spoke. Then Christopher got out of bed. He brought a clean cloth and towel to her and gently washed Rebecca's face, then her thighs, and dried them with the towel. Finally, he washed and dried himself. She was touched by his tenderness. Rebecca laid her head on his chest. He responded by wrapping his arms around her until they fell asleep.

Rebecca was awake before the first light of morning. She watched Christopher as he slept. Lying on his back, his breathing was heavy, and now and then his legs twitched. The room had grown cold, so she snuggled next to Christopher to keep warm.

She liked the feeling of lying next to him. Secure. Loved. At peace.

Rebecca gently kissed Christopher on the mouth. He opened his eyes and blinked several times before speaking. "Um… do that again." She kissed him on the cheek and quickly got up before he would try to change her mind.

She retreated to the bathroom. Her groin was still tender from last night. She gently washed her bottom and put on her chemise before returning to the bedroom. They both stared at each other as they got dressed. Christopher pulled on his tight-fitting, knee-length flannel drawers, then his undershirt. When Rebecca slipped on her dress, Christopher smiled and kissed her shoulder before buttoning it. Rebecca sat down and stretched her legs as she pulled on her stockings. She saw Christopher watch her, catching the gleam in his eyes.

"There's no time for breakfast. That's too bad. They're usually delicious," Christopher said, pulling on garters to hold up his socks and lacing up his black and white dress boots. "We'll have to wait till we can stay longer in the morning."

Rebecca turned her attention to her stockings, too stunned to think they would stay overnight again. It would be too risky. Her reputation was at stake, not to mention her career as a nurse.

On the way to the nurses' home, the reality of what she had done began to sink in. She felt like a hypocrite. Sleeping with a man… not married. Sneaking into the residence just like Maude. Reporting her roommate and getting her expelled. Ben. Betraying him. Giving in to her passion instead of using her head.

Baltimore's streets were mostly dark except for the gas lanterns flickering their y-shaped flames. The carriage ride was bumpy, the air cool. Christopher held her close till they reached the alley behind the nurses' residence.

Rebecca felt awkward. She didn't know whether or not to say something about the night they spent together. "Good night, Christopher. I mean good morning. Don't forget I'll be going home soon for a two-week vacation."

"Tell me you're not sorry about last night."

Rebecca sighed deeply. "No… I love you, Christopher, and look forward to seeing you again. But you must go now. Someone may notice us. Bertha will let me in through the window."

"Please come back to Baltimore, Rebecca. Goodbye. I love you."

Did Christopher suspect she may not return?

She climbed the wooden stairs to the flat roof, stepping silently on each step. Rebecca dreaded having to sneak into the building but it was too late now. She tapped on the glass with the heel of her shoe. After a few minutes, she tapped again. Bertha came near the window and shook her head no.

"Please open it."

With a muffled voice, she said, "I shouldn't let you in."

Rebecca leaned her face against the glass. "Please open the window."

Bertha quietly opened the sash and Rebecca crawled inside. Neither spoke while she quickly undressed and changed into her uniform.

"I know what you're thinking," said Rebecca.

Her roommate shrugged her shoulders. "Well, if it's about Maude, yes I am."

"Bertha, I'm so sorry. I was with Dr. Morgan. We love each other."

"I can't believe you were stupid enough to do that. What were you thinking? What if you get caught? I'll be alone if you have to leave."

Rebecca's throat tightened. She felt guilty about betraying her loyal roommate. "I know. I wasn't thinking about that."

"What about Dr. Morgan? Aren't you afraid now that you slept with him, he'll move on to someone else? You know these men—once you give them what they want."

"Oh, no. Not Christopher. He would never do that to me." But her roommate's bluntness caught her by surprise.

"How do you know?"

"I… I just know."

"Listen—you and I went to Miss Nutting to report Maude. Now you do the same thing. You're just a hypocrite. Say one thing and do another. I should report you too."

"Please don't. I'm sorry… I know I made a big mistake. I beg you. It won't happen again… I promise." But Rebecca felt the sting of being called a hypocrite.

"Good God, Rebecca. You took a big chance. I signed in for you last evening. But don't expect me to ever do it again."

CHAPTER 69

THE FOLLOWING SUNDAY WHEN REBECCA SAW CHRISTOPHER, there was an awkwardness between them. He was kind and affectionate, but to her disappointment, said nothing about their night together. And she was too embarrassed to bring it up. He did ask her how it went after she returned to her room that morning, but he didn't question her further. But right before she left on her two-week break, he sent her a note along with a single red rose.

> *I will miss you when you are gone and look forward with great anticipation when I see you again. Do be safe and return to Baltimore as soon as you can.*
>
> *I remain your devoted and loving companion,*
>
> *Christopher*

Rebecca felt somewhat better after reading his note, but Bertha's remark about Christopher moving on now that they had been intimate haunted her. And made her even more terrified to tell him about Ben. She also had mixed feelings about going home for summer break. She wanted to see her family and Back So Straight, but fear about facing Ben loomed ahead. To make matters worse, the train ride was deathly hot. Rebecca nearly gagged at the odors of sweaty bodies and coal soot that wafted through the passenger car.

Her thoughts drifted from Christopher and their night together… then to Ben. Then to Maggie and Lilly. She was eager to see them again but afraid her time in McAlisterville would be tainted by the dishonesty she was hiding from everyone.

Rebecca was startled when the train steward announced "Mifflin." Not already. Gathering her suitcase and satchel, she walked off the train and looked for the family wagon. She spotted her father and waved. Her spirits lifted as she watched Jenny pull the wagon to where she stood.

"Pop, I'm glad you came to pick me up."

Elwood grabbed her suitcase and threw it in the wagon before hugging her. "Nice to have you home, Rebecca. Been a long year."

"I know. It has been for me too."

She was startled by the way her father had aged. His face was thin and drawn. Lines she never saw before lined his forehead, and his hair had gray peppered throughout the brown.

"Pop, tell me the news. What's happening on the farm?"

Elwood waited to answer until he cleared his throat and took a drink of water from a jar resting on the seat. "More timber being cut all around our land. Big patch of bare land on Little Round Top next to the land I sold Eastman… but still don't know who cut them."

Rebecca tried to keep calm but she knew the timber meant more to her Pa than anything else. "I'm sorry Pop. What are you going to do?"

Her father cleared his throat again. "Not much. Can't prove anything. Trees are gone. Must keep the farm going as best as I can."

Rebecca scanned the forests as they traveled east along Main Street West. Large spans of mountains had been laid bare, knee-high tree trunks dotting the ground. Dirt roads crisscrossed the land, huge stacks of brush piled between them. Now and then she spotted small wooden buildings clustered together on the mountain ridges. When they crossed the bridge in Oakland Mills, she gasped. The water in Lost Creek was muddy brown and had debris and small branches floating in the current.

"Pop, what happened to the creek?"

"Had some bad thunderstorms and heavy rain. Washed the mountain ground and everything on it. Went into the runs and streams that feed Lost Creek."

Rebecca stared at the creek as they traveled past it until she couldn't bend her neck any further. "What about the fish and other wild critters that live in it?"

Elwood mumbled something under his breath Rebecca couldn't understand.

"What did you say, Pop?

"I said, how the hell should I know. Ask your brother."

Rebecca drew a deep breath. Her pop had never spoken to her like that. Only to Gary. She moved to the far edge of the seat and fought back the urge to cry. When they reached the farm, she jumped off the wagon and ran into the cabin.

Jane dropped her oven mitts and wrapped her arms around her daughter. "You're home at last. I've missed you so much it hurts."

"Me too, Ma."

"Let me look at you. You're even taller than I remember. Grandma, come into the kitchen. Rebecca's home."

Mary grinned when she came into the kitchen. She touched Rebecca's face. This woman, once meek and thin, looked robust and happy.

"Grandma, you look wonderful," said Rebecca.

"So do you. I can't wait to hear all about what you learned in nurses' training."

Rebecca heard the back door open and turned to see Back So Straight walk into the cabin. The Indian woman's eyes stared at her, a smile breaking across her face. Rebecca embraced her mentor, holding on to her for a long time. Home at last. All four of the women together.

That evening Jane made a big dinner of Rebecca's favorite food, chicken potpie. Gary had returned home late that day, but only gave Rebecca a perfunctory welcome. She chose to ignore him, only because she didn't want anything to spoil her first day home. Rebecca ate three helpings of chicken potpie and sweet-sour pepper cabbage and drank more meadow tea than anyone else. She was too full to eat apple dumplings but put one aside for later.

Rebecca didn't say much to her Pa, either. He was quiet throughout supper, and as soon as he ate, went out to the barn. That was all right with her. She was tired and couldn't wait to sleep in her bed. When she opened the door to her room, she stepped back. On her dresser, nightstand, windowsill and by her bed sat vases of wild flowers and pretty painted stones. Each one had a picture of a plant or flower. She recognized some of them—wild yarrow, lavender, mint, sage, plantain, echinacea and teaberry. Back So Straight.

Rebecca woke up the late the next morning to the familiar smell of the cabin, one of the things she treasured most about coming home. When she went downstairs, no one was there except Jane.

"Where is everyone?"

"They're busy doing chores. But Pop said he saw Ben at the blacksmith in town early this morning. I scolded him for not telling Ben you were home, so why don't you take Jenny and find out if he's still there? Surely you want to see him while you're home."

Rebecca faked a smile. "Of course, I do."

The ride to McAlisterville didn't take nearly long enough for Rebecca to gather her courage, but she rehearsed what she would say over and over. When she turned onto the main road in town, there he was, standing next to the blacksmith's furnace. He turned when he heard her horse, but said nothing.

"Hello, Ben. It's good to see you again." She got down from her horse and clutched her arms to her chest to calm her pounding heart.

"I'm surprised to see you. I didn't know you were home." The solemn look on his face struck Rebecca as a bad sign.

"Yes, I came home yesterday. I guess I should have written to you."

He shrugged his shoulders and turned to speak to the blacksmith. "We'll be leaving now. What do I owe you?"

Before the blacksmith had a chance to answer, a young woman appeared at the doorway of the shop. "I'm ready, Ben, if you are. It's way too hot in here to wait any longer." She took her bonnet off and pushed strands of blond hair off her forehead.

Ben answered, "Yes, just give me a minute to pay my bill." He took some change out of his pocket and handed it to the blacksmith. Then he turned to Rebecca and said, "I'd like you to meet my friend, Emma. We've been together now and she's been going with me to deliver carriages."

The young, plump but pretty woman extended her hand to Rebecca and smiled. "Nice to meet you. Ben told me all about you being in nurses' training school."

"I… yes… I am. I'm pleased to meet you, too," she lied.

"Well, we'd better get along. Good to see you again, Rebecca." Ben took Emma's arm and led her toward a buggy with a handsome palomino horse in front.

Aghast and flustered, Rebecca ignored her impulse to bolt away. But she stayed and regarded the way they sat close together in the buggy. They appeared to be familiar with each other, even affectionate. Rebecca stared in disbelief as they continued down the street until they turned east toward Mifflinburg. The shock of seeing Ben with another woman shook her to the core. She didn't know if she was jealous or relieved. Maybe both. Or maybe neither.

CHAPTER 70

THE IMAGE OF BEN WITH ANOTHER WOMAN HAUNTED Rebecca for days after her encounter with them at the blacksmith shop. She hoped to sort out her feelings by riding Jenny in the mountain trails and meadows. Even after being away for three years, the forests remained her solace, her way to clear her head. But there were so many memories of riding those very paths with Ben, it was impossible to clear her thinking. To make matters worse she found it increasingly difficult to avoid the trails that now crossed through clear-cut sections of land that had been rich with evergreen and deciduous trees just last year.

Late one afternoon when Rebecca returned from riding on the mountain next to Little Round Top, she guided Jenny into the barn and was startled by a bird that had flown inside. The barn swallow flew past her, its V-shaped tail nearly touching her head. As she followed its flight, she observed the large wooden beams and flooring overhead and recognized some of the wood by their grain and color. Oak, poplar, chestnut. Her father had taught her to how to identify the trees that grew on Juniata County mountains and how to differentiate the wood.

Rebecca unsaddled her horse, wiped down her sides and started to brush her coat. But her mind was on the timber it took to build the barn. Lumber would always be needed. But whose trees would be cut and how many?

Jenny nickered and tossed her head up and down. Rebecca sensed someone was in the barn. She stroked her horse's neck and talked to her softly, straining her ears to hear any sounds other than Jenny huffing. Then she heard a boot squeak and turned to see her brother standing behind her.

"Gary, what are you doing sneaking up on me like that?"

"Sorry. I'm not sneaking up on you. Just want to talk in private." He leaned his arm on the side of the stall and looked at Rebecca squarely in the face. "I haven't been very nice to you lately. Sorry. I'm pretty mixed up."

"Well, what's wrong? Might as well tell me about it. I've got to go back to nurses' training next week." Rebecca was genuinely worried about her brother's mental state. Last time she left for the train station, he didn't even say goodbye. Something was terribly wrong.

Gary hesitated, then sat down on a hay bale. "Remember the poem David wrote to me?"

"Yes, I do. I wrote to you about it. Have you and David worked anything out about your future?

"I'm not sure. Just when I think I'm going to stay away from him… I can't. We've spent a lot of time together this summer. He and I have become… well, I don't know how to tell you."

"Oh, no. Don't. I'm afraid of what you're going to say." She bit her lip.

Gary grabbed a pitchfork and tossed a clump of manure onto a pile. "I can't tell anyone else. I know you think I'm… don't say anything to anyone. You're the only one I can trust."

Rebecca drew a deep breath. "I won't. But you must hide this awful thing from Pop and Ma. They won't understand."

"But you do, don't you, Rebecca? Tell me I'm not a freak. I… David and I…"

"Stop. We already talked about the trouble you and David will cause. There are those who'll shun you and even hurt you if they find out."

Gary backed up against the stall and stared at her, his face squeezed together.

"I'm sorry." Rebecca reached out to put her hand on his shoulder but he jerked aside and trudged out of the barn.

"Wait. Gary, some back." But he ignored her.

She stood looking at the barn door, the pained look on her brother's face lingering long after he was gone. Jenny whinnied and pushed her nose against Rebecca's arm. She finished grooming her horse, each stroke of the brush reminding her of her night with Christopher. She tried to imagine two men loving each other. What did they do together? How did they touch each other?

A familiar voice startled her. "My child, I have been seeking you. It has been a long time since we sat on my bench."

"Back So Straight. I'm surprised to see you here." Rebecca embraced her mentor and kissed her gently on the cheek.

"Come with me. I want to speak to you."

Rebecca cocked her head to the side and frowned, puzzled that Back So Straight came seeking her rather than the other way around. "All right. I would like that very much."

They walked out of the barn and sat on the tree bench near Back So Straight's cabin just like they had dozens of times before, quietly listening to the sounds of the forest and waiting to speak. A black-capped chickadee landed on a feathery branch of a nearby hemlock tree and pecked the tiny seeds out of the small pinecones dripping from its tip. Soon Wind pushed open the cabin door and trotted to Rebecca's side, her tail wagging briskly.

Back So Straight slid forward and faced Rebecca. "I have been eager to hear about what you are learning. Do you have peace in your heart when you care for the people who come to you for healing?"

Taken by surprise, Rebecca fished to understand what the Indian woman was asking. "What do you mean?"

Back So Straight leaned sideways against her young friend. "There is much turmoil in this place. Some of our forests are no more. I struggle to find herbs and plants. Maybe there will come a time when these things will not be found anywhere. Perhaps your medicine will be all that's left to heal those who are sick."

Rebecca sucked in a deep breath. She hoped she hadn't forgotten what Back So Straight taught her before she left for Baltimore? "What will we do if they are gone forever?"

Her mentor didn't answer.

Hoping to soothe her fears, Rebecca said, "I learned there are many new medicines that do not come from the forests. We have special men who make something called compounds and they press them into little tablets that look like small stones. But I don't think they heal any better than the ones we make from the forest. Maybe the plants and trees will grow back."

Back So Straight sat quietly before she picked up a twig and broke it. "I pray to the great healer, Mother Earth, that this is so."

Rebecca spent her last week at the farm helping with chores and sitting on the porch talking to her Ma and grandma. Although she was happy to be home and away from the relentless work in the hospital wards, her mind raced with thoughts about Ben and his new girl, Gary and David, the cutting of the forests, and her own ambivalence toward all of them. She felt tired and she admitted to herself: she missed Ben. The farm held memories of their time together and her fond feelings for him surfaced again and again. But then she thought about Christopher. It seemed like a long time since they had slept together, even though it had only been less than a month. She pictured the inn and the look on Christopher's face when he begged her to stay with him. Rebecca wondered if Gary had the same feelings for David.

She didn't want to return to nurses' training in a state of turmoil, so early in the morning the day before she left, Rebecca trudged to Back So Straight's cabin. Wind sat near the open door and greeted her with wet licks. "May I come in?"

The Indian woman came out from behind the blanket that separated her cot from the rest of the cabin. She was wearing a cotton sleeping dress and her long, black hair was hanging loosely down her back. She sat down on a chair and motioned for Rebecca to sit on the bench.

Rebecca studied her mentor's appearance. She had never seen her dressed in anything but buckskin and skirts and cotton blouses. Trying to hide her surprise, Rebecca returned her eyes to Back So Straight's face. She saw sadness in the drooping eyelids and turned down mouth. But when the Indian woman reached down to pet her dog, her face brightened slightly.

"What is it that brings you here so early in the morning?"

"I'm sorry to disturb you but I need to ask you questions about something that is greatly troubling me. It concerns Gary."

Back So Straight placed a few small pieces of wood in the woodstove. She took a small rawhide pouch and emptied dried lemon balm leaves into a pot of water, which she placed on top of the stove. Then she set two cups made out of gourds on the table by the window. When the water started to boil, she poured the leafy mixture into each cup, followed by raw honey she scraped off a piece of honeycomb.

"Here, my child. Share some of my tea before the men come with their many saws and horses and take the plants away."

Ah, this was why Back So Straight wasn't dressed, Rebecca realized.

"Now, what is your question?"

Rebecca sipped the sweet-tart liquid. The familiar taste calmed her and gave her courage to ask what she desperately wanted to know. "I am almost embarrassed to ask you this, but what do you know about men who love other men?"

"Why do you want to know this?"

Rebecca took another drink of tea before she answered. "Gary read a love poem to me from his friend David, Maggie's brother. They became close friends and have been writing and seeing each other when David comes to McAlisterville in the summertime."

Back So Straight listened quietly, petting Wind's ears and head.

"The poem spoke of love between the two of them. I don't know what to say. I already told Gary to never see David again."

The Indian woman looked squarely at her young friend. "Let me explain how my people saw men and women who were attracted to other men and women. They saw them as spiritual leaders and teachers. Their spiritual gifts were highly valued. My great-grandfather told about a 'two-spirited' man who married a great warrior. His story was passed down from his generation to mine. The white man called them 'bercache,' but that was an insult."

"Why?"

"Because 'bercache' were sacred."

Rebecca shook her head. "That's hard for me to imagine."

"Yes, but you must try. My great grandfather also told stories about babies who were a boy or girl at birth but sometimes saw themselves the opposite. Our people saw this as being doubly blessed, having the spirit of a man and the spirit of a woman."

Rebecca cringed, her shoulders drawn up toward her ears. "How can that happen?"

The Indian woman reached out and patted Rebecca's hand. "I don't know. How do the sun and moon know how to shine? Or the wind to blow?"

"What should I do?"

"Do not think of your brother or his friend as evil. They are specially made. But they must be very careful. They will be rejected and shunned."

"Yes, I know, but it'll be harder for my family. They will be ashamed of him and our church will condemn them both. Tongues will wag. It'll be horrible."

Back So Straight held her hands up. "You must keep loving your brother no matter what others do or say. Try to be patient. He will need you to keep him from going mad or running away."

As Rebecca tried to understand what Back So Straight advised, an uneasy feeling crept up her back. She looked down at her tea leaves. They had all floated to the top, looking like small trees drifting on dark water.

CHAPTER 71

REBECCA TRAVELED FROM THE NORTHERNMOST OF THE FIVE train stations in Baltimore to the hospital in an electric streetcar. Men and women speaking Polish, Italian, German, and Irish crowded the seats and isles. She learned their dialects while caring for them in the free wards. Colored people tried to cram into the streetcar but were often left to hang on the sides or stand on the small platform in the back.

The sounds and smells reminded her of her first trip across town on a public wagon, just two years ago… the familiar screeches of the electric streetcars and the clomping of horses trotting on busy streets. She pictured the shops and markets that lined the streets and the remnants of oyster shells, rotting debris in the gutters, and ever-present horse manure.

She leaned back against the seat and held a handkerchief over her nose to mask the smell of the streets and the sweaty bodies of those around her. Her mind drifted to the wards and the odors of sickness and disinfectants. Then to the time she fainted and Christopher came to her aid. And finally to her night with Christopher and her first surrender as a woman.

Despite the noise and jarring streetcar, Rebecca nearly fell asleep. Her satchel fell on the floor and landed on her foot, waking her in time to step off the car and onto the street.

Bertha was in the parlor when she walked in the nurses' residence. "Rebecca. I was hoping you'd come back."

"Did you think I wouldn't?" Rebecca wasn't sure what her roommate meant.

"No, but I didn't know. Christopher stopped by hoping to catch you when you arrived."

Rebecca's heart skipped a beat. "Was he here?"

"Yes. He just left a few minutes ago."

"Did he leave a message?" She plopped her suitcase down and looked pleadingly at Bertha.

"Yes. He said he would come by on Sunday and take you wherever you wanted to go."

"But that's almost a week away."

Bertha looked annoyed. "Come on, let's get you unpacked and go to dinner. I'm hungry."

They sat at a table with senior students and exchanged stories about their time away. But soon the conversation turned to what lay ahead as senior student nurses. They were told that older students were often assigned to six months on special duty because it gave them more educational and practical experience, especially if they worked as private duty nurses after they graduated. They were also placed in charge of wards to save money that would have been paid to hire head nurses.

The next morning, the women in the senior class were called to meet in the large lecture room for their assignments. Miss Nutting gave descriptions of the various departments they would be rotating in: operating room, dispensary, private wards, maternity and children's wards.

Rebecca whispered to Bertha, "I hope I get assigned to the operating room first."

"Why? I heard it's pretty gory."

"I think I'm ready. Remember, I saw lots of gory stuff as a farm girl."

Miss Nutting scanned the faces of her students and added, "Keep in mind… you may be given other assignments such as working in positions of responsibility if your progress is satisfactory. I will now give you your first assignments."

Just as she hoped, Rebecca was assigned to duty in the operating rooms. She assumed she was prepared for what she was about to see since she grew up on a farm and witnessed accidents to their farm animals. Once a pig got her head caught in the fence and pulled off one of her ears trying to get it out. She also helped her father castrate bulls and put the mutilated testicles in a bucket to later empty in the woods. And Gary and Jake often brought home animals that they had trapped, and as they skinned them, threw bloody animal parts near her feet while they watched her jump away.

But these were people, not animals. Nothing prepared her for what she witnessed and what she had to do. At first, she, along with her classmates, viewed surgery up above from a surgical theater. Gauze sponges, retractors, hemostats, drains, hoses, sutures, and needles were arranged on metal trays surrounding the operating table. Nurses poured water into basins and handed clean towels to the doctors.

She watched a nurse give the patient anesthesia with a mask, only minutes later the surgeon made the incision in the man's side. The man screamed and the doctor motioned for the nurse to drip more ether on the gauze pad over his nose and mouth. Finally, the man became unconscious.

Doctors and prominent citizens also watched surgeries and talked freely while the surgeons removed what appeared to be a small tumor. Rebecca was appalled at the casual conversation that went on among them. Once in a while the surgeon looked up at their colleagues in the gallery above and nodded, or held up a bloody hand holding a piece of tissue.

Thankfully, her day off duty was her saving grace. Christopher took her to a restaurant and carriage ride to Federal Hill where they watched ships enter the basin. They rode an electric streetcar from the Electric Park in the northwest part of the city near Belvedere Avenue. He pointed out the Sharp Street Methodist Episcopal Church, one of the leading Colored Methodist and Protestant churches in the city. Rebecca was fascinated by the idea of a separate church for colored people.

Their final excursion was the newly constructed children's playground at Carroll Park in southwest city off Washington Boulevard. They watched children play on swings hanging from metal frames twenty feet high with ladders to climb to the top. Rebecca cringed to see children perched on the top bar and hanging from their knees. Groups of girls in white dresses and hats hung from ropes suspended from a Maypole, their bodies suspended as they circled the tall tower.

Christopher, however, was enamored by the massive brick power plant on Pier 4 along the East Pratt Street waterfront on the Patapsco River. Four tall smokestacks rose above the industrial plant, belching black smoke into the air above the brackish water. Rebecca thought about the patients she took care of that had difficulty breathing, wondering if they worked in this plant and the dozens of other buildings along the basin.

Christopher took her to a new restaurant and they went for a walk near the bay. They didn't talk about their night at the inn, but Rebecca wondered if he would ask her to stay with him again. She wasn't sure if she would feel glad or disappointed.

When they returned to the nurses' residence, one of Rebecca's classmates approached her. "I picked up this package addresses to you. The carrier must have been delivered yesterday but it was still in the mailroom. I thought you would want to have it."

Rebecca frowned. "Thank you. I can't imagine who would send me something."

Christopher said, "Look at the return address before you open it."

Rebecca turned the package and studied the writing on the corner. She quickly stepped back but it was too late. Christopher squinted and brought the package close to his eyes. "I think it reads McAlisterville . . . a Ben somebody. Who's Ben?"

Rebecca took it from him and tried to calm her shaking hand. "I… no… I'll open it later."

Christopher crossed his arms on his chest. "But who is Ben? Is that your brother's name? I thought you told me his name is Gary."

Rebecca swallowed hard. "He's… yes, my brother's name is Gary."

"Why are you so evasive?"

"Nothing. I… I'll explain the next time I see you." She gripped the package until her knuckles turned white.

"But Rebecca, I need to know who Ben is and why he sent you a package."

She stalled for time, feigning fatigue. "All right. I must go to bed soon. But Ben's just a man who lives in a small town near mine. We used to be special friends until I met you. He also has a new woman in his life, but he must have remembered my birthday for some reason even though it was months ago."

"Open it. I want to see what's inside."

Rebecca tore open the wrapping and pulled out a sliver reticule with a black braided handle. A note written with bold black letters dropped on the floor. They both stooped to retrieve it, but Rebecca reached it first.

"What does it say?" Christopher asked, putting his hands on his hips.

Not able to conceal the note, Rebecca answered in a shaky voice, "Happy Birthday. Love, Ben. See, Ben is just a friend who remembered my birthday." At least she thought that was true.

"Then why did he sign it—love, Ben?"

"I have no idea. He has a new girlfriend and I haven't been in touch with him for a long while." Not a lie but not exactly the truth either.

"All right. I'll say goodbye for now, Rebecca." Christopher walked away briskly and slammed the door.

She stood motionless. Ben. Why did her give her a belated birthday gift? What about Emma?

Christopher seemed angry. He probably didn't believe me. Nothing made sense.

She hid the reticule in her dresser drawer and got ready for bed. When Bertha returned, Rebecca pretended she was asleep, despite the light of the late September evening streaming through the window. Images of both men flashed through her mind. A wonderful day with Christopher, then a gift from Ben. Rebecca tried to sleep but sleep didn't come. She gulped down her breaths to keep from crying.

The next day Rebecca tried to conceal her worry from Bertha, despite the dark circles under her eyes. She had to report for duty in the operating room and steel herself for the tasks ahead. There was no time for figuring out what do about Ben and Christopher.

The first operation was on a young man whose appendix was enlarged and painful. Rebecca was pleased to see that surgeons wore sterile gloves. She couldn't imagine digging into the body and feeling the slippery fat and muscle as he cut through layers to find the organ, then cutting it free and reaching his hand inside to remove it. The smell of blood, antiseptics, and sweating bodies under layers of uniforms and surgical coats made her nauseated. She was glad when she could step to the side of the room for a moment and fold bandages.

Rebecca witnessed gruesome amputations that afternoon. Bones had to be cut with saws. The sound reminded Rebecca of the sawmills at home. Retractors held back muscles and tendons. Thick gauze sponges absorbed blood and other fluids, but some spilled to the floor and splashed onto their shoes. Sometimes a severed limb was given to her to place in a metal basin. A foot, black with gangrene. A leg above the knee crushed in a railway accident. Rebecca wondered what happened to the severed parts. Were they buried? Burned?

One surgery almost made her flee the operating room. A little boy had his hand amputated after a dog nearly bit it off. The small hand was mangled, tendons and bones showing through slices of skin. This time the surgeon did not speak, nor did the nurses. An aura of sadness fell over the room.

Over the next few days Rebecca helped with surgeries to remove tumors, goiters, and wombs. Boils were lanced—pus shot out and sometimes splashed onto her uniform. Some patients woke up before the surgery was finished, and were hastily given more ether or chloroform. Rebecca's job was to gather bloody cloths, take the surgical instruments to be washed and mop the floor.

Breathing in the smell of bloody rags made her gag; she took deep breaths to stop from vomiting.

When she worked on the surgical ward, she gave patients morphine for pain, but they often remained in a stupor for days. Some developed pneumonia from staying in bed too long and died as a result.

Again, Rebecca found it difficult to sleep. When she did, the nightmares of the sawmill and the severed arm jolted her awake. She woke up sweating, unable to go back to sleep. Her earlier excitement about working in the operating room disappeared. Now she just wanted the nightmares to stop.

CHAPTER 72

BERTHA OPENED A PACKAGE OF 'LISTER'S TOWEL SANITARY Towels for Ladies' and placed the pads in her dresser drawer. Rebecca envied her friend. She couldn't afford to buy pads. She had to use strips of cloth sewn into layers during her monthlies, and wash and dry them each day—a chore she hated.

She thought about the last time she wore her monthly cloths. It was right before she left for McAlisterville six weeks ago. She shook her head no. Couldn't be. Just working too hard and not sleeping at night. She folded her arm against her stomach and closed her eyes. Go to bed. Tomorrow her monthly would probably come.

But the next morning Rebecca felt nauseated while brushing her teeth. She mouthed no, no, no, this can't be happening in the mirror. The toothpaste dripped down her chin. She wiped it away and swallowed the saliva that gathered in her mouth. There wasn't any way this could be true. Christopher told her to trust him.

Rebecca pulled herself together and got dressed. No time for breakfast, nor did she have any appetite. She thought to herself, ironically, this was the first day of lectures in obstetric nursing, learning to care for women in the family way and their babies. Please God. She didn't want to be one of them.

With child or not, she hung on every word the teachers said. Instructors and head nurses gave most lectures, but doctors presented the lectures on obstetric complications. Rebecca willed herself to take copious notes, trying to block the thought of her monthly being late out of her mind.

After two weeks of intense, daily lectures, she was assigned to work on the maternity ward. Since most women gave birth at home under the care of midwives, the patients were largely women with complications that required hospitalization. But since the invention of forceps, some women of means wanted a doctor to deliver their babies instead of midwives.

On Rebecca's first day on the ward, she admitted a woman who came to the hospital with swelling in her feet and ankles. Her face was puffy too, and she admitted she had gained over fifty pounds during her pregnancy.

"When did you last pass your urine?" Rebecca asked as she helped her into bed.

"Not for two days."

Rebecca checked her heart rate and blood pressure. Pulse 96. Blood pressure 210 over 100. Much too high. She hid her concern from the patient, but quickly walked to the nurse's station to report it. When she returned, the young mother suddenly began to thrash about, her arms and legs jerking and her head and neck held rigid. Rebecca turned the mother's head to the side so she wouldn't bite her tongue or choke on her saliva. "I need a doctor!"

The woman continued to convulse, her entire body jerking. Rebecca tried to keep her from falling out of bed but was impossible to stop the convulsions or check on the baby. Instead, she covered her with a blanket to keep her from hurting herself. A staff nurse came to help, but it was too late. The woman gasped, then went completely limp and stopped breathing. Rebecca and the nurse stood silently by the bed, their faces locked in disbelief. Just when the nurse was reaching for the mother's wrist to find a pulse, a doctor rushed to the bedside. He stopped abruptly when he saw the mother lying there lifeless.

The nurse spoke up. "This mother had high blood pressure and went into a convulsion. Her student nurse came to get me after she took vital signs and found the patient in trouble. She did everything she could."

"Move away. Hurry!" The doctor placed his fingers on the side of the woman's neck and quickly moved his stethoscope around her swollen abdomen. Rebecca could tell by the solemn look on his face, mother and baby were dead.

"I'll go tell the husband," the doctor said, his voice shaking and his shoulders slumped.

Rebecca was terrified she had done something wrong. She stood by the bed, trying to hold back her tears, but soon sobs wracked her body. This mother was twenty years old. *Same age as I am. And her name is Jane.* But Rebecca was also crying because she was afraid this could happen to her.

She went over and over the scene in her mind searching for answers. God, why this mother and baby? Rebecca saw death before. Howard hanging from a rafter. The little girl who had diphtheria. Patients dying on the operating table. Or from typhoid. Or pneumonia. But somehow this was different.

On Sunday, Christopher didn't come to the nurses' residence. Rebecca waited more than an hour, but when he didn't arrive, she took a walk outside to help clear her thinking.

It didn't.

When she returned, there was a bouquet of red roses in a tall, leaded crystal vase on the table inside the door with an embossed linen envelope on top that read 'Rebecca.' She felt her heartbeat in her temples. She opened the wax seal and slipped the card from the envelope.

> *Amour, from Christopher. PS. Wear the blue dress next Sunday and be ready by one o'clock.*

Christopher had come. She didn't wait long enough. Rebecca walked outside again and looked both ways. He was gone. She'd have to wait until next weekend unless she could by chance find him in the hospital. She returned to her room and laid down. Thankfully, Bertha's parents had taken her out for the day, so there was time to be alone and think about the possibility that she was carrying a child. She couldn't escape the fact that she had missed two monthlies. Lately, her breasts were tender and swollen. Could Christopher have been wrong? How will she tell him?

Rebecca thought about how hard she had studied and worked for the past two years…how disappointed her mother and father would be…and Doc Headings and Peter North. What she would do if Christopher wouldn't marry her. Where would she live and who would take care of her and her baby?

Tears escaped from her watery eyes. She curled into a ball and rubbed her abdomen.

It was flat and warm. Maybe she wasn't with child after all.

But the next day when Rebecca awoke she barely made it to the bathroom before she vomited. Bertha knocked on the door. "Are you all right? Maybe you're coming down with something."

"No… I think it was… the soup I ate yesterday. Just give me a minute and I'll feel better."

Rebecca brushed her teeth and got dressed in her uniform, trying to hide her nausea from Bertha. After a breakfast of tea and toast, the walk outside to the hospital helped ease her queasy stomach, but the idea of caring for laboring mothers and newborn babies nearly made her stomach churn again.

The head nurse assigned her to a ward of laboring patients. Some were moaning and screaming, while others laid quietly, their eyes staring ahead. She tried to remember what she had learned about the stages of labor, how to check the baby's position by feeling its outline through the mother's abdomen, and how to find the heartbeat with a stethoscope. The memory of the mother and baby that died under her care added to her uncertainty.

According to her teachers, midwives or family doctors provided most maternity care at home in Baltimore, although some women came to the hospital because they were ill or the baby stopped moving. A growing number wanted to deliver their child in a hospital because they preferred to be cared for by a physician rather than a midwife. She had a difficult time understanding their reasons, because midwives always stayed with the mother while the doctor spent much of his time out of the wards.

One of her patients on the free ward was expecting twins. Rebecca marveled at the size of the mother's distended abdomen and the purple stretch marks that formed lines from her breasts to her pubis. She watched as a doctor examined the mother, teaching a young resident to locate each baby and place the stethoscope where he thought the babies' backs were located. He explained how he was going to manage the pain of labor and birth by using ether or chloroform.

Later that day and the next, Rebecca smelled ether gas on mother and babies. It was all she could do to keep from vomiting, especially when her patient threw up violently. She was also frightened because the newborn infants were slow to breathe after birth.

Another doctor explained to her and the resident, "In Europe, painless childbirth is becoming popular because of morphine and scopolamine. We are now using that technique at Johns Hopkins." He reported that he mixed small amounts of each drug and gave it to a woman he knew to be a well-known socialite from a wealthy family who lived in an exquisite home next to the nearly completed St. Patrick's Catholic Church. The doctor also bragged that many of his patients were from Baltimore's wealthiest families.

As she watched the drugged woman thrash about and scream in bed, Rebecca was fascinated and horrified at the same time. The mother had difficulty pushing the baby out, and when the baby boy had blue lips and hands, she was unaware. The obstetrician slapped the baby's buttocks and feet many times, trying to stimulate him to wake up. Rebecca held her breath along with the baby, not sure if the baby would ever breathe. Finally the newborn took a breath, but his color remained blue for almost half an hour. After the mother's drugs wore off several hours later, the she woke up and was delighted when her baby was brought to her. She told Rebecca she remembered nothing about her labor or the birth itself, or that she gave birth to a baby boy.

Rebecca did her best to care for his patient, torn between wanting to do her best and resenting the special attention she and many of his other privileged patients demanded.

She assisted with five more births that week, all public patients, one from Ireland who had ten other children, and three from Eastern European countries who didn't speak a word of English. The fifth was a colored woman who came to the hospital bleeding profusely. Her placenta had separated from the womb when she went into labor. Her husband brought her to the hospital in time for the doctor to use metal forceps to deliver the baby, who succumbed.

Later that week, after dinner and study time, Rebecca sequestered herself in the library, sitting on a wicker chase and ruminated on what she had experienced. She rehearsed each scene in the maternity ward, questions floating through her consciousness. Would the poor mother and baby who died have survived if they had had the same care and attention as the women of privilege? Will she be a woman of privilege if Christopher marries her? If he doesn't, will she go back to McAlisterville and will Dr. Headings deliver her child?

CHAPTER 73

THE COLORED DRIVER DRESSED IN A GRAY EVENING COAT, white gloves, and tall hat drove the coach in front of the nurse's home. He opened the door and Christopher stepped out, holding his hat and walking stick. Rebecca's heart skipped a beat, knowing what she had to tell him tonight.

She smiled, trying to hide her apprehension. "I'm glad to see you, Christopher."

"Rebecca, you look absolutely beautiful in your blue dress. I'm glad we have some time before the opera. I want to take you to my home first. We seldom have time together just you and me. My parents have gone to a party and will meet us at the opera house."

"Well, Christopher, if you think that's all right with them." Rebecca smoothed the waist of her dress and clutched her reticule. She felt guilty carrying the gift Ben gave to her but she had nothing else to carry her handkerchief and lip rouge she borrowed from Bertha, or fancy enough to wear with the exquisite dress. She held it in the folds of her dress, hoping Christopher didn't recognize it as the gift from Ben.

The young doctor helped her into the coach and tapped on the roof to signal the coachman. "Rebecca, I've been hoping to see you in the hospital all week. I asked your roommate about you—she always said you were working and studying."

Just looking at him made her fight back tears. "Yes, Christopher, I… I've been very busy."

"I've missed you, Rebecca. Are you well? You look lovely but your face is a little peaked."

Rebecca smoothed down the waist of her dress. "Yes, I… I'm well… just a little tired. I was hoping we could go for a carriage ride in the country before the opera. I need to talk to you about… about something important."

"That's fine. But the house is empty—we could relax there and take a walk around the gardens."

"All right, Christopher, if that's what you want." Rebecca felt a nervous chill go up her spine thinking of how she would tell him she was with child. She looked out the window of the carriage so he wouldn't see her chin tremble.

She hardly noticed the huge purple beech trees lining the driveway as they pulled up to the mansion, or the sculptured arborvitae surrounding a massive fountain. Christopher helped Rebecca down from her seat, and let his hands rest on her waist. He felt her stiffen.

"What's bothering you, Rebecca?"

She willed herself to be strong. "Why didn't you contact me for two weeks? I felt like you abandoned me."

Christopher raised his voice. "I did nothing of the sort. I tried to find you in the hospital. I sent you dozens of roses and a note. Did you receive them?" Before Rebecca could answer, he gently took her arm and led her through the portico and into the side door.

Rebecca managed to answer yes but when she stepped into the grand mansion, her composure plummeted. The house was even more imposing than she remembered last Thanksgiving when she met his parents and brother for the first time. Large fireplaces faced with blue deft tile graced the formal parlor in the side wing of the mansion. Tall windows had louvered white shutters on the lower halves. Windowsills over a foot thick held potted palms. Chrystal vases were stuffed with fresh flowers. A grand stairway rose up the middle of the parlor to the second floor, doorways to upper rooms spreading out like spokes on a wheel.

A colored maid quietly approached Christopher. "May I serve you a glass of fresh lemonade or some coffee?" Unlike her friend Lilly's maid Lucy, her English was perfect.

"Yes, some coffee would be nice," answered Christopher, as he took Rebecca by the hand and led her to an adjoining sunroom that overlooked a rose garden. Large green ferns rested on ornately carved wooden pedestals in front of each window, their feathery branches drooping to the floor.

They sat down on the wicker sofa and waited until the coffee was served. Christopher said, "Thank you Mandy. You may take the rest of the day off."

Rebecca's stomach started to churn at the smell of the coffee and the saliva ran together in her mouth. She swallowed several times to keep her lunch where it was supposed to be. "Tell me what *'amour'* means. I have no idea what you said in your note."

He smiled and cocked his head to the side. "It means love, Rebecca, in French. I'm sorry. I thought you knew." Rebecca clenched her jaw. "I didn't have the privilege of studying languages like you did, Christopher. Do you speak French?"

"Not fluently, although I know a few words. Actually, I speak German. It's only one of many things we have yet to learn about each other, Rebecca. But there's time for that."

Rebecca studied his face. He was freshly shaven, a small nick where his jaw met his ear. Christopher's hair shown nearly silver in the sunlight filtering through the sunroom windows. His clothes were well chosen, a finely woven, tan, wool day coat and a starched white shirt. Hands, nails perfectly groomed, rested on his lap.

He looked at her and took her hand. "What's on your mind, Rebecca? You look troubled. Are you still angry with me for my thoughtless message?"

"No. I can't be angry with you for saying love even if it was in French."

"Good. Please forgive me." His voice lowered to nearly a whisper. "I love you."

Rebecca took a deep breath and relaxed her body. "And I love you, Christopher."

Christopher's face burst into a broad smile. "Let me show you how much I love you. Please, Rebecca. Come with me to my bedroom."

Rebecca's voice caught in her throat before she almost blurted out she was expecting his child. But his face was near hers, his penetrating blue eyes pleading. His hand reached under her chin, lifting her face while he kissed her tenderly. She closed her eyes. He wanted to bed her again. She had already made one mistake. Dare she make another? Was she weak for wanting to say yes? She should tell him about the baby right now before the situation got complicated. But indecision won over reason. She sat silently, kneading her hands in her lap.

"Please. I promise it will be all right. No one is here."

Rebecca hesitated before she answered. "Christopher ... I ... I'm ..."

He kissed her again, this time pulling her to him and tasting her mouth. She stared to speak but he put his finger on her mouth and said, "Shhhhh."

Her resolve gone, Rebecca closed her eyes and nodded.

Christopher took her hand and led her up the massive stairway to a large, masculine-looking bedroom with dark green and tan flowered wallpaper and matching drapes. But it was the massive black cherry poster bed that caught her attention. A puffy burgundy silk comforter with short lengths of shiny cord tucked in the center of each square of silk fabric, covered the bed. Beyond the bed was an open door that led to a private bath with a water closet. Everything was perfectly clean and orderly as if no one had ever slept there.

After he pulled the drapes closed, Christopher took his outer clothes off and reached for Rebecca, pulling her into his arms. His mouth was hungry. As he kissed her, he loosened the buttons down the front of her dress. She nearly stopped him but was caught up in her own desire to please him. As his hand caressed her breast, she ran her hands through his soft long hair. They stepped backwards toward the bed and fell onto the soft comforter. He fumbled with her corset strings, cursing under his breath. The absurdity of it made her giggle. Soon they were both laughing and undressing each other with abandon.

When they were both naked, he rolled Rebecca over on her stomach and ran his hands over her buttocks and down her long, muscular legs.

"Do you know how desirable you are with your perfect body and beautiful bronze skin? I can't resist touching you." He lay on top of her with the full weight of his body until she started to squirm.

He laughed and rolled off her back. "Turn over, Rebecca and let me kiss you from head to toe." His tongue caressed her neck and breasts until she drew him to her, her arms encircling his body with all her strength. "I need you, Rebecca. Please let me pleasure you as long as I can before I have to stop."

Rebecca gasped as he entered her. She was shocked at her response to his movements. It was as though she had lost all inhibitions. At the peak of their passion, he withdrew from her, letting his seed fall on the sheet. Her body shuddered as he sat back on his legs and laid his head on her belly. They stayed like that, saying nothing, their heartbeats and breathing slowing.

Then, just like he did the first time they made love, Christopher washed Rebecca's body and then himself, drying them with a linen towel. She loved his tenderness but the weight of what she had just done made her cry.

"Rebecca, what's the matter? Did I hurt you?"

"No. Christopher, please lie next to me and hold me." She waited until he laid down on the bed and then cradled his head on her chest. In a soft voice she said, "I have something to tell you. I tried to do it before we came upstairs but I just couldn't. She pulled the sheet over both of them and rolled on her side facing him. Her ears were ringing and she felt nauseated again. "I ... I think I am with child. Probably about nine weeks."

Christopher jerked away. "What? You can't be."

Rebecca tried to remain calm but she was disappointed in his denial. "I have not had my monthly since before we went to the Inn. I have other signs as well—morning sickness and my breasts are tender."

"I don't understand how this could happen."

"You told ... you told me that pulling out would work. Well, it didn't."

"But… " Christopher stared at her in disbelief. His cheeks were flushed as he studied her with a deep frown between his eyes. "No. This isn't possible." His voice grew louder. "I'm just getting started in my medical practice. The reason I couldn't visit you these past few weeks is because my father and I have been setting up a surgical fellowship for me in Germany."

Rebecca covered herself with the comforter, panic rising in her voice. "Germany? How long will you be gone? And why didn't you tell me?"

Christopher got up and began to get dressed. "I was going to tell you about it after all was confirmed. This changes everything. We'll get married as soon as we can. But give me a little time, Rebecca. I need to figure out how to tell my mother and father. They'll suspect what has happened, and I must be honest—they'll be upset."

"What about my mother and father—and my sponsors? I'll have to leave nursing school. My life will change drastically." She fought to hold back tears. "I also planned on practicing my profession. I only have a short time until I graduate."

"You're right. I'm sorry. I just need time to think." Christopher sat next to her. "Let's not do anything right now until we can think more clearly. Meanwhile, you should see a doctor. I know a colleague who specializes in obstetrics. Let me contact him."

Rebecca sucked in a breath. "No, I want to be cared for by one of the midwives. I would be embarrassed to be examined by one of your colleagues."

"We'll talk more about this later. For now, we'd better get dressed." He pulled on his trousers and took a pocket watch out of his vest pocket. "I'll go to the stables and ask the coachman to pick us up. Come downstairs when you're dressed."

"Christopher ..." but he closed the door.

CHAPTER 74

DR. AND MRS. MORGAN WERE ALREADY SEATED IN THE UPPER balcony box when Christopher and Rebecca arrived.

"Good evening, my dear. You look lovely in that blue dress. You must sit down before the orchestra begins."

Stifling her anxiety, she stole a glance at Christopher, then his mother. "Thank you, Mrs. Morgan."

As if taking her cue, Christopher squeezed her hand and led her to their seats. "Rebecca has never seen an opera. I'm eager for her to hear Miss Schumann-Heink."

The elder Dr. Morgan said, "Yes, she is quite accomplished—sings many of Wagner's characters—don't you agree, Dorothea?"

"Of course. But it's the costumes that intrigue me. So lavish, even the men's. It must cost a fortune to put on such an extravagant production."

Rebecca remained quiet, her mind on everything but the opera. Within minutes the orchestra began to play and the curtain went up to gasps from the audience. Despite her anxiety, the pageantry, the splendor of the garb the singers wore, and the massive staging made her skin shiver with goose bumps. Miss Ernestine Schumann-Heink sang the opening aria, her voice unlike anything Rebecca ever heard, powerful and clear.

Christopher whispered to Rebecca now and then to explain the drama's story and lead characters. For the next hour, Rebecca tried to forget about her situation. When intermission was announced, Mrs. Morgan rose out of her chair and stood behind her. "My dear, how coincidental that this opera was written by the German composer Robert Wagner. Isn't that your last name? Perhaps your father was related to him."

Blinking rapidly, Rebecca tried to think of a proper answer. She slowly turned around to face Mrs. Morgan. "I don't think so. My father's people were farmers like he is."

The elder woman's frown made Rebecca regret her answer. But it was too late. Mrs. Morgan returned to her seat and leaned over to her husband and whispered in his ear.

Dr. Morgan patted her hand and glanced at Christopher. "Now Dorothea, don't be upset. Miss Wagner is a lovely girl."

Turning to his mother and father, Christopher said, "Yes, mother, she is. And it is important to me that you treat Rebecca with respect. She is my guest."

His mother put her hand to her throat, and said, "Of course she is. I meant no harm asking her about her ancestors."

Rebecca bit her lip, trying to calm her racing heart. Her fear of not knowing her way back to the nurses' residence kept her from fleeing. She looked down from their balcony seat, pretending to watch the people below.

"Please ignore my mother's remark. She didn't mean to be disingenuous," Christopher said, his face turning red. "I know how difficult this evening must be for you. It is for me, too, but let's try to make the best of it."

Before Rebecca responded, the curtain went up for the second act. She sat straight up in her velvet seat and vowed to stay calm. Christopher slid his little finger in hers and held it tightly. They fingers stayed locked together until the second act ended with a spectacular display of cast and orchestra on stage. They joined the people in the theater as they rose to their feet when the applause became thunderous.

While Dr. and Mrs. Morgan were clapping their hands and looking at the stage, Christopher took ahold of Rebecca's elbow and led her out of the theater.

They waited with throngs of people until their carriage stopped in front and the coachman opened the door. As it pulled away, Rebecca glanced out the window and saw the elder Morgans step through the theater door, their faces somber and their eyes following the carriage as it sped away.

Rebecca sat back in the seat and took a deep breath. "Christopher, it's very clear your mother and father don't think very much of me. There's nothing but heartache ahead for us, even if I become the mother of their grandchild." Her voice cracked. "I know it's not your fault, but I feel unworthy of your love. Perhaps it would be better if I just moved back to Pennsylvania and set you free."

Christopher put his arm around her and drew her close. "No. I'll not have them dictate my life and whom I marry. It's my fault you are in the family way and my responsibility to take care of you. Rebecca, we'll get through this together. I won't let you down."

She wanted to believe him but the sting of his mother's remarks lingered. Her body crumbled forward, the tears forming and escaping despite her efforts to blink them away.

He took a white linen handkerchief out of his breast pocket and wiped them away, then gave it to her. She unfolded it and held it to her eyes, gasping for breath between sobs.

When the carriage arrived at the nurses' residence, Rebecca pulled away from Christopher and reached out to unlatch the door before the carriage came to a complete stop. She swung the door open and stepped down into the street.

"Rebecca, wait!"

CHAPTER 75

BERTHA WASN'T IN THE ROOM BUT HER OPEN NOTEBOOK SAT on her desk. Rebecca was relieved she didn't have to face her roommate, not sure she could keep her secrets if Bertha showed her any kindness. She slipped out of her dress, gathered her nightgown and walked briskly to the bathroom. When she stepped out of her chemise, she noticed a small spot of dark blood. Probably nothing. She knew some women bled a little during the time their monthly was due, especially the first few months of confinement. After washing her face and the spot out of her chemise, she returned to her room and found Bertha waiting.

"I hope you had a nice time with... Rebecca, what's wrong? You look terrible."

"The... the opera was very sad. I cried the entire second act." Rebecca forced a smile and crawled into bed. "I am tired, though, so I'll say goodnight."

Bertha closed her notebook and approached Rebecca. "All right. But don't forget we have an examination tomorrow morning on the obstetric patient. Good night. See you at five thirty."

After reliving the day with Christopher and the rebuke from his mother, Rebecca drifted off to sleep only to awaken several hours later with cramps in her pelvic area. She tiptoed to the bathroom and found more dark blood when she wiped herself with toilet paper. Maybe her monthly was coming after all.

In the morning she stuffed two quilted cloths inside her chemise in case her own homemade ones weren't thick enough to keep her uniform clean.

Rebecca and Bertha reported to the free maternity ward by six forty-five. They each were assigned to care for new mothers and their babies. Several mothers were still groggy from ether or morphine and had to be awakened to feed their newborn babies. Rebecca gagged from the smell of ether but hid it by holding a handkerchief over her mouth and nose. Other patients only spoke Italian, Polish, or had strong Irish accents, making it difficult for her to teach them to take proper precautions to prevent infection.

By noontime her cramps became almost unbearable, and Rebecca felt a warm wetness on her upper thighs. She hobbled into the supply closet. Bleeding had soaked through her quilted pads. She wrapped them in cleaning rags and threw them in a trashcan. Then she grabbed two Lister's Towels and placed them inside her chemise to absorb the blood, which was oozing down her legs.

Opening the door a crack, she scanned the ward. Bertha was only a few bed lengths away, helping a mother put her baby to breast.

Rebecca whispered, "Bertha. Please come here. I need you."

Her roommate sneaked into the closet and saw Rebecca doubled over, holding her abdomen. "What's wrong? Are you ill?"

"I ... I need you to help me get back to our room. I'm bleeding ... and I think I may be ..."

Bertha took Rebecca's arm. "Sit down on this stool and tell me what to do."

"Please try to reach Dr. Morgan. I think he's in the hospital somewhere." Her body shook despite her efforts to stop it. "Bertha ... I think I'm having a miscarriage. Please promise you won't tell anyone. Just explain to the head nurse I'm having a heavy monthly and must change my clothes."

"Oh, no, Rebecca. Don't worry, I'll find him." She made sure no one was near before walking briskly out of the ward.

She found Christopher in the surgical theater. She climbed the steps to the viewing window and motioned for him to come near. "Dr. Morgan,

Rebecca asked me to find you. She's ... bleeding a lot. And has cramps. I'll take you to her but she made me promise not to tell anyone except you."

By the time Christopher reached Rebecca, she was still having severe cramps and bleeding heavily.

"Rebecca, what's happening? Please let me call Dr. Parthemore to examine you."

"No. I just wanted you to know I may be losing the baby. Bertha can walk me to our room because I don't want to call attention to myself."

"But you shouldn't be alone."

"Bertha can stay with me for a little while." Rebecca stood up and swayed to and fro, grabbing onto the doorknob for support. She held on to Bertha's arm while her roommate explained to the head nurse that Rebecca needed to go to her room because of cramps and a heavy monthly. They walked out of the ward, doing their best to pretend that nothing was wrong by smiling and talking softly. When they reached the nurses' residence, Bertha put Rebecca to bed and spread a folded sheet under her. An hour later, Rebecca asked to use the chamber pot. She passed small pieces of tissue into the chamber pail. Blood covered the clumps of tissue and the bottom of the pail. Rebecca looked at it and threw up on the floor. "Bertha! Please help me."

"I'm sorry, my friend. It's over. I think that was the remains of the afterbirth and fetus. Let me help you back to bed before I clean up."

Rebecca wiped her face on her sleeve but said nothing.

A knock on the door startled both of them. "Hurry, let's get you to bed."

Bertha covered the pail with a towel and quickly wiped up the floor. The room stank, so she opened a window.

The knock became louder. "Rebecca, open the door. I asked Dr. Parthemore to examine you. He should be here in a few minutes. Please let me in."

"Dr. Morgan, it's Bertha. Please give me a few minutes to help Rebecca change into a clean nightgown."

Rebecca remained quiet as Bertha placed clean Lister's Towels between her legs and slid her arms into a clean nightgown. She could barely see through the tears that ran down her pale cheeks, but she recognized the handkerchief Bertha placed in her hands. It was Christopher's from the night before.

"Blow your nose before I wash your face and hands. You'll feel better." Rebecca nodded and lifted her face while her friend gently wiped her forehead, cheeks and chin, followed by her hands.

Bertha gathered up the wrappings and dirty linen and kissed Rebecca on the top of her head. She opened the door slightly and said, "You may come in now, Dr. Morgan," and quietly left them alone.

As soon as Christopher came into the room, Rebecca broke down, sobbing deeply. The secrecy, the shame, the uncertainty was over. No leaving nurse's training. No forced marriage. The baby, hers and Christopher's, was gone. She hadn't allowed herself to think about the baby… as a real person... a boy or girl. Now her chance was taken away from her.

Christopher sat on the edge of the bed and put his arms around her. They held each other until Rebecca's sobbing changed into quiet tears that wet his shoulder.

"My dear, look at me. I would like you to allow Dr. Parthemore to examine you. He should be here by now." Without waiting for her permission, he stepped into the hallway to greet his colleague.

"Thank you for coming. I'm quite sure Rebecca has miscarried. I trust you to be discreet—it was our baby. She's very upset. Would you please examine her to make sure she's all right?"

Doctor Parthemore nodded. The two of them went into Rebecca's room.

"Miss Wagner, Dr. Parthemore is here to examine you. I'll leave the room if you wish."

She closed her eyes and turned away. He called her Miss Wagner. Why so formal? Weren't they on a first name basis? After all, they'd slept together. "I don't want to be examined. I know what happened—just leave me alone."

"But you must be examined to make sure that you've completely passed all the tissue. I've told Dr. Parthemore all the circumstances of this pregnancy. He'll be discreet."

"No, Christopher. I've asked Bertha to send for one of the midwives. She and the midwife will take care of me. You both can go now."

Dr. Parthemore looked at Christopher expecting him to argue.

Instead, Christopher sat down on the side of Rebecca's bed. He looked pale, his eyebrows severely drawn together. "My dear, I'd like to talk to you before we go. Please excuse us, Dr. Parthemore, Bertha." They quietly walked out of the room and closed the door. "Rebecca, there are some things I must say to you before you chase me away. First of all, I'm sorry this has happened to you. It's my fault. But I love you, my dear. In a few weeks this will all be behind us. Think on the bright side. Now you won't have to leave nursing school. I won't have to tell my parents or anyone else about the pregnancy. Our lives can go on as we planned before any of this stood in our way. You'll be able to complete nursing school and I can start my fellowship. We won't have to rush into marriage."

Her mouth fell open. "Christopher, this didn't just happen to me—it happened to us! We lost our baby. Is that all you can think about—our plans? I don't care that now we can go on with our plans." She dug her fingers into her palms, willing herself not to cry, but her chin quivered. Christopher tried to hold her but she stiffened. "Please, leave me alone. I don't want to hear any more." Rebecca turned away and curled around her pillow.

Christopher pleaded with her. "I'm so sorry I didn't say the right thing. Obviously, I've upset you. I'll go now but I want you to know that I'm sad about the baby, too."

"You sure don't sound that way. I ... I'm so tired, Christopher. Please leave. I just want to rest."

CHAPTER 76

Rebecca was relieved Bertha was able to convince Miss Nutting that she had an unusually heavy monthly and needed to rest in bed for a day or two. Her roommate brought meals to her and helped her with clean padding. They didn't talk about the miscarriage but she was worried Bertha had lost respect for her. It wasn't as though her roommate said or did anything to make Rebecca suspicious, but the guilt she felt about their reporting Maude for sleeping with a doctor ate away at her conscience.

Despite Bertha's kindness, Rebecca felt unsure about confiding in her about Christopher, convinced she would never understand what it was like to be lost in love. Bertha had never spoken about a relationship with a man, or even a boy from her hometown. Or being attracted to someone from a world vastly different from one's own. Wealth. Privilege. Culture. Bertha had been raised with all those, but Rebecca hadn't. She learned what it was like to have those advantages when she met Maggie and Lilly—and then Christopher—and to want them for herself.

Once Rebecca felt well enough to return to work, she tried to act as though nothing had happened. But something inside her changed. She felt detached from her work and her patients, facing each assignment without her usual passion. Weeks passed. Even the colors of the fall leaves didn't hold her attention.

Hoping to give herself time to recover and sort out her feelings about Christopher, Rebecca told her classmates to inform him she was not available if he came to the nurses' residence. She also left the letters he sent unopened in her desk. She lost weight. Her body worn down, her mind a swirling storm of self-doubt. Thoughts of leaving nursing school haunted her each night as she tried to fall asleep. She tried to rehearse in her mind how she would tell Dr. Headings and Mr. North. But nothing came—except rambling thoughts about her inadequacies as a third-year student nurse who was given more responsibility each day.

One evening after an exhausting day in the dispensary lifting heavy boxes, Rebecca returned to the nurses' residence and heard music coming from a device on a table of the sitting room. It was the scratchy sound of an orchestra with a solo from a violin. She stood still, enthralled by the magic sound that came from a wooden box that held a metal cone that looked like a trumpet-shaped flower. The music lasted almost two minutes. Her mind drifted to David Eastman ... then Maggie.

Maggie. Except for Back So Straight, she's the only person Rebecca could trust to tell about how confused she was about staying in nursing school and her feelings toward Christopher. Energized for the first time in months, Rebecca ran to her room and wrote furiously. Before she lost her courage.

Dear Maggie,

I hardly know where to begin this letter. Over two and a half years I left my small town to come to the Johns Hopkins Training School for Nurses. I was only eighteen years old and knew nothing about nursing or what I was about to enter into.

The human suffering I have seen is beyond my comprehension. I have seen things I never thought I would have to see and done things I never imagined I would have to do. Things like seeing a young man writhe with pain when he had his appendix removed without receiving adequate ether. Or watch a little girl die of diphtheria and witness her mother and father crying over her body. I cared for a little boy whose hand had to be amputated because he was bitten by a vicious dog.

Gangrene. Pus. Tumors so big they did not fit in the basin. People observing surgery in a theater as though they were watching a play. A young mother and her unborn baby who died from convulsions. Poor people nobody wants. Colored people and people from foreign countries who can't speak English and are at the mercy of those who do.

Most of the time I am helpless to save my patients and have to watch them suffer until they either get well or die in misery. The longer I am here the more I realize suffering and death are beyond human control.

My back and arms suffer from lifting bodies and hauling heavy buckets and washing beds. My hands are raw because I scrub them to keep from getting the very diseases my patients have, lest I succumb as they did.

My studies have been vigorous and demanding. Sometimes I fall asleep during the endless lectures because I'm on duty at night and attend classes during the day. I am grateful for the teachings and practice our instructors, doctors, and head nurses instill within us. However, oft times we students are judged more by our behavior and character rather than our competence. If we have a new idea or try to challenge a practice that seems antiquated, we are told to stifle our opinions. There is one doctor who tries my soul. He accuses me of being part colored and speaks ill of me to other doctors. But I am powerless to stand against him because he is a physician and I am only a lowly student nurse.

I have nightmares about my patients when I lay down to sleep at night. But one that haunts me still is the one of the severed arm at the lumber mill in McAlisterville. I dream this dream every time I witness an amputation or clean blood from a wound.

My private life is also trying. I have met a young doctor and my love for him led me to make serious mistakes. The first one was the hurt

I caused Ben Siebert when I betrayed him. I loved both him and the doctor. The second mistake, and it is a grave one, is that the doctor and I produced a child. But that life ended in a miscarriage and now I am left with nothing but sadness and anguish over my own lack of moral principle and my guilt at having hurt both men and a classmate I reported for doing the same thing. I still have fondness for this doctor but I yearn for the sweetness and forgiveness of Ben.

It is with sadness and confusion that I write to confess my failures to you in hopes you will not judge me unworthy of your continued friendship. Please write to me of your opinion. It is with much pleading that I ask you to have compassion for my wrongdoings.

With much humbleness,

Rebecca

CHAPTER 77

UNABLE TO MAKE AMENDS WITH REBECCA, CHRISTOPHER went on with his plans to study abroad and planned to leave for Germany in a few weeks. He spent much of his free time at his home in Mount Vernon Place studying articles about surgical techniques for hip replacement pioneered by German physician Themistocles Gluck. Hopefully, with recommendations from Dr. Osler and the elder Dr. Morgan, his application for a fellowship to practice under this noted doctor would be accepted.

The young Dr. Morgan suspected his mother and father were pleased that he no longer left the house on Sundays to spend time with Miss Wagner. But his brother, home from Harvard for a semester break, questioned Christopher about the change in his schedule.

"What's going on with you, big brother? You seem have your nose stuck in a book more than usual."

"What I do with my time is none of your business."

Michael chuckled, a smirk on his face. "And I haven't heard you talk about your beautiful friend. She's a mighty fine-looking woman. Not my type of course, too tall and much too outspoken."

Christopher's body stiffened. "I'll let those remarks go over my head. They're not worth answering. Besides, it's none of your damn business."

"Pretty touchy, aren't you? Something must have happened. Did she ditch you for someone else?"

"You ..." Christopher lunged at his brother and knocked him to the floor. As he fell, he hit the side of his head on the corner of a table. The red glass antique lamp sitting on top fell to the floor, shattering into hundreds of pieces. Blood ran from his brother's forehead and oozed onto his neck. He wiped it away with the back of his hand and glared at Christopher.

One of the housekeepers heard the crash and came running into the room, followed by their mother. "What happened to you, Michael? You're bleeding!"

Michael looked at Christopher with slanted eyes, then turned to Dorothea. "I ... caught my shoe on the carpet, mother."

Christopher nodded and handed his handkerchief to his brother. "Let me take a look at that cut. It may need stitches." He wiped the blood off Michael's wound while their mother watched, her eyes darting from one son to the other.

"The cut's not too deep but it will require a few stitches. Let me get my medical bag and I'll make sure there's no scar."

Michael backed away. "Not on your life. You're still learning. Look at all those books you're reading. Let father do it."

The wound on Michael's head was a minor one. However, the wound between Christopher and his brother was far more serious. Neither admitted to their mother the real reason for Michael's fall. But when Michael was ready to return to Harvard, he refused to talk to Christopher or bid him goodbye, despite the fact that they wouldn't see each other for a year or more.

Christopher regretted overreacting to his brother's remarks about Rebecca and his own response to her when she miscarried. Unable to understand the depth of his feelings and so filled with remorse was he that no amount of self-rationalization gave him peace. Finally, he resolved to find Rebecca in the hospital and try to mend their relationship.

A few days before he left for Germany he waited outside the nurse's residence until the students returned from their day shift and asked when Rebecca would be off duty. The student who answered the door told him she would probably get off duty within half an hour. He walked inside and sat in the parlor where he could see her the moment she arrived.

"Christopher… I mean Dr. Morgan. What are you doing here?" Rebecca looked down at her apron and tried to sweep away a stain.

"Hello, Rebecca. I was hoping I'd find you. Could we please sit together over in the corner beside the piano?"

She nodded and allowed him to take her elbow and walk her to a love seat. "Rebecca, please, we must talk. I'll soon sail for Germany and I want to clear things between us before I go."

After hesitating Rebecca said, "Whatever you have to say you can say right now."

Christopher leaned close to her face and whispered, "I love you and don't want to lose you. If I hurt you, I'm very sorry. Please forgive me."

"I forgive you, Christopher, but I need time to sort out my feelings. Maybe this year while you're Germany will give us both a chance to heal. Until you return, this is the last time I'll see you, but I promise to write. That's all I can promise right now."

He took her hand and held it for a long time. When he released it, he had tears in his eyes. "Goodbye, Rebecca. I will miss you."

"Goodbye, Christopher. I will miss you, too."

With a small leather attaché case in hand, Christopher strolled up the gangplank. He glanced back at his mother and father waving from the boardwalk below, but his eyes swept the people on either side, hoping by some miracle Rebecca had changed her mind. She hadn't.

He watched cargo being loaded onto the hull and into the belly of the ship by cranes and on the backs of sturdy men: barrels, crates, boxes, baskets of vegetables and fruits, trunks, suitcases, and stacks of hat boxes.

The horn blasted two times when the ship was completely loaded. Dockworkers unwrapped the heavy braided ropes from the mooring rings.

The precision with which the men worked to loosen the mighty vessel from the dock fascinated Christopher. He stood on the deck and watched the huge anchor made of cast steel and forged iron ascend into the hull of the ship. As the ship chugged its way out of the harbor, he gazed at the land that grew smaller and smaller, marveling at the short length of time it took for the White Star Liner RMS Majestic to leave behind any trace of the shoreline.

As soon as the ship was in open water, he approached one of the crew and asked about the vessel. In a heavy British accent, the sailor told him the ship was filled to capacity—1, 490 passengers. Three hundred were first class, but he wasn't sure about the number of crewmen.

His cabin steward showed Christopher to his cabin. He wondered if other first-class passengers had accommodations as beautiful as his. The first-class stateroom was larger than he anticipated. It held a double bed, an ornately carved desk, a built-in dresser, a chaise-like lounge chair and a small water closet with thick, white towels stacked beside the sink. Light streamed in through a round porthole over the bed. Just as lovely as the bedroom at the inn, he thought. But no Rebecca to share it with.

That afternoon he explored the ship. The White Star Liner RMS Majestic reminded him of a grand hotel. Skylights brought filtered daylight into the library, lounges, and the dining room. Plaster panels decorated the first-class salon, depicting early ships and naval battles. Except for the naval theme, the ship reminded him of the inn where he and Rebecca spent the night. Elegant, comfortable, romantic.

For the remainder of the next eight days, Christopher spent his time reading in the library, playing games with other first-class passengers, and attending concerts and readings. He delighted in watching little girls skip rope, their laughter echoing against the metal sides of the mammoth ocean liner. Boys with cardboard daggers ran up and down the deck pretending to be pirates. A flash of regret dampened his joy. Six months from now he would have been the father of a baby girl or boy.

He ate his meals in a splendid dining room that was inspired by a mid-16th century French chateaux. Ornately carved tables and upholstered swivel chairs made dining feel luxurious, but he hated dining alone. There were too many memories of lovely dinners with Rebecca, so most evenings he invited himself to eat with other passengers or was joined by those traveling without a companion.

He wished Rebecca could see the RMS Majestic. One day he'd take her on this ship and they'd enjoy it together. He'd give her everything—and anything she wanted.

CHAPTER 78

HER SENIOR YEAR CLASSES CONTINUED TO BE DIFFICULT AND tedious. Tests and more lessons on the wards. Lectures on Obstetrics continued from last fall: presentations and positions of the child, management of mother during the puerperium, and obstetric emergencies during pregnancy, labor, and postpartum. When it came time for classes on infant feeding in health and sickness, Rebecca wanted to put her fingers in her ears so she wouldn't have to listen. Her mind wandered and she stopped taking notes. She was embarrassed that several times Bertha had to nudge her to pay attention.

In April, Dr. Baker gave advanced lectures on general medicine. Rebecca's mood improved when he spoke about the anatomy and physiology of the nervous system. She was fascinated by the complexity of the brain and spinal column, and memorized most of the peripheral nerves of the arms and legs. Now she better understood the injury to Ben's legs. Ben. She hoped he was happy with his new girl, Emma. But there was a twinge of jealousy and regret that lingered far longer than she wanted it to. She had lost him. And it was her own fault.

Thankfully, nursing instructors provided classroom practice in the care of the nervous system before she and her classmates were required to care for patients in the ward. Once she passed vigorous examinations, Rebecca was assigned to patients with unexplained paralysis, spastic limbs, brain tumors, and mysterious illness that rendered them incoherent. More than a few times she imagined her own fatigue and poorness of spirit were symptoms of one of the diseases she was studying.

However, it was Dr. Charles Emerson's lectures on the blood and blood-forming organs, heart and blood vessels that struck her personal interest because of her grandfather Wagner. She grasped the material at an exceptional level, thanks to having read Dr. Heading's medical books.

By the time May arrived, Rebecca was so absorbed in her studies, she hardly noticed the budding and flowering trees. Bertha asked her to take walks in the nearby parks but all her roommate wanted to do was study and work. Nothing brightened Rebecca's mood. She grew thinner and went to bed most evenings right after dinner.

Her classmates were deciding where to practice nursing. Most were remaining at Johns Hopkins Hospital; some were even taking head nurse or other leadership positions. Five were going to work as private duty nurses for wealthy families in the Baltimore/Washington area. Bertha planned on returning to Richmond, Virginia, and practice at Reid hospital with her father.

Rebecca vacillated between remaining at the hospital—after all, in less than a year, Christopher would return from Germany—and returning to McAlisterville, although she realized it would be difficult to find work there. However, if she moved back to McAlisterville she could serve her neighbors and repay Dr. Headings and Mr. Eastman for sponsoring her. And she would be able to learn more from Back So Straight, that is if enough plants and trees were left untouched.

But Ben and Emma were there, too. And she had failed miserably at being a friend to Lilly, despite her promise to write.

It was late May. Soon she would have to make a decision. But the closer she got to graduation, the more uncertain Rebecca felt about her future. If only she could ask Back So Straight what to do. But it was a letter from Maggie that gave her the courage to make a decision.

Dear Rebecca,

Thank you for confiding in me about your losses. I am truly sorry you have endured these painful events especially when you are far away from home. I want you to know I will keep your confession sacred and I do not regard you any less for having told me. The same fate has befallen some of my classmates here at Bryn Mar, much to the disappointment of their mothers and fathers. I however, do not judge these young women, as it seems the young men who fathered these children suffer no consequences whatsoever.

Your studies seem far more difficult that mine, although I do have a heavy load of academics. My studies in Latin, Algebra, and Science II keep me engaged in studying many hours each evening. The German VI Review of Schiller's Das Lied von der Glook *and site reading have me quite engaged. But my favorite is History IV- European History from 1485-1686, especially learning about kings and queens and political pandering and arranged marriages among royalty for the express purpose of forming alliances. Just imagine those preposterous shenanigans going on in 1901!*

This semester I read The Truth Tellers by Winter and Chaplet of Pearls *by Yonge, and just last week completed* Old Dominion *by James. Before the end of the semester, I must read* A Soldier's Secret *by King. Our professors insist we must be well read, but their motives are somewhat based on their opinions that women should be excellent conversationalists if we want to find a suitable husband among the learned men of Philadelphia. My mother and father continue to want me to marry someone worthy of my stature and avoid becoming a spinster. That is not my plan at all. Several of my friends invited me to attend a meeting of the National American Woman Suffrage Association. I heard Carrie Chapman Catt speak about our "sisters" who have been arrested and harassed because they are advocating for women's right to vote. That is preposterous! When I graduate, I am going to join their movement. I am also going to serve in the tenement houses to help women who work in the textile factories. They have no rights and work in unsafe conditions, and because they are foreign born, they have to live in crowded, filthy buildings with no running water.*

It is because of you that I am dedicating my life to helping poor and oppressed women. You inspire me to serve humanity, just as you are doing by becoming a nurse. You are strong and intelligent and I have admired you ever since we met and you stood up to that man who tried to intimidate us at the cave. I also admire you for reading medical books so you could help take care of your grandfather and how brave you were when we nearly stepped in a nest of poisonous snakes. You saved our lives.

My lovely and intelligent friend, do not let the mistakes of the past prevent you from accomplishing your hopes and dreams. Go forward and start anew.

Your friend always,

Maggie

P.S. Have you written to Lilly or received a letter from her?

No. She hadn't written to Lilly. She wasn't sure why. Maybe she was unsure about what to write or fearful Lilly was still angry with her. Rebecca felt guilty. Regretful that she left her friend down. But in truth, she had let herself down. Just like she had when she slept with Christopher.

Rebecca read the letter again. And again. Maggie has everything—wealth, a good education, a privileged upbringing. But she admires her—a farm girl?

Go forward and start anew. But where?

CHAPTER 79

FOURTEEN PUPIL NURSES SAT IN THE LARGE LECTURE ROOM of the Physiological Building. They turned their attention to the opposite side of the platform where current and future faculty members and nursing leaders Adelaide Nutting, Elsie Lawler, Lavinia Lloyd Dock, and Anna Wolf sat dressed in their white starched uniforms and black stockings and shoes. Flanked on their left sat a representative from the newly formed National Nurses Association. Nursing caps from schools from which they graduated perched on their heads.

Next to them sat Dr. William Osler, Mr. Francis T. King, President of the Board of Trustees, and several other hospital officials. Dr. Osler stood and opened the ceremony with these remarks: "On behalf of Miss Nutting, members of the faculty of the Johns Hopkins Training School for Nurses and honored guests, I welcome you to the graduation of the class of 1901."

Rebecca's attention was riveted on Dr. Osler. Out of respect for him, she fought the urge to scan the room for her parents and brother in the audience.

He continued, "The practice of medicine is an art, not a trade; a calling, not a business; a calling in which your heart will be exercised equally with your head. Often the best part of your work will have nothing to do with potions and powders, but with the exercise of an influence of the strong upon the weak, of the righteous upon the wicked, of the wise upon the foolish." White capped heads on the platform nodded in unison. He continued to speak for a few more minutes before he looked out at the audience and smiled. "I now call upon Mr. Francis T. King, president of the board of trustees."

As Mr. King rose and walked to the podium, Rebecca looked beyond him to the seats in front of the platform. There, near the back of the room, were her father, mother, and brother, their necks straining to see her. When their eyes met, Rebecca's breath caught in her throat. They came!

Mr. King spoke briefly about the new era in hospital care and the fiduciary responsibility of the board of trustees to provide support for the growing need for trained nurses. The student nurses remained stiff in their seats as he droned on.

Finally, Miss Adelaide Nutting was called to the podium. She walked erectly, her head held high. When she spoke she looked directly at the graduating students, her eyes resting on each one. "Your greatest service will be the prevention of the spread of disease. You also have a pivotal role in advancing the status of nursing as a profession. I have just learned that the Army Reorganization Act was passed by our Congress and signed by President McGinley, establishing the Army Nurse Corps. This will allow employment of women nurses in the military hospitals of the Army."

A buzz of voices could be heard increasing in volume until she started speaking again. "Never regard yourselves as second-class citizens. You are on the cusp of a growing movement of highly trained nurses who know more about the patient's condition than anyone else. And you will become the nursing leaders and educators for this century and beyond."

Turning to the guests seated before her, Miss Nutting said, "These young women have been subjected to the harshest tests of stamina and courage. They worked until their backs ached and their hands grew raw from washing. They were subjected to all manner of disease and wretchedness, while not complaining or faltering. Their private lives have been interrupted in order for them to serve the sick, the poor, the old, and the young. We commend them for obeying their honorable calling."

Bertha tapped Rebecca on the arm and whispered, "I am glad we endured, aren't you?"

"Yes ... I am."

Miss Nutting motioned for Miss Dock to walk to the table on the side of the platform. Her colleague moved quickly. "And now it is time for the awards."

The distinguished woman lifted up three envelopes and placed two of them back down again. Miss Dock spoke clearly and deliberately. "The first award is to the pupil nurse who exemplified nursing by her intelligence, skill, judgment and moral character. This award goes to Miss Bertha Perkins."

Bertha gasped. Dr. and Mrs. Perkins rose from their seats, clapping. The entire audience joined them. Bertha accepted her award and sat down clutching the envelope to her chest.

"You always were the best of the four of us," Rebecca said, as she squeezed Bertha's knee.

Miss Dock continued. "And now the second award for the pupil nurse who excelled in her clinical practice and displayed outstanding professionalism throughout her rotations." Miss Dock scanned the faces of the student nurses before continuing. "Miss Amelia Hanway, please come forward and accept your award." The applause carried throughout the room and echoed through the hallways.

"For the third award, we have reviewed the academic standing of each pupil nurse throughout her three years of preparation to become a trained nurse. There is one student who has maintained a near perfect record." She paused and studied the student nurses who sat perched on the edge of their seats. "Will Miss Rebecca Wagner please come forward?"

Rebecca wanted to float away but she managed to put one foot in front of the other until she reached Miss Robb. There must be some mistake. She didn't deserve this award. Too many mistakes.

"Congratulations, Miss Wagner."

"I ... thank you."

Miss Dock reached her hand to her mouth and whispered, "Miss Nutting told me you have a great mind. Use it wisely."

"Yes ... I will try." Rebecca returned to her seat, Miss Dock's words burning in her ears. Use it wisely. What did she mean?

Before Rebecca had a chance compose herself, Miss Nutting crossed the platform and stood before them. "Pupils, please rise for the recitation of the Nightingale Pledge."

On cue, the voices blended as one. Bertha linked her little finger around Rebecca's.

"I solemnly pledge myself before God and in the presence of this assembly, to pass my life in purity and to practice my profession faithfully. I will abstain from whatever is deleterious and mischievous, and will not take or knowingly administer any harmful drug. I will do all in my power to maintain and elevate the standard of my profession, and will hold in confidence all personal matters committed to my keeping, and all family affairs coming to my knowledge in the practice of my calling. With loyalty will I endeavor to aid the physician in his work, and devote myself to the welfare of those committed to my care."

Rebecca's throat tightened. She said the words and vowed to keep them. But one was too late: purity. Her sense of regret was overwhelming. The room grew warm around her. People in the audience stirred, their murmurs growing louder. She imagined they were talking about her; she did not deserve the award.

But then Miss Nutting spoke again. "Pupil nurses, please be seated. Miss Dock and I will now award you with the Johns Hopkins Nurses' Alumni Association pin. Class of 1901, I admonish you to wear this Maltese Cross because it was chosen as the symbol of the Alumni Association when it was founded just nine years ago. On the reverse of the pin is the word 'Vigilando', which means forever watchful. It serves to remind us every day of our commitment to those we serve and the strong ethical and moral foundation for nursing practice." She called each newly graduated nurse in alphabetical order. The 14-carat gold Maltese pin was presented in a beautiful felt-lined box. As soon as each young woman returned to her seat, she affixed the pin to the uniform of the student next to her, who then reciprocated. Rebecca pinned Bertha, then strained to watch her friend thread the gold and navy blue cross through the collar of her own uniform. After her pin was secured, she looked out into the lecture room and fixed her gaze on her family, eyes thick with tears.

I did it. But now what? Nothing left for me here. The baby's gone and so is Christopher. And Ben has Emma.

Juniata County… the trees… the mountains… my family… Back So Straight… are all I have left—and my resolve to be a healer. That's where I belong. I'm going forward and I'll start anew.

I'm going home.

BIBLIOGRAPHY

Cronon, William. *Changes in the Land—Indians, Colonists, and the Ecology of New England.* Hill and Wang A division of Farrar, Straus & Giroux, 1983.

Devall, Bill, Editor. *Clearcut: The Tragedy of Industrial Forestry.* Sierra Club Books and Earth Island Press, 1993.

Ellis, F. and A.N. Hungerford, Editors. *History of that part of the Susquehanna and Juniata Valleys, embraced in the counties of Mifflin, Juniata, Union and Snyder, in the Commonwealth of Pennsylvania*, 2008.

Fedkiw, John. "National Forests and the Performance of the Organic Act of 1897," 12-17. Forest History Today, 1998.

Gagliano, Monica. Thus Spoke the Plant: *A Remarkable Journey of Groundbreaking Scientific Discoveries & Personal Encounters with Plants.* North American Books, Berkley. 2018.

Gates, Gary. *How to Speak Dutchified English.* Good Books, 1987.

Holmes, Bonnie. *When The Doctor Rode in a Gig: Dr. William Hamlin Banks, 2018.*

Hulse, Arthur; C.J. McCoy; Clensky, Ellen J. *Amphibians and Reptiles of Pennsylvania and the Northeast.* Cornell University Press. 2001.

Jennings, Francis. *The Invasion of America: Indians, Colonialism, and the Cant of Conquest.* W. W. Norton & Company, Inc., 1975.

Johns, Ethel and Pfefferkorn, Blanch. *The Johns Hopkins Hospital School of Nursing 1889-1949.* The Johns Hopkins Press, 1954.

Kimmerer, Robin Wall. *Braiding Sweetgrass: Indigenous Wisdom, Scientific Knowledge and the Teachings of Plants.* Milkweed Editions, 2013.

Kirkpatric, Jane. *A Name of Her Own: Book 1 in Tender Ties Series.* Waterbrook Press, a Division of Random House. 2002.

McClure, Elmyra P. *Short Tales and Long Tales.* (No date given)

Merritt, Joseph. *Guide to the Mammals of Pennsylvania.* University of Pittsburg Press, 1987.

Orth, Richard L. T. *Folk Religion of the Pennsylvania Dutch: Witchcraft, Faith Healing and Related Practices.* McFarland & Company, Inc., 2018.

Ostman, Ronald E. and Little, Harry L. *Wood Hicks and Bark Peelers: The Photographic Legacy of William T. Clark.* The Pennsylvania State University Press in collaboration with the Lumber Heritage Region of Pennsylvania and the Pennsylvania Historical and Museum Commission, 2016.

Reverby, Susan M. *Ordered to Care: The Dilemma of American Nursing, 1850-1945.* Cambridge University Press, 1987.

Rinehart, Mary Roberts. *My Story. (Beyond Bed Pans: The Life of a Late 19th- Century Young Nurse.)* Farrar & Rinehart, 1931.

Savinelli, Alfred. *Plants of Power: Native American Ceremony and the Use of Sacred Plants.* Native Voices Book Publishing Company, 2002.

Shaffer, Larry. *Pennsylvania Amphibians and Reptiles.* Pennsylvania Fish and Boat Commission, 1999.

Simord, Suzanne. *Finding the Mother Tree: Discovering the Wisdom of the Forest.* A. A. Knopf, a Division of Penguin Random House, Toronto, 2021.

Taber, Thomas T. III. *The Goodyears: An Empire in the Hemlocks. Book No. 5 in the series Logging Railroad Era of Lumbering in Pennsylvania,* 1971.

Tekiela, Stan. *Birds of Pennsylvania Field Guide*. Adventure Publications, Inc., 2021.

---*Trees of Pennsylvania Field Guide*. Adventure Publications, Inc., 2021.

Varner, R. L, Tim Varner, Editor. Written by Getz, Gail; Lauver, Bob; Leitzel, Tom; Shallenberger, Roger. *McAlisterville and Fayette Township Bicentennial Book: A History of Fayette Township 1810-2010.*

Wagner, Sally Roesch. *Sisters In Spirit—Haudenosaunee (Iroquois) Influence on Early American Feminists.* Native Voices Book Publishing Company, 2001.

Warren, Mame, Editor. *Our Shared Legacy: Nursing Education at Johns Hopkins, 1889-2006.* The Johns Hopkins University Press, 2006.

Wert, Miriam Taylor. *People, Places & Passages of Tuscarora Valley and other Parts of Juniata County*. Port Royal, PA. (No date given)

SPECIAL ASSISTANCE

Jodi Jameson, Assistant Professor, Mulford Health Science Library, University of Toledo, Toledo, Ohio 43610-2598.

Juniata County Historical Society. 498B Jefferson Street, Mifflintown, Pennsylvania 17059-1424.

Marjorie Kehoe, Reference and Accessioning Archivist, Alan Mason Chesney Medical Archives, Johns Hopkins Medicine, Nursing, and Public Health, 5801 Smith Avenue Suite 235, Baltimore, Maryland 21209.

Pennsylvania Lumber Museum, 5660 US Route 6 W, Ulysses, Pennsylvania 16948.

Shirley Covert, Volunteer and Researcher, Juniata County Historical Society and life-long resident of Juniata County, Pennsylvania.

ABOUT THE AUTHOR

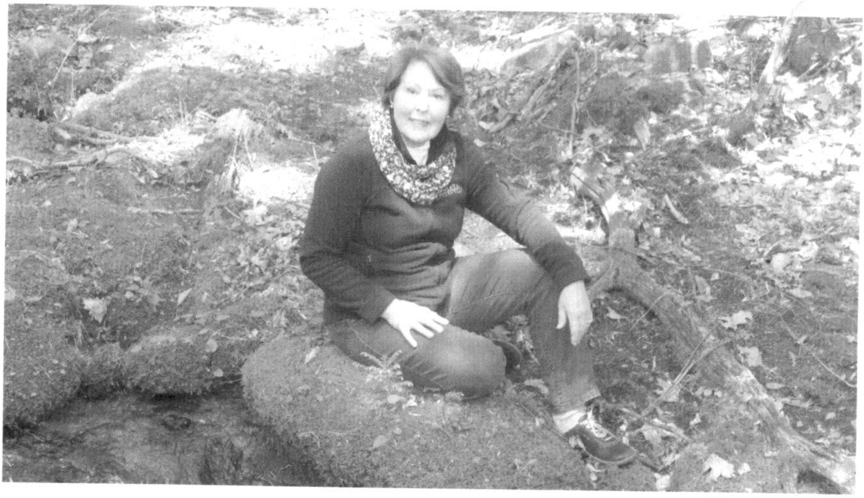

I'VE ALWAYS LOVED TREES. SO, WHEN I HELPED BUILD A LOG cabin in the Shade Mountains of Pennsylvania on land severely timbered nearly thirty years before, my imagination grew like the thousands of sprouts springing up from the mother trees that had been cut down.

As the forest matured, some of the sprouts thrived, resulting in an overstory of hemlock and white pine, as well as dozens of species of hard and softwood trees. And an understory of small trees and plants, their roots forming an underground network that defied my attempts to plant new seedlings.

I walked the dirt roads, imagining what life was like when virgin trees covered the mountains near the little town of McAlisterville. When Pennsylvania was the epicenter of American logging. Where a young farm girl who grew up in the late eighteen-hundreds in a rural village had few choices to become anything other than a farm wife or work as a domestic.

Years later, when I retired from nursing, I began the six-year journey that gave birth to The Trees Remember Trilogy. I imagined a farm girl who struggled to help her father save the family's forestland from the lumber barons. A girl who wanted to preserve the forests because her Indian mentor taught her to respect the trees, plants and herbs her ancestors used for centuries to sustain life. A young woman who conquered her fears and graduated from the Johns Hopkins Hospital School of Nursing, and took care of the men who clear-cut the very mountains she loved.

I thought back to the farm stories of my mother and grandmother—tales of hardship and loss—and my own experiences as a young naïve student nurse. I spoke to people who have lived in the Juniata Valley all their lives. I did research into the history of the lumbering industry, Native American use of plants and trees, nursing in the late 1800s and early 1900s, and local history of the places and people of the Juniata Valley. What I uncovered was a story rich in fact and fiction, a story of inspiration, endurance, and remembering. A story I felt compelled to tell.

JOYCE L KIEFFER

P.S. Some of you may remember me as the best-selling author of *To Have… To Hold… A Parents Guide to Childbirth and Early Parenting*, seven editions from 1979 to 2001. I hope you enjoy my new writing adventure.